Robert Wallace

The Phantom Detective: 5 Murder Mysteries in One Volume

OK Publishing 2021

Robert Wallace

The Phantom Detective: 5 Murder Mysteries in One Volume

Published by

Books

- Advanced Digital Solutions & High-Quality book Formatting -

musaicumbooks@okpublishing.info

2021 OK Publishing

ISBN 978-80-272-7874-9

Contents

Empire of Terror

Chapter One
Killers in Black

The bright, dazzlingly clear Arizona sky gave no hint of the ominous.

Outside the two-story frame building housing the temporary national radio network concentrated at Rock Canyon Dam, a midday sun gleamed brazenly down upon the several thousand sweltering, enthusiastic citizens and officials expectantly milling about the giant dam a half mile away.

Within the unpainted radio headquarters, on the second floor, three engineers with an assistant each, and three United States Army soldiers acting as guards under a hard-boiled infantry lieutenant, waited alertly for the hands of the electric clock on the drab wall to point to the hour of noon.

At the precise stroke of twelve the President of the United States, broadcasting in person from Rock Canyon Dam, would dedicate and formally open the greatest Federal irrigation project in the history of the country.

Lundbalm, the stocky chief radio engineer, touched a volume dial with tensed fingers and said over his hunched shoulder to Lieutenant Howard in charge of the army guards:

"Twelve minutes to go. The Marine band is hooked in now from Washington. It'll be hell if something goes wrong here."

"Nothing can go wrong," the lieutenant snapped. "This isn't the Tennessee Valley flood disaster, if that's what you're thinking of. We're prepared, this time. The entire section here is under guard. It's fool-proof!"

A frown darkened the square face of the chief engineer, and for a worried moment he stared grimly at the battery of signal lamps in a panel along one wall.

A duplicate set of signal bulbs, a brief month ago, had given him and the world the only warning of that ruthless devastation. Those lamps had flared violently a minute before the public opening of the famous Tennessee Federal power project.

Then the lights had shattered in the terrific, unexplained explosion that had blasted free the pent flood waters of the vast system and turned the valley into a torrential cataract of death.

That disaster, and others smaller but similar throughout the country, it still remained unexplained. But their origin had been traced to mysterious human hands. There, the Federal Bureau of Investigation, the G-men, had run into a blank wall. They had been stopped by a strange, impenetrable emblem —a small grey seal cut in the shape of an hour-glass, with a crimson capital "I" drawn perpendicularly through the stem.

The challenging, mystical emblem had appeared but once, pasted on the forehead of the murdered Public Works engineer in charge of the demolished Tennessee Valley Project. But the weird seal had started wild, imaginative tales of terror. And ugly, mob-inspiring rumors were persisting.

"I was out on that emergency Tennessee broadcast for two hellish weeks," Lundbalm growled dourly. "It was a ghastly experience. I'll never get over it."

"Well, it can't happen here!" Lieutenant Howard guaranteed flatly. "You tend to your gadgets. I've got us all locked in this room. Leave the protection to me."

Lundbalm reached for a phone. "I'll check again with Lewis over in the main announcer's cage at the dam." He started to plug into one of a row of connections.

His hand never finished the movement.

Behind him, from a silently opening trap in the ceiling, a yellowish egg-shaped object dropped to the floor, cracked open with a quick hissing sound. Instantly, an acrid, faintly greenish gas curled swiftly upwards, filling the long room with paralyzing, blistering fumes.

Lundbalm staggered back from the instrument table, his hands clutching his throat. He stumbled against Lieutenant Howard who was blindly trying to fire his heavy service Colt up at the hideously masked face leering down at them through the opened ceiling trap.

A black-sleeved arm laced across the opening, and a knife flashed downward through the curling, greenish vapor.

The raised Colt clattered to the floor from Lieutenant Howard's fingers as the steel blade plunged hilt deep through his neck. He fell, twisting in death, his clawing hands dragging Lundbalm's gas-strangled body down with him.

Blood spurted from his throat, spilling redly over the chief engineer's beefy back as the other radio control men and the three heavily armed soldiers collapsed and fell where they stood.

Not a strangled cry had broken the swift, silent action, so rapidly had the deadly gas choked out their lives.

A black-robed, hooded figure dropped quickly through the trap and stood reaching up, his face hidden within the startlingly weird gas mask covering his head.

"Hand it down!" he ordered in a terse, gratingly harsh voice.

The black-robed arm of a similarly hooded and masked figure reached through the hole in the ceiling, passed a round, flat leather-covered parcel into those extended hands. Then the second man swung down through the opening, dropped to the floor.

With scarcely a glance at the ten dead engineers and soldiers sprawled in grotesquely pitiful huddles about the room, the two robed figures crossed wordlessly to the control switchboard. Working with expert speed, one of them disconnected several wires while the other opened the flat leather case, removed from it a black wax radio recording disc.

The first man turned abruptly, strode directly to a far corner of the long room, and came back carrying a standard studio electric portable phonograph. He hooked it up to the broadcast wires he had unfastened, glanced briefly at the wall clock, and put the black wax record on the machine.

"Good timing," his rasping voice commented. "One minute to twelve!"

His fingers flicked beneath his robe, came out holding a single small grey seal. Its design was an hour-glass, and a blood-red capital "I" was drawn upright through the stem.

He stepped quickly over to the body of Lieutenant Howard, moistened the back of the strange emblem with the army officer's blood, stuck the mysterious seal on the dead man's forehead.

His movements were swift, nerveless, as devoid of emotion as though he'd merely hurriedly pasted a stamp on a letter. He stepped back to the instrument desk, started the phonograph disc revolving, and poised the sensitive reproducing needle above the fine outer lines at the edge of the record.

"The President's uninvited ghost goes on the air in exactly thirty-five seconds," he said with low-voiced, exultant grimness.

The second robed figure, standing ready with one hand on a master-control switch, asked in a flat, dried voice:

"You sure we can get out of here all right?"

"Yellow?" Sneering contempt grated in the first man's quick, snarling retort. "The Imperator's experts never miss! We'll walk out, you fool, like ministering monks in the confusion when the dam blows!"

Slowly, nervelessly, the needle lowered toward the ominously whirling black record —A half mile away, at Rock Canyon Dam, the sweltering crowds shuffled restlessly in the hot noonday sun that beat down upon the colorful pageantry.

Enormous American flags draped the sheer walls of the gigantic dam, ready to be raised majestically on gaily bannered wires when the sluices opened at the President's pressure on an electric control key. The President himself, with his chosen administration officials and vigilant Secret-Service guards occupied a temporary, flag-draped stand in a niche cut into the rock wall above the dam.

From the horns of the public address system the National Anthem, played by the Marine Band in the nation's capital, swayed the eager watchers crowding the canyon's rugged, railed rim, and poured inspiringly from the radios of millions of listeners.

The Arlington-timed clock in the main announcer's cage at the near end of the dam showed ten seconds to noon. Mort Lewis, the veteran radio announcer, nodded to Toby, his assistant, and leaned tensely close to his microphone.

As the final rousing strains of the Marine Band faded, Lewis' clear baritone voice came over the air and through the canyon speakers along the rocky walls:

> "And now, ladies and gentlemen of America, the nation's Chief Executive is about to speak from Rock Canyon Dam-the President of the United States!"

A pause. Then the President's kindly, sincerely convincing voice: "My friends —"

Without warning, the President's voice was cut off by a sharp, amplified click.

For a bare fraction of a second there was a scratching sound, followed instantly by a swift, brassy, metallic flow of startling words:

> "This is the Imperator of the Two Americas speaking for the citizens of the rising Invisible Empire! Rock Canyon Dam, a futile project of a weak, incipient government, will be destroyed by explosives in exactly one hundred seconds. Future public disasters will follow until the purpose of constructive anarchy has been attained. Sixty seconds now remain before the explosion. I, the Imperator, have spoken!"

The chilling, metallic voice stopped with a clipped snap that was like a hammer blow on glass.

For a terrifying, suspended moment dead silence fell upon the air and gripped the assembled officials and spectators at Rock Canyon in a paralysis of helpless dread. Then pandemonium broke loose.

The crowds surged back away from the canyon's railed rim-fighting, shouting, cursing. Army officers, soldiers and state police rallied vainly to direct a swift, safe escape for the hysteria-crazed mauling mob.

Women and children were trampled underfoot. Strong men were knocked down by the wild, blundering rush. Screams drowned out the frantically shouted commands of the officers.

Three Secret Service guards grabbed the President bodily, rushed him back off the platform, hurried him out into a cleared roadway where they, with the willing help of his official party, made a white-faced, desperately protecting ring with their bodies.

Down on the rim of the dam, Mort Lewis shouted futilely into his dead mike in a frantic, heroic attempt to direct the crowd caught and jammed in the lower approaches. He waved Toby, his assistant, toward the exit bored into the canyon wall, rushed after him at the last second.

The veteran announcer was three yards from the narrow exit when the first terrific detonation rocked the canyon from deep in the bowels of the mighty dam. The rock walls trembled.

He stared down, hypnotized into rigidity by the enormous snake-like cracks appearing in a patternless maze across the solid face of the man-made water barrier. The greenish expanse of imprisoned flood, extending for miles back of the dam, rippled and shuddered.

And suddenly, as a second shock reverberated, Lewis' widened eyes narrowed on the black-hooded, cloaked figures emerging from a leaking sluice slot at the dam's base, running for shelter. A moment later, with three more thunderous explosions shattering the masonry, the center of the dam split open into an enormous, writhing V.

A harsh, angry roar arose drowning out the rumble of the rocking blasts, and the strangled water poured through the split, tearing away huge pieces of the dam, widening the vital opening.

The two fleeing black-robed figures disappeared, whirled away in the first rush of the flood that blotted out the power houses and buildings at the foot of the dam as though by, magic in a hellish cataract of thundering destruction.

The churning water rushed on, sweeping everything in its path. The helpless spectators, workmen and soldiers caught beneath the rising tide of the whirling, serpentine monster of death, were gone like straws, their despairing cries lost utterly in the horrifying roar of the plunging flood.

Mort Lewis swayed dizzily, leaped for the dangerous safety of the narrow exit at the end of the completely crumpling dam. He lunged halfway through the tunnel opening, was knocked down as part of the wall gave way.

Rocks and shale pounded down on his twisted legs, pinioned him helplessly to the stone floor. He lay there writhing, sweating in agony, while behind him the snarling torrent drowned out his shouting, fading voice.

Chapter Two
Red Warning

Lowering purplish storm clouds had hovered menacingly over New York City all day, seemingly caught and held stationary by the sharp spires and pinnacles of the towering skyscrapers. At three o'clock in the afternoon the storm hadn't broken yet, and the spasmodic rumble of thunder was just beginning to become annoying over radios in crackling static.

But it wasn't storm interference that broke in upon the swing music floating from the hidden radio in the large Moorish reception room of the stately Fifth Avenue residence of Mr. Frank Havens, the nationally known publisher. It was the announcer's smooth voice cutting in from Radio City:

> "Ladies and gentlemen, through the facilities of the National Broadcasting Company, you are about to hear the President of the United States speak from Rock Canyon Dam, Arizona, where he will formally open the largest irrigation system in the world. One moment, please —"

As the fading strains of the National Anthem, played by the U. S. Marine Band, swelled into the big, gaily crowded reception room, Muriel Havens stopped dancing and smiled whimsically up into the lean, tanned face of Richard Curtis Van Loan.

"Something official like that would have to break into my afternoon tea-dance," she protested with a little laugh, and started to signal a butler to dial in another program.

Dick Van Loan stopped her with a quick shake of his head and moved with her nearer the wide window where the radio was camouflaged in a flower-covered wall table.

"Mind if I listen to him?" he asked politely, and added, "The daughter of Frank Havens should be able to inflict the President's voice on her guests for a few min —"

His bantering words broke off abruptly as his sharp eyes flicked to the window.

Out across Central Park, rising high above the skyscrapers of the Roaring Forties to the south, blinking red lights on Frank Havens' towering Clarion Press Building gleamed now, flashing warningly, vividly against the purplish background of foreboding storm clouds.

The Phantom's signal! Neither exclamation nor tremor betrayed the vitalizing shock that whipped Dick Van Loan's nerves into tensed alertness. His signal-from Frank Havens-Around him the gay party went on, heedless and merrily ignorant of the dire call. Even Muriel Havens, the nationally powerful publisher's beautiful daughter, had no inkling of the grim Phantom drama being signaled in by those rapidly winking lights atop her father's Clarion tower.

Dick Van Loan's cryptic smile gave no hint of the driving turmoil seething within him as he deciphered that flashing code message:

> Calling the Phantom-Come to my office —
> Hurry-This is a murder call-Havens —
> Calling the Phantom —

The dots and dashes kept on winking ominously, would continue to blink that secret message until the Phantom himself contacted Frank Havens. Van Loan damned himself mentally. He'd been idling here, dancing, unalert to that urgent message.

But before his brain could hit upon an acceptably logical excuse to offer Muriel Havens for an abrupt departure, the familiar voice of the veteran radio announcer, Mort Lewis, broke in upon his consciousness:

> " —From Rock Canyon Dam-The President of the United States!"

Then the President's warm voice: "My friends —"

Dick Van Loan's eyes narrowed at the sharp click that interrupted the President's kindly greeting.

The next instant, as the first chilling words of that strange unannounced metallic voice came brassily over the air, Van stooped low over the radio table, his tensed fingers twisting off the volume. He motioned Muriel Havens away, dialed the icy flow of words until he alone in the room could hear:

" —the Imperator of the Two Americas speaking for the Invisible Empire. Rock Canyon Dam will be destroyed in-one hundred seconds. Future public disasters will follow-Sixty seconds —I, the Imperator, have spoken!"

Grimly, his knuckles white against the dial, Dick Van Loan spun the volume on full as the icy metallic voice stopped with a brittle snap that was like glass broken by a hammer blow. But now only a vague rumbling sound and the crackle of distant static came from the suddenly stilled station.

Tight-lipped, Van turned down the power to normal volume, dialed in a dance orchestra on a minor local station, and rose to face Muriel. No use disrupting her afternoon party with this new, grimly spectacular radio mystery. Damage enough, that millions of listeners had heard that dire, threatening voice.

"Something went wrong with the President's address," he said to her with a convincing smile of apology.

"I'm a very hard-boiled stockholder in that broadcasting company, so you won't mind. Muriel, if I run off from your very pleasant soiree to see what's happened?"

How much she minded was evident in her gently veiled, disappointed gaze as she let him go. But it was not a polite lie that Dick Van Loan used to excuse himself from the Havens home.

He did own stock in the National Broadcasting Company. In a number of other industrial corporations, too. And in Frank Havens' coast-to-coast chain of newspapers, including the New York Clarion. Richard Curtis Van Loan was wealthy, but not cumbersomely so.

But the tall, athletic Park Avenue clubman and man-about-town had cleared his mind of Muriel's tea-dance before he reached the curb. And he had no intention of driving first to Radio City, as he jumped into his fast, powerful coupe. South of Central Park, the Clarion tower lights were still flashing their urgent secret code for the Phantom.

And the Phantom was answering that call! Answering it now in the fast run of Dick Van Loan's dark blue coupe down Fifth Avenue and across town to Eighth.

He parked a block from the towering Clarion Press building, but did not immediately get out of the car. Instead, bending low in the coupe's seat, he produced from a panel beneath him a small, compactly equipped make-up kit.

Working rapidly, with swift glances of caution at the hurrying pedestrians passing a few feet from the car windows, he began the familiar task of disguising his features. It was an old story with him, this quick change of character.

Always, when the inevitable Clarion call came to war on crime, it was Van's deft, experienced fingers that brought the Phantom into being again-as those sure, artistic fingers had done in the beginning. For the Phantom was Dick Van Loan's own creation, a product of his restless energy, his fearless demand for action, and his determination to put his wealth and talents to the best use.

Van hated crime and criminals instinctively. But it was Frank Havens, a far older man, who had shown him that always, behind the scenes of every series of modern crimes, some one brain, some one man, was the ruthless guiding genius, untouchable by the usual forces of law or the police.

The Phantom was Richard Curtis Van Loan's answer to the death challenge of lawlessness. The Phantom, a sinister figure without name, without identity-more untouchable and grimly mysterious than the slipperiest of those crooks and killer geniuses of crime whose ravages he was fighting.

It was the Phantom's real identity, the identity of Richard Curtis Van Loan behind the varied character disguises of the Phantom, that had to be ultimately and desperately protected.

Without that complete anonymity, all the aids he used-the different character roles, the three hideouts, his gift of ventriloquism, even the red code lights still signalling him from the pinnacle of the Clarion Building-went for naught.

Dick Van Loan slid the make-up case under the seat into its trick compartment. But it wasn't the Park Avenue clubman who sat upright in the coupe now.

The lean, tanned face had disappeared, replaced by a square featured, sallow-skinned man twenty years older than Van Loan. The hair was combed unbecomingly on the opposite side of the greying head, and the eyebrows curled upward belligerently.

A twist of the necktie, a slip of two notches in the soft leather belt, and an awkward, ill-fitting hitch of the grey suit coat, rounded out the convincing picture of a rugged, aggressive but personally sloppy and rather shopworn character of no particular qualifications.

What unknown talents the character possessed, were added to by a shoulder-holstered Colt .38 automatic, a carefully pocketed black silk mask, a pencil flashlight, and a peculiarly designed platinum and diamond badge.

It was seventeen minutes after three o'clock in the afternoon, and the delayed storm was just beginning to spatter the pavement with the first big drops of a heavy rain, when the Phantom, alias Jim Doran, jammed a crumpled panama low over his eyes and faded down the street away from the locked coupe.

He paused abruptly at the corner of Eighth Avenue, lighted a cigarette as he listened to an announcer's tense voice cracking from a loudspeaker in a radio shop doorway:

> "Flash! The giant government irrigation project at Rock Canyon Dam, Arizona, has just been destroyed by a series of devastating explosions. The entire dam has been demolished and the canyon itself is a raging torrent. Loss of life is estimated at well over a thousand, with the toll mounting.

> "Property damage will be incalculable until the water now sweeping the whole Arizona valley spends itself. The President of the United States was saved by quick action on the part of his Secret Service guards and members of his staff. This report comes by telephone from Phoenix, all radio facilities at Rock Canyon having been destroyed by the disastrous explosions.

> "A mysterious voice, cutting in upon the President's dedicatory address at the dam a few seconds before the series of blasts, threatened this fatal national disaster and others to follow.

> "Federal investigators are flying to the scene. This is the first report that has been received. More details will be broadcast as they are relayed to us."

The voice stopped, and people on the street stared blankly at one another, stunned, heedless of the increasing rain.

Jim Doran's squarish face became rocky, his keen grey eyes smoldering as he strode grimly a half block north. He ducked into a subway kiosk, came up into the Clarion Building on the other side of the wet street.

The Phantom was reborn.

Chapter Three
Special Corpse

The editorial offices of the Clarion were on the eleventh floor and Frank Havens had a bullet-proof glass cubicle there, raised above the floor level in a far corner.

But the publisher's real office was a triplex suite on the eighty-fifth and top floors of the towering press building, reached only by a private express elevator entered through a sliding panel in that non-shatterable glass cubicle overlooking the editorial rooms.

Turmoil and cyclonic confusion seemed to have hit the enormous editorial office when Jim Doran stepped off the public elevator and was stopped by the wise-eyed blond receptionist at the railing gate. Telephones jangled, typewriters and teletypes clattered, adding to the bedlam of excitedly shouted orders and rushing copy boys.

But the suspense-ridden, grinding overtones of the Clarion's frenzied editorial department, the Phantom realized grimly, was only a larger duplicate, of the frantic commotion occurring in every metropolitan press editorial room in the country at this moment. The universal, terse newspaper cry was:

Hold that Rock Canyon wire open!

"Jim Doran, to see Mr. Frank Havens," Van told the girl curtly. Jim Doran was one of the score of names that Dick Van Loan and the publisher had agreed upon as Phantom aliases. "Mr. Havens is expecting me," he added as the girl at the desk hesitated.

She gave him a sharp, respectfully curious glance as she finished putting through the call to Havens' quarters, and a moment later Jim Doran was slouching through the familiar maze of editorial desks, guided by an alert copy boy.

Toby, the publisher's trusted elevator guard, rode him up in the private express car from the glass cubicle, watching him warily but without recognition. Toby had known Richard Curtis Van Loan for some years.

Van's veiled grey eyes hid his satisfaction, as the keen scrutiny of the operator failed to catch the slightest flaw in the quick character make-up of nondescript Jimmy Doran. Toby's shrewd, bold eyes were always an infallible first test.

At the eighty-fifth floor, the swarthy operator slid back the elevator door. Jim Doran stepped out of the car, stood a moment in the ornately furnished reception foyer staring belligerently at the uniformed policeman eyeing him suspiciously. Behind him, the car door slid shut silently as Toby took the elevator down again.

"I'm here to see Mr. Havens," Van announced in a deep, gruff voice that was not at all the smooth baritone of Richard Curtis Van Loan. "Didn't expect to find you cops up here."

Before the policeman could question him, Judkins' tall, bald-headed figure appeared on a balcony at one end of the room. The publisher's confidential secretary called down to the cop:

"If that's Mr. Doran, send him right up, officer."

Van nodded to the cop, brushed past him and mounted the staircase to the balcony.

Judkins' sallow glance was nervous but his worried brown eyes were without recognition as he led Jim Doran through a doorway into a large room that was more lounge than office.

"Mr. James Doran," he announced, and withdrew, closing the door.

Frank Havens' penetrating gaze darted up sharply as Dick Van Loan crossed to the wide, polished walnut desk behind which the publisher sat drumming his fingers anxiously. Six other men, one in the uniform of a police captain, looked up quickly from the armchair about which they were grouped.

But the figure slumped in that chair did not move.

As Van's swift glance took in the unusual tableau, his right hand swung across the desk toward Havens in a hearty handshake that hid the small platinum-and-diamond badge palmed in his long fingers. The significant emblem of a mask outlined by the brilliant gems was the only design on the smooth platinum surface of that cryptic shield. But it was enough.

Frank Havens' worried eyes glinted with recognition as Van's swift fingers gave him, but not the others, a flashing look at that Phantom badge. The emblem disappeared again in Jim Doran's hand.

"Gentlemen, Mr. James Doran!" Havens said and stood up from behind his desk. The name had weight now as he spoke it. Jim Doran was no longer a password name, but had become a reality. "Mr. Doran will represent me in this investigation." He nodded his grey head toward the silent figure in the armchair.

Van stepped over to the armchair, his eyes on the domelike head of the middle-aged man slumped there. A small fleck of blood stained the fellow's white lips as the Phantom raised the lolling head and studied the fixed expression of sheer surprise stamped on the dead man's face.

Rigor mortis had not yet set in, and there were no visible marks of violence on the neatly dressed body.

"This wants some preliminary explaining," Jim Doran grumbled. "I didn't think anybody'd be interested in just one corpse, after what happened at Rock Creek Canyon."

"We know about that," the officer in the captain's uniform said. "This happens to be New York City, not Arizona."

Van glanced up, curiously aware that Havens, in his repressed excitement, had not named him as the Phantom, although two of the men in street clothes were obviously homicide detectives.

The other three men in the room were big, well dressed fellows. Frank Havens made the brief introductions.

One of the strangers was Warden Jack Bluebold of Alleghany Penitentiary at Mountainview, Pennsylvania. The next man was Dr. Maurice Jessup, resident surgeon at the Alleghany prison. The third was ex-Congressman Harry Arnold, a Pennsylvania politician. The three of them stayed close together in a compact, capable group.

Havens eyed the lifeless figure in the armchair, frowned and said:

> "Lester Gimble is-was-one of the leading metallurgists in this country. Because I wanted an article on the subject, I induced him to interview Dr. Waldo Junes, the famous scientist who is conducting some unusual experiments in metals at the General Electric laboratory at Niagara Falls. Gimble was on his way back here —"

Havens broke off, nodded to the plainclothes men.

"Simmons and me," the taller of the two dicks said, jerking his head at his partner, "were standing in Grand Central Station near the taxicab entrance about two-thirty this afternoon, when this fellow Gimble shows with a suitcase and a briefcase, coming from the lower level train platforms.

"He starts to get into a cab, when two guys take a shot at him from behind. He dropped his bags and swung round. One of the gunmen grabs up his suitcase and the other one got the briefcase. Simmons and me opened up on 'em then and there was a hell of a lot of racket and commotion.

"I killed the bird with the suitcase before he got ten steps, but the one with the briefcase got into the crowd where Simmons didn't dare shoot. So far as we heard yet, the second guy got away. A lot of cops were after him by that time, so Simmons and me took care of this Gimble who'd been shot at.

"He claimed he wasn't either hit or hurt, and had to get over here to see Mr. Havens in a hurry —" The tall detective shrugged and glanced deprecatingly at Captain Walters.

"Well, we knew who Mr. Havens was, so we took Gimble and his suitcase and brought him over here."

Frank Havens nodded. "The right thing to do, under the circumstances." His blue, penetrating eyes swung to the Phantom. "Mr. Gimble came in here with these two officers and sat down in the chair he's in now, he hadn't said anything on the short ride over, and he was looking rather white. Before he had a chance to talk, he slumped over and died.

"I had the Clarion's staff physician rush right up here from downstairs, but nothing could be done. We found that Gimble had been shot in the spine."

"That's why we didn't see any blood," Detective Simmons stated. "Them kind of wounds don't hardly bleed at all, and the victim don't feel he's been shot because he's numbed. He don't die until the fluid in the spine drains out like an internal hemorrhage. But how was we to know—"

"The Clarion physician exonerated both of you," Havens declared. "I've heard of similar cases, particularly during the war. Gimble would have died anyway. But what are we going to do now?"

He turned to Van. "I phoned for Captain Walters and asked him to keep this free of the regular police routine for one hour. I'm glad you got here so quickly, Mr. Doran."

"If you haven't found anything of importance in Gimble's suitcase, or on his person, and if that scientist, Dr. Junes up in Niagara Falls, can't give you a lead of some sort," Van growled, "you don't need any help until the police catch the gunman who got away with Gimble's briefcase." He shot a look at Captain Walters. "That is, unless the man this detective killed can be identified."

"We're working on that angle," Walters snapped, and said pointedly to Havens, "If it's okay now, let's have the Homicide Squad and the Medical Examiner in on this."

Havens eyed Van questioningly, and when Jim Doran nodded, the precinct captain picked up the phone, asked for Headquarters.

"There was absolutely nothing in Gimble's pockets, nor in his suitcase, that points to a clue," Havens said emphatically. "We went through everything while we were waiting for you. And I've put a call through to the General Electric Experimental Laboratory, but Dr. Junes refuses to be disturbed and won't answer the phone."

He motioned Van to follow him across the large room to a teletype machine in the corner. The tape, twisting snakelike over the rim of the overflowing receptacle, was still uncoiling the grim account of the life and property toll at Rock Canyon Dam.

Havens fingered the ticker-tape with a trembling hand, looked searchingly at the Phantom. "I didn't tell them"—he nodded toward the three police officers, and lowered his voice —"who you were, because I thought you'd want to work on that Arizona disaster, Van."

Jim Doran's slatey eyes were inscrutable. "I saw the Clarion tower lights signaling just before the N.B.C. network started to put the President on the air. Yes, Frank," he agreed in a grave, low-pitched tone, "I'd like to go after the brain that is directing these catastrophes. I heard his voice-if that was his voice, making that threat over the radio. Somebody will have to stop him!"

The Phantom looked keenly at the famous publisher. Havens was staring out through the wide windows overlooking Manhattan and the New Jersey hills green against the background of dark, scudding rain clouds. The older man's blue, moody eyes seemed to be envisaging the calamity that threatened those peaceful, rolling lands and the vast country beyond, presaged in the thin, endless record of the tape sliding implacably through his fingers.

"Somebody must stop him!" Havens repeated with a note of despair in the almost-whispered words.

Van asked shrewdly, "What did you send Gimble to Niagara for, Frank? It wasn't just a news article you wanted!"

"You're right," Havens confessed. "Dr. Junes is trying to unite two metals, aluminum and calbite, heretofore impossible of fusion because high enough temperatures couldn't be reached. It's an experiment a lot of steel and munitions manufacturers would like to know about.

"If those two metals can be fused, the result will be the most impenetrable armorplate in the world, a new metal ten thousand times harder and stronger than the toughest of modern steels!"

"At least tough enough to get Lester Gimble murdered," Van commented, and glanced at the three big men from Pennsylvania. "What are those fellows here for?"

"Ex-Congressman Arnold came here with the other two prison officials to ask me to stop giving publicity in my newspapers to the graft and corruption that's been reported at Alleghany

Penitentiary. They were here when Gimble came in. Harry Arnold is chairman of the Pennsylvania Board of Parole and Pardons. He and Bluebold and Jessup claim the publicity I've been giving their prison has interfered with their attempts to ferret out and clean up the prison rottenness. I'm convinced they're right, too."

Van nodded, and said to Havens as the police captain called to them, "Keep the Phantom out of this, Frank, until I tell you otherwise."

Captain Walters had finished phoning, with flustering results.

"A sour mess this is turning out to be!" he exclaimed. "Doran, you wanted to get a line on that bird Jackson, the detective, killed."

Van's voice slipped into character again, became a harsh, demanding growl.

"If it's a lead, hand it out," he grumbled.

"It's a lead that's going to raise hell over in Pennsylvania," Walters declared. "That gunman Jackson shot is Snakey Willow, a lifer at Alleghany Penitentiary!"

The three brawny prison officials eyeing Captain Walters glanced sharply over to Frank Havens and Jim Doran.

"Snakey Willow —" Warden Bluebold's voice was a dry rasp. "He was in the prison three days ago, when we left. By —"

"Yeah," Walters said caustically. "He ain't there now! And I didn't see any police teleflash about his escape yet, neither. But that's not all. The rogues gallery picture of him we had at Headquarters don't fit his face. He had a fresh operation on his mug! If he'd been able to erase his fingerprints, we'd never have found out who he was!"

Dr. Maurice Jessup, the prison's resident surgeon, frowned, and glanced sharply at Bluebold. "I don't think the report you received is correct. Not in intent, anyway, sir. I remember Willow —I should, because he had an accident in the prison foundry and I operated to save his life. His face was very badly burned, so I did my best to patch it up. If that's what you refer to, Captain."

"Well," Walters said grudgingly, "that's different!"

Harry Arnold, the ex-congressman from Pennsylvania, broke in with, "It's a mistake that Willow was able to escape at all! Mr. Havens, you can see the state things are in at Alleghany Prison. If there's any more adverse publicity, we're apt to have a prison riot or an organized jailbreak. If you'll give us some help, by stopping advertising the conditions, I'll guarantee the prison is cleaned up!"

"You're right, Mr. Arnold," Havens said determinedly. "I'll do my best to keep this escape quiet. But see that the prison is reorganized at once, or I'll have to expose the whole situation, and you're apt to have the Federal Prison authorities step in!"

Jim Doran's slatey eyes had become the color of muddy marble. He nodded abruptly to the men in the office. "The police can handle this. I'll get the details later from them," he announced curtly, and strode out of the room.

But only Frank Havens caught and appreciated the determined, eager gleam that had crept into Jim Doran's sardonic gaze.

Several police officials, two internes and a man from the medical examiner's office were waiting in the bulletproof glass cubicle down on the eleventh floor when Van got out of the elevator. The editorial room was still a bedlam of cyclonic confusion.

Out on Eighth Avenue a persistent rain was wetting the shouted Clarion extras:

TITANIC EXPLOSIONS WRECK
HUGE FEDERAL PROJECT

Weird Radio Voice Threatens Further Disasters

Chapter Four
Dread Snatch

Snakey Willow's body lay flat and deflated on the cold morgue slab when Van pulled back the disinfected white sheet and bent close over the dead killer's wax-like face. Even in death, the escaped murderer's features were menacing and evil.

Special attention had evidently been given Snakey Willow's face-lifting operation by the Bellevue Hospital medicos, for the recently healed incisions under the tight-skinned jowls and along the high cheekbones had been slit open again by the autopsy scalpels.

Studying those freshly reopened incisions keenly the Phantom smiled thinly to himself.

He was no M.D., but mechanized crime hunts had led him deeply into the study of modern drugs, hypnosis and medicine. He recognized here, in Snakey Willow's now mutilated features, the sensitive hand of an exceptionally fine surgeon.

The criminal's nose had been remoulded, shortened and widened in a manner that tended to broaden the appearance of the unchangeable bone structure of the narrow head. No wonder the sharp eyes of the New York City police had failed to recognize that revamped face.

But it was the deft, startlingly liberal application of skin grafting that held the Phantom's concentrated attention. He fingered a small, powerful magnifying glass from his vest pocket, focused it upon those hundreds of individual skin grafts that had covered the incisions of the original plastic surgery operation.

Each graft, he knew, had been a separate detail taking time and infinite patience-and taking, also, a dangerously large amount of live skin.

Van pulled the white sheet all the way off the nude figure, examined the body carefully from shoulders to feet for scars of skin removal. He found none, and slid the sheet back up over the corpse slowly, his grey eyes moody and thoughtful.

Some other person had provided the live skin for this facial operation. And from the amount of skin grafted, it had been a dangerous venture for the donor.

Snakey Willow was not a type to have sacrificing friends. And prison hospitals didn't provide such donations for convicts. Somebody had been paid a big sum for the skin used. Or else force had been used to take it.

Before Jim Doran replaced the magnifying glass in his pocket, he examined the dead man's fingertips. They had been tampered with, showed the marks of acid burns, but the tell-tale whorls had not been eradicated.

Even skin grafting could not stop those true fingerprints from growing back again to identify their owner. Snakey Willow had, it seemed, tried to polish off for criminally practical purposes a job the prison surgeon had done to save his life.

Van Loan left the Bellevue morgue with three convictions:

The prison surgeon who had repaired Snakey Willow's face had performed one of the finest technical and artistic operations the Phantom had ever seen. The skin grafting job had taken more live epidermis than any one donor could safely give. And the entire operation had cost far more money than Snakey Willow could ever have paid.

Beyond those three conclusions the Phantom refused to confuse his mind with speculation. He made a phone call from a drug store booth to his garage, asking that his coupe be picked up near the Clarion Building.

A second telephone message got Wild Jerry Lannigan at the mid-town apartment where the Phantom kept sanctuary quarters under Lannigan's name.

"Holmes Airport at eight this evening, Champ," he said curtly when the big red-headed man's voice boomed over the wire. "We're flying the Beechcraft to Buffalo."

At the other end of the line he could hear Jerry Lannigan's explosive exclamation of enthusiasm. "Champ" was the familiar name that only the Phantom used for the beefy, reckless ex-army mechanic and pilot. It served as a confidential and friendly identification, for not even Lannigan knew the Phantom was Richard Van Loan.

"Okay, Skipper!" Lannigan was too close to Van personally to use The Phantom appellation, and too smart to bandy it over a public phone. "The ship'll be gassed and oiled. It's about time something happened. I heard that guy with the screwy voice break in on the President's radio broadcast—"

Van cut him off with a cryptic, "So did too many other people, Champ. The man at the airport will be Professor Bendix," and hung up.

The Jim Doran disguise had sufficed for the hurried Phantom appearance at the Clarion, but a character of far more ponderance would be needed for the difficult interview Van planned. And there was some special technical information he wanted before he visited Dr. Waldo Junes at the General Electric Experimental Laboratory at Niagara Falls.

The place to effect both of these needs was in the seclusion of that sound- and explosion-proof lab in the old abandoned river-front building up on the East Side.

There was nothing of the scientist in the appearance of the slouching figure of Jim Doran as he swung off a First Avenue bus at Ninetieth Street and ambled with wary carelessness toward the East River.

At the dock end of the street a deserted red brick warehouse loomed on the left, its dirty windows staring vacuously through the still drizzling rain of the late summer afternoon. Jim Doran paused as he reached the corner of the decrepit building, glanced furtively about him.

The next instant he had faded into the darker shadows beneath the dilapidated loading platform.

A gaping, broken coal-chute window let him drop through into the darkness of the warehouse basement. He crossed the musty concrete floor with quick, familiar steps, produced a small brass key from a hidden crevice in the masonry at the opposite end of the silent cellar.

A moment later and he'd unlocked and pulled open a heavy counter-balanced steel and concrete trap door in the floor.

The Phantom lowered himself down a metal ladder, closed the trap above him, locked it and snapped on a light switch. He stood in the large steel-walled sub-cellar laboratory of Professor Paul Bendix.

Three-quarters of the long, low-ceilinged chamber was equipped with indestructible work tables upon which were an array of glass jars, racks of test tubes, Bunsen burners, heat-resisting crocks. A large electric arc furnace filled one corner of the modern lab. And along two walls were rows of compactly stacked shelves of chemical supplies.

The remaining quarter of the long room was a well stocked scientific library of modern chemistry, physics and crime literature in bound volumes, in professional technical magazines, and in those privately printed abstruse brochures published by the more learned scientific societies for purposes of research. The library represented seven languages.

There were no windows in the room, but a hidden ventilation system operating through a disused chimney in the warehouse tended to the air and chemical fumes when Professor Bendix used the laboratory. Behind a screen in a corner of the library was a couch, a dressing table, a shower and a large steel wardrobe case with a combination lock.

Jim Doran stepped over to that wardrobe, unlocked and opened it with four deft turns of the dial.

Inside hung an array of clothes-the rough garments of Gunner McGlone, a Chinatown character as mysterious as he was tough; the loud-checked suit of Lucky Luke Lamar, the swaggering gambler; the tuxedo and dinner clothes of Maxie Herman the Hermit, a unique Broadway figure who emerged bat-like from some undiscovered seclusion to frequent the night clubs, cabarets and expensive gambling and vice dens of Manhattan after dark.

There, too, hung the greenish, antique frock coat, the wing-collared shirt and the baggy striped trousers of that strange, erratically brilliant scientist, Professor Paul Bendix, the owner of this underground laboratory.

A brief smile of appreciation curved Dick Van Loan's lips as his grey eyes slid over that array of garments.

He touched the sleeve of Maxie the Hermit's tuxedo reminiscently.

The last time he'd worn that disguise, the Hermit had exchanged hot lead with Trigger Dwyer, now dead, across the crooked roulette table of the extinct Gold Casino Club.

The Phantom's smile faded, shutting out the past. This was a grimmer case he was facing. The tough disguise of Gunner McGlone might prove more appropriate in combating the murderer of Lester Gimble. But right now Professor Paul Bendix was needed.

He took down the faded, greenish frock coat and the rest of the professor's eccentric, old-fashioned clothes. From the bottom of the steel wardrobe cabinet he lifted a metal make-up box, opened it on the mirror-backed dressing table.

Sitting before the triple mirror, with a strong electric light focusing his reflection, the Phantom's trained fingers went to work. Jim Doran disappeared, became Richard Curtis Van Loan again.

Then the lean, tanned face of the Park Avenue clubman faded rapidly beneath the squarish, bearded features of Professor Bendix.

Fifteen minutes later the Phantom closed and locked the steel cabinet and adjusted the worn frock coat on his padded shoulders.

Professor Bendix was a big man physically as well as scientifically, and spoke with a slightly guttural accent. Van made a few practise gestures before the mirrors, then turned to the shelves of specialized technical books and magazines.

For a solid hour he pored over involved treatises dealing with metallurgy and explosives. Rock Canyon Dam was supposed to have been engineered to withstand even T.N.T. and the newer picric acid explosive compounds.

And for another hour he studied various medical journals, confining his research to articles on plastic surgery and skin grafting. Dr. Jessup's operation on Willow might not have been a matter of sheer coincidence.

By seven o'clock he was finished, his mind a bit fagged from the strain of such continuous concentration. But his confidence was backed now by definite knowledge of the specialized and seemingly unrelated subjects he appeared to be up against.

He let himself out of the laboratory through the heavy steel door that opened directly onto the stubby concrete dock jutting out into the East River. Van had bought and equipped this abandoned warehouse under the name of Paul Bendix, so in character he was free to come and go as he chose, without the handicap of secrecy —a stooped, hulking and harmless old gentleman steeped in abstract problems of pure science.

He phoned Frank Havens from a booth, caught him still in the Clarion office, and identified himself with a clipped: "Jim Doran."

"I'm going to Niagara, flying with the Champ," he said cryptically. "Dr. Bendix. But unannounced, Frank. Anything new come up?"

Haven's voice was irritable with worry. "Yes. Mort Lewis, the radio announcer at Rock Canyon, was the last man alive off the dam. He was found partially buried in a tunnel exit, but was revived. He reports that two men wearing black robes and black hoods ran out of the bottom of the dam after the first two explosions, and were drowned in the flood. Several soldiers claim they saw two similarly robed figures walking away from the building there that was used for the radio control station. Every man in that radio station was murdered, including the guards!"

The Phantom whistled tunelessly through clamped teeth. Havens' voice went on:

"Somebody tried unsuccessfully to break into the ore exhibit of the Smithsonian Institute at Washington, D. C., last night. An F.B.I. man has been added to the building's regular watchmen.

"How do you figure a connection?" Van asked. "The Smithsonian is a long jump from a revival of the Ku Klux idea in Arizona."

"I'm not figuring," Havens' voice snapped, and the publisher added apologetically a moment later, "It's only that I know Dr. Junes visited the Smithsonian a month ago and was given a chip off a meteoric fragment on display there. He was using it, how I don't know, in his Niagara experiments with aluminum and calbite. I rather expected you'd go out to that Alleghany Penitentiary, after finding Willow had escaped."

"There's the two choices," the Phantom explained. "Remember, Gimble was murdered evidently for information he'd got from Dr. Junes. If I can see Junes first, I might have something positive to work on from the prison angle, afterward. You'll hear from me."

He hung up. Out on the street, he bought a late Clarion extra. The dam disaster in Arizona, the headlines screamed, was still spreading destruction through the lower valley of the enormous Federal project.

Arizona state militia had taken charge of the paralyzed flood district, and the Federal Bureau of Investigation had a number of men on the job. But as yet nothing definite had been unearthed regarding either the mechanics of the terrific explosion, or the fiendish operators who had set off those devastating blasts.

On a back page, crowded in with the comparatively inconsequential local news, was a short item about the shooting that afternoon in Grand Central Station. It was given out that Lester Gimble had died suddenly on his way home from the attack, with a bullet lodged in his spine, But the fact that he had actually died in the Clarion Press Building was omitted.

The motive was given as probably robbery.

Professor Paul Bendix left the newspaper on the counter of a diner where he ate a hurried meal, and climbed into a taxi. As the cab rolled over Queensboro Bridge toward Holmes Airport, the nearest aviation field on Long Island, the cab radio began announcing late news.

The Phantom listened moodily to more flood reports from the Arizona area. But suddenly his eyes narrowed as a flash announcement came over the air:

> Niagara Falls, New York. Dr. Waldo Junes, noted chemical scientist conducting secret metallurgical experiments in the General Electric Research Laboratories in that city, was driven from his underground workshop late this afternoon by an explosion that demolished a portion of the laboratory and wrecked his experiment. The Doctor is at home, recovering from shock, and claims he cannot explain the cause of the blast, but will never attempt the experiment again that he was conducting, because of the danger to humanity —a danger which he also refuses to explain.

Professor Paul Bendix leaned forward in the cab seat, his grey eyes sharp and penetrating beneath their shaggy brows.

"Faster!" he called to the taxi driver in a terse, guttural voice. "A bonus for speed!"

The cab spurted ahead, raced along Northern Boulevard, swung left through the entrance to Holmes Airport.

The swift red and silver Beechcraft cabin biplane was waiting on the line, its propeller already turning.

The Phantom threw a five-dollar bill to the cab driver, lurched out of the taxi, loping in hurrying strides to the plane. The fiery red head of Big Jerry Lannigan, visible through the open window of the cabin's cockpit, turned as Professor Bendix pulled himself into the ship.

"Hiya, Skipper!" Lannigan said, and grinned. "We're going places again, eh? Reminds me of—"

His good-humored voice broke off and the grin on his freckled, weathered face faded abruptly as he recognized the grim determination in the Phantom's darting eyes.

"Get going, Champ," Van then snapped. "Full throttle! We'll talk in the air. Head for Buffalo."

Jerry Lannigan's beefy shoulders hunched over the controls, and the powerful motor roared. The ship taxied rapidly, swung into the wind, thundered down the runway.

A minute later Long Island was dropping swiftly away below them as Jerry wound up the retractable landing gear. The climbing plane banked and headed north across the Sound.

Chapter Five
Hooded Kill

Darkness had descended over the nation's capital. Yet Washington, sweltering in the heat, was a murmuring hive of excitement and near panic. The Rock Canyon Dam disaster was on everyone's tongue.

The lights in the Smithsonian Institute had been turned out, but that building of strange antiques and specimens was being guarded by a Secret Service man.

Standing in a window on the second floor of the Smithsonian Building, Jud Marks, the Federal Bureau of Investigation operative stationed in the building, was staring out at the red marker lights atop the shaft of the Washington Monument. He was a large, rawboned man, with sharp blue eyes, a blond mustache and a jutting jaw.

He turned quickly as a slight shuffling noise caught his ear, but it was only one of the regular night watchmen making his rounds.

Jud Marks signaled the man and turned back to the window. He lighted a cigarette, smoked half of it leisurely, and suddenly dropped it to the floor, scrubbed it out with the toe of his shoe as his narrowed eyes stared down at the driveway below.

A long, black sedan, its headlights extinguished, was rolling to a stop beside the delivery entrance to the building. But nobody got out of the car immediately.

Marks watched the car a moment longer, then moved away from the window toward the stairway. There was, so far as he knew, no official of the Smithsonian Institute who had stayed in the building after it had been closed up for the night, no person here who would have a car call for him.

He started down to investigate, but flattened abruptly against the wall halfway down the staircase as two shadowy figures darted across the corridor below.

Jud Marks jerked out his gun, ran silently the rest of the way down the stairs, following those two fast-moving, furtive figures. He lost them among the glass cases of stuffed reptiles on exhibition in a room of the west wing.

Out in the big dark main foyer an electric flashlight in the hand of one of the regular night watchmen made a thin, yellowish shaft across the stone floor. A second later the light blinked out, clattered onto the flagging, and there was a quick, stifled moan, then the dull thud of a falling body.

Marks ran back into the foyer, his own torch shooting a shaft of light before him.

In the moving beam the watchman's body was a huddled heap on the floor, and a flow of blood coursed redly from a wound in the unconscious guard's back. The protruding black handle of a knife was visible.

This, the tall F.B.I. operative saw in a sliding glance as his torchlight jerked across and outlined for an instant a black-robed, black-hooded figure running through a doorway into the mineral exhibit room.

Marks bent down over the watchman on the floor, saw that he was dead, then plunged after the hooded killer. And as he swung through the open doorway a human catapult hit him.

A knife blade ripped his coat in a swift downward plunge. He whirled aside, slammed into a wall behind him, snapped on his flashlight to get a target for the automatic in his right hand. The light struck full against a corpse-grey mask covering a face hidden beneath a black, monklike hood. The Federal operative's gun fired low, purposely. The robed murderer would be more valuable alive than dead.

But in the split-second it took to change his aim, the grim target spun aside, leaped at him again with poised knife. Marks' slug chipped the stone wall harmlessly.

Then the killer was on him again, cursing with harsh, rasping oaths. The long-bladed knife slashed at Jud, ripped through his sleeve, burned paralyzingly through the flesh of his warding forearm, knocking the electric torch from his grip.

As the light dropped, its rays for a split-second swept down across two more robed and hooded men crouched over an open glass display case. They were lifting from its bed a silver-colored rough ball-like piece of metal the size of a small goldfish bowl-the meteoric fragment Dr. Hugo Junes had taken a chip from.

The torch cracked out against the stone flooring, blotting off the strange tableau. From somewhere off in the darkness another gun exploded and a scream of agony started and broke off. The powerful arms closed around Jud Marks' body, lifting him into the air.

He fought now like a wild man, his gun hand gripped in the viselike fist of his smothering opponent. The man in that weird hooded garb had the strength of a gorilla. Ju jitsu and judo were useless tricks in this swaying, gasping, silent battle.

Marks kicked back with his heels, tried to dislodge the footing of the man holding him off the floor. The grip about his waist only tightened.

He was vaguely aware of blurred movement across in the darkness. A torch gleamed in the doorway at the rear of the room, advanced toward them. The man he was struggling with shrieked out a curse, called for help.

The next moment a second hooded unknown ripped the gun from Marks' grip, cracked him in the jaw with a driving fist. Jud's senses rocked as the second and third blows crashed against him.

"He's not a watchman," an authoritative, icy voice stated. The torch shone blindingly in Marks, eyes. "Who is he?"

"I'll kill him and find out afterward!" The powerful arms took a fresh grip about the F.B.I. man's body.

Jud felt fingers jabbing into his pockets as the light blinked out. He stopped struggling, breathing hard, waiting for an opportunity to break free. He could feel the sharp point of the long knife against his ribs.

"Federal agent of the Bureau of Investigation," the first voice grated as the flashlight jabbed its beam at the badge that had been taken from Marks' vest pocket.

"All the more reason to use the knife on him," the growled voice of the man pinioning Marks' arm said ruthlessly.

"A damned good reason not to!" the man with the electric torch snapped. "Give him the pencil and we'll take him along. We've got what we want here. The chief wants one of these Federals for questioning. Wants to find out how much the bureau knows about him. Use the pencil on him and toss him in the car. We've got to get out of here!"

"I ain't got one of them pencils with me —"

"You're a damn fool!" The hooded, white-masked face in front of Jud Marks came closer, taking a thick black pencil from his pocket.

Marks' slitted eyes glared fearlessly, helplessly.

The hand holding the pencil thrust it close to Jud's face.

"Have a nice nap, copper!"

"I'll see you in hell!" Marks grated defiantly.

"Well-you'll get there eventually yourself," the black-robed man promised.

A cruel, sadistic chuckle sounded behind the Federal agent. A faintly bluish puff of odorless gas squirted suddenly from the pencil into Marks' face. The F. B. I. man gagged, coughed once, then went limp as unconsciousness swept over him.

"Tape him up and lock him in the luggage trunk on the sedan," the one with the electric flashlight directed as he put away his gas pencil. "Everything else is ready. Hurry up. We've got a long hard trip."

The unconscious Secret Service operative was picked up bodily, carried to the delivery entrance, dropped on the floor while adhesive tape was plastered over his eyes and lips and wrapped around his wrists and ankles.

As he was carried out and crammed into the trunk on the rack at the rear of the car, the rough ball of heavy metal the meteoric fragment taken from the glass case in the ore exhibition room, was being wrapped in a blanket and placed in the bottom of the car. Ten minutes later that long, black sedan was purring across the Potomac River into Virginia where it turned to the right and headed north in the night.

Chapter Six
Torture Death

All through the fast two and a half-hour flight against a strong crosswind, Dr. Paul Bendix sat in the front seat beside Lannigan, and seemed half asleep. His cryptic answers to the big red-headed Irishman's questions were enigmatic and curt.

"We'll have to wait, Champ," he told Lannigan flatly, "until we find out what's been going on with Dr. Junes' metallurgical experiments. With murder at one end, and an explosion at the other, there's more than the ordinary crime-for-money motive behind this peculiar affair."

"Some big mob is working again," Jerry declared. "Another gang of crooks like that arson outfit that tried to blackmail New York City, eh? I'd like to get my hands on 'em!"

Van veiled the fragment of a wry smile behind his drooping eyelids. Jerry Lannigan was a whirlwind in a fight, fearless and trustworthy beyond reason, and far from dumb. But it was sometimes a tough job to hold the big fellow back from too sudden action that might warn off the unknown brain operating back of a sequence of crimes.

Jerry Lannigan had been the top sergeant-mechanic in charge of the pursuit squadron that Richard Curtis Van Loan had commanded as a flying major during the World War. And Lannigan, loyal and faithful, kicked and shoved by chance three times around the world since then, had tried to find the man who had been his C.O. in France.

He'd not succeeded, so far as he knew. Four burly but polite doormen had unceremoniously tossed him into the street from the aristocratic entrance to the exclusive London-town Apartments on upper Park Avenue atop which Dick Van Loan had built his penthouse bachelor home. Van Loan owned the building, in fact, but had been away when Lannigan had tried to visit him.

Van had found Jerry by accident, subsequently, during the blowing up of a Bronx River bridge, but had been disguised and Lannigan had not recognized him. Remembering the battling qualities of the big red-headed mechanic. Van had immediately hired him, letting Jerry know only that he was being employed by the Phantom.

It still stood that way now.

For Dick was afraid that Jerry's pride, damaged at having been thrown out of the swanky London-town when Lannigan had tried to look him up, would drive the Champ away if ever the likeable, fiery Irishman found that the one-time flying major he was searching for and the wealthy Park Avenue clubman were the same.

Lannigan knew some of the Phantom's disguises. He would never know the real identity of the man he sought behind those ingenious characterizations.

The Beechcraft's powerful Wasp motor beat a rhythmic, staccato monotone as the late evening sky darkened into night, making conversation difficult. The rain storm of the afternoon had blown north, but the speedy ship outdistanced it. At ten-thirty the glow and flash of Buffalo's lights were under them, and the Phantom swung the control wheel from Lannigan's seat over to his own.

"I'll land at Niagara," he told Jerry. "We'll lock up the ship. You come with me to Dr. Junes' home. I don't know what we'll run into there."

A gleam of anticipation shone in the Champ's greenish eyes as Van cut the throttle and swooped down toward the small unlighted airport at Niagara. Across the dark, thunderous canyon of the mighty falls itself, the glimmering lights of houses and hotels winked mysteriously at them from the Canadian side of the rapids.

A grim reminder of the flood force of the disaster at Rock Canyon Dam seemed to echo through the darkness from the mighty falls as the Phantom set the ship down on the field and snapped off the landing lights.

"What we want," he told Lannigan as they locked up the plane, "is a talk with Junes, if I can get him to talk. He'll know something about Dr. Paul Bendix, because I've managed to get several science articles published in the journals he reads. Then, we want a look at his laboratory, whether he'll take us there or not."

"We've cracked open tougher spots than labs," Jerry reminded him confidently. "We'll get in!"

Ten minutes later Van and Jerry were pulling up in a cab in front of a small, neat cottage on a dark, quiet street at the residence address of the famous metallurgist.

"Just in case," Van whispered to Lannigan, "I couldn't come armed. If I need a rod, how about it?"

"I'm rodded, so don't worry," Jerry told him. "I wouldn't want to answer a phone call from you without a roscoe on my hip."

Several reporters stood on the tree-shrouded sidewalk, talking in low tones with a detective and a uniformed police lieutenant.

"I'm looking for Doctor Junes," the Phantom announced as he got out of the cab. He spoke with a slightly guttural accent, his eyes studying the men and the dark surroundings from beneath the shaggy greying eyebrows of Professor Paul Bendix. "Is the Doctor at home, gentlemen?"

One of the reporters, wearing a ticket in his hat band, eyed the odd, stooped figure in the faded frock coat with interest. "Who are you, Mister?" He added, in a brazen aside to the other men, "This old-timer looks as screwy as Junes himself, eh?"

"I am Professor Paul Bendix!" Van said haughtily. "I am a man of science, so you have doubtless never heard of me!"

The police lieutenant stepped up close. "Didn't you know that Dr. Junes had a nasty explosion in his laboratory early this evening?"

"We just flew up from New York City," Lannigan said gruffly.

The plainclothes detective, watching them suspiciously, glanced at the lieutenant. "If they flew up, they were in the air when the report went out. They wouldn't know, I guess."

The lieutenant nodded, asked bluntly, "What did you want to see Dr. Junes about, Professor Bendix?"

"A purely scientific matter," the Phantom's foreign-accented voice answered curtly. "Doctor Junes is conducting some valuable experiments in metallurgy in which I am interested. My visit here is sponsored by Mr. Frank Havens, the eminent publisher."

"I guess I can tell you, then," the police lieutenant said, his eyebrows going up at mention of the Clarion owner's name. "Dr. Junes had a very mean shock when the explosion happened. Nobody was killed, fortunately. He was brought home by two of his assistants, and refused to talk, except to say that he was finished forever with what he was working on — I don't pretend to understand that part of it, naturally. Anyhow, he suddenly changed his mind about a half hour ago, and went back to the laboratory with the two assistants again."

"If the doctor is at the laboratory, then I should see him there," Van stated. "Is there any reason why not, sir?"

"I suppose you can go there," the officer admitted. "I'll tell you, though, Professor Bendix — a fellow from New York City visited Dr. Junes yesterday, and was murdered in Grand Central Station today when he returned to your city. The New York police notified us, so we are sort of trying to watch out, for the doctor's protection. In fact, we've got a couple of detectives hanging around as close to Dr. Junes as they can get. Which isn't very close, in that lab of his. He's a touchy old codger." The officer studied Dr. Bendix warily.

"What could that have to do with me, sir?" Professor Bendix shrugged, turned toward the cab. "I am concerned with science, not with crime. Thank you for directing me, officer."

He climbed into the taxi with Jerry, ordered the driver to take him to Dr. Junes' laboratory. As the cab pulled away, he turned sideways in the seat, watched narrowly through the rear window.

In the vague darkness behind, he caught a glimpse of the police lieutenant and the two reporters darting across the sidewalk toward Dr. Junes' cottage, evidently intent on using the phone.

"Checking on us," he said quietly to Lannigan. "Perhaps warning the detectives to watch us, or let us go through. We'll soon see."

"If we're going in, we're going in, dick or no dicks," Jerry declared flatly.

Van's eyes clouded, then became sharply alert, determinedly alive again as the taxi stopped in front of a long, squatty low building of bleak stone that stood apart from other dark buildings on a black private lane near the rumbling falls. He got out, paid off the driver, and stood for a minute with Lannigan as the taxi turned and rolled away.

A high iron picket fence surrounded the tree-shaded grounds. The large vehicle gate was locked, but a narrow pedestrian passage beside the empty watchman's booth let them through onto a winding cinder path leading to the dark laboratory.

Van led the way, making no attempt at caution. There was no sign of the detectives the police lieutenant had mentioned.

At the arched main entrance to the squat building he tried the door, found it locked, and rapped resoundingly with his knuckles.

There was no answer for fully two minutes. Then the door opened a few inches and a flashlight gleamed blindingly in their faces.

"Yeah?" a harsh voice demanded suspiciously. "What'd ya want?"

The Phantom ignored the gun visible in the hand of the man with the torch.

"Professor Paul Bendix to see Doctor Hugo Junes," he announced impatiently.

"I'll have to know more than that," the man inside growled.

"Tell the doctor," Van ordered, "that Professor Bendix has arrived from New York City and is to see the doctor in behalf of Mr. Frank Havens, the publisher."

"Wait here." The door shammed shut on them.

"I should have shoved in while he was arguin'," Jerry exclaimed.

Van shook his head. There were other means of getting inside that laboratory, if this direct method failed. If possible, he wanted Dr. Junes to connect Professor Bendix with the murdered Lester Gimble before they met, so the General Electric scientist could be prepared to give him, unobserved, the information Gimble had carried to his death. But he didn't want to use Havens' name unnecessarily.

There was another wait of several minutes before the door opened once more and the torch gleamed at them.

"Come on in," the harsh voice directed.

They shoved into the blackness anteroom. The door shut and the smell of a thousand chemicals assailed their nostrils. Van recognized the predominant odor of fulminated sulphur which increased as they followed the stocky figure who motioned them along with the revolver he held.

Ahead of them the beam of his flashlight outlined the bare walls of a concrete corridor, and steps going down. They descended, their footsteps echoing hollowly.

Another corridor turned off at right angles behind a heavy steel door which the stocky man opened and closed behind them. Van got one good look at his hard features before he padded on ahead again. There was another left turn, a second stairway going down, steeper and longer than the first.

At the bottom they stopped before a massive circular steel vault-like door cut into what appeared to be no longer concrete but solid rock. Their guide could not have come this far and returned during the short few moments they had waited outside the front entrance of the building. He must have phoned down here.

As the man swung open the heavy round door, Van said to him:

"How do you know I'm Professor Bendix?"

The fellow eyed him belligerently. "That'll be up to the doctor. He's down there." The stocky man stood aside, waiting.

Van looked through the circular doorway. A ladder disappeared into the well-like shaft, but light showed at the bottom some twenty feet below as he peered down. Except for a rangy shadow that moved momentarily across the light at the bottom, the hole had every appearance of a death trap.

The Phantom glanced warningly at Jerry Lannigan, nodded swiftly, and stepped onto the steel rungs of the ladder fastened into the circular stone wall. Above him, as he lowered himself, Lannigan's descending bulk blotted out the light of the electric torch above.

A moment later the Phantom stood at the bottom of the hole. He stepped away from the ladder, turned and moved into the queer octagonal laboratory of Dr. Hugo Junes.

One whole side of the laboratory was a wreck. An electric arc oven was blasted apart, and a slab of the rock wall behind it had been blown off. The debris-burnt metal, ore and scorched, blackened stone had been brushed into a heap and partly covered by a collapsed iron screen tipped over it.

The compact but barren-looking equipment across the room that had not been demolished by the explosion was now in use.

Dr. Junes himself-Van recognized the man from his pictures in several of the metallurgical journals he'd studied-was standing tall, gaunt and frightened beside a shelflike high-voltage electric oven which was already glowing whitely beneath the plates covering its heat producing arcs.

Two men, wearing heavy welder's goggles covering their eyes and faces, were watching him alertly, and a third stood back of them at a large rheostat in the wall. He, too, wore similar heavy glasses and face protector.

There was no other equipment in the room except, on a stone slab that made a workbench jutting from the wall opposite the rheostat, a heavy twenty-four-pound sledge hammer, a chisel and a steel handsaw. Beside the hammer was a small chip of silver colored ore the size of a silver dollar.

The tall, gaunt man nearest the furnace looked across at Van with an almost beseeching gleam of hope in his heat-moistened eyes. His gaze shifted a moment to Lannigan, who now stood behind the Phantom, then settled helplessly upon Van again.

"I am told," the unsteady voice of the gaunt, frightened man said with an attempt at formality, "that you are Professor Paul Bendix, of New York City. I believe I have had the pleasure of reading several of your scientific brochures. I am Dr. Hugo Junes."

The Phantom nodded gravely, and his grey eyes veiled their wary alertness beneath the drooping lids of Professor Paul Bendix.

"Excellent, Doctor," he said austerely. "And I am familiar with your remarkable work." He glanced at the glowing furnace. "I observe your experiment is already in process, despite an unfortunate explosion."

"What you observe," Junes stated with suppressed passion, "is the ultimate defeat of all my experiments with aluminum and calbite. I have returned here only to burn up what the attempted fusion reaction did not completely destroy."

The eyes of the others in the room were inscrutable behind their heavy goggles. For the moment, at least, they seemed content to listen and dart quick glances at the furnace.

"I understand your experiments are designed to fuse calbite and aluminum," Van said appreciatively. "But the explosion —"

Dr. Junes' gaze shifted to the others, then to the oven, and back to the Phantom, blinking confusedly. "I have refused to continue, or to leave any trace of my work, because of that revealing accident this afternoon. I am unable to understand what was the real cause of it, sir, but only a few grains of the composite metals, not quite fused, suddenly exploded-with the result you can see for yourself." He waved a hand toward the debris at one side of the room.

"Powerful," Van commented, his nerves tightening as the impact of that information struck him. "A few grains, you say? No more?"

"A very few grains, Professor Bendix. And —" Junes smacked his palms together sharply — "it happened! My assistants do not agree with me in my refusal to continue. But consider-what would happen to humanity if the explosive power of the formula I nearly discovered became a reality! The whole world would be at the mercy of whoever could control that metallurgical combination. It is too dangerous, too terrible to contemplate. So I have refused to go on!"

"It's an endothermic compound, I presume," Professor Bendix suggested, and when Junes nodded agreement, "At what temperature did you expect to make the aluminum-calbite fusion?"

"Impossible to say," Junes declared warmly. "These furnaces produce the greatest heat of any man-made generators yet devised. And they fall considerably short of a real fusion. I've added ammonium nitrate —" He paused, frowned. "But enough. I am done. I will not jeopardize humanity."

The man at the rheostat said sullenly, "Dr. Junes is very stubborn, Professor Bendix. The explosion this afternoon has him imagining too many things a scientist should never consider."

"Bah!" Junes exploded. "You-all of you! I will not be driven, nor forced! Nor bribed. Nor threatened!" His voice rose to a suddenly terrified screech, a pitch that seemed without reason.

Two of the assistants grabbed and held him. The rheostat man nodded curtly, asked Bendix:

"Could you, Professor, finish the doctor's experiment-if you were without his hysterical prejudices?"

"Perhaps," Van answered evenly. "Given time."

Dr. Junes' tall figure jerked violently, shuddered, and suddenly collapsed as the two men let him loose. He staggered, stepped backward, his eyes wide with quick terror, staring at the opening behind Van where the steel ladder led up to the sub-cellar corridor above.

The Phantom whirled, knocking against Lannigan's big hand that almost automatically was reaching for a hidden revolver. Van gave Jerry a warning signal to wait. Then Professor Paul Bendix settled his gaze on that exit.

Standing in the well-like opening was a tall, powerfully built figure dressed in a caped black robe with a black hood over a head whose face was masked in white. The next moment the terrifying figure moved into the room.

A frightful scream of agony slashed the silence, shot a blood-chilling shock through Van as he spun back, stared with momentarily paralyzed muscles at the gaunt, writhing form of Junes.

The scientist was sprawled backward halfway across the top of the white-hot furnace plates, his body held there by the adhesive, scorching flesh that stuck to the plates and was filling the room with a nauseating stench. A final shriek died on the doctor's lips. The whole upper half of his body shriveled; the arms alone waving spasmodically in unconscious, dying reflexes.

The Phantom sprang for the rheostat, knocked aside the third masked man standing near it. He spun off the electric dial control, turned to watch the scientist's limp body slide down off the furnace.

For a fleeting second, as one of the men wearing the welding mask bent over Junes' dead body, Van caught a glimpse of the handle of a hypodermic syringe in the fellow's coat pocket. The next moment the handle had slipped down out of sight.

"A regrettable accident," the hooded figure stated sullenly, and glanced at Professor Paul Bendix with icy determination. "Did I hear you say you could carry on the unfortunate scientist's work?"

"This furnace wasn't hot enough for the experiment, anyhow," the masked man who had been at the rheostat declared. "We've been watching this stove seven hours, and the metals won't fuse."

The Phantom's seething mind clicked to a grim conclusion. He was being asked to take the place of the dead scientist. Junes had refused to aid these men in what ever plan they had proposed. Van had not positive proof, but already suspected that the doctor had been shoved onto that furnace and murdered. He decided to join them, let them force him into their scheme.

He nodded, inclined his head gravely, saw even then out of the corner of his eye what was going to happen, as he indicated Lannigan.

"Yes, it is entirely possible that I could conduct the unfortunate doctor's experiment," he said. "If I have my assistant."

At a nod from the hooded figure, one of the men had stepped close to Jerry Lannigan. A faintly blue vapor curled up swiftly from a pencil in the man's hand, and Jerry dropped unconscious to the floor.

"You shall have your assistant," the icy voice promised with a note of satanic humor. He pocketed the small chip of silver-colored ore on the stone bench, and advanced on Van.

The next instant a second pencil ejected a shot of that bluish brain-fogging gas straight into the Phantom's bearded face. The room whirled dizzily for a second that seemed endless, while the hooded face leered. Then oblivion blotted out the room.

Chapter Seven
Destination Darkness

Jolting movement and the sound of rushing wind and an automobile motor's powerful throbbing rhythm beat into the Phantom's drugged brain.

He tried to open his eyes, but the tight pressure of tape on them kept the lids shut. His hands were fastened behind his back with tape. He lurched helplessly with each swerving plunge of the car, his body held upright between two men in the seat beside him.

His parched lips were taped shut, and hunger gnawed at his stomach, giving him the only measure of the passage of time. Eight hours or longer, he judged, since he had been knocked out with those bluish odorless fumes.

The last physical sensations he remembered were the smell of fulmigated sulphur and the heat in that sub-cellar of the General Electric metallurgical laboratory. But now the fresh odor of pines, an occasional lingering whiff of burning coal, and the rush of cool air assailed his senses.

He listened keenly, trying to pick up the rumbling roar of Niagara Falls, but could hear only the hum of the motor and the swish of the wind. The totality of his blind impressions was of steep long climbs, quick descents and open spaces.

The two men sitting beside him began to stir restlessly. A match scraped, followed by the pungent odor of cigarette smoke.

"Making good time for a long ride," one of the men said in a tired voice. "Almost there now. The other car'll be there already."

"Yeah," the other rider agreed. "Not a hitch on this trip. That's what organization does. You going to try for a sergeant's circles?"

"I ain't killed nobody yet," the other grumbled. "Anyhow, not officially. Soon's I do, though, I'll sure apply for the next rating. Sergeant's get plenty of authority."

"You won't have to wait long for a chance to get a killing credit," the second man prophesied knowingly. "I heard, from one of the district majors, that th' State Militia is commin' after us."

"Better not talk too much," the man on Van's right warned. "I heard somethin' about that, too, but you know what the penalty is for not keepin' your mouth shut!"

Van could tell by the movement of the man's body that the guard had gestured significantly at him.

In the prolonged, moody silence that followed, the Phantom tried to fathom the motives and extent of the mysterious organization that three times now had reared its ugly, poisonous head, There was but the one conclusion-some secret society was plotting to overthrow the government of the United States, and was relying upon some new unannounced discovery of modern science to effect their treacherous ends.

And that the dead Dr. Hugo Junes' metallurgical experiments with aluminum and calbite had something to do with those murderous plans appeared obvious. The Phantom was convinced that Dr. Junes' death had not been accidental, but a deliberate killing.

The doctor's pleading fear and final wild hysteria, the hypodermic syringe visible for an instant in one of the masked men's pockets, the whole set-up in the General Electric underground heat laboratory, in fact, pointed at murder. Junes must have been drugged and thrown against the top of that furnace.

But why should these hooded and masked members of such a secret organization kill Dr. Junes, a scientist whom they were using?

The obvious answer was that Junes had refused to conform to their demands. And now the Phantom himself was purposely letting himself be forced to take the murdered scientist's place in their subversive scheme. The disguise of Professor Paul Bendix had proved more real and convincing than Van had ever hoped.

His unanswered and unvoiced questions were interrupted by the slowing of the car. It stopped and, judging by the sounds, they had driven inside some building which, nevertheless, did not smell like a garage. The binding tape was ripped off his ankles and he was shoved out of the car.

His shoes crunched on cinders and there was a trace of coal gas in the air. Then he was being guided along an earthy-smelling, cool passageway that had the confining feel of a tunnel.

There were four men with him now, their rough voices sounding loud and echoing. They stopped him a hundred paces beyond. Van could feel unsteady board footing beneath him.

Something slammed suddenly, sounding like a gate. Mechanism grated and groaned into action. The Phantom, his pinioned arms still held by two of the men, experienced the sensation of being lowered slowly in an elevator.

The complaining, slow descent went on it seemed endlessly. Van had no way of reckoning how far down into the earth he was being carried, but the air became rapidly more gaseous and damp, the pressure heavier.

The guards with him had ceased talking, but their casual, almost illiterate conversation before had given him no inkling of where he might be, except for an occasional miner's phrase.

The elevator car stopped finally and Van was pushed into a narrow passageway. His shoulders rubbed against damp dirt walls, and he had to stoop to protect his head from the low, wooden beams bracing the roof.

From the voices only two men were with him now one in front and one behind. He was herded through an interminably long and crooked tunnel and several times he could feel with his shoulders different openings leading off. Whether or not they were following the main tunnel or any one of its branches, he had no way of knowing.

The floor was a steady decline, some parts steeper than others, but always descending. Five times, the Phantom counted, he was stopped while the exaggerated clicking and grating noise of a door being unlocked, opened, closed behind them and locked again, filled the accentuated silence about him.

The passage leveled out beyond the fifth door. He felt several more openings in the walls as he was shoved ahead. The tunnel twisted continuously, and the odor of gas increased, made breathing more labored.

Another door barred their passage, but there was no key in the possession of the guards for this one. One of them beat against the panel with what sounded like the butt of a gun-five swift blows, a pause and a single sixth.

On the other side a key turned with a click that echoed like an explosion in the compressed atmosphere. A bar scraped as it was slid away from the door on the opposite side. A moment later the door swung inward and the Phantom was pushed through, shoved up against a wall.

He heard the door being closed and locked. Then without preliminaries the tape was ripped off his wrists, torn off his eyes and mouth. Van opened his eyes slowly, slitting them against any unexpected light that might blind him after his long siege of complete darkness. But only a poor indirect glow lighted the cavernous room in which he found himself.

The two men who had brought him in stood on either side of him and one of them held a heavy long-barreled revolver. Both were dressed in overalls and miners' caps in which gleamed small electric bulbs.

Across the chamber stood a tall figure in a black-caped robe. The man had a black hood over his head and his face was covered with a mask through which his eyes glittered ominously. He might have been the same grim specter who had appeared at the General Electric sub-cellar laboratory. Even his voice when he spoke sounded similar in the deceiving echoes of the cavern.

"Professor Paul Bendix," he said contemptuously, "I hope the trip hasn't upset you."

Van eyed the hooded figure defiantly, wet his parched lips. "What manner of science is it," he demanded in the guttural voice of Professor Bendix, "that makes such humiliating experience necessary?"

The hooded man shrugged indifferently beneath his robe.

"Asking questions is not a part of your job here," the tall man stated flatly, and added significantly, "You witnessed what happened to your predecessor, Dr. Hugo Junes."

The Phantom stepped away from the wall, flexing his cramped muscles. In another corner of the cavern his eyes, accustomed to the peculiar light now, slid and settled on the bound and gagged figure of Jerry Lannigan. The big Irishman was watching him eagerly.

"You have my assistant here, I see!" the Phantom exclaimed, making his words ring with anger that covered the relief he felt. "Untie him!" This was no time for feeling his way. They evidently still thought he was an eminent scientist, and he had to continue his bluffing characterization.

"I had your assistant untied before," the cloaked leader in the room said. "He became unmanageable and fought, so I had him tied again to keep him from getting hurt. I hope that the fool will behave himself now that you are here."

"I'll guarantee that he will," Professor Bendix declared gravely. Yet within him was a warming glow at the thought of what damage the Champ had probably done before they overpowered him.

The hooded leader nodded to one of the guards, who went over and ripped the tape bonds from Lannigan's ankles, wrists and lips. The red-headed Irishman got to his feet, came over and stood belligerently beside the professor.

"This joint is ratty!" Lannigan growled at the man in the hood, and turned to Van. "The whole place is overrun with these guys dressed up like Ku Kluxers."

"Enough of that!" the leader snapped. "You'll find our organization very effective if you try any foolishness."

"Quiet," the Phantom warned Lannigan, and addressed the man in the black robe: "If I am to be put to work, I must see the laboratory. And I would appreciate knowing where I am."

The tall, hooded figure again jerked his head at the two mine guards and moved to another door in the chamber.

"You will find where you are," he said over his shoulder, "when the time comes and you are a blood member with us. For the present, the temporary laboratory is directly under us."

The two guards, both of them with guns in their hands now, motioned Van and Lannigan to follow their leader. Van, while he had been talking, had been using his hands casually, feeling of his clothes and secret pockets. His captors appeared not to have taken time to search him thoroughly.

Even though unarmed, he and the Champ might have put up a fight in an attempt to break free. But the information he wanted was evidently down here, not elsewhere.

Escape now would have defeated his purpose.

Guarded by the two armed men, Van and Jerry followed the robed figure through the door which he opened, down a steep incline that turned twice at right angles and brought them out into a deeper, smaller cavern cut into the earth directly below the subterranean chamber above.

Heat greeted them as they entered this room.

Four burly men, stripped to the waist, eyed them curiously. A fifth man who appeared to be a hunchback looked up leeringly with small pale eyes set deep and wide apart in a distorted, twitching and scarred face.

But it was the glow in the center of the room that held Van's attention. Through a small opening in the rock a thin flame stood up from the floor for almost a foot in height. The rock from which this jet spurted was white hot, and the flame itself was perfectly colorless at the base but flowered into vivid blues and yellows before it expended itself.

The room was filled with a constant hissing sound, a miniature roar that made speech difficult.

The Phantom tore his eyes from that fascinating light, and for a moment as he looked away he was blinded. Then vision returned swiftly, but he kept his eyes off that flame, and noticed that about the necks of the four workmen and the hunchback hung thick goggles.

The cloaked leader indicated the short squat man with the hunched back, and said to Van, "This is Doctor Kag. Professor Kag was one of the foremost metallurgists in the world until one of his experiments blew up and crippled him. He is temporarily —" He emphasized the word forebodingly —"in charge of the experiments we are conducting here. The gas flame in this room, with the addition of oxygen, is the hottest torch that has ever been discovered-two thousand degrees centigrade higher than that electric arc oven of Dr. Junes at Niagara Falls."

The Phantom's eyes showed a sharpened interest that he did not have to fake.

The man-made oven of Dr. Junes, built by the General Electric Company for experimental purposes, had the highest temperature of any arc furnace thus far designed. And arc furnaces were the hottest known to man.

Yet, by the statement of one of the engineers in this hooded organization, seven hours of that arc heat had failed to fuse the two metals whose union had been the aim of Doctor Junes. Van did not doubt the statement of the leader standing before him now. And two thousand more degrees of heat, he realized, would be more than sufficient, if properly controlled, to effect that world-important fusion of those two metals.

He was about to speak, when Kag came swaying toward him, leering, pawing with gnarled, crippled hands.

"Professor Junes!" Kag's voice was shrill, piercing.

"He's not Junes," the hooded man shouted. "He's another scientist. Junes is dead, burned up in his own furnace!"

Kag's pale eyes rolled wildly in their sockets. "You're not Junes?" he cried querulously.

"No," Van admitted, watching the man narrowly. There was near insanity in those crazy, rolling eyes.

Suddenly the hunchback's fawning attitude changed. Crazed genius glittered in his rocking gaze.

"Ach!" he screamed. "A scientist, are you? It is I who am the scientist-the greatest scientist in the world! What do you know of science-of fire-of metallurgy?"

"I was a friend and contemporary worker with Dr. Junes," Van answered as calmly as he could. This hunchback, he knew, could trip him with questions, show him up as an impostor. "Tell me, Professor Kag, what experiments you are working —"

"Kag!" The hunchback's shrill voice trembled with frenzy. "Kag! I shall tell you nothing! I shall ask you questions! You do not even know who I am. Kag!"

The Phantom saw the mistake he had made, tried to stop the man's wild screeching by correcting the error. This man was unquestionably Dr. Gulliver Vonderkag, once the foremost metallurgical scientist in Germany-but now only the shell of him, yet his genius still raged.

But Van could not make himself heard.

"A metallurgist, are you? Tell me quickly the fusion point of antimony and copper."

The Phantom's muscles tensed at the suddenness of this crisis.

"Antimony and copper —"

Van had to hesitate, grope an instant before the answer came to him. Then he gave it, watching the hunchback nervously. If the German scientist shot many more such questions at him, he'd be stuck, and his Bendix role unmasked.

"Slow," Kag cried in disgust. "Dr. Junes, he would have been quicker. I could have used him in my work. But you —"

"You've no choice in the matter, Kag," the hooded leader said flatly. "Test him again."

The Phantom's mind fought against Vonderkag's warped brain, beat the crippled scientist's formulating question by sheer audacity and drive.

"Doctor!" Van shouted. "Let us stop this kindergarten child's game. I am interested only in your knowledge of Dr. Junes' work-his experiment which he refused to continue."

"Refused to continue?" Kag demanded shrilly. "What is that?"

"Fusing aluminum and calbite," the Phantom declared in a loud, challenging voice. "Dr. Junes, as you've been told, was killed, but before he died, he had refused to carry on the fusion. He was afraid. I know what he feared. Do you?"

"Afraid?" Kag screeched the word as though it had come from a foreign tongue and had no meaning for him. "Are we men of science?"

Somebody pounded on the door. The hooded leader swung round, unlocked the door, let in a man dressed similarly in hood and robe but without a mask. On the sleeve of the newcomer was a green circle with a zigzag line running through it.

"What's the trouble, Sergeant?" the masked man demanded.

The hooded sergeant saluted briskly, swinging his arm in toward his stomach and out again. He stepped around a water pail, his leg brushing the dipper sticking out of it as he handed over a sealed envelope.

"Something that demands immediate attention," he stated.

As the man in the mask ripped open the envelope and extracted the folded sheet of note paper it contained, Van signaled Lannigan to be ready, and edged closer to the leader whose eyes narrowed dangerously as he read the penciled notation.

For a swift instant, Van caught a glimpse of that note, got a flash view of the words:

Professor Bendix suspected of being sent as a scientist spy from the capitalist publisher —

He managed to catch the name Havens in the note. As he moved, Van remembered he'd used Havens' name in Niagara Falls. The invisible organization had caught up with him!

But what he did now he had already planned to do in that continued moment of suspense when Vonderkag had challenged him as a metallurgical scientist. The crisis demanded instant action; Kag was forgotten for the instant.

With one quick swing, so swift as to be almost undetectable, Van's right arm shot out and downward as his hand gripped the water pail, lifted it, swung its contents straight into the hissing gas flame in the center of the floor.

Instantly the entire room became a dense fog of swirling, blinding steam. The Phantom whirled, and his fist cracked against the jaw of the nearest mine guard. He yanked the gun from the falling man's hand, heard the harder crack of Lannigan's hamlike fist as Jerry slugged the other guard.

"Out!" Van barked.

The next second he was through the door with Jerry puffing behind him. Back of them in the furnace chamber, shouts and shots sounded as slugs pounded into the wall after them.

Chapter Eight
Lannigan's Trick

Near the first turn in the inclined passageway, the Phantom stopped to make sure Lannigan was still coming. The big Irishman plunged past, carrying something heavy over his shoulder.

They raced on up, lunged into the larger cavern above. The place was empty.

Van slammed the door shut, slid down an iron crossbar, locking it. He jerked out his pencil flashlight that the guards had not taken away from him. In its thin shaft he saw Lannigan dumping the hooded figure of the sergeant on the floor.

"How long can we hold them off?" the Irishman demanded. "I brought this guy along so that you could use his costume."

"Not very long, Champ," the Phantom said tersely. "They'll shoot the door off its hinges." He looked quickly at the sergeant. The unmasked face was ordinary, unintelligent. "Get into those robes yourself," the Phantom directed. "One of us has got to get out of this mine and get to Havens. You're elected." He bent down over the unconscious man, began unfastening the black hood.

Shots began crashing into the barred door as Van handed up the costume to Lannigan.

"I'd rather stay here and let you go up, Phantom," Jerry growled as he shrugged into the black outfit.

"I've got to stay. Got to find out more about this organization and the metal they're fusing with that heat," Van insisted. "You get to Havens and fly back here. He'll know what to do when you tell him what's happening. Come on!"

Van's light guided them through the door through which they had first come. Behind them, the barred entrance to the passageway below was trembling on its hinges under the onslaught of the hooded leader and Kag and the hunchback's four burly helpers.

With Lannigan running ahead in the disguise of the sergeant they ran swiftly along the level tunnel toward the first guarded gate. Suddenly, Lannigan ducked into one of the side passages as a bobbing electric headlight on the cap of someone approaching gleamed in the darkness ahead.

Van slid in beside Jerry. The racket of shots and shouts back along the passageway echoed and re-echoed against the walls.

"That's the guard at the next doorway," Van warned. "You've got the black uniform, Champ. Go get him!"

Lannigan's grunt of satisfaction was eager. He took Van's pencil flashlight, stepped out in the path of the advancing guard.

"What's going on down there?" the man shouted excitedly.

The torch in Lannigan's hand gleamed, caught the guard full in the face, outlining his hood and robe and the revolver in his fist.

He jerked to a halt, stopped by the blinding glare of the flash. Jerry gave him no chance to ask anything more. The big Irishman's hammerlike knuckles hit the guard's jaw. The fellow seemed to bounce up off the floor of the tunnel, hang suspended in the air an instant before he dropped back and lay still.

The Phantom darted out, snaked the black costume off the man's body, got into it himself. He took the man's gun, ran on again, urging Lannigan ahead of him.

They were both outfitted in organization uniforms now, and both had two guns apiece. But there was a maze of black, guarded passageways and doors ahead of them, and they had still no identification or countersigns to get them through.

A powerful flashlight sent its beam into the tunnel behind them as the imprisoned men broke loose from the cavern. The Phantom and the Champ raced through the now unguarded first gate into the upgrade underground passage ahead. There was no way of locking those doorways on the entrance side, for only the guards on the inside of the tunnel openings could bar them.

"Take the first turn to the left that looks like something!" The Phantom directed. "We can't take time to lay out every door guard we come to."

A moment later, as the light grew larger behind them, they whirled off the main corridor into a side passage that led up sharply. As he ran, the Phantom tugged off the tell-tale Van Dyke of Professor Paul Bendix. That character was done now, so far as this mysterious subterranean organization was concerned. He thrust the beard up into a crevice between the wall and a wooden tunnel brace, and caught up with Lannigan again.

The passage broke unexpectedly into a large cavern along one wall of which cement sacks were stacked to the roof. In the opposite wall was a large steel door built into a heavy concrete and stone abutment. The door was locked with several large handles and two wheels that gave it the appearance of a steel vault. The construction was recent. Van recognized it as a watertight compartment lock, built to hold back one of the subterranean lakes found in all deep mines. This lower level series of shafts and channels under the operating portion of the coal mine had evidently been used and abandoned, for there was no sign of recent operation this far down and they had come upon no workmen.

There were three exits from this cave, one of them unmarked, the other two marked respectively in chalk on their frame braces: SHAFT 9 and CAGE.

"Which way, Skipper?" Jerry asked.

The Phantom stopped running, glanced back and listened. For a moment there was no sound of pursuit.

"The cage," Van answered, and led the way. "We'll probably run into someone. Don't shoot if you can use your fists."

They advanced more cautiously, and as they went forward along the slightly rising tunnel, Van manipulated some of the make-up of Dr. Bendix that remained on and inside his face.

His nose became more normal as he removed the two small aluminum pieces that had given it the broadened, heavy appearance. The injection of the specially prepared compound that he had shot into his cheeks and jowls had already been partially absorbed and dissipated. He ordinarily had to renew his make-up for any disguise every twenty-four hours. It was, he realized, only the dumbness of his captors and the demand for speed on the part of their leaders, that had made them forego the opportunity they had had to strip him while he had been unconscious.

Even so, it required the expert, trained eye of a physician to detect the fact that one of his complete characterizations was a fraud. By the time he and Jerry had gone another two hundred yards through the shaft, the face of Professor Paul Bendix had completely disappeared, although beneath the black robe Van wore, the frock coat was still a dangerous piece of evidence.

"If this tunnel don't end pretty soon," Jerry panted behind him, "we don't need any elevator. We'll have walked out of here!"

"Just so we get you free of this place, Champ," Van replied.

A half minute later a voice challenged them from somewhere ahead, and another voice, harsher than the first, repeated the warning.

"Keep going," the Phantom whispered to Lannigan, and answered the challenge with a terse, "Show your light, you fools!"

A strong torch beam caught them immediately in a blinding glare. Van stopped, tried to look beneath that light.

"Password!" the harsh voice demanded.

The Phantom's eyes glinted. "Two suspected men have escaped from Professor Kag's shaft!" he snapped, ignoring the password demand. "If they haven't got this far, send word ahead!"

"Whose orders?" the first voice asked sharply from the intense blackness behind the flashlight's unswerving beam.

"Sergeant Flannigan is with me," Van said angrily. He glanced over his shoulder. "Sergeant —"

Jerry stepped to the front, glowering, showing the gun in his hand. His rough voice bellowed: "Who th' hell is giving orders here?"

"I am!" the harder voice snapped, and a tall, hooded and masked man stepped partway into view. On his robed sleeve was the green circle with two crossed yellow zigzagged markers through it. "I'm Commander Rotz!"

The authority in his voice was unmistakable. Van tensed, and gave the peculiar salute he had observed back in Kag's cavern. Lannigan, too, saluted uncertainly.

And at the same instant, the Phantom's keen ears heard the first faint sounds of the pursuit far back along the tunnel.

They were trapped!

Commander Rotz heard that growing sound of voices footsteps also, for he suddenly whipped up his gun, covering them menacingly.

"Stand where you are!" he ordered grimly. "I've seen deserters try to get away like this before."

The Phantom's left hand jerked abruptly at Jerry Lannigan's stolen black robe, a hard, unexpected tug that yanked the beefy Irishman off balance. If Lannigan had made that quick movement himself, some slight flick of warning would have given him away. But Van's quickness had precluded that.

In the split-second that the commander with the leveled gun took to correct his aim, the Phantom's right foot kicked up, hit the masked man's hand at the wrist behind the revolver.

A sharp cry of pain broke from the fellow's hidden lips. The gun spun from his fingers. And Van's fist exploded against the man's jaw!

In the sudden violent confusion, the light fell to the floor of the shaft as Jerry leaped at the other guard. For a matter of seconds there was only gasping, strangled breathing. Then the muffled sound of quick movement and the rustle of cloth.

It was less than a full minute, all told, when Van's fingers found the powerful torch on the dirt floor and snapped it on briefly. In its bright light, Lannigan was bent over the dead figure of the guard, his big hands going through the fellow's clothing.

And the Phantom was standing erect in the black robe, hood and white mask of Commander Rotz. The lifeless, frock-coated body of a man who might have been, beneath his masked features, Professor Paul Bendix, lay at his feet.

Even Lannigan stared twice at the swift, complete transformation before he recognized the Phantom's voice ordering him to action.

"Drag that guard out of sight somewhere," Van directed tensely. "Dump him some place where he won't be found immediately. Get on ahead of me and if you get a chance to get out of here, take it!"

"Okay, Skipper! That's the fastest make-up change I've ever seen you put on." Lannigan grabbed up the dead guard as the light in Van's hand turned toward the sloping end of the shaft up which they had come. The glare of the torch completely hid Jerry's movements behind it as he carried his burden further up the tunnel.

The Phantom kept his light on, faced the pursuers who were already shouting to him above the hard, echoing pounding of their feet. Behind the white mask, his lips were a thin, determined line.

"Halt!" he shouted above the increasing clamor. "Password!"

His voice was harsh and sharp now, like the voice of Rotz. He recognized in the beam of the electric torch the foremost of the advancing crew-one of the mine guards who had been with him in Kag's cavern. The others were strange faces, men picked up in the search that had split into several parties.

"September Third!" the guard snapped back at him and saluted.

September Third! There was grim significance in that countersign.

Van pointed his light down at the figure on the tunnel floor. "You're hunting for that?" he demanded harshly.

The guard and the others with him stared. The identity of the dead Rotz would eventually be discovered, but for the moment the resemblance to Bendix was close enough to fool them. The guard nodded, glanced up.

"There was another one —a big, heavy man with red hair."

"Didn't come this way," Van stated with a ring of authority his voice. "This man was sneaking along here and refused to stop when I challenged him. I've sent the guard stationed here to report this in Shaft Nine. Take your men and come with me. I'll send you up to report on top."

He turned, started up the inclined tunnel in the direction Jerry had taken. There was a sharp curve in the shaft that ended fifty yards beyond at a rough gate that barred the entrance to an elevator car.

There was no sign of Lannigan. The Phantom breathed easier.

"This car shouldn't be left down here now, with a deserter loose. Take it up," he ordered.

"The fellow wasn't a deserter," the guard leading the others told him. "He was a spy —"

"He'll be a dead spy if we catch him," Van promised. "Now get going with that car and report topside!"

The guard saluted again, got onto the car with the three men who had come with him. The elevator trembled in its loose, rough framework as it started to move upward.

The Phantom's light was on it, watching. Where in hell was Lannigan? —The question was answered a second later. Only the protection of the white mask he wore kept back the jolt of sheer shocked surprise that twisted Van's features; He stared, almost unbelieving.

Jerry Lannigan's beefy bulk was hanging beneath the rising floor of the shaft cage, his ham-like hands gripping the cross-bracing under the car! The Champ let go with one hand, waved to Van, and pointed down under him.

The Phantom understood. Lannigan had dumped the body of the dead guard into the elevator well. There was no need even to look.

Van switched off the electric torch, stood in complete darkness.

Chapter Nine
Find the Imperator!

Half a second later he was running noiselessly back along the narrow tunnel. Jerry might be able to get through up above. If audacity and courage counted, Van was confident he would. But there was more information needed about this subterranean organization down here, before any outside help would be of value. Without more knowledge than he had, a raid would only drive the members of this mysterious society of revolt deeper into their hidden holes. Somewhere there was a leader, a single brain, governing and directing this mob-mad legion of doom. Not until that leader was ferreted out could this terror-inspiring organization be broken up and destroyed.

The Phantom decided upon a bold stroke. He had got rid of the clothes of Dr. Paul Bendix, wore now the complete equipment of the dead Commander Rotz.

And he had the password-September Third!

He retraced the path up which he and Jerry had fled from Kag's cavern. In his stolen commander's uniform there was no difficulty in getting by the reguarded barriers he and Jerry had fought through before.

He went directly to Kag's cavern. The hunchbacked scientist was still there, with two of his stripped helpers, and two hooded but unmasked guards whom Van had not seen before, but who eyed him with considerable respect.

"I understand there's been some trouble down here," the Phantom rasped in the voice of Commander Rotz as he entered.

The men, excepting Kag, saluted him with that same peculiar and suggestive movement of the clenched fist across the stomach.

"A dangerous scientist sent to spy on us for the capitalists," Kag exclaimed with renewed excitement, and gave a garbled account of Professor Bendix and his beefy assistant who had been caught and escaped. "An ignoramus!"

As he talked, the crippled scientist unfastened a blanket from a heavy, round object on the floor, began stroking the rough, silver-colored ball of metal.

"What's that?" Van demanded, keeping his eyes off the white jet of flame shooting up through the center of the floor, but motioning at the ball with his hand.

"Ach!" Kag's wild eyes rolled and glistened. "A meteoric fragment!" he exclaimed. "From the Smithsonian Institute. It was the only proof in the world that aluminum and calbite could be fused-but the world lacks that proof now. The Imperator and I alone hold this secret. Not even the famous Dr. Junes could do what I have done!"

"I've heard about it," the Phantom said. "And you too, Dr. Vonderkag."

The hunchbacked German expert in metallurgy smiled at the mention of his real name, and grew more voluble.

"You are interested, I see," he cried. "I will tell you —I have fused calbite and aluminum in that flame there, and have made the lightest, toughest metal ever conceived by man! Soon, we plan to manufacture this for our own purposes, in quantity!"

Kag's statement ended in a series of shrieks and idiotic chuckles of secret merriment. Van wanted to ask him more, but at that moment another sergeant entered, stared round and saluted him, handing over a note. The Phantom accepted the piece of paper, read the order printed in pencil:

IMPERIAL BOARD STAFF MEETING
IMMEDIATELY IN THE SHAFT 9
BARRACKS. KINDLY ATTEND.

THE IMPERATOR.

Van stared at the order through narrowed eyes, his every nerve alert and tingling. He nodded at the sergeant, shoved the paper into a pocket under his black robe.

"I shall call upon you again, Professor Vonderkag," he said, and strode out.

As he went back up the incline and out into the main corridor, he noticed with surprise that the passageway was now heavily guarded, with sentries stationed every thirty or forty yards. Each of them threw their electric torches upon him and saluted him as he passed.

Several other men were standing along some distance ahead, receiving the same crisp salutations as himself. It didn't seem possible that he was soon to meet the Imperator in person. Yet the Imperator's name was the authority on that order in his pocket.

He passed through the cavern where the steel water door was set in the concrete, followed the two men ahead of him into the underground corridor marked SHAFT 9. The tunnel curved to the left away from the passage that led to the elevator cage up which Lannigan, he hoped, had made his escape.

Two guards at a heavy wooden door took up his written order, passed him on into an extraordinarily large and long chamber of cavernous height. The place, lighted by lanterns that threw grotesque shadows along the walls, was already a scene of weird assembly.

All of the men present were robed, hooded and masked. Each of them wore upon his sleeve a green circle of the clan. And through each circle ran the double zigzag emblem that marked them as ranking officers.

There was no fraternizing. The men did not gather in the usual small groups while they waited. Each man stood aloof from his companions, as though afraid of being caught discussing their mutual organization affairs.

The Phantom moved over against a wall, looking about eagerly for some centralizing nucleus to this strange silent gathering, There was no dais, no raised platform.

Suddenly, without preliminaries, an incisive, chilling and metallic voice filled the cavern-the same voice that had come over the air to announce the Rock Creek Dam disaster sixty seconds before it happened.

Van's darting eyes slid over the room, searching for the source of that metallic flow of words. Of the fifty men present, not a lip moved. Yet the voice went on:

> "Attention, officers of the Invisible Empire! Rock Canyon Dam has been successfully destroyed! Not a clue that could be traced to us was left. And only ten of our men were obliged to sacrifice their lives to protect our Order. Their families, according to our constitution, will be financially independent now for seven generations."

Van's eyes glittered behind his white mask as the full significance of that statement struck him. With such a guarantee of financial security as a reward for sacrifices to this carefully schemed out organization, there was practically no limit to the hysterical courage which such a bait engendered.

The cold, inhuman voice went on: "Our next attack upon the government will occur at dawn on September 3rd. I myself, at that hour four days hence, will bomb the United States Treasury Building at Washington, using the airplane that has been built of the aluminum-calbite metal being manufactured here. A new explosive, more powerful than the explosive used at Rock Canyon, will be dropped from my plane. I shall detail a detachment to carry here the United States Treasury gold."

Throughout the cavern there was a sharp intake of greedy breath as this announcement was made. But the invisible speaker continued emotionlessly:

> "One other matter at this time. Through our intelligence service I have been warned that a capitalist scientist, Dr. Bendix, has attempted to gain admittance to our headquarters here. It is suspected that Mr. Frank Havens, an enemy publisher, has employed this man.

"A Professor Bendix and an assistant did appear here. I have two reports, neither of them checked sufficiently. One is that these two men escaped. The other is that one of them, presumably Bendix has been killed. I shall send at once a man disguised as Doctor Bendix to visit Mr. Havens in New York. This envoy will remove the publisher. I call for a volunteer."

Instantly, the Phantom's hand was raised in the air and his voice rang out:

"I, Commander Rotz, offer myself for that honor!"

There was an imperceptible silence while the eyes of every officer in the room turned toward him. Then the chilling voice of the unseen speaker again:

"Commander Rotz is accepted. He will advance at once, at the conclusion of this meeting, along the unnumbered gallery next to Shaft 9. He will be met. That is all, gentlemen. I, the Imperator, have spoken!"

The Phantom's pulse pounded wildly. He out-stared the eyes watching him, turned quickly and strode out of the barrack cavern, the Imperator's icy words ringing in his ears:
    "Advance along the unnumbered gallery."
    He would be met.

Chapter Ten
Horror Cave

Van was gripped by the first real hope of unmasking the power-mad genius behind the Invisible Empire. It quickened his senses, keyed him to alertness.

Not once since he had tricked his way into this maze of subterranean passageways had he been able even to guess at the position of the headquarters of the organization. It would have been impossible to track out the black, labyrinthian corridors of this vast series of connected mines and expect to stumble upon the center of the hooded society.

Nor had he heard anyone except Kag mention so much as the existence of a leader. He suspected none of the robed members or the guards had ever seen the Imperator face to face. There seemed to be some unwritten law against speaking his name.

That was the most baffling phase of this strange underground hunt-the utter and impregnable silence of the members.

The Phantom had considered Vonderkag as a suspect, but the hunchback scientist seemed too excitable, too unstable to govern such a ruthless association of men. Yet, apart from Kag, who was there, of all those masked and hooded members, that he could challenge as being the Imperator? A single such open attempt would only end in his immediate death.

The fifty masked officers who had attended that cryptic meeting in the cavern barrack were automatically eliminated as ultimate Imperator suspects, for that cold, emotionless speech had been delivered from some point outside that underground chamber.

Van had thought of trying to escape from this subterranean warren, to contact Havens and get help. He'd have to get out and warn the publisher, after this last threat. But to have these tunnels surrounded by police or soldiers would be useless. The Invisible Empire would only fade deeper into the mines and emerge at will from a hundred different exits.

He was stopped by two guards at the entrance to the tunnel leading off from the cavern that had the concrete walled water door of steel. They let him through at mention of the name Commander Rotz.

He went on alone, his flashlight outlining the earth walls of the sharply rising passage.

The tunnel curved several times, and ended at an iron door that was unlocked. He swung it open, found that it was the entrance to an elevator. The car was empty.

Van stepped into the cage, closed the iron door, and tried the operating lever. The elevator would not lower, but it went up rapidly when he reversed the control.

So far as he could determine, there were no stage landings until the car stopped of its own accord. He opened the door again, stepped out into a short corridor.

Two more guards in robes, masks and hoods, stood before the only exit, a narrow steel door set in a wall of cement at the end of the passage. There was an electric battery lamp over their heads.

The Phantom advanced, gave his name again. A key jangled in the lock, and the door swung open for him. He stepped through the opening into a lighted room of solid white concrete, heard the door close and the lock click behind him.

An odor of disinfectant and medicine permeated the place which was a combination surgical ward and operating room. Against one wall was a glass cabinet holding several trays filled with delicate, razor-sharp instruments. Beyond it was another door opposite the one he had entered, closed and evidently locked from the other side.

In the center of the room stood two operating tables, with space to work between them.

Van's eyes slid around the place, and a low moan sounded behind him. He turned, stepped behind a screen, looked down at a cot. On that stiff bed lay a man whose face was scarcely recognizable as human!

Van gazed pityingly into the agonized eyes of the helpless patient, and drew in his breath sharply. The skin on that mutilated face had been removed from more than two-thirds of its area. The cheeks, jowls, jaw and nose were raw flesh, and both ears had been amputated. The pillow upon which the head rested was bloodstained, sticky with gore.

The man's eyes clung to the Phantom's masked face wildly, then roved to the bed stand at the head of the cot. Van followed that tortured glance, and started at what he saw.

On the enameled top of the stand lay a gold badge and an identification card. He picked them up, his own eyes narrowing as he read the name:

JUD MARKS
Federal Bureau of Investigation

Van's hand shoved back the black hood he wore, and jerked off his white mask. He reached beneath his black robe and his fingers dug into a pocket in the belt he wore under his clothes.

Then he bent over the man on the bed, and held before the Secret Service operative's eyes a small, flat platinum badge studded with bright diamonds set in the shape of a mask-the Phantom's seal. Few men had ever seen that badge, but its legend was a by-word of accomplishment in police circles, an emblem of terror among criminals.

The eyes of the tortured F.B.I. man became alive with recognition and hope as he stared at the diamond mask in Van's hand. He tried to nod, and his bloody lips formed the word "Phantom!"

Dick Van Loan replaced the badge in his belt, bent again over the man on the bed.

"Can you talk?" he asked eagerly. "Who brought you here?"

The G-man's mangled face shuddered with the effort to answer. His words came slowly, painfully weak:

> "An attempt had been made to rob Smithsonian Institute —I was-guarding it-Hoods-like yours" —his agonized glance roved over Van's black costume — "jumped me-stealing a —meteor from-ore case. Been trying to make-me talk about the Bureau-since I woke up here —"

Van's eyes gleamed. That meteoric fragment he'd seen and that Kag had boasted about down in the furnace cavern-it had come from the Smithsonian Institute. Kag had gloated over its theft.

"Who did this to you-here?" he urged.

"A doctor-big man-couldn't see his face —I'm dying."

The F.B.I. man's hand moved beneath the thin, stained sheet.

Van pulled back the bloody covering, saw that Jud Marks was shackled to the bed. More skin had been cut from his arms, chest and stomach. The G-Man's fingers gestured-desperately.

The Phantom gripped that bony hand, held it warmly, while his narrowed gaze clung to Marks' glazing eyes. The man was dying, and knew it.

Van swallowed back the burning, hard lump choking in his throat. This was death, ruthless, horrible, yet a blessed relief for Jud Marks from the torture of unceasing pain.

The G-man's fingers in the Phantoms' hand slowly relaxed. The Federal agent's eyes became glassy, vacant, staring sightlessly.

Van lowered the limp hand to the bed, pulled the sheet up over the dead man's ghastly face. Gravely, a bleak look of intense determination growing in his eyes, he picked up and pocketed Jud Marks' badge and identification.

If Van escaped from here alive, those two grim articles would be returned to the Federal Bureau of Investigation at Washington. And the name of Jud Marks, G-Man, would appear on the engraved honor roll there, another hallowed addition to that heroic record of courageous warriors who had lost against crime.

As he stood there moodily, his thoughts still on the murdered Federal investigator, the Phantom's fingers toyed nervously with a physician's thermometer on the bed stand. He shook himself out of his brief, grisly reverie, glanced about the room, preparatory to giving it a quick search. His eyes shifted back to the thermometer in his hand.

He held it closer, looking for the manufacturer's stamp. And suddenly an eager gleam leaped into his narrowed grey gaze.

Printed on that sliver of glass, the two words partially rubbed away by use, was the ownership legend:

Alleghany Penitentiary.

As he stared at that name, Van's mind leaped back to Frank Havens' office in the Clarion Tower, and the tableau of death that had been enacted there.

The picture was startlingly vivid-the murdered metallurgical expert, Lester Gimble, lifeless in the armchair beside Havens' desk; the two homicide detectives with Captain Walters; Havens himself; and the three officials from the Alleghany Prison.

Warden Jack Bluebold; Dr. Maurice Jessup, the resident physician: ex-Congressman Harry Arnold, Chairman of the Board of Pardons and Parole. Van hadn't forgotten them.

Even at that time, it had struck him as odd that they should have been sitting in the Clarion publisher's private office at the precise moment when an escaped lifer from the Alleghany stir was identified as the dead murderer of the metallurgical specialist employed by Havens.

The Phantom stepped resolutely across to the instrument tray between the two grim operating tables, took from it the metal container for the thermometer that someone had left there. He thrust the thermometer in its cover, put the case in his pocket.

That slim glass tube of mercury would be used as evidence, if the time ever came when the facial surgeon and skin grafter was caught. And he should be here now, if the Imperator still meant to disguise Commander Rotz and send him as Professor Paul Bendix on the murderous mission to Havens.

Van glanced at those fine, sharp knives and instruments in the glass cabinet against the wall! The Imperator's genius for evil went beyond any make-up table, and resorted to surgery that cut any moulded living flesh to suit its deadly purposes.

Grimly, the Phantom decided to see it through, despite his discovery of the thermometer clue and his realization that he himself would be recognized as Dr. Bendix again. It was an immediate chance to meet the surgeon, probably the Imperator himself. He pulled the ghost-white mask back up over his face, tugged the black hood down over his head.

The two revolvers he had appropriated with Jerry Lannigan down there deeper in the mine warrens felt good in his belt under the black robe.

And suddenly he heard harsh, clipped voices outside in the short corridor where the two masked guards kept watch. Judging by the different tones that came through the steel door, five or six more men had just come up in the elevator and joined them.

The Phantom crouched at the door, listening. Some of the words out there came through distinctly:

"—found Commander Rotz dead down below—"

"What're the orders? Do we wait?"

"Open up! Imperator's instruction-He won't be here now. Get in there and kill the spy—"

The voices lowered to whispered directions.

Van's nerves steadied under the desperate change in the situation. He realized clearly what had happened. The Imperator had already discovered that the dead man wearing the clothes of Professor Paul Bendix was not Bendix at all but Commander Rotz himself.

Eventually, that discovery had to be made, and the Phantom's quick change of disguises shown up. Van had hoped it would not happen so fast, but now that it had-He darted across the room, tried the opposite door, but found it was too securely barred on the other side.

Out in the corridor the voices faded to an ominous silence.

Van's glance raced to the dead, ghastly face of Jud Marks outlined rigidly beneath the stained sheet. He leaped over to the narrow bed, tossed the bloody covering aside, carried the mutilated body to the operating table nearest the corridor door.

The G-man's body was limp. He propped it up facing the entrance through which the masked guards would come, managed to get the right arm and hand in a braced position so the lifeless fingers pointed accusingly straight at the door.

Outside, the key was scraping against the lock.

Van sacrificed his flashlight, turned it on and set it on the instrument tray so that its rays centered upon the grisly figure.

With a final swift movement, he turned out the powerful oil lamp in the room, sprang to the wall and flattened himself beside the steel door as it swung open.

A horrified oath broke from the lips of the first two guards as they rushed in. Their momentum carried them past the door, but the ghastly, spotlighted spectacle held them momentarily frozen in their tracks.

And in that split second, the Phantom plunged through the doorway out into the short, dimly lighted passage, his two guns pistol-whipping the five stunned guards outside!

He knocked three of them down before they could recover from the charging shock of his attack.

Springing past them, he reached the open elevator door, whirled into the car.

Both his guns blasted back into the corridor as flaming shots slugged at him. A masked guard screamed and flopped to the floor. A bullet nicked Van's knuckles as he jerked the door shut, grabbed the control lever.

The cage started down swiftly, the grating rattle of its descent drowned in the echoing barks of gun fire above.

Chapter Eleven
On Top

There was no guard at the bottom of the elevator shaft when Van stepped out of the car.

He made his way back to the big cavern where he had entered the unnumbered tunnel. The two hooded sentries were still posted there, but they let him pass when their torch lights showed the green circle with the two zigzag yellow stripes of an Empire officer on his black sleeve. Evidently no general alarm had been sent out for him, since he was supposed to be securely locked up in that subterranean concrete operating room.

The Phantom passed on into the main tunnel from which he and Jerry Lannigan had fled to make their escape from their original guards. He turned left, away from the direction of Vonderkag's gas cavern.

He was moving without a light, but the guards at the tunnel gates ahead of him, were satisfied with his officer's insignia and with the password, September Third.

When he had got by the last of the six doors he'd counted on his way in blind, he discarded the robe, mask and hood. A quarter mile further on he came to a fork in the shaft, and took the tunnel that had the heaviest bracing.

The passage climbed steeply, opened into a broader shaft up which ran a cog-wheel rail line for coal cars. There were no cars operating now. Van struggled up the long, sharp incline, came out upon a slag dump beneath stars and a bright moon.

He ran off the dump, darted along a mountain side, and dropped down to a dirt road. The fresh night air that filled his lungs gave him new energy. He followed the road, heard a railroad train laboring up a grade somewhere in the near distance.

Van had no definite idea where he was, except that he was in the heart of a coal mining district, probably in Pennsylvania. But fifteen minutes later, when he walked into a small town, his location assumed a grim significance.

The name of the town, Mountainview, was the post office address of the Alleghany State Penitentiary!

Van had Frank Havens on a long-distance phone connection to New York City within ten minutes. He was talking from a booth in the waiting room of the local railroad station. He didn't dare say much, and used the name of another Phantom alias, Jimmy Lance.

"I'll be at the Mountainview Hotel," he informed Havens. "Is Lannigan back yet?"

"He is," Havens stated. "And he'll fly me right out there."

"That saves me asking you to come," Van said appreciatively. "It's hotter here than you think. Bring along all the authority you can. If I'm not at the hotel there'll be a message for you. Anything else happened?"

"Yes," Havens told him tersely. "The Twin-City Power Dam at Minneapolis was destroyed by a blast-one single blast did it-to-night! And several more hooded men were reported seen at the disaster immediately after the explosion. The Twin-Cities are in a panic, partially without light, and the State Militia has been called out by the Minnesota governor!"

The Phantom kept back the flow of words that leaped to his tongue. One single explosion-the new explosive Kag had perfected!

Havens' voice came over the line again:

"I'm leaving for Mountainview at once!"

Van cut off the connection. Enough had been said over the phone. The clock in the hotel lobby showed ten P.M. when he registered for a room and locked himself in.

There was still time to visit the prison, if he could get inside the grim walls. Jud Marks' F.B.I. badge should help him there.

The Phantom spent five more minutes at the mirror and wash basin, removing the grime of the mines from his face, brushing off the blue suit he'd taken from Rotz. When he finished, he looked like a hard-traveled man who might have been a salesman.

It took him twenty minutes to get a local taxi and ride to the penitentiary on the outskirts of the town. The prison appeared bleak and grey, and fortlike in the night. It was built on a mountain side, one high stone wall almost abutting the rock-ribbed mountain itself.

About the tough prison was an atmosphere of menace and mystery that seemed to hover even over the wooded, thickly undergrown background of rugged ranges and deep, boulder-strewn valleys.

Van announced himself to the prison turnkey as a Federal agent named Jim Lance checking up on the escape of Snakey Willow, shot to death in New York City. He flashed the murdered Jud Marks' gold badge, asked to see the warden at once.

A rangy fellow named Rowan listened to the Phantom's preliminary questions irritably.

"Can't give you no information," the deputy grumbled. "You'll have to see Bluebold himself. He's in a huddle right now with Mr. Arnold who's Chairman of the Board of Parole. Dr. Jessup, the prison physician, and the wall and cell captains are with him. We got Killer Kline, that two million dollar mail robber and murderer, coming up here from Pittsburgh to be electrocuted next week. We do all the state's killings up here, since we built the big new chair."

Van studied Rowan's dull features keenly. The deputy wasn't impressed by the presence of Jim Lance, G-man, but was obviously in considerable awe of the Pittsburgh big shot who was to be locked up here for the last brief week before his official execution.

"Kline gets delivered here in the morning," the deputy went on, "so we ain't taking no chances on anything happening to him while he's with us, until he gets the jolt in the electric chair. Bluebold and the others are in the Board Room getting up their plans to handle this killer now. So you'll have to wait until they're done."

He took Van into the warden's office inside the prison behind the double gates of the turnkey's cage, and sat with him for a half hour until Bluebold and the men in the conference came out of the Board Room door at one end of the prison chief's office.

During that wait, Van's attempts to get the deputy to talk about the prison's management failed dismally. The rangy officer was obviously under orders not to give out any information at all concerning the activities behind these grim walls.

Rowan had run completely out of conversation when the Board Room door opened and the conference filed out.

The Phantom eyed the seven men in turn as they entered the warden's office. They were all big, powerful sharp-glanced, with the hard look of prison officials accustomed to handling convicts ruthlessly. The two cell captains and the two officers in command of the prison wall guards went out immediately. The deputy introduced Jim Lance, told what he'd come for.

In the austere environment of the penitentiary, Warden Jack Bluebold was even more rugged and capable looking than he had appeared when the Phantom had first seen him in Frank Havens' office. He sat aggressively in the chair behind his desk, eyeing Lance with shrewd, suspicious appraisal.

Ex-Congressman Harry Arnold, the Parole Board chairman, seemed no different than he had been in New York. His bearing was confident, his manner unruffled and assured. The responsibility of handling Killer Kline and electrocuting the tough murderer hadn't disturbed the politician's suavely alert and open-minded appearance.

Dr. Maurice Jessup, Van observed, seemed to be the only one of the three who was not fully satisfied with what had been decided upon in that Board Room meeting. He kept darting unexpected glances at Arnold and Bluebold, as though on the verge of declaring himself on some point which he never quite voiced.

The three officials were no more impressed by the presence of a G-man investigating Snakey Willow's escape than Deputy Rowan had been. They listened tolerantly to Van's questions, and Warden Bluebold became the spokesman.

"Snakey Willow was working in the foundry, welding a job, when some of the metal kicked back into his face. His welding glasses saved his eyes, but we had to patch up his ugly map or he wouldn't have had any face at all. Dr. Jessup's pretty proud of how he fixed Willow's face."

Dr. Jessup nodded. "I took my time on him," and shrugged. "Willow told me nobody'd know him, if he ever got out again."

Bluebold jerked open a drawer, thrust a printed "Wanted" police broadside at Van, The folder gave Willow's Bertillon and fingerprint measurements and his picture before the lifer had had his face lifted. The date of release printed on the police notice was four days old.

"Hell!" Bluebold exclaimed. "Deputy Rowan here, who was in charge of the prison while I was on a trip to New York, reported the escape as soon as it was discovered, and had that broadside sent out. I admit we've had some graft and corruption going on here under our noses, but we're getting that cleaned up. I fired eight inside guards today!"

"Yeah," Rowan nodded. "Those eight screws won't be sneaking in any more contraband."

"Besides bringing in whiskey on their hips," Dr. Jessup exclaimed caustically, "those guards were bringing in dope!"

Van handed back the police broadside to Bluebold.

"I'm not through cleaning up this prison," the warden declared determinedly. "But it takes time to ferret out these rats who've been wearing guards' uniforms around here. Mr. Arnold is going to appear before the state legislature with a bill that will make it a felony for a state penitentiary employee, guards and civilians both, to be caught carrying in or out anything that isn't permitted in the book of prison rules. The way it is now, all I can do is can these birds whenever we catch them trying to slip something over on us!"

The Phantom nodded, letting them talk.

"All they lose is their jobs," Harry Arnold emphasized. "We can't prosecute them. This is the toughest prison in the state, a sort of Alcatraz where the hardest criminals are sent. Those crooks usually have plenty of money and friends outside the walls, so you can understand, Mr. Lance, the profit there must be in bringing contraband in here to the prisoners."

Dr. Jessup, Warden Bluebold and Deputy Rowan jerked their heads in agreement, their eyes on Van.

"I'd be safe in saying," Harry Arnold went on, "as I'm going to say to the state legislature, that without a law putting a high felony penalty on such violations of our penitentiary rules, the crooked guards and civilian employees can, and do, make ten times their salary carrying in contraband and taking out uncensored letters to be mailed without our knowledge!"

Van asked bluntly, "How do you figure Snakey Willow got out?"

Warden Bluebold's eyes glinted. "Outside help did it!" he snapped. "This prison is escape-proof from within. There's a double count when the cons are locked in their cells at night, and again when they're let out to go to the shops in the morning. That count is checked twice each time before the cell doors are locked. At the shops and wherever the men work, there are between two and four guards who are responsible for the number of cons they handle. Willow's changed face might have helped, but you can't blame Dr. Jessup for that."

"If the guards are corrupted with money outside when they're off duty," Arnold put in, "all the warden and his deputies can do is wait until something arouses their suspicions, or until a convict disappears. We know the cons can't get out without help. It's the screws and the civilians who aid in the few escapes we've had. We're organizing a spy system among the guards themselves, which should help us detect crookedness before anything serious happens."

The four prison officials talked on, emphasizing what they'd already said, repeating themselves in different words. The Phantom recognized the hard logic in their statements, but could not break through the defense barrier they were building against him. The whole story was not coming out, whatever it was. They were ganging up on him, holding him off with reiterated generalities.

"How about the hospital?" he demanded. "Prison hospitals are apt to be a breeding place of corruption, due to the necessity for less iron-bound rules."

Dr. Maurice Jessup glanced at him with a gleam of contempt. "Perhaps that is true in other penitentiaries. It isn't true here!"

Warden Bluebold thrust out his jaw. "Our hospital is the hardest spot in this institution to get into. A convict is damned sick before he's admitted. We don't even allow visitors to go through that part of the prison without a special guard as a guide. Dr. Jessup is as much a disciplinarian as I am, besides being a very exceptional doctor and surgeon."

Van's eyelids flicked. They were putting this on heavy now-too thickly for him to swallow whole. There wasn't going to be a single loop-hole for him or any other investigator to use as a starting point.

He switched his attack, asked suddenly, "Ever had any trouble with any secret societies around here?"

The four men looked at him with set blankness in their eyes. Then Arnold chuckled good-naturedly.

"I see what you mean, Lance," he said tolerantly. "The papers are beginning to play up the old Ku Klux Klan idea in connection with the Arizona dam disaster. About twelve years ago, if I remember right, there was an organization of Ku Kluxers in these parts, but they sort of petered out after the national exposure of their political aspirations."

Warden Bluebold scowled. "If you're really investigating Snakey Willow's escape, Mr. Lance, you won't get anywhere chasing screwy newspaper scareheads. The payoff on that was cold cash on the line, outside, and not any nutty Ku Klux hocus-pocus. I'd suggest that you try to find the surgeon who fixed up Snakey's mug. That's the angle that Mr. Arnold, Dr. Jessup and myself are working on."

Van nodded, his veiled gaze hiding the sharp alertness behind his drooping lids. If that thermometer he'd found, with Alleghany Penitentiary stamped upon it, meant anything, Warden Bluebold's words were a direct challenge.

"I guess you're right, warden," he said, as though he'd begun to lose interest in the Willow case. "If you don't mind, I'll go through the prison tonight, so I won't have to wait over until tomorrow. I've got to make a routine report on this, anyhow."

"That'll be all right," Bluebold stated. "Deputy Rowan will show you around."

Van shook hands with them, then followed the deputy into the main corridor opening into the two big dormitory wings of the institution. Rowan seemed voluble enough now, so long as the Phantom stayed on generalities.

They walked along railed and lighted galleries past row upon row of gloomy cells in which the convicts slept restlessly. An occasional cry of some prisoner in his sleep was the only sound that broke the peculiar monotone of four thousand men breathing in weary nervous rhythm.

The great dining hall was a dark, deserted auditorium of long, narrow tables that gave the vague impression of deserted tombstones, where their footsteps shuffled ominously loud in the echoing silence.

In the shops, where shoes and cheap mining machinery were manufactured by convict labor, the rows of lathes, presses, cutting machines and drills were grotesque shapes poised in grim stillness, waiting for the maw of morning when they, would grind again into endless, heart-breakingly monotonous motion.

Van took particular notice of the enormous foundry as he and the deputy passed through its shrouded darkness. The high-ceilinged shop with its two big blast furnaces was peculiarly well equipped, and there were extra night guards stationed around its thick walls.

"That's the hospital over there," the deputy announced when they came out into the prison yard again.

He pointed at a four-story stone building set against the grey prison wall. It was dark, except for a red light over the entrance and a glow from one of the windows on the top floor.

"I'd take you in there," Deputy Rowan stated with finality, "except there's an iron-bound rule against visitors, official or not, going there at night. Black-Jack Bluebold would kick hell out of me if I let you in. Anyhow, the place is locked and I haven't got the key on me."

"Who keeps that key?" Van asked.

"Dr. Jessup, when he's inside the prison," Rowan answered and eyed Van distrustfully. "Other times it's locked up in the warden's safe. There's a fire exit that can be opened from inside the hospital, if that's what's worrying you."

The Phantom shrugged. There was no use his trying to break through the official reserve of these prison officials any longer. They were telling him just so much, and no more. But there was another way of getting past their loquatious, calculated barriers.

"Where's the death house cells?" he asked.

"See that light on the top floor of the hospital building?" Rowan said, his voice hardening. "That's it. There's two guys in there now, Sam Robbins and Joe Sholtz. We're frying Joe tonight. The electric chair is where that light shows. They're getting it ready."

The Phantom studied that grim window with the drawn shade a moment, his grey eyes slitted, his features masking the intensity of his sharp scrutiny. The shade of death would be drawn across that window in a few brief hours.

"I've seen enough," he said abruptly. "I'll fix up my report to the bureau from what information you've given me."

Relief showed on Rowan's face as they walked back to the main cell blocks and on through to the turnkey's double-doored cage.

Van thanked the deputy, shook hands with him, and was let out into the starry night. But the Phantom's eyes had become strangely restless.

Chapter Twelve
Fast Flight

When he got back to town Van stopped at an all-night restaurant. He had almost forgotten that he was ravenously hungry. But his mind was not on the food he ate.

He calculated the flying time from New York City to Mountainview, Pennsylvania, decided that Lannigan and Havens would land at the small local airport at about two o'clock in the morning. He needed sleep, but he could sleep in the plane, after he'd convinced Havens of the necessity for the queer, dangerous action he was planning.

Speed was essential; and next to that, Havens' influence as a public figure. He'd need Jerry Lannigan, too.

Van had left nothing at the hotel. He went directly to the airport from the restaurant, found the two small hangars locked and the field deserted.

He waited impatiently at the edge of the single short runway, keeping himself awake with cigarettes and frequent nervous pacings, while his mind went over and over the details of his plan.

At ten minutes past two in the morning, an hour and a half after the Phantom had reached the forsaken airport, he heard the first faint drone of an airplane motor. He stared skyward, caught sight of the red, green and white triangle of the ship's flying lights.

The moon was still out, making landing flares unnecessary. A half minute later the beat of the motor ceased and the ship drifted down toward the field, spiraling as Lannigan maneuvered for a short landing. The twin wing lights flashed on as the ship slid down and settled on the ground.

Van was at the door of the plane's cabin before Havens had it unlocked. He jerked it open, flashed his platinum and diamond insignia at the publisher, and pulled himself into the cabin.

"Get into the air again, Champ!" he ordered.

The roar of the motor as Lannigan taxied rapidly and turned into the wind, taking off again, gave Van a chance to greet Havens and slap the big red-headed Irishman on his beefy shoulder. When the ship was above the mountain ranges, leveling off, Van said determinedly to Havens:

"You've got to see the governor of Pennsylvania for me right away, Frank. Is he at the capitol in Harrisburg?"

Havens shook his head, reached forward and tapped Jerry on the arm. "Pittsburgh, Lannigan," he directed, and turned to Van. "Governor Young is in Pittsburgh tonight. I talked with him on long distance after Lannigan got through to me and said you were down in a Pennsylvania coal mine near Mountainview."

The publisher smiled wanly and added, "I wanted Young to have a detachment of National Guardsmen ready in that district, in case I didn't hear from you within the next twelve hours."

"That wouldn't have helped any," the Phantom declared flatly. "That region is honey-combed with connected mines, for miles around." He glanced at Lannigan, asked him. "How'd you get out, Champ?"

"I hung onto that elevator until it stopped," Jerry said over his shoulder as he banked and headed for Pittsburgh. "Then I got into the shaft bracing beams and climbed on up. I was still in the mine, but those hoods had disappeared, so I smacked a couple of guys that got in my way, and found a drift that led me out finally. Jeez, I had to walk about five miles to get to a phone. A miner drove me to the Mountainview airport and I chartered a plane. What happened to you after I scrammed?"

Van's eyes held a faraway look for a moment as he recalled the burly figure of Lannigan hanging to the bottom of that mine cage. Then he gave the two men a swift account of his own attempts to penetrate the hooded mystery.

As he talked, Frank Havens' age-lined face darkened into a frown of grim worry that matched the graveness of his steady gaze.

"Phantom," he said, "you've taken too many risks already." He looked down through the cabin windows at the dark, ragged tops of the mountains. "But we've got to keep on until the Imperator is stopped! Governor Young will use his soldiers —"

Van cut him off with a shake of his head.

"It can't be done that way, Havens," he insisted sternly. "Even if the entire district was surrounded, these members of the Invisible Empire could come and go as ordinary miners-most of them are workingmen who've been duped into joining this legion."

"Got to nail the bird who calls himself the Imperator," Jerry declared. "I was in those mine tunnels myself, and I know! You couldn't even blast 'em out with that stuff that blew up Rock Canyon Dam!"

"You see, Frank," Van went on, "the members are too afraid of their leader to talk, even to save themselves. And he knows that nothing can drive them out into the open so long as he remains an unseen emperor, and continues to pay them off. Remember, if any member is killed, that man's family is guaranteed financial independence for seven generations! It's a weird idea but it holds them, makes them willing martyrs."

"Can't he be cut off through his finances," Havens demanded. "Money can be traced!"

"Not the way he handles it, evidently," Van persisted. "Don't forget all the small bank robberies, the blackmail pay-offs, the things he can do with that explosive of his. And now he's going after the United States Treasury. You can't trace gold, you know. And he does not keep his money in public institutions, I imagine. That hospital room he's got underground, is proof enough he can, and probably does, have vaults buried in those tunnels."

"What's all this got to do with Governor Young, then?" Havens demanded. "You say you can't use state militia to any purpose."

The Phantom's grey eyes glowed. "The heart of this secret organization is in that prison at Mountainview, Frank, I've told you I made a pass at it tonight, and ran into a blank wall. But there's that thermometer with Alleghany Penitentiary stamped on it. There's the fact that three men from that institution were in your office at the time your man was to report to you on Dr. Junes' aluminum-calbite fusion experiments-and that man was murdered.

"There's the killing of Junes by these hooded devils, witnessed by Jerry and myself! There's the theft of that aluminum-calbite meteoric fragment from the Smithsonian Institute in Washington, and its delivery to Vonderkag down in the mines. The whole thing ties up with the fusion of these two metals—a fusion demonstrated as a possibility by that fragment itself!"

Lannigan called over his shoulder, "I'm with you, Skipper, whatever it is you're leading up to. Maybe you didn't get much chance to keep up with your reading, down in the mine, but the newspapers are reporting, now that two or three hooded guys were seen at that Mississippi River explosion in Minneapolis. Mort Lewis, remember the radio announcer, says he saw two of them hoods himself after the Rock Canyon blast."

The Phantom nodded to the publisher "Havens told me on the phone, and the Imperator boasted, in his speech down in the cavern, that the Arizona disaster had been a huge success for the organization, and that the new explosive-the stuff they used in Minneapolis-would be dropped from the air on the Treasury Building."

"All right," Havens said curtly. "The prison, you've discovered, is right on top of this mine district. What's your plan?"

Van looked searchingly at the publisher, and said "I want to get into that prison in the disguise of Killer Kline!"

Havens jerked in his seat. "That's an impossibility! Kline is the present Number One criminal in the United States. They're going to electrocute him almost as soon as they get him into the death house. He's to die some time during the week beginning September second-and that's tomorrow!"

"Yes, it's tomorrow," the Phantom agreed tensely. "And on September third, the day following, the Treasury at Washington will be blown up at dawn-if we don't stop the Imperator in the next" —he glanced at the clock on the ship's instrument panel —"fifty hours!"

For a long minute the grey-haired publisher pondered. Then he asked: "Suppose something goes wrong, Phantom? Suppose you're in there as Killer Kline, and they decide to hold the execution at once?"

Lannigan turned and eyed them. "They'd have a hell of a time, if I was there as a witness to that frying! And I'll be there!"

Havens' head moved slowly in negation. "You, nor anyone else, not even Governor Young himself, Lannigan could stop the warden if he should decide to strap Kline in that death seat at any hour after the week set for the execution starts."

"You mean, if somebody there-maybe the warden himself-got suspicious of Kline, or the Phantom?" Jerry demanded.

"That is exactly what I mean," Havens said. "The Phantom is convinced that the Imperator operates from within that penitentiary. If that is true, then the Imperator is one of those officials, or controls them. If he gave the word to electrocute Kline, nothing could stop that execution."

"Nothing can stop the Imperator's wrecking the financial heart of the country, until he's caught," Van insisted grimly. "I'm willing to take my chances in there." Defiance crept into his voice.

Havens eyed him sharply.

"In which instance," the Phantom added pointedly, "you couldn't ever be sure that I didn't manage to substitute myself for Kline. I could do it, you know."

A peculiar light, that had no malice in it, gleamed deep in the publisher's somber eyes. He smiled inwardly, but said sternly:

"That's a threat, Phantom. A challenge. I might even call it blackmail. In fact, it was I who asked Lannigan to fly us to see the governor in Pittsburgh."

"I'm glad you agree with me, Frank," Van grinned. "You can make things so much easier, when you quit fussing about my safety. Here's a few other things I'd like to have you work on while I catch some sleep. Get a line on the history of the executives and their assistants at Alleghany Penitentiary.

"And you, Jerry! Somewhere in the Mountainview district is a hangar, probably built underground like the new army field hangars. You won't be flying me back, but you can report to me as a visitor at the stir, and tell me how your hunt for that all-metal ship the Imperator has built is coming. Blow it up when you find it."

The Phantom's tired glance covered the two men a moment. Then he stretched back in the seat, adjusted the safety belt, and cocked Havens' hat over his eyes.

"Wake me up," he said, "when you get things fixed."

Chapter Thirteen
Killer Kline

It was six o'clock in the morning. Killer Kline was shaken awake and hurried from his cell in the Pittsburgh jail out a back exit into an armored car that sped him toward the airport.

In the car with him was another prisoner-the Phantom.

But that second prisoner had not been booked in any Pittsburgh jail. Van had been locked in the truck before it had left the sheriff's garage, as a precaution against spying eyes in the jail. Only the driver and the two guards-three special deputies assigned by Governor Young to make the Kline delivery knew that that second passenger rode in the steel box behind them. And even they did not know who he was.

Van studied the shrewd, ruthless features of the mail robber and machine-gun killer crouching on the iron bench in the armored box as the truck whirled through the streets. Kline's greenish grey eyes darted about the interior of the car ceaselessly, in search of a way of escape.

He was close enough to the Phantom in size, to make a switch a reasonable risk. Van's gaze noted brazenly the mannerisms of the criminal, the way he moved his hands, the leering twist of his lips:

"Going all the way?" he asked Kline bluntly.

"Not if I can help it," the murderer snarled. "They jolted Joe Sholtz up there in the stone house early this morning, didn't they? I ain't seen a morning paper yet."

"Yeah," the Phantom answered, getting the tone and inflection of Kline's sharp, harsh voice. "Four minutes it took to burn him dead. That's a long time to jerk against those death chair straps."

Beads of sweat began to stand out on Killer Kline's forehead.

"I do it in four seconds with a tommy gun," Kline growled. "It don't hurt so much, either. By God, I wish I had a tommy gun in my hands right now! They ain't going to fry me —"

He broke off, glowering at Van distrustfully.

"A smart, tough guy like you," Van encouraged, "shouldn't have to take the juice."

"Yeah." Kline's voice grated boastfully. "I ain't never stayed locked up long before. Parties make passes at me to get me out so I can help 'em pull jobs they ain't smart enough to do themselves." He shut up abruptly, eyeing Van with suspicion.

"I'll bet you got propositioned that way since you've been in the Pittsburgh can," the Phantom suggested.

Kline's gaze froze up. "I don't know what the hell you're talking about!" he declared belligerently.

Van didn't press him further. The Killer's manner implied that he'd already been approached with a chance to escape. It was what the Phantom had been expecting and hoping for.

A few minutes later the armored truck stopped at an outlying precinct station. The only door in the box opened and one of the three deputies called in:

"Come on out, Killer. This is as far as you go, this trip."

"What th' hell is this?" Kline demanded, and peered out the door. "This ain't the Alleghany stir?"

That was as far as he got. The deputies yanked him out of the car, manhandled him into the precinct station's alley entrance.

Nobody except Van and the three officers knew the transfer had been made. Kline would be booked under another name and hidden in a constantly guarded cellar cell until the Phantom or Governor Young sent word to have him finish his last ride.

The armored truck door slammed shut on Van and the car rolled off again. The Phantom forgot everything else for the next ten minutes as he concentrated on the make-up task confronting him. Before the truck reached the airport where a plane was waiting to fly Killer Kline to Mountainview, Killer Kline had to be reproduced.

From beneath his coat Van took out a paper sack containing the make-up kit he'd got on such short notice through the influence of Governor Young.

He set up a small pocket mirror, went to work swiftly. The Kline character had to be done entirely with the face, for Van would be stripped and re-dressed in prison clothes at the penitentiary. For the rest, he had to rely on his own ability to portray the Killer's characteristics in voice, mannerisms and action.

Fortunately, there were no Bertillon figures or fingerprints of Killer Kline on record at Mountainview. Those records would be taken there at the stir, and a copy of them mailed to the State and Federal identification bureaus-where they would be seized and promptly destroyed. Van had insisted upon that, to protect the Phantom's identity from being discovered. Later, if he survived the Alleghany Prison affair, the records there would be burned, too.

A moment before the truck swerved into the airport gate, a crumpled paper sack and a small pocket mirror fell from a gun slot in the steel car wall. The truck drove directly to a waiting ship, its door was opened, and Killer Kline was hurriedly transferred to the airplane.

There had been no hitch, no error. And there was none when the plane landed at the small Mountainview flying field and was met by a prison van.

Within thirty minutes Killer Kline was booked into Alleghany Penitentiary, without a hint of suspicion concerning his real identity, and the commitment papers were being signed by Warden Black-Jack Bluebold in person.

The same four men who had talked to Jimmy Lance in the warden's office the night before, now confronted the Phantom in the same room.

Ex-congressman Arnold and Dr. Maurice Jessup eyed Killer Kline in austere, watchful silence. Deputy Rowan, with three prison guards, kept the two doors into the office blocked. They were taking no chances with the notorious murderer.

"Still think you're the toughest guy in the United States?" Bluebold demanded harshly.

The Phantom put across his initial act with a snarl of defiance.

"I've got part of a week to live, starting tomorrow, you big punk! If you can think up anything during that time that's too tough for me, give me a crack at it, Peanut-brain! And that goes for the rest of you bottom rate chislers."

He swung upon them all. "Hell, there ain't a one of you smart enough to make yourself a buck outside. If it wasn't that the state paid you a salary, you'd all starve to death! Come on, let's take a squint at the death house you're so damned proud of."

"You'll take more than a squint at it, Killer," Bluebold snapped.

"Take him away and give him a bath, Rowan!"

But Rowan didn't take him alone. The three uniformed guards came along, crowding Van, yet watching him with nervous respect. He'd told off Black-Jack Bluebold! Killer Kline was the toughest con they'd ever handled.

Van shed his clothes, and took a secret satisfaction in making the muscles ripple under his skin as he moved about under the shower. These screws would think twice before they tried to maul him around. And his toughness and prowess as a hard guy would get talked about, which was what he wanted.

He wasn't sure the Imperator had sent an envoy to the real Kline in Pittsburgh jail. But he intended to give that mystery commander of the Invisible Empire a reason for wanting him as a member, if brazen courage and insolent fearlessness would do it.

Deputy Rowan threw him an outfit of prison clothes, drab, worn garments of faded muddy color that blended with the bleak, hopeless surroundings. Bluebold himself supervised the Bertillon and fingerprint records. Then he was herded over to the hospital.

Van's eyes sharpened as Dr. Jessup examined him, in the presence of the warden and Rowan and Arnold. The four men seemed to take a grisly delight in observing his physical qualifications.

"If you'd turned out to be a prizefighter or a professional wrestler, Kline," Dr. Jessup advised, "you'd have got some place in the world." He glanced at the others. "A wonderful specimen of a physique, gentlemen. It's really a shame to destroy it by electrocution."

"Count up the number of innocent and helpless guys Kline has killed," Harry Arnold said gravely. "Kline, you can't be executed but the one time. How many men do you figure you've murdered?"

"Who th' hell are you?" Van demanded. "Another punk screw?"

"Mr. Arnold," Bluebold said dryly, "is the Chairman of the Board of Parole and Pardons."

"If I added you to that list of guys I've rubbed out," Van rasped, "it would be a hell of a swell idea. Go on back to the Pardon Board and tell 'em that!"

"You're not going to ask Mr. Arnold for any help, I take it," Dr. Jessup remarked dryly.

"Nuts to him!" Van exploded. "I wouldn't take a pardon from none of you dopes. When I crash out of a stir, I do it my way!"

"Let's see you beat the death house, Kline," Black-Jack Bluebold challenged grimly. "I'll be waiting to shoot you!"

"Yeah!" Killer Kline snarled contemptuously. "You, with a gun. I can imagine! Hell, punk, I'd take it away from you and blow your damned face off with it!"

"Upstairs with him," Bluebold ordered.

The Phantom was ushered out of the prison physician's office into an elevator. There were no stairs, he noticed. At the fourth floor, which was the top, he was shoved out of the car into a steel-walled corridor at the end of which was a door painted a sickly green.

Bluebold, who had come up with him, pointed to the corridor's end. "That's the last door you'll ever enter, Kline. The chair is waiting for you on the other side. It's not a long walk."

Van did not answer. He'd put on his Killer Kline act enough, he imagined, and didn't want to overdo it. The guards shoved him into a cell, slammed shut the door which was entirely of steel bars.

There were seven other death cells on the corridor, four on each side, but none of them were occupied. Since Joe Sholtz had gone last night, Killer Kline appeared to be the only occupant of the death house.

But Deputy Rowan last night had mentioned a second murderer awaiting a future execution-Sam Robbins. And convicted men who entered this short corridor weren't supposed to be removed except through that fatal green door at the end, or by order of the Board of Pardons. If there'd been a pardon for Robbins, Governor Young would have mentioned it.

Robbins wasn't in the death house now.

Warden Bluebold and Rowan left him a few minutes later, after a whispered conference with the two guards on duty. The Phantom sat on the edge of the iron bed fastened to the wall, staring moodily through the bars at the empty cell opposite him.

He was on his own now completely. Not even Frank Havens could reach him on short notice, without the consent of Black-Jack Bluebold.

And suddenly Van remembered a mistake he'd made. He'd told Jerry Lannigan to visit him here, keep him informed about the hunt for the mystery plane. But Lannigan had been seen by the Imperator, or by several of the Imperator's men; in Dr. Waldo Junes' laboratory at Niagara Falls, and again in the mine, where Gulliver Vonderkag, the hunchback scientist, worked with the subterranean gas flame.

During those two periods, Lannigan had been stripped of the adhesive tape bandages over his eyes and mouth. And Jerry wore no disguise. If he showed up here, visiting Killer Kline, and one of the Imperator's men saw him-The Phantom shrugged off the thought of the consequences. At any rate, then the Imperator would guess the ruse that had been put over on the prison officials, and would show his hand in action.

Presently the elevator door jangled open and two men came into the corridor. Van could get only a passing look at them down the hallway, but they were in civilian clothes. He heard one of them mention his name: "Tough guy Killer Kline."

The two guards stepped over to his cell, unlocked the door, let in the two strangers, and locked the door again. Van heard them both go into the electrocution room beyond the green door, evidently so they wouldn't hear the conversation.

He stared at them sullenly, with the baleful contempt of Killer Kline himself. The two men were stocky, blunt-featured, shifty-eyed. They flashed state troopers' badges at him. They looked like brothers.

"Remember us, Kline?" one of them demanded.

The Phantom's eyes narrowed. Was this a trap? "So what?" he evaded. "I'm Garbo —I wanna be alone."

"Still the wise guy, eh?" the second one growled. "Well, you got this far along the route, sap. Want to let 'em fry you?"

"It's me that's gettin' fried, ain't it?" the Phantom snarled. He was stalling for time, trying to lead them into making some remark that would let him know what they were after, who they were. "I guess I got some rights left. If I wanna let 'em cook me, that's my business, ain't it?"

"That's what you said in the Pittsburgh can," the first of the two men grumbled. "You haven't got much time to make up your mind."

"I got a week," Van declared, eyeing them slantwise from the bed.

"That's what you think, chump. Listen!" The two men bent over him, as one of them prodded the air emphatically with a stubby finger: "Bluebold's got the authority to squirt the old juice into you any time after midnight tonight. Your last week starts then."

"Bluebold ain't in no hurry," Van exclaimed mockingly. "The publicity Killer Kline is bringin' him is plenty. He's eatin' it up!"

"Balance that publicity against the hundred grand you salted away out of that last mail robbery. It still adds up to cash on the line for your liberty. We ain't saying how soon Bluebold is figuring on watching you burn. He's sore. We offered you a chance at a proposition down in the Pittsburgh can. Want to talk business now?"

"You ain't very free with the details," Van growled.

The other stocky stranger elbowed his partner aside, and said:

"Look at the facts, Kline! For that dough, you get snaked out of here without any fireworks. You join up with our outfit and get an equity in your own money, and that's a damned sight more than you'd get trying to buy your way out through a regular stir delivery."

"Keep talking," the Phantom urged, and let himself show some growing interest.

Evidently Killer Kline had more of an inside track on his proposed escape than anyone had even dreamed. But Van still didn't know who these men represented.

"And another thing," the stocky man persisted. "You get taken care of after you get out of here. That comes with joining with us. The hideout is free, and you don't have to keep yourself locked up in no cheap room for a year, or keep jumping from town to town dodging cops, either."

Van spoke with a gleam of challenge in his sharp eyes.

"For a hundred grand you guys are going to make over the whole world so everybody'll love me or something? Me-the top killer of 'em all! Yeah, sell that plot to the movies, you lugs!"

"Don't get like that Kline," the second man grumbled. "You ain't heard it all yet. Our outfit's got a croaker that does the best job of face-lifting in the country. And he's working on a way to keep fingerprints from growing back again after he grafts new skin on the fingertips. All that medical stuff goes along with the hundred grand, soon as you join up."

"You won't recognize yourself, Kline," the first stocky stranger declared, "after that medico gets through with your map. You'd pay fifty grand alone for an operation like that, outside."

"Who's the croaker who does those operations?" Van demanded bluntly. "Why ain't I never heard of him before?"

"Yeah, a lot of smart guys would like to know that," one of the men told him. "Hell, Kline, we don't even know ourselves who he is. And what's more, we don't ask."

"And all my dough goes to that doctor?" the Phantom said.

"The dough goes to the organization, the mob," the other fellow told him. "You'll find out about it when the time comes."

"Gimme a little while to think about it," Van said after a pause during which they eyed him eagerly. "I'll probably come on in with you. But I gotta think about it." He saw their eyes cloud, and added quickly, "I can't pluck that hundred grand of mine out of the air in this damned stir. I'll have to figure how you can get it."

"Okay, Kline. You got until midnight tonight." The two men glanced confidently at each other. "You'll be seen before then, if not by us, by somebody who'll be in the know. And don't forget that midnight your death week begins. Black-Jack Bluebold ain't a nice guy to be waiting on, when it's your life he can burn up."

They rattled the door to attract the guards.

"Suppose I get quizzed about your visit," the Phantom said in a low voice. "What's the angle?"

"We're a couple of state cops, like our badges show," one of the men winked at him and grinned. "We're trying to find out what you did with that dough from that mail robbery."

The guard with the cell key let them out, and the elevator at the end of the corridor made a scraping noise as it took them down.

"Guard," Van called when the two men had gone. "Gimme a cigarette." And as the guard lit one and handed it to him through the bars: "Say, I thought I was having a guy named Sam Robbins for company. Where they got him now?"

"The prison physician, Dr. Jessup, moved him downstairs into one of the wards," the guard answered indifferently. "Sam complained that something he ate didn't agree with him. Then he got pretty blamed sick all of a sudden right after breakfast."

"Ate something that poisoned him, eh?" The Phantom's veiled gaze was sharp and hard behind the drooping lids.

Chapter Fourteen
Behind that Door

The Phantom had three more visitors that afternoon.

Congressman Harry Arnold was brought up by Deputy Rowan, who left immediately, and the interview was conducted with the bars of the cell door between them. Arnold was on his official dignity at first, but he became shrewder and more human as they talked.

"My purpose in coming here," the Congressman stated, "is to fulfill a formal duty. As Chairman of the Board of Pardons, I'm obliged to talk with every man condemned to death by the state, to make sure that he is given an opportunity to try for a pardon if his lawyer or friends or relatives have not done so."

Van stepped away from the bars and sat down on the end of the uncomfortable iron bed, studying the politician shrewdly. The man was rather handsome in a rawboned manner, and the inflection of his speech was flawless.

"I take my oratory sitting down," Van cut in on him. "After you get through about the pardon I couldn't get in a couple of million years, what're you going to talk about?"

Arnold raised his eyebrows appreciatively, and a faint smile twitched his lips.

"Aside from the fact that you're here in the death house, Kline," he said interestedly, "which means that you blundered —I'd say you were a pretty smart man. I suppose you won't be afraid to die, until the last minute or two. Or don't you give a damn any more?"

"What makes you think I don't?" the Phantom asked curiously.

Arnold shrugged mildly. "Your toughness, your hardness, Kline. The name you've acquired-Killer. Admirable qualities, sometimes. But-there's always the chair at the end."

"Nerts!" Van snapped at him. "I figure I'm in for a battle over that hundred grand I'm supposed to have tucked away-and what do I have to listen to? A sermon!"

"Dr. Jessup's point of view is rather apt," Arnold remarked, his glance still amused. "It ought to be a shame to destroy a specimen like you." He turned away abruptly toward the elevator. Over his shoulder he said, "I may see you again before Bluebold's nerves get the better of him. I'm afraid your reputation is working against you this time-speeding the last hour."

Van lay back on the bed, pondering. Arnold had been present in Frank Haven's office when the three officials from the Alleghany Penitentiary had appeared. That was about the only suspicion Van could attach to him.

Yet Arnold, being a politician, had to be a public speaker and organizer. It would take a shrewd organizer to build up and control such a fear disciplined mob of hooded devils as Van had run into.

Arnold didn't seem to possess the ruthlessness needed, hadn't evidenced such hardness at any rate. Nor had he displayed any knowledge of either medicine or chemistry-the two requirements the leader of the Invisible Empire must possess besides a genius for organization in secret.

Anyone, the Phantom reasoned, could hire a surgeon to transform the criminal faces of crooks who chose to become members. He was trying to consider the prison executives one at a time now, and kept Dr. Jessup out of the mentally probing picture for the moment. And anyone could hire a scientist, such as Kag, perhaps.

But the rub was, that no shrewd-minded commander of such a society as the Imperator controlled, would sensibly care to trust both of the main mechanical factors in his organization to hired men. He'd almost have to be an expert in at least one of the two major lines himself, over and above his executive capacity.

Van's thoughts were interrupted by the arrival of Warden Bluebold. Van stood up, leaned against the bars, eyeing the prison chief sharply.

"How do you like your temporary quarters now?" the big man asked. He handed Van a fresh pack of cigarettes. "The guards give you lights for your smokes and tend to your whims okay, Killer?" His attitude was not sour, but unexpectedly cheerful.

"I'm doing fine," the Phantom told him. "Decided when you're going to tuck me into the chair and turn on the juice?" He eyed the warden sharply. "Your pal Arnold is afraid I'm getting on your nerves."

"Arnold? Humph!" Black-Jack Bluebold's voice was a tolerant growl. "Mr. Arnold isn't tough enough, I'm thinking, to make a good prison warden. Kline, it takes guys with nerve-like you and me, Killer! I'm going to get a kick out of throwing the switch on you."

"Tomorrow morning?" Van asked pointedly.

"That'll be up to you, in a way," Bluebold told him flatly.

"Saving me for something?" The Phantom's voice was caustic.

"I want to find out where that money is you got on your last robbery, Kline. The insurance company put it at a hundred thousand dollars. Want to talk about it now-or later?"

The Phantom covered his own surprised reaction in a Killer Kline shrug of contempt. "I was waiting for something like that, you big punk! Personal shakedown, eh? Suppose somebody beat you to it?"

Bluebold's eyes narrowed dangerously.

"Kline, I've stood about all the insults from you I'm going to take! I can fry you at midnight tonight, and by God, if you don't control that dirty tongue of yours, I will turn the heat on you then!"

Van's voice cracked back at him:

"Why the hell don't you? What's stopping you? What the devil are you waiting for?"

The warden's face reddened. He started to shout something, but bit off the words with a snap of his heavy jaw.

"If you've got a proposition to make," the Phantom told him flatly, "let's have it, Bluebold. You ain't the only one making passes at me."

"Listen, you rat!" Bluebold growled, his eyes smoldering with hate, "I ought to come in there and beat that information out of you. But there's other ways of finding out." His manner changed suddenly, became icy and deliberate. "I'm not after that dough for myself. There were two dicks up here to see about that money a while ago. What did you tell 'em?"

The Phantom's eyes glittered. Was Bluebold in with those two phony state trooper detectives, afraid they were doublecrossing him?

"I told them," Van answered, "what I'm telling you, Bluebold! Before I cough up about any dough I may have parked somewhere, I want time to figure out where I come out on the deal."

"I see," Bluebold said stonily. "All right, sucker! Figure it out your way, but don't figure too damned long. Midnight tonight!" He strode away from the cell door, stomped heavy-footed into the elevator and went down.

Van began pacing the narrow cell floor.

He couldn't figure Bluebold out. The man was harder, tougher than Arnold. And he had a reputation as a ruthless disciplinarian-an essential requirement for a man handling any secret society like the organization that called itself the Invisible Empire.

The Phantom's mind kept reverting to that underground surgical room where he'd found the Alleghany Penitentiary thermometer. It was obvious that, if there was a connecting passage from the prison down to that operating room-and Van believed such a tunnel existed. Warden Bluebold would have the greatest opportunity to use it.

With a degree of medical and scientific knowledge that he might easily be hiding beneath his harsh outward bearing, Black-Jack Bluebold could be the Imperator.

Van was still thinking about the warden when one of the guards brought him his supper. And Van's third visitor didn't show up until almost ten o'clock that night.

It was Dr. Jessup.

"I'm going to ask you a favor," the M.D. said without preliminaries when he came up to Van's cell door. "You don't have to submit to my request."

From the way he said it, though, there was little doubt that Killer Kline would conform, or else!

"Going to try to make a specimen out of me?" Van demanded.

"I'm conducting some very detailed experiments and analysis of the effect of electricity on the human body and brain," Jessup explained gravely. "I want to examine you more thoroughly than I've done-before the electrocution. I'll make the other part of the tests and experiments, of course, when I perform the autopsy on you."

"Glad you're so cheerful about it," Van said sardonically.

The cold, distant eyes of Dr. Maurice Jessup surveyed him with sharp eagerness. "Very good, Kline. We'll go down to my laboratory."

He summoned the two guards, had the cell door opened, and the four of them got into the elevator.

"Of course," Jessup said as they rode down, "I do this with the consent of the prison authorities."

The car stopped at the basement, and the Phantom was ushered across a barren concrete floor into a three room laboratory that was a strange combination of operating equipment and electrical instruments. The two guards had come into the main laboratory and stationed themselves near the door.

"The X-ray pictures come first," Dr. Jessup said, and led Van into a smaller room on the right. The place was furnished only with a large X-ray machine, a plate cabinet, and the one chair used for seating the subject. "Be seated, please," Jessup directed.

The Phantom parked himself in the chair, watching the doctor move swiftly about the small, compact space. Jessup's cold eyes seemed to be watching everything at once, and there was no lost motion in his movements.

Van's back was toward a narrow door opening into the basement proper, and a screen blocked his view of the larger main laboratory.

"Damn!" Jessup exclaimed suddenly. "I'll have to get fresh X-ray plates. Just sit where you are, Kline."

The doctor seemed to have forgotten that he was preparing to examine a criminal convicted of murder and capable of murdering again. He hurried round the screen, out into the main lab. Van could hear his footsteps cross the floor to the third of the three rooms. A door opened and shut.

For almost a minute there was silence.

Then, without warning, a screaming voice shrilled somewhere out in the dimly lighted basement.

The Phantom leaped from the chair, reached the narrow door that opened directly into the basement. As his hand shook the knob, the voice sounded again, screaming words. "You tricked me! I'm making explosives for your brainless empire —I'll expose you —I'll-aaahhh ! —"

The frenzied words broke off in a piercing wail of terror that chopped off into abrupt, ominous silence, punctuated by the thud of a falling body.

Van's hand jerked away from the locked door. He swung round the screen, saw one of the guards still standing by the main door, poised, a gun in his hand. The other prison guard was running out into the basement. Dr. Jessup was nowhere in sight.

The Phantom ran into the large laboratory as the second guard snapped out of his paralyzed posture. The two of them rushed out toward the uniformed screw bending over a huddled figure on the basement floor.

"Who is it?" the running guard shouted.

"Don't know," the other called. "Never saw him in my life."

But Van had seen that odd, grotesque form before.

It was Gulliver Vonderkag!

The Phantom stared down with narrowed, unbelieving eyes at that hunchback German scientist. The crippled man was already dead, but as Van and the two excited guards bent over him, no wounds or marks of violence were visible.

Remembering the gas fumes that had knocked him out in Dr. Junes' laboratory, the Phantom stooped suddenly between the guards before they could stop him, smelled Kag's lips, depressing the no longer breathing lungs. But there was no odor of gas, no sign of the purplish discoloration of asphyxiation.

The two guards yanked him back away from the body, and the two of them lifted the dead hunchback, carried him away into Jessup's laboratory.

As they laid the body on one of the operating tables, the prison physician emerged from the smaller room on the left, opposite the X-ray office. Dr. Jessup was carrying a packet of X-ray plates. He stopped, stared at the tableau, hurried over to join them.

Van eyed the doctor covertly, noted that the man's seeming surprise was replaced almost at once by a sharp, professional interest.

"Who is this man?" he demanded. "What happened?"

"We don't know," one of the guards exclaimed. "We heard a screech and some screw hollerin' about explosives —"

"I heard that part of it myself," Jessup declared, shutting off the guard's answer. "Thought it was a patient in a fit, up on the floor above." He glanced sharply at Van. "Where were you?"

"Right where you parked me, Doc!" the Phantom snapped. "What killed him?"

Jessup set down the plate case, started examining the body, while the others watched him. The doctor's fingers moved expertly over the dead cripple, removing the clothing, prodding, probing.

When he'd finished, he glanced up, frowning.

"Not a mark on him," he said. "Not a scratch!"

"A guy don't scream like that just from heart failure," Van remarked and stared keenly at the dead face.

Those wide eyes that had rolled so terribly in Kag's head were fixed now, concentrated straight ahead in glazed contemplation of eternity. Staring down at their vacuous expression, the Phantom's keen gaze caught a tiny fleck of blood that looked like a thread thin blood-vessel on the white eyeball. He bent over the still, agonized face, pushed the wrinkled flesh away from the eye socket.

"Mind, doc?" he asked, but didn't wait for permission.

On the outer corner of the left eye was a minute blood clot covering a needle hole that had penetrated the brain.

Van pointed it out to Dr. Jessup, noticing the worried, lines that appeared on the surgeon's features.

"Maybe the guards can find the needle that made that puncture," the Phantom suggested boldly. "Anyhow, Doctor, it took a medical man to know how to kill a guy that way."

Dr. Jessup looked at Van sharply, startled, but was too slow to stop him as the Phantom stepped back and crossed to the small room from which the doctor had emerged a minute after the murder.

Van reached the open door, stared swiftly through. A man moving fast could have got out of that room through a door, met and killed Kag, and got back into the room again before even the paralyzed guard could have seen him.

He scowled, stared again through that open doorway. A single glance covered the whole of the small room. There was not a door or a window in it, and the walls, like the walls of the other rooms, were of solid concrete.

Dr. Jessup couldn't have got out of there unless there was a trick door. Van had no chance to search for one. He was still Killer Kline.

Chapter Fifteen
The Voice

As the Phantom swung back into the main laboratory, heavy, quick footsteps sounded out on the basement floor, and a moment later Warden Black-Jack Bluebold stood staring at them all through the doorway.

"What the hell's going on down here?" he demanded angrily.

Then his eyes saw the naked hunchback on the operating table, the clothes strewn on the floor. His gaze hardened and his face became rocky as he advanced into the room. But by neither expression nor gesture could Van detect recognition in the beady-eyed prison chief's manner as he stared down at Vonderkag's white face.

Dr. Jessup told him grudgingly what had happened, and why Killer Kline was present. Still, the stolid features of the warden betrayed no emotion other than anger and resentment. Bluebold was either a consummate actor, or else his thick-skinned reactions were limited to ruthless malice.

"Where's Rowan, that damned deputy of mine, the lazy devil!" Bluebold growled. "I want this body got the hell out of here in a hurry! What am I running here, a prison or a madhouse?"

"How about finding out who killed that hunchback?" Van demanded.

"Yeah?" Bluebold's beady gaze glittered dangerously. "Since when did Killer Kline start worrying about catching murderers? You shut up, or I'll hang this bump-off onto you!" He went to one wall, grabbed the phone receiver off its hook, barked into the instrument:

"Get me my office, Muldoon-Hello, Rowan? —Send a guard detail down to the hospital basement. Man killed here —I don't know-Oh, he is, eh? Be right up."

He turned back to Jessup. "Arnold just came into my office. Wants us to bring Killer Kline up there right away."

"We'd better go along then," Dr. Jessup said. "I'll finish with Kline afterwards."

"If we don't fry your specimen first," Bluebold said sourly.

Van went with them through a heavy door in the hospital basement wall, down a flight of steps into an underground concrete connecting passage, electric lighted, that brought them out into the corridor behind the warden's office.

Rowan and Harry Arnold were alone in Bluebold's private room when the three of them entered.

"Lock Kline in the Board Room with a couple of guards," Arnold said curtly. "I've got a surprise for you." He smiled blandly at the prisoner. "We'll let you in on our surprise in about ten minutes, Killer."

Jessup was repeating the circumstances of the killing, back in the hospital, to the Pardons Board chairman when Rowan took Van into the Board Room through the door that opened from the warden's office. Rowan put two guards in with the Phantom, went back and joined the other three men.

Van borrowed a smoke off one of his guards, began wandering about the long, high-ceilinged room. Bookcases containing the bound laws and penal records of the state lined one wall. Opposite were full length pictures in oil of the state governors over a period of more than a hundred years.

A long oak table with stiff chairs pressed against it occupied the center of the room. Two tall heavily barred windows at one end of the room gave the only outside light-showed now dark night sky above a row of gloomy pines.

The impression the room gave was frigid, ominously bleak for those condemned men who faced the Pardons Board here to argue for their lives. But for the Phantom, as he moved around the gloomy room, the place seemed to exude a sinister, premonitory warning.

The murderer of Kag, under the hospital, had disappeared as though the walls had swallowed him. Yet that killer had left a clue, the deft mark of a medical man. And Kag's last shrieking words had irrevocably tied that unseen murder to the Imperator in a binding union of identity that could never be broken.

But of the Imperator, the killer of Kag, there was still not the slightest trace. Van had been so positive, for a moment, that Dr. Maurice Jessup was the man, that the weird, grim mystery of the Invisible Empire had seemed to solve itself in a single flash of comprehension. And then there had been no visible second door out of that one basement room. The obvious and narrow deduction that Jessup had killed Kag had become a problematical, unproved chance again!

What, now, was going on in the warden's office, Van had no idea. One of the guards was stationed near the door, barring him off from any attempt to listen at the panel.

Had he been alone, the Phantom would have searched even this austere room for a possible secret opening into that hidden passageway which Van was positive existed, connecting the prison with the subterranean operating room and the labyrinthian mine shafts below. He had to content himself, under the hard, suspicious eyes of the two guards, with spotting possible likely places where such an exit might be concealed in the long room.

The door to the warden's office swung open abruptly, and Deputy Rowan appeared, his eyes burning grimly at Killer Kline.

"Come on in," he rasped, and snapped at the two guards:

"You screws beat it."

Van watched him let the guards out into a corridor exit. Rowan locked the door again, nodded at him. "Okay. Let's go!"

The Phantom entered the warden's room, and the Board Room door locked behind him. He faced Black-Jack Bluebold who glowered at him from across the heavy desk. Jessup and Arnold were standing to one side, and Rowan joined them.

"Well, Killer Kline," Bluebold grated, "this is the end for you!"

"Going to fry me tonight?" the Phantom asked harshly.

The four men nodded.

Van's eyes slid over the room-furniture, walls, ceiling, doors, barred windows. There wasn't a chance to escape! And there was neither pity nor patience in the four pair of grim, ruthless eyes glaring at him. In the tight, watchful silence of the office, the only human element of contact seemed to come from the faint, metallic hum of the radio in the corner where it had been turned down but not quite off.

"We've decided," Bluebold stated in a deadly voice, "that the sentence imposed upon you by the trial judge in Pittsburgh will be carried out one minute after midnight tonight! Thirty-five minutes from now." He glanced at his watch. "Anything you've got to say, Kline?"

Van stepped closer to the desk. "Lemme write a note," he said. "You can read it."

"Stalling?" Bluebold asked sharply.

"It's about that hundred grand I'm leaving behind," Van said.

"We're not interested in that —" Bluebold started, but the politician broke in on him with:

"Write the note, Kline! It's his privilege, warden. That hundred thousand dollars belongs to somebody."

The Phantom glanced about him as he picked up a sheet of stiff writing paper. Dr. Jessup was picking up the phone, starting to give orders about his medical kit being taken up to the execution chamber. Rowan was on another phone, giving directions to the guards who would be on duty during the licensed killing.

Van's gaze flicked and his lips twitched.

"Getting nervous, eh?" Bluebold sneered.

"Not much." The Phantom put fear into his voice, and suddenly slid the sharp edge of the paper across his thumb. "Hell! I guess I must be getting jittery —"

Blood spurted from the deep cut, smeared the edge of the warden's desk, made crimson blotches on his papers. Bluebold swore, jerked open a drawer, slapped a first-aid kit on the desk top, pulled out a roll of bandage.

Van held out his hand, thumb up, watching Bluebold keenly. As the warden began wrapping the bandage around the cut, the Phantom jerked his hand awkwardly, wincing.

Bluebold cursed and the bandage slipped off onto the desk.

"Here!" Arnold snapped. "Let me, warden. You're as nervous as he is." He caught the bandage in his fingers, wrapped it securely, twisting it around Van's wrist. "All right, Kline. You won't need to wear it after your heart stops beating."

"Thanks," the Phantom said. His voice had a sudden steely ring. "Before I put on this party, suppose you let me in on the surprise you've got."

"Sure, sure, Kline." Bluebold glared at him. "Part of that little surprise is something maybe you can help explain, Killer. You've got some queer friends."

"Bring him in," Arnold advised. "Let's get it over with."

Bluebold punched a button on his desk. There was a brief pause. Then a key grated in the lock of the corridor door. It swung open with a bang.

Four burly prison guards crowded into the office, holding a fifth man-Jerry Lannigan!

The Phantom's narrowed eyes smoldered and he fought for control of his tensed, twitching muscles as he recognized the big, powerful, red-headed Irishman.

Lannigan's face was raw from a beating, but his blue eyes blazed defiance. He growled a curse at the screws holding him, and his gaze settled on Killer Kline.

"Know this guy?" Bluebold roared at Van.

For a fraction of a second, the Phantom hesitated, trying to signal Jerry to silence. But Lannigan's jaw was already clamped shut.

"Hello, Champ!" Van called to the burly fighter. "Thanks, pal, for the try!" He turned swiftly to Bluebold and the others. "Sure I know this bird. Champ O'Hara, from Frisco. He's an airplane pilot, and he was going to make a pass at chiseling me out of this stir. What tripped you, O'Hara?"

"Hiya, Killer," Jerry growled disgustedly. If he'd forgotten that one or more of these men might have seen him twice before, he'd now caught Van's cue, was putting on a swell act. "I cracked up my ship, and was trying to swipe a new one."

A wry grin split his bloody face as he went on:

"Did I pick out a good one, or didn't I? Jeez, it turned out to be a sort of kind of earthquake an' volcano! The damned thing blew up on me, Killer! Blew all to hell —"

Van's slatey eyes flicked. Lannigan had found that mystery ship, and demolished it!

"Tough going, Champ," he offered. "What was the trouble?"

"She was loaded with bombs, or something worse," Lannigan declared. "I found some airplane tracks in a deserted field, and there was this brand new crate hid in an underground hangar. It looked like what I wanted, so I went after it. Some hoods tried to shoo me off with gun slugs, but I had a rod and tossed some back at 'em. The ship didn't get hit, but I guess some of the bombs they were loading did. When I come to, Killer, the birdies was singing and I was asking for Killer Kline."

"Looks like you found me," Van said, and noticed that a deathly silence had fallen over the tensed office.

Black-Jack Bluebold was watching them both, catlike. Every eye in the room was on them.

Van saw the guns appearing in the hands of the four guards. Rowan and Jessup were edging toward him. Bluebold was getting to his feet behind the desk, fingering a long, sharp paper knife with a steely, ragged-edged blade.

Ex-Congressman Arnold's eyes were bleak as he moved away from the Phantom and Lannigan, toward the wall, his voice calling across the stilled room:

"Warden, this is your affair! I'd suggest you lock O'Hara up until you're officially finished with Kline." He jerked his head significantly at Lannigan. "Dr. Jessup, it looks like you've got a nice big new human specimen."

"Yeah!" Bluebold grated. "I'm running this pen! I'm frying Kline, and his tough gorilla pal can be a witness. Then I'll tend to him! Let's take 'em up, men!"

The broken silence of the office became a quick, restless stir. Across the room Van saw Jerry's blue eyes begin to burn and his neck muscles bulge. Bluebold was advancing, the knife held low, poised.

"It won't be your thumb that's cut this time, Killer!" the warden rasped. "I'm going to make your innards trail from here to the electric chair!"

The Phantom's eyes flicked at Lannigan again, and his face slid sideways, his jaw hunched close to his shoulder, his lips parted in a voiceless snarl.

And suddenly, from the corner of the office where the radio still hummed in dull, mechanical monotony, a metallic, chilling flow of words poured into the room:

> "Attention, members of the Invisible Empire! Alarm! Calling the Imperator! Gas has broken into the officers' cavern! Warning! Calling the Imperator! Danger of explosion!"

The lights in the warden's office blinked off abruptly. The voice stopped. Instantly, the room became a pandemonium of shouts, curses, bodies hurtling into each other, fists thudding, screams.

A steel door slammed across the room, crackling like a pistol shot above the bedlam.

The Phantom hurled his lean body through the crowd, his hands pawing aside the blindly fighting, panicked men in his path as he leaped toward the sound of that door. His voice roared: "Champ! Champ!"

Then his fingers clawed open the exit that had crashed shut, and he darted through, found himself in the darkness of the long, high-ceilinged Board Room.

Across in the blackness his narrowed eyes caught the vague movement of one of the full-length oil pictures as it swung shut against the wall.

As, he sprang toward it, he heard Jerry Lannigan's harsh breathing behind him.

Chapter Sixteen
Hell's Goal

Van reached the picture he'd seen move in the darkness. He ripped at its frame, swung it away from the wall. He pulled himself up into the black opening behind the canvas, reached out and touched Lannigan's groping arms.

"In here, quick!" he whispered.

Back of the big Irishman, across the length of the Board Room, the guards and prison officers inside the warden's private quarters were ham-mering at the steel door that Lannigan had slammed after him. The Phantom pulled Jerry up into the narrow hole behind the oil painting, swung the frame shut against the wall again.

"Here's a ladder," he muttered as his dangling legs knocked against iron rungs. "Got a light?"

"That's all I got!" Jerry growled. Van was already climbing down into the black well hidden in the Board Room wall. Above him, Lannigan's electric torch sent down a wavering, eerie glow as Champ followed him.

The hole seemed bottomless, but the Phantom didn't take time to listen for the sounds of that fleeing figure who had preceded them. Their own rapid descent made hollow, echoing thunder in the narrow well as their feet struck each iron rung.

When Van's feet hit solid dirt, finally, all noise from above had ceased.

Lannigan dropped down beside him, shifting the dim, fatigued gleam of the flash.

"Gawd!" he exclaimed. "Those guys up there don't know about this hole!"

"Lucky for us," Van said tersely. "A dozen shots pouring down would have finished us. Come on, Champ. Through here!"

A low opening in one side of the well let them crawl on hands and knees through a down-grade, twisting tunnel. Van reached back, took the electric torch from Jerry, crawled on ahead rapidly. Behind him, the beefy Irishman was having a tougher time getting his bulk around the sharp curves.

Then the tunnel widened, dropped off abruptly into a chasm.

Van's flashlight beam petered out into darkness before the glow touched bottom. He flung the beam across the empty space, centered it on a plank on the other side.

"Smart lad," he muttered to Jerry "He pulled his bridge across after him."

"Well, we can't sit here and catch him," the Champ growled.

Van measured the gap with a sharp eye. It couldn't be leaped without at least a short run. And nobody could run out of that hip-high tunnel through which they'd just squirmed their way.

"Might swing you over," Lannigan ventured.

The Phantom shook his head grimly and suddenly stretched out full length, his feet against one side of the passage, his hands against the other. By stretching out, he could make the long reach and brace himself a little.

"You may have to stay here, Champ," he warned. "If I miss!"

Then, stretched horizontally, Van began inching his body out over the chasm. Lumps of loose dirt slipped through his fingers, dribbled silently into the fissure, making no sound against a bottom too deep to send up even an echo.

Lannigan, watching him, began to sweat.

For a full half minute the Phantom was a straining human bridge from wall to wall above that bottomless pit. Then he dropped to the tunnel bottom on the other side. He took a deep breath, shoved the plank across for the Irishman.

Lannigan crawled over to him, pulled the plank back.

They went on, standing upright now in a higher passageway. And as they stumbled on, the Phantom began to recognize some of the landmarks he'd spotted during his escape from the mines.

He led Jerry on, down grade, twisting, turning.

"Where'd that devil go?" Jerry panted as Van hesitated a moment at a fork.

"He's headed for the water gate," the Phantom answered. "He thinks gas has broken out somewhere down below." Van spotted the turn he wanted, ran on again.

The gate to the elevator shaft Van was looking for almost broke as they crashed into it, but the car was at their level. They leaped in, started down.

"We'll split off from each other at the bottom," Van directed. "You take the left tunnel, follow it straight through to the third door, and turn right. You'll come out into the cavern where that water door is fastened into the cement retaining wall. I'll probably be there ahead of you."

"Suppose you're not," the Champ demanded.

"Then you'll run into this Imperator yourself, Jerry. I guess you'll know what to do with him. Pull a Frank Buck on him, Champ."

"I'll bring him back," Lannigan promised, "conscious, but in pieces, if you say so, Skipper. How do I know him when I see him."

The Phantom chuckled.

"You'll know him, all right. He'll be wearing a gas mask, and that damned robed outfit. But he won't have a white mask. If there's more than one, pick on the bird with the gas mask, Champ, and you can't go wrong."

"Okay," Lannigan agreed. "But where're you going?"

"I'm going to try to beat you there."

The elevator car hit bottom, stopped. Van grabbed Lannigan's hand in a firm grip. "Good luck, Irish. But if you hear water, run like hell! Get out any way you can!"

The pressure left Jerry's hamlike palm, and the electric torch was thrust into the Champ's fingers. Then the Phantom was gone, moving swiftly through a wide, dark passageway straight ahead of the elevator shaft.

He felt his way along, touching one side of the tunnel with his hands, feeling the ground ahead for his unseen footing. He wasn't positive, was relying upon his knowledge of mine tunneling, to locate the shortcut that reason told him should be here.

If he didn't find it, he'd have to run back and try to catch up with Jerry before the Irishman got to the cavern and the steel water barrier. But he'd sent the Champ on that route for another reason-to have a way cleared for a running escape. Lannigan, he knew, wouldn't leave anyone behind who'd have an ounce of fight left.

Then, two hundred yards from the elevator shaft, the Phantom found what he was hunting. It was a drop-off in a narrow shaft, leading at right angles from the main passage.

He could tell by the type of bracing his hands encountered that he'd guessed accurately. He was moving through an auxiliary shaft that served as an emergency exit into the mine further on.

Van slid down the sharp incline of the drop, bumped his way along uneven down-grade steps cut into the dirt, and emerged into a wider passage that opened suddenly into the cavern he wanted.

Even in the blackness, he could discern the feeling of movement in the air about him. Labored, harsh breathing guided him across a blank space where his hands touched only heavy, moist air.

As he advanced, crouching, a thin shaft of bright light slid along the further wall, caught and hung for a moment on a concrete foundation, then slid on again to circle the round steel water door.

The Phantom's pulse calmed now. He moved forward cautiously, silently. The light ahead blinked out. There was a prolonged silence. Then a dry creaking sound.

Van reached the concrete wall, flattened against it, edging closer to the steel door. He could hear the quick, hard gasps of breath again, each followed by another straining, louder creak of metal against unoiled metal.

And suddenly the torch flashed on without warning, skidded over the door, caught the Phantom full in the face.

Blinded by the unexpected ray, Van dove straight at the light. His shoulder hit a shifting human body, and his hands closed in on the familiar feel of a long robe.

Then the electric torch crashed down on his skull!

The Phantom twisted, half stunned and ducked a second blow as the light shattered into intense blackness. He slugged upward, hammering into a flat, hard stomach.

Then fingers gripped his throat, tightened.

With a wrenching lurch, Van threw himself sideward, tried to claw off those throttling fingers. He could feel his own senses reeling. The fingers, clawlike, closed down.

The Phantom relaxed abruptly, let his whole body go limp.

But the next moment, as the robed, writhing weight floundered down on top of him, his knees doubled under him, his heels kicked out, hit solid bone.

The crack of that blind kick was like the snap of a whip. He hung onto the cloth in his fingers, was jerked forward onto his chest, sprawled across the suddenly inert form beneath him. His fists smashed into an unprotected jaw with crunching force. There was no answering struggle.

But beneath him, now, was a trickle of water, and filling the cavern was a suppressed but growing rumble.

Van lunged to his feet, grabbing the limp figure. He half dragged, half carried it back toward the tunnel exit, shouting once more for Lannigan.

An answering bellow drowned out for a moment the increasing roar of the still dammed water.

"Skipper! Skipper!"

Then Jerry Lannigan's feeble torch gleamed in the darkness ahead, the weak rays caught Van's struggling figure.

A moment more, and the Champ was at Van's side.

"Carry this fellow!" the Phantom gasped. "Run! The bulkhead is breaking open!"

He grabbed the torch from Jerry, ran beside him. They reached the first incline at the cavern's exit as the water lapped at their heels. As they got into the tunnel, the dull growl back of them broke into a violent, angry roar.

"There it goes!" Van shouted. "The bulkhead gave way!"

They had a fair start, for the narrowness of the tunnel acted as a brake against the crowding water of the subterranean flood. And the up-grade helped beat the churning wall of dank water that, lunged at their heels.

But the flood was knee deep when they reached the elevator shaft, and waist deep before the creaking cage dragged them up out of the roaring, clutching current.

As the car climbed, Van jabbed the light downward through a crack in the flooring. The beam reflected only churning, rising water.

"That," he said, standing up again and putting the beam on the robed and hooded figure Lannigan was holding, "is the end of the Invisible Empire, Champ. They're finally, flooded out."

He lifted the head of the man slung limply over Lannigan's powerful shoulders, and jerked the gas mask off that pallid face.

"And this —" He shoved the light close to the no longer robust but now sagging features.

Jerry Lannigan said, "Yeah, I guessed who he was already. Warden Bluebold! It couldn't have been Jessup, the prison croaker, because I slugged him, chasin' you into the Board Room." The Champ grinned proudly at his own smartness, and turned his head to look.

A chuckle broke from the Phantom's bruised lips as Lannigan, his blue eyes widening, stared into the face of ex-Congressman Harry Arnold!

Chapter Seventeen
The Phantom Fades

Minutes later they were still in the mine, but the flood was swirling unseen, deep in the shafts below them. Lannigan was shifting Arnold's inert body on his shoulder when Van announced:

> "Here's the passageway I've been looking for, Champ. I came up here on another elevator, but there had to be some back way in, because there was a locked door I couldn't get out of."

He stood facing a steel door set in concrete-the rear entrance to the underground operating room-after they'd gone a few rods up a sharp incline. An up-elevator opened several yards further on.

The Phantom examined the lock on the door, took keys from Harry Arnold's pocket. One of the keys fitted, opened the door.

Van stepped swiftly across the threshold, got a light lit and stared about the Imperator's operating room. Only one thing in it had been changed since he'd escaped from there last:

The place of the dead, nude body of the F.B.I. operative, Marks, on the operating table was empty now, but a live man occupied the narrow hospital bed behind the screen.

As he crossed to that bed, the Phantom said over his shoulder, "Champ, get some tape and do a job on Arnold, but leave his mouth free." Then Van looked down at the new occupant of the room.

The man on the bed was stocky, dark-skinned, with dark, glittering eyes that darted over the Phantom's face in startled, hopeful recognition. His hands and feet were shackled to the bed, and his mouth was taped, but he had not been touched yet with a knife.

The Phantom worked the tape off the fellow's lips, stood back, waiting for the man to get his tongue moving again. A mumbled volley of oaths spewed from the prisoner's throat, and his words became rapidly intelligible.

"You're Killer Kline, ain't you!" he declared as soon as the profanity wore out. "The toughest crook of us all, eh? What'd you do, crack this stir?"

Van turned without speaking, set the screen aside so the fellow could see Lannigan and the Imperator in the robe and black hood. The man's eyes smoldered, then burst into darting flames of fresh hate:

"Him! The dirty, sneakin'—"

"Who're you?" Van barked.

"Me-you ain't forgot me, from the Pittsburgh jail! I'm Joe Sholtz. God! That guy you got there, he was going to skin me alive, he told me, so's he could use my hide on you, Killer! He was goin' to do a face-liftin' job on you, use you for somethin' he was planning. That's why I wasn't cooked in th' hot seat last night." Terror suddenly pitched Sholtz' voice. "You ain't gonna let him skin me now, are you, Killer?"

Van thought fast, sizing up the hard-looking con on the bed.

"I won't, if you'll talk," he snapped. "Maybe I can get you free of the hot seat, get 'em to commute your sentence to life."

"I'll tell every damned thing I know!" Sholtz declared. "I've been in this stir awhile. I seen some queer things."

"How'd you know it was Arnold who brought you here?" Van asked.

Sholtz' glittering eyes darted to the ex-Congressman's taped body. "The dirty rat! He was dressed up like the prison surgeon when he took me down here, handcuffed. He didn't think I'd ever get out. He took off the gauze he was wearin' over his face, after he'd chained me to this damned bed, so he could talk better."

Van turned to Lannigan. "Champ, that elevator out there'll take you up—"

"It'll take you up into the prison hospital basement," Sholtz cut in. "Lets you out through a fake dumbwaiter. But there's a halfway landing up the elevator shaft that opens into a tunnel leading to a rock quarry outside the prison walls. I was brought down from the hospital, but you can skip th' stir that other way."

"Get that?" The Phantom nodded to Jerry, who'd finished with Arnold's bindings. "Use that quarry exit, Champ. You'll find Havens with the National Guards the governor sent up to Mountainview. Tell them to take over the prison, and bring Havens, Bluebold, Jessup and the militia commandant back here with you. Lock up Deputy Rowan and his screws until we find out how much they're in on this."

Lannigan grinned, went out, and when Van had locked the door he swung back to Sholtz.

"Who told you about that quarry tunnel?" he demanded.

"The hood who was with Snakey Willow on that New York killing," Sholtz said grimly. "He came in here that way, an' Arnold jumped him for using that entrance. I seen and heard the whole thing."

The Phantom's eyes flashed. "What happened?"

"The guy come in here and met Arnold," Sholtz growled. "And give him a briefcase snatched from the fellow shot in New York-Grand Central Station, he said, was the spot. Arnold raised hell because the thing had been bungled, and stabbed the hood to death right here in front of me. Gawd, it was bloody!"

Harry Arnold had opened his eyes and was staring at Killer Kline with growing comprehension and fear. Van turned on him:

"Where's that briefcase now, Arnold?"

"To hell with you!" Arnold's voice was shrill, choppy with sudden rage. "Find it, if you're so damned clever!"

"Know where that case went to, Sholtz?" Van demanded.

"I seen him hide it under the instrument cabinet," the con answered, gloatingly. "There's a trick drawer below the bottom shelf."

The Phantom had the briefcase a moment later, was opening it on the operating table, examining its contents, staring keenly at Gimbel's reports on Dr. Hugo Junes' aluminum-calbite fusion experiments.

He studied the reports briefly, then turned to Arnold, and his voice was icy when he spoke.

"You intend to talk, Arnold? Or do you think you can hold out?"

"You're not Killer Kline," Arnold snarled abruptly. "You'd be out of here before now, if you were. I got nothing to say, to you or to anybody else. What the hell can you prove, in court?"

"You're in court right now," Van told him tersely, and turned to Sholtz. "Think you can make him talk, if I let you at him?"

"I'll peel him alive if he don't!" the murderer guaranteed, but he eyed Van now with intent sharpness.

Arnold was trying not to show his mounting terror. He glared at Van, stuck to his question:

"Sholtz couldn't make me talk. But-who are you?"

For a moment Van hesitated, advancing close to Arnold, And there was something so terrifying in the steely grey eyes boring into the Imperator's that Arnold winced, glanced away, trembling. Van's hand reached down, jerked the ex-Congressman's jaw around so that he couldn't avoid that impelling, piercing stare.

"I'm your judge!" Van said in words that seemed to chill the walls of the concrete room. "I can do with you anything I choose! Arnold, you are facing the Phantom!"

As the dread name filled the strange subterranean room, and the full realization of the power of the man he was up against struck Arnold's consciousness, he slumped back against the wall, seemed suddenly to collapse within himself as a balloon collapses when it is punctured.

Over on the bed, Sholtz began swearing, making low, animal noises, while his eyes, bitter and defeated, stared at the Phantom with a stunned expression of amazed bewilderment.

Harry Arnold's lips moved. His voice came out, dry, grating:

"I've heard-God! I'll talk!"

"I think," Van said flatly, "you're beating Bluebold to the punch. I never met a bull-whip like him yet who wasn't yellow. How'd you happen to pick on him as your right-hand man?"

Arnold's eyes glowered hopelessly. "I had to use him, because of the prison and the men I could take from it. I —"

Arnold, the Imperator, kept on talking, while the Phantom checked his weird, dominion-mad story with Dr. Junes' reports on the operating table, with Sholtz's growled comments, and with his own piecing together of the murderous crime pattern.

The ex-Congressman didn't shut up until, a full hour later, Van unlocked the door and let in Lannigan. With the big Irishman were Bluebold and Dr. Jessup, both handcuffed, Frank Havens, and Colonel Leusik, the tall, sharp-featured National Guard commander.

"Colonel Leusik's men have command of the penitentiary now," Havens said, introducing the colonel and eyeing Van's make-up curiously.

"Lannigan says you have caught the Imperator —" He looked at Arnold and at Sholtz.

The Phantom nodded. "Take the cuffs off Dr. Jessup, if you will, Colonel. I'll try to give you the incriminating facts quickly, since I presume you'll want to turn over the evidence to the governor along with the prisoners. You'll have little difficulty, I'm sure, getting the signatures now of Arnold and Bluebold."

The warden's face whitened and he shot a frantic look toward Arnold. "I'll sign no confession! I'm being railroaded!" He took a menacing step nearer the ex-Congressman. "You-you talked?"

"He beat you there, Bluebold," Van cut in and shoved the big man back against the wall. "You can recriminate after it's over."

Bluebold's jaw dropped as he glared at Van. "Arnold's a liar, whatever he told you! He's behind all this. And you, Killer Kline —"

"The Killer Kline you're looking at," Lannigan said with a growling laugh, "will have to do until the real Kline comes up from Pittsburgh, Bluebold. You signed your death warrant when you signed the commitment papers letting him into your stir!"

The Phantom stepped back to the table, picked up the reports spread there, while the others watched him with mingled emotions.

"As a matter of fact, Bluebold," Van said, "Harry Arnold didn't have to tell me a great deal, although Sholtz and I convinced him it would be a healthy idea. But what he did tell me was startling-the part I couldn't grasp at first:

"Arnold conceived this gigantic idea of the Invisible Empire, gentlemen, not for money. He wanted power. He wanted to be another Hitler, another Mussolini, in America!

"He couldn't do it by votes. He was washed up politically because of a conviction against him in California for an illegal operation on the face of an escaped San Quentin convict. He was known there, he admits, as Dr. Harold Arrnster. His fingerprints and the American Medical Society would have caught up with him if he'd tried to become more than a congressman anywhere in public life.

"But he thought he could get control of the country without votes-by terrorism, by destroying enough well chosen industries and governmental projects, to throw the nation into a helpless, undirected revolt.

"Then he planned to step into control, take over the armed forces with his own trained lieutenants, and set up a new government with himself as dictator."

The Phantom paused, shuffled the reports on the operating table.

"It was the aluminum-calbite fusion experiments of Dr. Hugo Junes at Niagara Falls that first gave me the trail that has ended here in this room, gentlemen! Colonel Leusik, if you'll follow my deductions you'll find the presentation of evidence against Arnold and his assistant, Bluebold, not so complicated.

"I realized, when the Rock Canyon Dam was blown up, that a new explosive had been discovered. For the Arizona dam, and some of the other industrial projects that had been wrecked, had been built to withstand T.N.T. Metallurgical chemistry is a rare enough field, so that any new or outstanding development in it can be traced. Dr. Junes was known to be experimenting with a new metal fusion.

"And then Gimble, carrying a report of Junes' work to Mr. Havens, was shot to death and the reports stolen. I have them here, for they were delivered to Arnold by the killer who escaped.

"Almost immediately, Dr. Junes' experiment blew up in his face. But I'd already realized that, since in all endothermic compounds, terrific heat is necessary to their formation, the sudden releasing of those fused elements, by accident or design, must produce the same amount of heat energy when the elements separate.

"That breakdown makes, rudimentarily, all endothermic explosions, and is the basic rule for the manufacture of trinitrotoluene and the amatol, picric acid and ammoniurn nitrate mixtures we use for blasting and bombs.

"The fusion of aluminum and calbite would be an unstable union, apt to disintegrate in an explosion, without the addition of some stabilizing element. Dr. Junes was using a chip from a meteoric fragment on exhibition at the Smithsonian Institute, so I was sure there'd be an experimental tie-up with that ore.

"There was. The meteorite was a stable fusion of the two metals Junes was trying to unite, But the fusion had happened on another planet. The only way he could find out what the third ingredient was that held them together was by melting them down. And he couldn't do it. The hottest furnaces man had ever made wouldn't do it.

"I had most of this knowledge before meeting Junes. Of course, it was obvious that somebody else was trying to find out what the metallurgist had discovered, how far he'd gone in his fusion, and how close he was to getting sufficient heat to finish his work.

"In fact, the Imperator had his own men working there in Junes' laboratory. And his own metallurgist, the half crazy Vonderkag, was doing things with aluminum and calbite down here underground-things that Junes couldn't do. For Kag had the heat, a natural compressed gas from a subterranean reservoir that would, and did, melt the meteorite and give him the third vital element.

"In the course of Kag's experiments, the metal that Junes was trying to make was perfected. Lannigan found it in discovering the airplane Arnold had got built. But more important, for the Imperator, was Kag's working out of an even higher powered explosive in the disintegration of the new metal.

"It was that latest explosive compound that Arnold relied upon to blast into being his plan for an Invisible Empire that would be no longer invisible but actual and operative. It was the near discovery of that explosive that stopped Junes from continuing his fusion work. He was very close to it then, and saw the danger to the world if such a chemical formula should be perfected."

Van paused again, put down the reports and notes he'd been scanning while he talked.

"I'm telling you this in detail, Colonel," he explained, "because this phase of the investigation won't come out in court. You'll have evidence enough without using it, and it will be better that the public doesn't know of Kag's too dangerous findings. Fortunately, Kag is dead. And the stolen meteorite, along with Dr. Junes' chip from it, have been lost forever in the flooded mine under us.

"And now for the record: It was an accident that Snakey Willow was shot by a New York City detective when Gimble was killed. That was a lead here to this prison —a lead, however, which wouldn't have broken the case. All it would have proved was that one or two convicts had escaped. For Dr. Jessup knew nothing of what was going on, and would have been of no help. Arnold and Bluebold, naturally, would have, and did, cover up nicely any attempt to pry too deeply into their affairs.

"But it wasn't an accident that Arnold and Bluebold were in Frank Havens' office the day Gimble was to have appeared. They were there to see that he didn't get a chance to talk, if Willow and the other gunman missed. And again, Dr. Jessup was brought along as a figure who would help clear them of any suspicion, should there be a slip in their calculations somewhere.

"The chronology of events, Colonel, you can get from Mr. Havens at your leisure. I'm sure he'll help you organize the prosecution against Arnold and Bluebold.

"It was the Imperator's desire to get somebody to replace the erratic and untrustworthy Dr. Vonderkag, that led me here. I submitted to a form of kidnaping, and met Kag. I knew about the stolen meteorite, and was expecting it when it showed up in the underground laboratory under the mines.

"That cinched the location of the Empire and its center as being there. The rest of the job, from my angle, was to force the Imperator into the open. But it wasn't until I tricked him into using me as a murder volunteer that I found this room, and the thermometer with the Alleghany Penitentiary stamp on it. Finding Marks, the Federal agent, a prisoner here, furnished the surgical information needed.

"Thereafter, it was a process of thinning down the suspects up in the prison to a doctor who had the other necessary qualifications to fit the character such a role as the Imperator demanded.

"Death, at the hands of Arnold-although I didn't know who the murderer was at that point-eliminated Vonderkag. It also very nearly eliminated Dr. Jessup, for Jessup would have had to move faster than I'd ever seen him move before, to get in and out of that hospital basement laboratory to kill Kag. Jessup wasn't eliminated then, as a suspect, but my attention turned more suspiciously to the others.

"That brought the choice down to Jessup, Bluebold, Arnold and Rowan, with the emphasis on Bluebold and Arnold. So I cut my thumb with a piece of stiff paper when Jessup and Rowan were occupied phoning. Bluebold was clumsy when he tried to bandage my cut, but Arnold did a very neat spica wrapping —a technique only a doctor or a nurse would be apt to use.

"So I knew that Arnold had once been a medical man. The last move was to force him into the open. I resorted to a bit of ventriloquism, using the radio as a medium and the threat of escaped gas in the mine as a motive for immediate action. The Imperator had to stop that gas-actually, he flooded it out with water, which was the only emergency measure he could take.

"I was ready when he got the lights out, and followed him, with Lannigan. I'd already spotted the water door he'd have to open, down in the mine, so I knew where to catch him. And because of the supposed gas, he'd be wearing a gas mask, which precluded his smelling that there wasn't any leak, and at the same time marked him as the only man in that section of the mine who would not be wearing an Empire face mask.

"There was no difficulty, then, in taking him and bringing him here."

The Phantom smiled thinly, glanced at Bluebold.

The warden was muttering oaths, his eyes glaring at Arnold.

"Bluebold will, I think," Van said drily, "clear up any little details I may have missed."

"By God," the warden exploded. "I heard you! Arnold's talked, you've talked. Damn you, it's my turn now!"

With a slight shrug, Van went to the door, opened it, and stepped out, closing the door upon the violent, cursing recriminations of Black-Jack Bluebold, the Imperator's befuddled lieutenant. Nobody in the room except Lannigan and Havens noticed Van's silent departure.

He used the elevator, got off at the halfway stage, and entered the tunnel, using his deft fingers on his made-up features as he followed the shaft. Killer Kline was disappearing.

When he emerged into the rock quarry, he stood for a moment in the freshness of night, breathing deeply, freeing himself of the atmosphere of the mine.

But it wasn't as Killer Kline that he stared skyward at the silent stars. Nor was it the Phantom who finally lowered his hands from a smudged, rather handsome and weary face. For the Phantom was fading...

Yet a memory that was growing in the strange annals of criminal investigation —a nervous, restless figure in a mask who would, when the vipers of crime bared their poisonous fangs again, stalk once more the dread streets of darkness.

But for the moment, amongst all the teeming millions of the land, there stood alone, here in the quarry, a tall, silent, nondescript figure who was without name, without any tie.

Then that moment was gone. And the lithe form moved swiftly through the shadows of rocks and trees, disappearing toward the road —a road that led back again to the old life and to the Park Avenue penthouse of Richard Curtis Van Loan.

Only a brief sigh that was like a faint, vagrant breeze through the boughs above, signaled the Phantom's transition.

Death Flight

Chapter I
Murder of a Hero

The glaring white floodlights mounted on top of the great hangar building lit up the airport like day. They illuminated brilliantly the long main runways of the landing field, the low rope barriers that had been stretched on posts around the field, and the solid sea of humanity surging against those ropes. Scores of policemen struggled to keep the excited crowd from bursting through the ropes.

From a myriad throats came a deafening buzz and hum of voices, and in them one name was repeated over and over.

"Lucky James!"

A policeman turned toward a cool-eyed, craggy-faced man of wiry build who was passing along the line inside the ropes.

"Captain McCord, we'll never hold this crowd back when Lucky James' plane gets in!" the policeman panted.

Detective-Captain Thomas McCord told the officer crisply:

"You'll have to hold them somehow. If this mob is on the field when James' plane lands, some of them will be hurt." McCord went rapidly down the field, his wiry form striding toward the floodlighted hangar building. A group of about twenty-five or thirty men were gathered in front of the hangar, including airport officials, pilots, and newspaper men who had been allowed inside the ropes.

One of the group saw McCord and gripped the detective-captain's arm. He was a blond, good-looking young man whom McCord recognized as Blair James, pilot of a passenger airliner and cousin of Lucky James, the flier they were all awaiting.

Blair James cried to McCord:

"Lucky's plane was sighted over Bayshore ten minutes ago! He'll be here any moment! I guess this proves Lucky is the best flier of them all. A non-stop solo flight from Cairo to New York-and a fifty-thousand-dollar cash prize!"

"I've done a little flying," McCord said dryly, "and I wouldn't try a flight like that for fifty million."

He added, "I've got to see Stangland a moment."

He pushed past the excited Blair James toward Robert Stangland, the superintendent of Gotham Airport.

"Don't you have any way of putting up more barriers?" McCord asked the superintendent. "That crowd is going to —"

McCord stopped speaking. He and the superintendent and the others became suddenly rigid, staring up into the northeastern sky, from out of which, now, was coming a distant, deep-toned droning.

The crowd was staring too, and a hush had fallen over it. A dead silence in which the only sound was that humming drone that grew louder each moment, waxing into a roar.

Down into the glare of the airport lights came a big silver monoplane that roared low across the field, and then banked around and came back, dipping toward the runway.

McCord heard over the thundering motor, the frantic yelling of the crowd, and felt his own pulse hammer with emotion. Tow-headed, reckless young Lucky James had spanned a hemisphere and was dropping out of the stars to fortune and fame and a crowd gone mad.

The great monoplane's wheels touched the runway in a perfect landing and it rolled down the field, coming to a stop a few hundred yards from the floodlighted hangar.

McCord found himself running with Stangland and Blair James and the others toward the silver ship. They reached the monoplane as its motor was cut off, and a reporter pounded on its side.

McCord saw the door of the little enclosed cockpit open. And there in the opening stooped a rangy youngster with a grinning, tired white face, his blue eyes blinking at the flare of the photographers' popping flashlights. He raised his oil-smeared leather-clothed arm in greeting.

"Well, fellows, it looks like I've made me fifty thousand bucks."

Thuck! That brief, sinister sound cut through the din of popping flashlights and yelling voices around the monoplane.

Then McCord and the others, abruptly frozen in rigid, horrified silence, stared at the flier in the open cockpit door. Lucky James' grin had taken on a sudden surprised quality. His hand went uncertainly to a little hole that had appeared in the left breast of his leather jacket. Then he crumpled stiffly forward.

McCord and the men around him stared incredulously at Lucky James' body lying sprawled half out of the cockpit. Then Blair James, his face white and frantic, darted to the stricken flier.

McCord was close after him and helped him lift the limp body to the ground. Lucky James' wide blue eyes stared up at them unwinkingly, unseeingly.

"Lucky!" cried Blair frenziedly. "For God's sake —"

"It's no use, Blair!" rasped McCord. "He's dead-murdered."

McCord's eyes gleamed like crumbs of ice in his craggy face, sweeping dangerously over the staring, horrified group.

"Someone in this group around the plane shot Lucky James with a silenced pistol!" the detective-captain exclaimed.

A reporter turned to push his way out of the group, a wild yell coming from the other newspapermen as they, too, suddenly realized that they had witnessed the scene of a century. But McCord, his pistol flashing into his hand, sprang before them and halted them.

"Not one of you leaves here!" he grated. "Someone in this group is the killer and he's not going to escape."

"But you've got to let us break this story!" cried a reporter.

"Get back there, everyone of you," McCord menaced them. "You're going to be searched right here and now for the gun."

Frenziedly protesting, the newspapermen fell back toward the monoplane. As they did so, Stangland, the airport superintendent, cried out and pointed to the ground near the ship.

"There's a pistol, McCord!" he exclaimed.

McCord leaped and picked it up by its muzzle tip. It was a stubby automatic whose butt, trigger and trigger-guard had been wrapped with soft cloth. It had a silencer on it.

"The killer wrapped this so it would show no fingerprints, and dropped it right after he shot Lucky," McCord said. "He must have shot from under his coat, standing right here among us."

There came to McCord's ears a vastly increased roar of voices from the great crowd around the field. A police lieutenant, coat torn and ruddy face pale, burst through the group toward the detective.

"McCord, the crowd's gone crazy!" he cried. "They know Lucky James was just murdered and they're wild with rage-they'll tear to pieces anyone they suspect of being the killer!"

McCord whirled, saw that the crowds were now struggling to get through the rope barriers to the monoplane. The policemen along the lines were trying desperately to restrain them.

The idol of this crowd, the tow-headed youngster it worshiped, had been murdered, and the crowd wanted blood.

McCord's voice crackled to the pale group around him. "We can't stay out here-we'll have to continue this investigation inside the hangar until that crazy mob gets calmed down considerably.

"Stangland, you and Blair James carry Lucky's body," he ordered, and then spoke to the disheveled police lieutenant: "Davidson, you post your men outside the hangar's doors once we're inside."

The stunned Blair James and the airport superintendent picked up the dead flier's body and started with it toward the hangar. The others followed without need of urging, glancing nervously toward the raging mob outside the ropes. McCord followed last, gun in hand, watching to see that none of them slipped away.

When they reached the hangar, McCord waited outside a moment. Lieutenant Davidson and his torn, bruised officers were running toward the building, the vast crowd surging after them.

Davidson panted as he ran up.

"McCord, if you find the killer don't let this mob know it. They'll tear the place down to get him."

"You've got to hold them back!" rasped McCord. "Use your guns to scare them, and meanwhile I'll phone for reserves. Someone of that group is the killer, all right," he continued swiftly, "and they're going to stay here until I find out who."

Davidson yelled to his officers, and they spread out around the hangar, posting themselves at the doors with drawn pistols.

The mob rolled up to the building and halted with a menacing growl at sight of the glinting weapons. McCord saw that the guns would hold them back, and he strode swiftly into the hangar.

The interior of the hangar was a vast, dark space more than two hundred feet square, its floor of smooth concrete and with a spidery network of steel beams and girders under its low roof. A few suspended lights fought the darkness and showed the dim shapes of several large airplanes parked along the side.

The group of men gathered beside the body of Lucky James were listening with pale faces to the menacing voices outside. McCord singled out Stangland and said to the airport superintendent:

"There's a telephone in your office, isn't there? Then phone Headquarters to rush reserves here at once."

Stangland hastened across the shadowy hangar to the door leading to his offices. In a few moments he was back.

"The reserves will be out here as soon as they can make it," he reported.

"They'll take care of the crowd when they come," McCord said. "Meanwhile, we're going to learn who killed Lucky."

He turned toward the silent body on the floor. Someone had thrown a tarpaulin motor cover over it, and now Blair James stood gazing dazedly down at the unmoving, shrouded form of his cousin.

Blair's face was working, and he choked through trembling lips:

"To think that Lucky flew all those hours, across half the world, and all the time he wasn't flying to fame and fortune as he thought, but to death-flying to death!"

McCord nodded somberly. He asked:

"You and your cousin were pretty close, weren't you?"

Blair James nodded, his face still quivering. "He was more like an older brother than a cousin, I guess, because I was his closest relative. He taught me flying, got me my job, and was always lecturing me about wasting my money and gambling. We lived together, you know."

"Then maybe," McCord asked him keenly, "you can tell me if you ever heard anyone threaten his life, or heard him mention any such threats?"

Blair shook his head.

"Lucky was everybody's friend and nobody would —"

He stopped suddenly, his face changing as though expressive of an abrupt inward revelation.

McCord, watching him intently, saw the change and instantly fastened on it.

"You did hear of threats of some kind against him, then?"

"I just remembered something," Blair James said slowly. "You know, Lucky's flight was backed financially by Gotham Airlines, the company both he and I were pilots for. They thought it would be good advertising for them if one of their pilots won the prize, and to the pilot it would mean fifty thousand dollars.

"Several other of the pilots tried to get the company to choose them to back for the flight. Tuss McLiney and Wallace Jandron and Leigh Bushell were the others who applied, and they were pretty sore when the company turned them down and chose Lucky. It was rumored around the airports that some of the three had declared that Lucky James would never live to spend that fifty thousand dollars, even if he succeeded in making the flight."

"I heard talk like that around the field too!" exclaimed a mechanic beside Blair James. McCord asked tautly of Blair, "Were any of those three pilots in this group that was around the plane when Lucky landed?"

"Yes! They're all three of them here!" Blair exclaimed.

Out of the group there stepped quickly a stout, strong young fellow with chubby face and slightly protruding blue eyes.

"I'm Wally Jandron, one of the three you're talking about," he told McCord. "But I want to deny right here that I ever made any threats against Lucky James' life."

A sharp-faced, nervous young man behind him spoke up rather hastily.

"Neither did I ever threaten him —I'm Leigh Bushell," he said. "I was rather angry, but I wouldn't threaten a man's life." He added: "But I want to suggest that we slip out of here by a back window or something and continue this investigation elsewhere. That mob might do anything if it breaks in here!"

"That's right!" seconded a reporter. "If the crowd fastened on one of us as the murderer, it'd kill him right here."

"No one is going to leave here!" rasped McCord. "The murderer of Lucky James is going to be found before any of you get out. What about the third pilot, McLiney?" he demanded.

A tall, browned, hard-bitten man with a short mustache, thin hair, and a hard mouth and eyes, stepped forward.

"I'm Tuss McLiney," he said truculently, "and I hate lying and liars. I did make threats against Lucky James and so did Jandron and Bushell, though they deny it now. We were all three burned up because the company turned us all down to back Lucky, and I admit I talked wild and made angry threats. But it was just talk. No matter how resentful I was, I wouldn't kill Lucky or any other man."

"Why did you come here tonight to be on hand when he landed?" McCord demanded.

"Simply because I wanted to see if he made it," McLiney answered defiantly. "Naturally I was interested in the flight. I admit, mean as it sounds, that I hoped he'd never make it."

"And you admit you had threatened his life?" rapped McCord.

"I've told you that those threats were just angry talk," retorted McLiney.

McCord spoke to Blair James.

"Blair, you were nearer the plane than I was when the shot was fired. Were any of these three pilots near Lucky?"

"Yes," Blair said slowly. "Bushell and McLiney were at my right and Wally Jandron was just in front of me."

McLiney, his hard face unmoved, said to the detective-captain.

"But that doesn't prove that one of us killed Lucky. Anybody in the whole group around the plane could have done it."

"Yes, but who else in the group had a motive to do it?" McCord demanded. "Who else had made threats against Lucky's life? You three hated Lucky bitterly for edging you out and getting the chance to make the flight. And in this group, only you and Jandron and Bushell —"

McCord suddenly stopped, his craggy face tightening.

"Where is Bushell?" he demanded suddenly.

They stared around their own group, then around the dim, dark hangar; but the nervous young pilot with the sharp face was nowhere in sight.

"Bushell wanted me to let him and the others slip out a back window!" the detective-captain cried. "If he's done that —"

McCord sprang toward the door of the hangar, and tore it open and leaped out into the glare of the floodlights.

He collided squarely with Davidson, the police lieutenant, who had been about to enter the hangar.

The lieutenant's face was pale and his words poured forth in an excited flood.

"McCord, the crowd's got hold of somebody who tried to slip out the back of the hangar! They're yelling that it's the killer of Lucky James trying to escape, and they're going to lynch him!"

Chapter II
Mad Vengeance

The scene that met McCord's eyes on the floodlighted field outside the hangar was an appalling one. The immense crowd was pouring away from the building, giving voice like a great, baying beast.

In the lights flashed a sea of contorted, vengeance-lusting faces. Some one was being carried along on the shoulders of the crazed mob, struggling vainly to free himself, his face terror-stricken.

"String him up! He murdered Lucky James and then tried to get away!" roared the crowd.

"Hang him on this pole over here!" voices were yelling.

The mob was bearing the struggling victim toward the tall steel tower of a beacon light, yanking down ropes from the barriers around the field to use for the hanging.

"That's Leigh Bushell they've got!" McCord yelled to Davidson. "They must have got him as he tried to escape from the hangar. We've got to take him away from them-it may be a wholly innocent man they're lynching!"

He raised his voice and the police outside the hangar came running to him. McCord swiftly ordered two of them to remain and see that no one inside the hangar left.

Then with the other officers massed compactly behind him, McCord plunged into and through the mob that was bearing the terrified Leigh Bushell to his doom.

The officers' clubs bounced off heads right and left as they smashed through. The little phalanx of police drove through the formless mob like a spearhead, and in a few moments reached the beacon pole where a rope was being tied around the neck of the struggling Bushell.

McCord and Davidson knocked back the would-be lynchers with quick blows, and jerked the stunned pilot in among the officers.

"Back out with him now, Davidson!" yelled the detective-captain "Quick!"

"They-they think I killed Lucky!" the livid pilot was gasping.

McCord did not heed him, he and his fellow-officers fighting now to get Bushell out through the mob.

The crowd was yelling in redoubled fury as it comprehended that its victim was being snatched from its grasp. It surged around the little group of officers, struggling to recapture Bushell.

The advance of the police phalanx was slowed, then halted. McCord jerked his pistol from his pocket and fired a stream of shots over the heads of the crowd. The members of the mob nearest him retreated in sudden alarm, and the police group crashed ahead toward the hangar.

As they neared the building there was a screaming of sirens, and police cars and motorcycles came speeding onto the field. The crowd, that had started in pursuit of McCord and his group, fell back before this unexpected onset.

"Thank God the reserves got here!" panted Davidson. "They're not any too soon."

The captain in charge of the newly-arrived forces approached. "What's been going on here, McCord?" he wanted to know. "We heard that Lucky James was murdered when he landed."

McCord nodded grimly.

"He was, and the crowd thought this man was the murderer. Can you clear them off the field?"

"We'll disperse them," the other promised briefly. "And the Homicide Squad will be out before long."

The fleet of police cars and motorcycles soon was scattering the thousands of people still on the field, dashing among them in repeated charges.

The crowd, its mob anger cooling rapidly now, dispersed in all directions.

McCord turned and found that Leigh Bushell had slumped to the ground, half conscious, his white face bruised by blows. He and Davidson picked up the limp pilot and carried him back across the floodlighted field to the door of the hangar.

They set the pilot down inside and Davidson went back out to post his scattered guard around the building. Blair James and Stangland and the others came running across the dim interior of the hangar toward McCord.

"God, I thought you were all done for out there!" cried Blair James. "Did they kill Bushell?"

"He'll come around all right, I think," McCord said.

Stangland was clawing at the detective-captain's sleeve.

"McCord, while you were out there I remembered something that I think is a straight clue. It's a letter that —"

"Wait just a minute," McCord told the airport superintendent. "Bushell is coming around now."

Leigh Bushell had opened his eyes. As the detective-captain helped him to his feet, an expression of terror crossed his face.

"They nearly hanged me!" he cried. "Because they caught me escaping from here, they thought I was the murderer of Lucky."

"Well, aren't you the murderer?" McCord demanded grimly. "If you aren't, why did you try to get away?"

Bushell's face quivered with fear.

"I'm not the one who killed Lucky!" he cried. "I only tried to escape because I was afraid that the mob would break in here and maybe lynch us all. I told you I was afraid of that."

"It looks bad for you, Bushell," McCord said. "It may be that that mob had the right man." He swung toward Stangland. "Maybe you can clinch it, Stangland. You said you had a clue."

The airport superintendent nodded, his keen face alive with excitement. "Yes, and it makes me sure Bushell isn't the killer," he said. "It's a letter Lucky wrote me several weeks ago, in which he told me confidentially that he'd had trouble —"

Click!

The dim lights of the interior of the hangar suddenly went out, interrupting his words. They were plunged instantly into a Stygian obscurity relieved only by the faint glimmer from the small, high windows at the back of the hangar.

McCord's voice rasped through the thick darkness.

"Don't any one of you move! I'll shoot anybody I hear trying to escape! Stangland, you know where the switch of these lights is?"

"Yes, right by the door," came the voice of the airport superintendent through the dark, followed by his steps. "I'll —"

His words were abruptly punctuated by a dull, thudding sound. Then came the muffled impact of a body striking the concrete floor.

"Stangland!" yelled McCord in the dark. "What's happened?"

There was no answer from the superintendent.

"Everybody stay put! I'll fire if I hear other footsteps!" McCord cried, and darted forward in the darkness in the direction of the door.

In a few strides he stumbled over something lying on the floor. He knelt and struck a match.

And there Robert Stangland lay, on his side upon the floor, his face lax and unmoving. His skull had been fractured by a terrific blow from the side. Beside him, lay a short wrench whose end was smeared with blood.

The match went out, and in the dark someone screamed.

Chapter III
The Trap of Flame

It was the voice of one of the reporters and he shrilled: "The murderer has killed Stangland, too, to silence him!"

"Stay where you are, everybody!" thundered McCord.

He struck another match. In its glow he found the light switch beside the door, but discovered that instead of being turned off, one of the exposed wires of the switch had been torn out by a quick pull. The lights could not be turned on again.

McCord stooped with the lighted match and examined the blood-smeared wrench. There were no fingerprints on its handle. The killer had evidently wrapped it with a handkerchief before using it.

McCord looked up. Before him stood the chubby Wally Jandron, and beyond him Tuss McLiney and Blair James and the others.

"You two were both near the switch!" he said to Jandron and McLiney. "And since Stangland, just before he was killed, said he was sure Bushell wasn't the killer, he must have been about to name one of you two as the murderer. Which one of you took that wrench out of your pocket and killed him to keep him from telling what he knew?"

"It wasn't me!" bleated Wally Jandron hastily. "But I thought I heard someone moving in the dark beside me."

"Well, you didn't hear me, because I didn't move from my tracks," declared McLiney.

The match went out at that moment, leaving them all again in darkness.

McCord jerked the door open and yelled out through it.

"Davidson!"

Davidson's voice came from close at hand.

"What's the matter? I saw the lights in there go out."

"Some one turned them off," McCord told him swiftly, "and then killed Stangland. You get some kind of lantern quick, and I'll prevent any of 'em escaping."

As Davidson raced off on the errand, McCord turned back into the dark interior of the hangar.

Holding his gun leveled in the rayless obscurity, the detective-captain was fumbling in his pocket for another match when a sound, hitherto unheard, arrested his attention.

It was a liquid, gurgling sound that appeared to come from the side of the dark hangar where the line of airplanes was parked.

"What's that sound?" McCord cried.

Blair James exclaimed in the dark:

"It sounds like one of the planes leaking gasoline —"

His words were abruptly interrupted. Someone in the dark struck a match and then quickly tossed it, as soon as it flamed, through the darkness toward the parked airplanes.

The flaming match described a little arc of fire in the darkness and then flipped down into a gleaming pool of liquid that lay on the concrete floor beneath one of the airplanes.

Instantly that pool burst upward a great puff of flame that enveloped the ship above it in a fraction of a second.

Blair James yelled:

"Some one slipped over in the dark and opened the dump valve of that plane's tank, then flipped a match into the pool!"

"Let us out of here!" cried a photographer in alarm. "This whole hangar will go now!"

With a soft, loud roar, the flames spread to the next airplane, a small biplane.

Burning gasoline spattered the walls-patches of living fire that were swiftly spreading over the sides of the roof of the hangar.

"I'm not going to stay here and burn to death!" cried a reporter, bolting for the door.

"Wait a minute!" yelled McCord.

But with wild shouts of terror, the whole group was stampeding for the door. They charged past McCord before he could prevent them, and rushed outside in mad haste to escape the blazing inferno which the hangar was rapidly becoming.

Blair James had stopped to clutch McCord's arm. He yelled over the soft roar of the flames. "You'll have to get out of here too, McCord! Nothing can save the hangar now!"

"We've got to get the bodies of Lucky and Stangland out!" McCord told him.

He reached down for the still form of Stangland, while Blair James seized the body of his cousin.

As they dragged the two bodies toward the door, the fires were roaring terrifyingly, all along one side of the hangar, enveloping the airplanes there in sheets of bursting flame.

They got outside with the bodies. The floodlights on the roof had gone out, and the darkness was relieved only by the flickering glow from within the burning hangar.

Davidson ran up to McCord. He said: "I was getting a flashlight from the car when I saw the fire. Where's the group you were holding inside?"

"They stampeded out and now they've all escaped," McCord told him. "You and Blair get the officers together and try to round them up. Find McLiney and Jandron!"

Davidson nodded in understanding and raced along the side of the burning hangars, shouting for the policemen who had been posted around it.

Automatic alarm bells were now ringing wildly inside the squat, great building, and the roaring flames seemed spreading swiftly to that side of the building, that held the administrative offices and machine shops.

Blair James remained behind Davidson a moment to cry a question to the detective-captain, who had whipped a handkerchief from his pocket and was rapidly tying it around his mouth and nose.

"McCord, what are you going to do?"

"I'm going back into that building, to Stangland's office," McCord told him.

"Stangland said that a letter Lucky wrote him gave a direct clue to the killer. That letter must be in his office file. The killer fired the hangar to destroy that letter, and I'm going to get it before —"

Blair held him back.

"McCord, for God's sake don't try it! That building is a death trap now!"

"You go and help Davidson find McLiney and Jandron," McCord told him, pushing him after the police lieutenant. "I'll find that letter and be out in a couple of minutes."

With the words, McCord ran along the front of the burning hangar and around the corner to a side of the building not yet burning so fiercely.

He tore open a door and plunged into a dark hall, from whose ceiling smoke was curling ominously. He ran down it, bumping around a turn and into another corridor at whose end bursting flames were rapidly advancing with a steady, crackling roar.

McCord looked tensely ahead. There were a few doors down at the burning end of the hallway and he darted toward them. The heat of the flames just ahead scorched his hands and masked face, and the heavy smoke made him cough and choke.

Through tear-dimmed eyes he saw that one of the doors had on its glass panel the legend:

AIRPORT SUPERINTENDENT

He darted into a little office whose one wall was burning, filling the room with quivering light. The shifting glow showed beside a desk a letter file of green steel. McCord tore open the file, rapidly rummaged the mass of papers in its drawers, examining them with smarting, blinking eyes by the light of the flames.

His desperate search failed to discover the letter he sought. Heedless of the creeping fires, he continued to ransack the contents of the file. Choking from the stifling smoke, he suddenly uttered a hoarse, exultant exclamation as he found a carelessly scrawled letter with the signature, "Lucky," and a date of a few weeks back.

A swift glance through it told McCord that it was the letter he sought.

Stuffing the letter into his pocket, he darted through the now burning door frame and raced down the corridor away from the advancing fires.

McCord rounded the turn in the hall and was running down the dark section of the corridors when out of the blackness at the side of the hall a foot suddenly projected to trip him.

McCord sprawled headlong, and pinwheels of light spun in his brain as he struck the floor. Out of the darkness leaped the shadowy form of a man who hammered McCord with swift, deadly blows as he sought to rise.

McCord, already half-dazed by his fall, felt his attacker's savage blows swiftly beating him into unconsciousness.

His numbed brain apprehended what had happened. The murderer of Lucky James and Stangland, seeing the detective-captain enter the burning building in search of the damning letter, had also entered the flaming hangar to see that McCord and the letter both perished in the flames.

McCord made a supreme effort of will and body to save himself from the horrible fate that awaited him if he allowed himself to be beaten into unconsciousness. He reached out desperately, plucked at his attacker's ankles, jerked them hard. The assailant fell to the floor.

In the moment of respite this allowed him, McCord dug frantically in his pockets for his gun. He got it out, thrust it forward and squeezed the trigger.

The gun only clicked. Too late McCord remembered that he had fired all its shots in his effort to save Bushell from the mob.

He dropped it, clawed in another pocket for the stubby, cloth-wrapped automatic with which Lucky James had been shot, and which the detective-captain had been carrying ever since.

He got it out, but before he could use it, the killer had grasped his wrist and was trying to wrench the gun out of his hand. They struggled there in the dark corridor, the noises of their combat drowned by the roar of flames now advancing around the turn of the hall.

McCord swung his left fist hard. He felt a crunching shock as it struck the other's face. The man uttered a cry of pain, recoiling a little, and McCord seized the opportunity to wrench his gun-hand free.

He fired instantly, the crimson streak of the shot blazing across the corridor, but the murderer had thrown himself aside, and now his feet were pounding down the corridor as he ran down it toward the outside.

McCord, still on his knees, fired down the hall again as he heard the outside door slam. Then he was on his feet, plunging down the corridor after the fleeing criminal.

But before he had made two strides, there was a cracking crash ahead and a mass of burning wood broke down through the corridor ceiling ahead of him, blocking his way with a barrier of flame!

McCord spun around. The way behind him, too, was still blocked by the fires that were swiftly creeping around the corner of the hall toward him.

He was caught in a horrible trap whose jaws of flame were rapidly closing upon him. He glanced swiftly about, his craggy face and cool eyes showing no sign of fear, but tensely weighing every possible chance of escape.

Chapter IV
Struggle in the Sky

A quivering glow of the advancing fires, now illuminating the corridor brightly, showed McCord a door a few feet from him. He ran to it and ripped it open.

A mass of flames filled the office or room inside, almost as terrifying as the fires at the ends of the hall.

But McCord's smoke-dimmed eyes glimpsed a window on the other side of the flame-filled room.

McCord knew that to dash across that burning room was to take tremendous risks. Yet to stay in the corridor meant meeting a horrible death without even an attempt at escape.

Rapidly he stripped off his coat and wound it around his head and face. With one swift glance he gauged accurately the position of the window, then pulled the coat across his eyes and threw himself blindly like a human projectile across the flaming room.

He felt tongues of fire scorch his arms and legs, and then with an impact and crash of shattering glass he burst through the window and fell to the ground outside.

McCord unwrapped the coat and got to his feet, heedless of his singed limbs and the slight lacerations which the glass had inflicted on his body. He ran around the corner of the flaming hangar.

In front of the burning structure, fire trucks were dashing up with bells clanging, and a crowd of firemen and policemen were already toiling frantically to connect hoses with fire mains.

Davidson ran out of the group toward the scorched, disheveled detective-captain.

He cried:

"McCord, what in God's name happened to you in there?"

McCord, disregarding the other's excited question, asked swiftly:

"Did you see anyone else come out of the building?"

The police lieutenant shook his head:

"I just got back here from rounding up your group of suspects. We found the reporters at the nearest telephones, but haven't found McLiney and Jandron yet."

"McLiney and Jandron still at large?"

Then McCord suddenly cried, "By heaven, I know where the killer has made for, now that he knows I have the letter. Lucky James' plane!"

Before the astounded Davidson could comprehend him, McCord had turned and was racing down the runway into the darkness, away from the flaming hangar.

From the dark ahead there came to McCord's ears the sudden clatter of an airplane motor starting.

He sprinted forward frantically, Davidson and others coming yelling after him a few hundred feet behind.

Now the detective-captain descried in the dark ahead of him the big silver shape of Lucky James' great monoplane being taxied around to point down the runway. The silver ship started to roll forward, its motor roaring. McCord was abreast of it and dove for its side.

He got the handle of the cockpit door in his grasp and clung to it, trying desperately to open the door as he was dragged along with quickly increasing speed.

The door suddenly opened under McCord's frantic efforts. He reached in and got a hold inside, and with a convulsive effort drew his body partly in through the little door.

His legs still hung out of the door, and cinders flying up from the runway stung them. Then the cinders ceased to sting, and McCord knew that the roaring monoplane was rising into the air.

The wind tore viciously at the detective-captain's legs as he sought to climb completely inside the cockpit. Then, with a surge of desperate strength, McCord pulled himself up into the cramped little space.

A black figure, sitting at the controls in the front of the dark, crowded little cockpit, whirled in his seat. McCord jammed his pistol into the other's back and yelled over the roar of the motor:

"Take this plane back down and land or I'll kill you right here!"

The man, his face invisible in the dark, laughed wildly.

"You don't dare kill me, because if you do the plane will crash and you'll die, too!" he cried.

"Don't fool yourself!" snarled McCord. "I worked with the police plane division two years and I've done a little flying. If you don't turn —"

Before he could finish the sentence the man, whose hands had been busy a moment swiftly adjusting something at the controls, turned and struck suddenly at McCord with a gleaming tool.

McCord was knocked back against one of the big tanks at the rear of the little cockpit, and the shock sent his gun flying from his hand. The killer scrambled over his seat to strike at him again.

The monoplane was roaring along at an unvarying altitude on a straight course. McCord, squirming desperately to avoid those deadly blows, knew that the killer had made use of the automatic pilot device which Lucky James had had installed for his lengthy flight.

He knew, too, that the murderer meant to knock him out and then heave his body out of the open cockpit door.

McCord grasped the other's hand and they squirmed and struggled, on top of the parachute pack and thermos bottles and other objects on the cockpit floor. The killer fought to use his gleaming weapon.

Suddenly the roar of the thundering motor faltered. Almost instantly it faltered again, then abruptly died.

The monoplane's interior was filled with the screaming of the wind outside, shrill and keen. The cockpit in which the two men struggled tilted crazily this way and that.

McCord knew instantly what had happened. The gasoline in Lucky James' ship had been almost completely exhausted by his long flight, and now had given out altogether. The ship was drifting downward with its motor dead!

The murderer abruptly tore loose from McCord and clawed beneath him for the parachute pack, trying to struggle hastily into the harness.

He scrambled with it toward the open door of the cockpit. But McCord had scooped up the metal tool the other had dropped, and struck quickly with it.

The thunk of the blow on the killer's head was followed by his limp collapse on the cockpit floor.

McCord scrambled into the seat to the controls of the ship. He tore off the automatic pilot device and got the monoplane under control, then banked around in the darkness.

Down there below in the dark, some distance away, the big hangar of Gotham Airport was like a vast, red torch, flaming high.

He headed the monoplane straight down toward the field in front of the burning building.

A few minutes later the silver ship swooped silently down and made a ragged and bumpy deadstick landing near the flaming hangar.

When it rolled to a stop, McCord salvaged his stubby pistol and then was climbing out of the cockpit when, from the burning hanger, a group of shouting men ran toward him.

Davidson was the first to reach him, with Bushell and McLiney and the others behind him.

"McCord, you're all right?" cried the lieutenant.

McCord nodded. "I'm okay, and so is the murderer, though he's not conscious right now."

"You got him, then?" cried Davidson.

For answer McCord reached into the cockpit and pulled out the unconscious form of the murderer.

Lying there in the red glow of the burning hangar, sprawled half out of the little cockpit door just as his first victim had sprawled a few hours before, lay —

"Blair James!" yelled Davidson in utter amazement.

They stared unbelievingly.

"But it can't be that Blair killed Lucky James, his own cousin!" cried the police lieutenant.

"He did, though," said McCord somberly, "and he did it for the same reason that many a closer relative has been killed: for money. Lucky James, by completing his flight from Cairo to New York, automatically became worth fifty thousand dollars as soon as his plane landed tonight. Blair, as he told us, was Lucky's only near relative. As such, he was Lucky's heir, and would inherit the fifty thousand." McCord took from his pocket a scorched and crumpled letter. He looked up from it a moment.

"You'll remember that Blair himself told us Lucky had lectured him about his gambling and spendthrift ways? Well, this letter which Lucky wrote to Stangland from Cairo explains why Blair needed money so badly and was willing to kill his cousin for it."

McCord read:

> Stangland, I wish you'd keep an eye on Blair until I get back. I had quite a quarrel with him before I left. It seems he's lost several thousand dollars in I.O.Us, gambling, and is being pressed hard for payment. You know he'll lose his job as pilot if the company officials find out about it.
>
> He wanted me to give him part of the money the company advanced to back my flight, and when I told him I'd never give him another cent to pay gambling debts, he became very resentful and bitter. Try to keep him from doing anything rash, for he seemed in a desperate mood. Lucky.

"That explains it," McCord said. "Blair, bitter at Lucky and desperate for money, decided to kill his cousin when he landed and thus inherit that fifty thousand. He killed Stangland when he guessed that Lucky had written Stangland about his gambling debts and the quarrel, and he fired the hangars to destroy the letter. When I went in after it, he went in after me."

"And because McLiney and Jandron were still at large, I was sure one of them was the killer!" Davidson exclaimed. "But we found it was they who went to turn in the alarm that brought the firemen here."

McCord nodded toward the unconscious man. "We'd better take him and lock him up-we had a hard enough time getting him."

"We will," Davidson said, "and then you're going to come with me and have a drink. You look as though you need one."

McCord, his craggy face relaxing into tired lines for the first time that night, nodded assent.

"We'll all have one," he said, "and make it in honor of a kid who must still be flying, some-where. We'll drink to Lucky James."

The Sinister Dr. Wong

Chapter I
Blood is Shed

John Bracket, head of the United States Secret Service, was about to speak. When Bracket spoke, men listened. And when he called a group of his star operatives into the big sound-proof room that was his sub-rosa chamber, there was something mighty important in the wind.

Rolling his cigar from one corner of his mouth to the other, Bracket studied the faces of the men seated before him, his own eyes grave with the concern of the knowledge he had just gained. "Gentlemen," he said crisply, removing the cigar from between his teeth, "I have to tell you a bit of very disturbing news." Here he paused for a single, impressive instant, while he observed that every eye in the room was fixed on his face. Then — "Doctor Wong is back!"

For a moment following his announcement the men gathered before him made no reply, uttered no sound. Then slowly, gradually, they turned their faces, one toward another, lips parted as if to bite off some lurid oath, eyes narrowed grimly.

So the dirty fox of a heathen was back, eh? And what was he after this time?

Bracket did not keep them waiting long. When he had satisfied himself that his announcement had sunk in firmly, that the full import of his words had struck home with all the force that the wily Oriental's name deserved, he continued.

"Every man of us here," he stated now, "is familiar with Wong's reputation. We have dealt with him before and he can set a tough pace for the best of us. But this time we will get him, and get him right. The man is making himself a power among his people in this country and has now reached a stage where he constitutes the greatest menace to the peace and safety not only of this nation-but to the entire world."

The attentive operatives nodded grimly. The Chinese, as they still remembered, was a ruthless fiend-cruel, resourceful, with a brain as keen and clever as the best among the government's highest officials. But Bracket was still to disclose alarming facts.

"Within the past week," continued the Secret Service chief, "two of this country's greatest scientists have disappeared. This, of course, would be only two citizens under ordinary circumstances; two professional Americans among our millions. But-these gentlemen happen to be something more. They were experts associated with the Bureau of War Gas and Investigation, and they have disappeared. The combination of facts connected with the complete vanishing of these gentlemen, together with information which I have at hand, prompt me to confess to you here in utmost secrecy that Doctor Wong is behind the case."

The chief paused for a moment and glanced toward one of the men in the audience, then added:

> "Wong either has these two scientists or-he has disposed of them. I don't have to suggest to you what their fate has likely been. However, we have among us here one man who is equipped to deal with Wong. Most of you know who I refer to, for this man has been in at the kill on more than one case in which Orientals have figured with this department. Will you rise for a moment, Mr. Graham?"

Richard Graham, or Dick, as he was known to his fellow operatives, stood up, slightly embarrassed, and nodded to his chief. He was a tall man, perhaps five feet eleven inches in height, with a noticeably erect figure, square shoulders and a slim but well-knit body. His face was tanned almost to the hue of a native of the flowery kingdom, but it was his eyes that dominated the picture he presented. They were grey eyes, and when he looked at you they gave you a feeling of seriousness.

"Mr. Graham," explained Chief Bracket, "is, as some of you know, the son of a missionary to China. He was born there and spent his early youth among the natives of many provinces. Graham speaks, or is familiar with, most of the leading Chinese dialects. And I have decided to assign him to this job of running down Doctor Wong."

Dick Graham nodded again, thoughtfully, and resumed his chair while a score of his associates cast envious glances in his direction. There was no question in their minds about the judgment of John Bracket in assigning Graham to this job.

Dick was one of the aces of the service; had been for seven years. True, he had been born in China, and had started out as a student of Chinese customs and lore. He was the logical choice for the work, and as far as his courage and ability were concerned-well, that was beyond question. Graham was one of the nerviest men who ever carried the government authority into the realm of organized crime.

"When do I start, Chief?" inquired Graham now, as he noted that Bracket seemed to have finished and was frowning at the hot end of his cigar. "I'd like to move out on this right away."

Bracket looked up, rubbed his smooth-shaven chin with the capable fingers of one big hand, and nodded to his interrogator.

"Whenever you're ready, Graham," he agreed. "I merely called the boys together here so everybody would be informed. In case anything happened, you know. They'll know what you're on. You've made your arrangements already, I suppose?"

Dick Graham got up promptly, declared that he had, and without further ceremony, or even a handshake, walked to the door and went out.

Every man left in that room behind him knew that Dick Graham would either "get" the infamous Doctor Wong, or-go down in the smoke.

* * *

Fog enveloped the night in a cloak of dully grey gloom. The street lamps shone like pale gobs of phosphorus through the misty veil that hung in draperied festoons, swirling fitfully in the drafts that whispered about the dirty corners where streets that were alleys tangled with one another in the heart of the city's Chinatown.

Soft-slippered feet shuffled amid the drifting, ghostly fog like the padding of velvet-sheathed claws of jungle beasts hunting the night for prey. Under the spell of the dreary gloom there seemed to stalk at large the very spirit of some evil monster; some hissing, many-headed dragon whose giant body lurked behind, secure in its darkened den, where the bones of its victims crunched beneath its horny saber-shod claws.

Chinatown!

Tonight it pulsed with the very throb of the evil power that crouched beneath its mantle of serenity, for a great force had come to take possession of the quarter, a force masterful enough to command, to move a finger at which the yellow horde would cringe and bow low to the earth. Doctor Wong!

Wedged snugly between two dirty, ill-smelling tenements, where the lodgers were crowded like vermin in foul, dark dungeon rooms, stood a bleak-fronted building that had one day been the home of a merchant prince. Rusting elaborate fire-escapes clung like rotting skeletons to its front. The windows, streaked and crusted with the dirt of years, stared like the sightless eyes of a blind man into the thickening fog. There was no outward sign of life about the building; no sound filtered from the windows and the door.

Yet here was hidden Doctor Wong.

Back of these musty, dank walls he had established his headquarters, and here he waited, like a spider squatting in a web.

And along the Chinatown street a figure shuffled. Nearer and nearer to this house it came like a fluttering phantom, until, at last, with furtive glances behind through the mist it darted into the solemn, darker shadow that was the doorway.

A yellow, wiry hand snaked out from beneath the voluminous folds of a huge sleeve and one long thin finger moved unerringly to a signal bell hidden cleverly in the pattern of the wall.

Quickly and without a word the caller stepped inside. To the casual passerby this house was a forlorn, drab face of brick with dead eyes. Inside —a palace. As the muffled visitor shuffled along the hall, his slippered feet deep in the soft luxury of priceless Oriental rugs, his slant eyes glittered in full appreciation of the richness of the furnishings, the gorgeous beauty of the hangings, the splendor of the polished teakwood and ivory.

The man in the great hall breathed a prayer to his ancestors as he halted before a portal of polished ebony.

Once again his finger was pressed to an electric button, a signal bell fixed cleverly in the eye of a dragon whose sinuous body glittered with jewels.

This time, from somewhere beyond, in the depths of the building there was heard the resonant clang of a brass gong. The huge panel of ebony slid silently into the wall, revealing a broad, sumptuous chamber into which the visitor stepped.

One step he took, a single move that carried him across the groove where the massive ebony panel slid, and here he halted while the door itself closed swiftly behind him.

"Greetings, most high-born prince, from the humble slave Ho Lee," bowed the newcomer, his tone filled with reverence, his body almost doubled in his salutation.

From a dais at the far end of the room, a handsomely gowned yellow man stared at his guest with eyes that were motionless. Like a figure carved from ivory and yellowed with age it gazed down from a veritable throne, stiffly, emotionless; while on either side of him stood six towering giants, armed with heavy Oriental two-handed swords, their only sign of life a slow blinking of beady black eyes.

Ho Lee waited with proper respect for the majestic figure on the throne to reply, to recognize him. It was like waiting in a tomb for a mummy to arise from a sarcophagus. He heard the breathing of the huge guards flanking the figure on the throne, and saw that their bodies were stripped to the waist, smooth and hairless in the soft light that seemed to sift through the room from nowhere.

But his eyes could not remain long from the imposing occupant of the throne. Ho Lee, expressionless, immovable, saw the eyes of the other yellow man. They were hungry eyes, lustful, set in a tight-skinned mask of parchment shade, behind which a fiend might have watched, seeking his chance to kill, to reek a bitter hatred on all of the world.

Then Ho Lee saw a finger move and his eyes were drawn to the hands. They were slim as a woman's with long tapering fingers that might have been the steel-sharp claws of a tiger. And yet these fingers were graceful; the beauty of the gem-studded rings that adorned them swept away all suggestion of force, of the surging power that smoldered in the man's eyes, until one let his gaze rest on the hideous nails which were protected by jeweled guards.

Ho Lee saw but he did not tremble. It was not good for one to tremble within sight of-but lo, silence. The lips of the man on the dais were about to move. "Ho Lee," the lips intoned. "You have come, and it is well. You bring me the word as I wish it? Speak!" Shuffling forward three steps nearer, Ho Lee prostrated himself, and rising, began in a sing-song:

> "Ahn Wong-the celestial born-the king of kings! This miserable slave cherishes
> the honor of serving. He comes to report that Ahn Wong's well-conceived plans
> are carried out. The guards will be at the house of the infidel Raynor at mid-
> night. All is well."

Wong stared at Ho Lee, and his slant eyes narrowed until they were slits that blended with the crow's feet in his polished skin.

"Ho Lee is wrong," snarled Wong, leaning a trifle forward on his perch, his rich satin garments rustling with the movement. "All is not well, my slave!"

Lee lifted his suddenly frightened eyes to those of his master. What he saw there caused a chill to clutch at his heart. His bland face lengthened in a terrified start.

"But master," he pleaded. "What is it that I have done. I only —"

"Hold your tongue! You know what you have done. You administered the potion of the living death to the infidel, Naylor, did you not? Confess this to me. Speak!"

Ho Lee cringed. He seemed hypnotized by the dominating stare of Ahn Wong, who shouted:

"Answer me, you fool with the eyes of a fish. Confess!"

Ho Lee fought with his throat, tore at it with his hands, slid his parched tongue over his lips. "Yes, master," he managed to blurt, "but —"

"Enough!" thundered Ahn Wong, his wrath giving him the look of a demon aflame. "He is dead. You gave him too much. Our friend Naylor was a most valuable-yea, priceless plaything-alive. He is nothing dead. Your stupidity has cost me the price of the earth's ransom. And you-will feel the same death!"

A cry of terror escaped Ho Lee's dry lips. Ahn Wong drew a deep breath. The tortures of seven devils made Ho Lee writhe in agony at the fate that had been spoken for him. He threw out his hands in suppliance, pleading with his clutching fingers, his staring eyes and his speechless but moving lips. The same death!

Ahn Wong was unmoved. The block of yellow marble that was his head, turned toward the giant guards at his left side. Wong's snake-eyes fastened on the leader.

"You have heard me," Wong's words were scarcely whispers. "He dies the same death. Take him!"

Like great trained beasts the huge half naked guards strode forward, jerked the inert body of Ho Lee from the floor. The sudden clutch of powerful hands snapped Lee into semi-consciousness, a scream struggled from his lips, and a big hand was slapped over his mouth. Ahn Wong's slave was doomed.

Then came a lifted sword, flashing in the softened lights like the under-wing of a vulture in the blazing sun. Strong hands gripped the helpless Ho Lee while the cruel knife point of the blade was jabbed deep into his arm.

Ahn Wong watched silently, his metallic eyes alight with a fiendish pleasure, as another guard produced a vial and bit out the stopper. A liquid of the same color as the fingers that poured it splashed over the wound.

Drop. Drop. Drop.

Blood and poison. Swift and deadly the potion did its work. The man held in the viselike grip of the mammoth guards jerked, stiffened. His eyes visible above the monster's hand that was clasped across his mouth, bulged in agony.

"Fool," grunted Ahn Wong, with a grin that was his first facial expression.

Blood dripped from the wound to the richly hued rug beneath him. Ho Lee tried to struggle once more, spasmodically. His face and body began to change color. Spots of rusty ochre spread around his eyes, appeared on his throat. His eyes grew dull, lusterless. A tremor convulsed his whole frame. And then he went limp.

The guard whose hand had been clamped on Ho Lee's mouth stepped away and bowed low to Ahn Wong. He made no sound, but the man above him on the dais motioned with one jeweled finger.

"Take him away," he ordered.

As the Manchu giants carried the limp corpse off, Ahn Wong mumbled softly to himself. It was well. Blood had been shed this night. But this was only a moistening of the finger tips to the gory trail he planned for his triumphal march to the throne of the world. Blood would run in rivers, but Ahn Wong was destined to flood the earth in a sea of crimson.

Chapter II
The Yellow Hand Strikes

Steel nerves are essential to a man who goes up against the cold steel. Some of his fellow operatives of the Secret Service claimed that Dick Graham had no nerves at all. On the other hand, Graham himself admitted to nerves; he was just as human as the next fellow.

But an almost constant association with danger over a period of years had hardened Graham against the risks his duty made him face. At the same time the stalwart young operative was aware of the closeness with which he walked beside Death. It was the chances he took that thrilled him. This Ahn Wong case now was going to try the mettle of a real man.

"You see, Professor," Graham was discussing the situation for the third time in as many days, "this Doctor Wong is no ordinary criminal by any stretch of the imagination. He's some sort of a mad genius who is determined to acquire a power over the whole world. Has a monarchial complex. He —"

Professor Raynor interrupted with a shake of the head.

"Really, Graham," he argued, "all this elaborate precaution strikes me as entirely unnecessary. There's no reason for anyone to harm me. If your friend Doctor Wong wanted to offer me a little fortune for my invention, it was his privilege. Just as it was mine to refuse him if I chose, I'm just a simple inventor. No one would bother about me."

Graham, however, was not to be denied. He was under orders from Headquarters in Washington, and he could not afford to leave any loopholes for the plotting Oriental.

"My dear Professor," he insisted emphatically, but with the proper attitude of respect for the venerable scientist. "You have just perfected the invention of a gas which you claim-and have proved in your laboratory tests-could destroy the entire world. Do you not realize that there are men who would murder in order to obtain the secret of this gas?"

Professor Raynor shrugged and stroked his beard.

"If this fiend Wong could get the secret of this gas into his possession," continued Graham, "his mad desire for world dominance would be within his reach. Don't you see? And further-what about Naylor and Ralston? Does anyone know where they are; what happened to them? Do you? No!

"Well, I'll tell you what we think, what the Department has every reason to believe. Doctor Wong has got Naylor and Ralston. They may be alive or they may be dead, but you can take my word for it. Wong wormed their secrets from them, or slaughtered them in some torture chamber in an effort to draw it from them. And you'll be next. Unless —"

"Ridiculous," snorted the professor stubbornly. "My friends are working secretly. They have gone into seclusion. The idea of your placing all of these men here is simply preposterous. The guard you speak of from the War Department is ample-quite ample."

Graham savagely bit off the end of a cigar and flung his gaze about the room. Striking a match he applied it to the end of his cigar and puffed a moment, thoughtfully.

Professor Raynor was a hard old fellow to handle. Well, there was consolation in the knowledge that outside that door stood a half-dozen of Graham's men. In the street, too, there were six more rough and ready fellows keeping a strict vigil.

The scientist sat back in a comfortable arm chair and shoved an ash tray toward Graham. The secret service operative, nodded, and the silence was unbroken except for the ticking of a tiny desk clock. Both men had relapsed into their own thoughts. Graham looked at the clock now and began figuring mentally.

By midnight the War Department men would arrive from Washington. They would take back with them a small case containing a canister of Raynor's new poisonous gas; the only sample extant of this powerful lethal vapor.

"It's nearly time," mused Graham, comparing the time of the desk clock with that of his own wrist watch. "Once we turn this can over to the G boys we can stop worrying."

"I never worry," chuckled the professor. "The things I've searched for in my life have generally been years away. One always reaches them in time."

"It isn't the worry," corrected Graham. "I don't mean that exactly; but the responsibility. I'm anxious to get rid of that thing." He pointed to the innocent looking, specially made metal can-shaped thing on the desk. There was undoubtedly enough of the deadly gas in that sealed container to wipe out the millions that filled the crowded city. "Once the G-men have got it, it will be pretty safe. But they haven't got it yet. I wonder what's delaying them?"

As he spoke he raised his head quickly. Both men could hear the sound of feet in the hall outside. There were voices, too.

Then, as if in answer to Graham's question, the door was pushed open and two of his own men entered, escorting a quartet of strangers.

O'Leary, one of Graham's right-hand men, saluted.

"The men from Washington, sir," he announced, as the door was closed behind them.

Dick Graham nodded to the newcomers and Professor Raynor arose from his chair to reach over for the precious canister. There was a cheery smile on his face as he turned to the Secret Service operative.

"You see," he said. "It was just as I told you. No trouble. Everything is quite regular. Where is the danger you have been hinting at?"

The four from Washington moved to the desk, and one extended a small slip of paper, like a label, toward the professor. Graham peered across the desk at this, and chewed his cigar. He was trying to place these men in his catalogue of faces. If they were men from Washington, he should know them readily.

"We'll want you to sign this, Professor," declared the man with the label. "Have to paste it on the can to identify it as the original for records, just sign-here. Yes, sir."

Raynor took the paper.

Leaning over the desk, he picked up a pen which lay on a blotter there and with a queer twinge of his facial muscles, began to write his name. Then, as if he had been stabbed to the heart, he broke out with an odd cry, dropped the pen and stared in bewilderment and horror at his fingers.

In that instant Graham was beside him, looking at the same thing they all saw. Blood was on Professor Raynor's thumb and index finger. Terror sprang into the scientist's eyes and he glared horrified about him, gasping. Graham swore explosively, reached quickly for the fallen pen, and froze.

Nobody but Graham seemed to realize what had happened, for none moved. Graham stared now at the pen, its handle near the writing end, still sticky. And in the stickiness there glittered the fine particles of sprinkled glass chips. They were there on the blotter, too, where the pen had been lying when Raynor picked it up.

"What have I —?" The scientist tried to call out. He staggered and collapsed, falling backward into the chair from which he had but a moment ago risen.

The Secret Service operative snatched up Raynor's wrist and felt of the pulse. He looked up, startled, for the aged body was pulseless now.

"What the hell!" O'Leary broke in. "What's it mean, Dick?"

"Get an ambulance!" cried Graham, excitedly. It was no time for conjecture. It was a case for swift action. "A doctor! Quick, for God's sake!"

With an oath, O'Leary sprang to the telephone. The others stared blankly from Graham to the inert body of Professor Raynor. O'Leary was shouting angrily into the receiver, demanding immediate service, then swung around to reach for the pen where it lay on the desk.

"Damn funny," he declared, frowning, making a move to pick up the thing.

"Don't touch it, you fool!" warned Graham, knocking O'Leary's hand away roughly. "You'll die. Don't you get it, yet? Somebody dusted that stuff on the pen while it was lying there. Quick now, step outside and see if anybody's been seen hangin' around here. Someone's been in this house."

O'Leary followed orders quietly, swiftly, and returned with a baffled look. Graham shook his head.

"I never guess," declared the interne, then: "What do you want to do about him? It's Professor Raynor, isn't it?"

Graham frowned. "Yes, and you'd better just —"

"Maybe," offered the man in white, "we could rush him over to the hospital and try —"

"Do it," Graham broke in desperately. "Get him over there as fast as you can. Hurry. We may be able to save him. I can't understand how he could go so quickly."

The driver and the interne wasted no more words, but swiftly placed the body of Professor Raynor on a stretcher and carried him out of the house.

As the door closed on them, Graham's gaze turned to the four men by the desk, the four from Washington.

"What about us, now?" demanded the fellow who was evidently the leader. "We came for this can of-whatever it is. I'll just take this now and we'll be going."

"Wait," ordered Graham. "Just hold your horses. I'll make a little call first. This case is getting hot."

Picking up the telephone he listened for a moment, puzzled. No, the wire was not dead, but it was certainly odd. Somebody's voice was on the line. A man's voice.

"Who the devil is this?" demanded the Secret Service man gruffly.

A chuckle answered him, and from the other end came a calm "What number are you calling?"

"Get off this wire!" shouted Graham. "This is an emergency call and I'm in a hurry."

"Don't make me laugh, Richard Graham," taunted the voice, and suddenly Graham realized. Something about the accent, the tone of the speaker at the other end. A fierce fighting rage gripped his brain and he clutched the instrument with fingers that threatened to crush it to splinters.

"You are very unfortunate in your connections, Mr. Graham. This wire was cut in early in the evening. You can speak only to me-to the potential prince of the earth."

"Wong," snarled Graham, "you yellow devil! You're a liar. We just put through an ambulance call from here." Laughter followed this—a hearty, cruel, crackling laugh.

"My ambulance, Mr. Ace of the Secret Service," explained Doctor Wong. "I had to have the professor. And I've got him. I am certainly grateful to you for offering no resistance. My plans are working—"

"Your plans," snapped Graham into the mouthpiece, "are shot to hell. You got Professor Raynor, yes; but we have the can of gas. So what good will the man's body do you?"

"Just a moment, my friend," purred Doctor Wong in a voice that was smooth as satin. "You say you have the gas. I am certain that if you raise your eyes and look to your right, you will change your mind about the gas. Ahn Wong times his plans to the flutter of an eyelid."

Dick Graham unconsciously followed the suggestion of the Chinese at the other end of the wire.

There before him, arms elevated high above their heads, stood O'Leary and his comrade, grim, silent and still amazed. The four men who had "come from Washington" were in complete control of everything.

Big, businesslike automatics were pressed into the kidneys of Graham's two guards. A third mysterious gentleman was covering Dick himself, a yawning black muzzle aimed at his heart. The fourth fellow, evidently in charge of the party, stood with feet spread, one hand hooked into a sagging pocket, the other toying with a vicious-looking bulldog pistol.

Before Graham could move or utter a word, this gentleman, with a step nearer, spoke.

"We'll start somethin' any time you say, fella. All we're after is this little can here, and I don't guess you mugs'll give us much of an argument. Will yuh?"

Graham, his body rigid, glanced from one to another. It looked like a burying detail.

They were a tough, reckless looking quartet and a move by Graham or O'Leary or Marquiss would start bullets flying.

Chapter III
A Tryst with Death

Pushed literally to the wall, Dick Graham's brain was filled with a panic of raging thought. With a flash came the realization that he had been smoothly tricked by Doctor Wong and these men of his. These were no G-men; they were the hired thugs of the Oriental devil himself, gunmen who had either waylaid the real government guards and murdered them, or turned them off on some ruse.

Powerless now, Graham faced his captors, tensed for the chance he hoped might present itself. O'Leary and Marquiss, he knew, would stand by him in any pinch, and they could make a real fight of it if —

That was the catch. Graham's eyes searched for an opening and as he glanced about he wondered. Had it been one of these very four here who was responsible for that poisoned glass powder? And if so, how had it been accomplished?

Grimly silent, he cursed himself for the slip that made him now actually a prisoner. What was going to happen?

The leader of the quartet did not keep him in suspense. With a motion of his weapon, this fellow spoke.

"If any one o'you fellas try to yell out," he began his threat, "or you make a break for the door-blooey! Yuh get it. See? So far the mugs yuh got outside ain't heard a thing, an' if yuh wanna die right here now, try and let 'em know how we gotcha jammed."

"Hold on," sneered Graham angrily. "I never welched for a rat like you —" He had sprung like a terrier at the leader, reaching for the weapon, and smashing out with his clenched fist, when the other shouted.

Crash! Every man of the four brought his gun down with a smash on one of the three. Graham was struck front and rear, and felt himself crumpling under the double thunder of the blows.

O'Leary and Marquiss, too, went careening drunkenly, to sprawl face down on the floor.

Graham tried desperately to clutch at his adversaries, but the power of those gun smashes was too much. He was dazed, and struggled to lift his face and shout. With a smothered curse, one of the gang was upon him, engulfing his parted lips in a hard broad palm, and stifling the cry for help.

Collapsing in a heap on the floor, Dick Graham felt himself slide off into unconsciousness, but like a man who struggles in the grip of some wild dream, he was vaguely aware of rushing feet, and the voice of one of his enemies.

"Fast now, fellas," ordered the leader, grabbing the canister of gas. "Come on. Up the old fire-escape. Wun So has got the guys on the roof all peaceful by now."

Without a sound the four vanished through a window. It was as if they had been swept away on a magic carpet. There was not even an echo of the carnage or the escape. Only the little clock on the desk ticked on, its impassive face fixed on the mysterious, deadly pen.

Professor Raynor was gone. The hired assassins of Doctor Wong were gone. Dick Graham and his double guard lay in tiny pools of blood where they had fallen. Had Death claimed these also in the ruthless path of the dreaded Chinese madman?

* * *

And so it was night again. Darkness lay like a dirty blanket over the crowded section of the city known as Chinatown. There were few lights glowing in the grimy windows along the streets. In a doorway, here, there, a still figure leaned, motionless, garbed in somber black.

A Bowery bum, ragged and footsore, shuffled wearily along Mott Street from the Square.

Now he paused as he came to the corner of Pell Street.

Here was as good a place as any to rest himself, and with this decision he edged back against the tiny stoop that was the entrance to the sordid tenements above the stores.

Dick Graham felt as dirty as he looked, but under the mask of grime and paint, under the disguise that made him one of a thousand human wrecks that float with the tides of the city's underworld, he was as confident as ever, and determined to get the yellow fiend who called himself the prince of the earth.

Standing there out of the path of a dim light in the nearby store, Graham reflected bitterly. He had looked in at the door of Death. He and his companions, O'Leary and Marquiss, had faced the grim reaper and were still alive. That had been a narrow escape, a lucky break for them.

"Damn him!" mumbled Graham, as he remembered the affair in Professor Raynor's study and the close shave the three of them had when the scientist met his death.

As soon as the Secret Service operative was patched up and marked for duty, he had rushed back to pick up the trail. There was that ambulance matter. Graham set promptly about tracking down that odd business, and he was at last able to learn that, upon the night in question, an ambulance had also clanged its way through Pell Street. Two friendly tramps had seen it and Graham had pumped them cautiously for information.

"No," the speaker of the pair had said. "We didn't watch it where it went. Ambulances ain't nothin' new to us. Are dey, Joe? But we saw it comin' back, pal, 'bout ten, fi'teen minutes a'ter."

"Pell Street, huh," repeated the inquiring bum.

"Sure," the man agreed. "We seen it turn in dere. But how could we tell yuh where it wuz goin'?"

"Swell, pal, swell," chirped the curious bum who looked not at all like Dick Graham of the Secret Service. "Well, s'long, pals."

The tip, however, had availed Graham nothing. He had tramped the streets hour after hour. Perhaps the wily Wong was even watching him then, for all he knew. Well, he was an easy target for a Chinatown slug, and he had to play the game as he started it.

Somewhere in this labyrinth the Evil One, as he had come to think of Wong, was hidden safe, secure. The thought made him uncomfortable, itchy, and he pushed off from his lounging place and started along the street once more.

Chinatown seemed just coming to life. There were more people about him. Figures passed him, slowly, swiftly, like so many shadows. Here the glare from a shop window lighted a cruel grinning heathen face; there a bloated, pot-bellied denizen of some dungeon, once a white man, now a sodden wreck that cheated Potter's Field with every hour he breathed.

There were women, too; dark, sad-eyed creatures who strutted boldly, almost savagely among the figures on the streets, dodging the barrels and open cellars, flaunting their painted faces in the fluttering shadows, like bats that float with the night wind in search of prey.

Suddenly Graham halted in the middle of this whirl of black, white, yellow and grey. The passersby sped back and forth; yellow men, white men and black. But Dick Graham saw none of these now, for his eyes were staring at a girl.

"Here?" he moved his lips in awe. What was such a creature doing in this vile breeding-ground of the gutter whelps? She was beautiful, and her clothes were rich.

He could not help but stare at her, and then he felt a second start, for she was staring straight at him. As he caught the direct gaze of her eyes he saw her blink and look away.

But she continued toward him, unswervingly. In another moment she was close, almost touching him. He tingled with the fragrance of her perfume. Then her voice awoke him with a shock. For it was harsh, mechanical, like a phonograph.

"You seek the Doctor Wong?" was what she said.

It was a question. Did he look for Doctor Ahn Wong? What did it all mean? How could she know that he was there for that very purpose? But the girl was gone. He could follow her with his eyes, as she sifted in and out through the crowds, winding a trail along the narrow street.

Graham made up his mind swiftly. If it was a trap he would have to take his chances. He wanted, more than anything else in the world, to come up with Wong. If this girl could lead him to the crafty Chinese-why not? Moving after her, Graham began to gain on her. Soon he was at her shoulder.

"All right, girlie," he whispered close to her ear. "You lead the way to Doctor Wong."

"If you are alone," she replied in the same drab, mechanical voice, "follow me. If you try to play any tricks, your life is not worth-that dead cat there in the gutter."

Dick Graham gritted his teeth, and kept walking at a pace that permitted him to see the girl's profile and one eye. She was certainly a beautiful thing, but on second glance he was now as certain that there was that about her eyes which gave him a strange feeling. They were cold, expressionless and might have belonged in a plaster casting for all the life that shone in them.

Something about her manner, her bearing, made him feel that this girl was not a conscious tool of the Oriental master criminal. Fear seemed to guide her every step, her slightest motion of the head.

In his pocket Graham felt with reassurance the bulge of the pistol he carried there. A .38 police special. The girl continued through the night, crossing streets, down one block, around a corner, and on.

At last they came to a dark dilapidated house. He was aware that she had halted and turned in; saw her finger press an almost invisible button.

Taking a deep breath, he watched the door open, and in another moment he and the girl were across the threshold.

At once the Secret Service agent knew he had walked too swiftly into the dark. As the door shut behind them the place went black as a pit. Graham drew his gun and froze.

"What's this mean?" he demanded of the girl, who, he felt as he touched her arm, was now trembling with uncontrollable fear.

She was unable to reply, and the man from Washington could hear the sob that broke from her lips. He raised his pistol, finger snug on the trigger. There was something about the atmosphere in the place that made his blood chill.

Somebody was near him, somebody besides the mysterious woman. He wished now that he had a flashlight.

"Ah!"

The voice came at him from behind, and he was about to swing and shoot when, like a period dotting the single word, he felt something on the back of his neck.

His blood ran cold. His body tensed. It was the razor-keen edge of a hatchetman's tool of his trade. Gently as the caress of silken scarf it was pressed against his neck. A single move would be the end.

"So you looked for Doctor Wong?" laughed a voice behind him. "And you found him! Now, my foolish infidel friend, you will find death without looking further. Stand still. Do not move!"

Chapter IV
The Devil's Courtroom

Chinese tapestries crowded with dragons and other mythical monsters richly embroidered in red and gold, covered the walls of the big chamber. Row after row of low teakwood benches were arranged to reach from wall to wall, the full width of the big hall-like room, and stretched from the rear end almost to the edge of the dais at the front.

On these benches, packed tight like caterpillars in the branches of a tree, sat Chinese. Row upon row of gleaming yellow faces, countless golden moons shining in the mellow radiance of light reflected by the mingled silks and satins, the polished brass and magnificent jade. A slice of old Canton set down in the crowded quarter of a great metropolis in the United States.

Resplendent in the gorgeous robes of a prince of the Ming Dynasty, Doctor Wong sat majestically on the dais. The beady eyes swept back and forth over the throng seated out there before him and there was triumph in his eyes as he recognized the reverence in the worshipful stare of these stupid countrymen of his.

Five hundred of them sat there, waiting, paying him homage with their awed silence, and already they were pledged to the sacred cause of this self-ordained king of the "new empire."

This was the Chinese fiend's court; his palace where death and plunder were plotted. And before the dais stood a white man: an American.

It was Dick Graham. Bound hand and foot, he stood, half leaning against a pillar which rose from the floor to meet the teakwood beams of the high vaulted ceiling.

In grim contemplation of the scene around him, the Secret Service agent bided his time, making plans and discarding them as futile. Again and again his eyes returned to the coffin-like chest of ebony that stood in solitary splendor close to the side of Wong's miniature throne.

The chest was richly inlaid with purest ivory and aged perhaps by centuries in its native land beyond the seas. From the chest, Graham would let his eyes rove to the inscrutable face of Doctor Wong, then to the white woman who stood servilely at Wong's side.

Further, too, he could see more: two white men. They lay beyond the edge of the dais, also bound hand and foot. But they were apparently bound in addition by some mysterious potion that had dulled their senses. Occasionally they would stir feebly, as if struggling for freedom, then relax and grow still.

"Wonder what the connection is?" mused Graham as he glanced from the white girl to the yellow man.

What made the Secret Service operative most enraged was the servile attitude of the white girl toward the yellow devil. Well, he'd come to that all in good time-if he lived to get out of this dive. What a fool he had been to risk his chance with that girl! Looking for Wong. And all the while the cunning Chinese had had him followed, knew his every move; was just waiting for the psychological moment to snare him in his death trap.

What was that?

Graham roused himself at the sound of a gong. Deep and ominous its note boomed from somewhere as if muffled by soft draperies. A low rumbling murmur rose from the huddled Chinese, grew louder, swelling almost to a thundering din.

The American saw Wong's face light up with cruel scheming as he listened. Then, with a sweeping gesture of his jeweled hand, Wong rose majestically, and faced his audience.

From the assembled Chinese a great roar of approval answered Ahn Wong, and the inspired doctor turned on Dick Graham.

"I am holding court, infidel," he announced. "The future emperor of the world holds court to condemn the fools who would oppose me, and to reward those who are loyal."

Graham did not speak. He was working desperately, slyly, showing no slightest sign of his struggle, to free his wrists of his bonds.

Even now how could he know but that one of the audience had observed his efforts to slip the rope? One hand was almost clear. He kept his eyes on Doctor Wong who continued, addressing his countrymen:

> "My courageous servants," began Wong in a dialect of southern China, "we are on the threshold of great treasure. Follow my banner and we shall exterminate the white race from this earth. Obey me and I promise you the riches of the world. Oppose me and you are marked for death. At my side you see two of these infidels. They shall give us the key to the gates we march through. Their brains possess great weapons. One will give us a gun which can destroy cities a thousand miles away; the other furnishes us in two moons. We will deal with these dogs shortly.

> "But first we pronounce two sentences of death." Wong paused here and glared around, his eyes resting on Dick Graham. "One is for temerity in daring to meddle in the affairs of the Ahn Wong. The second is for treachery. This infidel, here, will be first." All eyes were fixed on Graham. Then Wong pointed his bespangled finger beyond. "There stands Ah Sin, whose crime is treachery!"

Graham saw a yellow giant who stood some distance to his left, clad in silken trousers. A gleaming knife was thrust through his brocaded belt. The man looked as if he had been struck by a stab of lightning. Blood faded from his lips and his eyes stared in terror. The muscles of his arms and hands flexed in spasms and sweat oozed down his muscular torso.

"Did you think to act without my knowledge?" demanded Wong of the horrified Chinese. "Your duty was to slay a traitor-Wun Foo. You failed. And for that you die!"

"But, Most High Prince," he pleaded, "Wun Foo is my blood brother. I am sworn to friendship with him. He is —"

"My word is supreme," he shouted harshly. "Loyalty to the Realm transcends the tong oath. Ah Sin has broken faith and for that he dies. By the fluid of the living death."

Ah Sin cried in mortal terror as his doom was pronounced and Wong pointed at Graham.

"The death of the white hand," he snarled at the white man, "is for you. You die first!"

Wong turned now to the girl at his side.

"Ariadne," he intoned in a peculiarly chanting voice, "do you hear me?"

"I hear, O Prince."

Her voice was hollow and empty, as if it came from far away. It seemed to Graham as if she spoke like an automaton.

"Then you will take this." Wong drew a gleaming blade from his belt and placed the hilt in her hand. "Take this," he repeated, "and with it tear the life from that white pig who dares to interfere with the plans of the Celestial One."

Chapter V
The Death of the White Hand

The girl's dark beauty had suddenly become a thing diabolical. What Graham saw in her face turned his heart to ice. Satan was staring from her eyes. The transformation was horrible. A vampire was creeping slowly toward him.

Tense with excitement, the crowded Chinese sat spellbound, eyes fastened on the moving figure of the girl, the glinting blade in her white hand. It was the magic of their master. Graham, too, was wrapt in the spell of the thing. She was without a doubt, the complete slave of Wong; her every move dominated by his will.

Closer and closer she approached. The knife in her hand was lifting. She was no longer that woman of the street, the strange, half conscious creature who had drawn him like a magnet to this den of crime. Now she was all fiend. She was the Death of the White Hand. The executioner of Doctor Wong.

And while he watched, she closed in gradually, as if she measured each step, each move. The knife was high, its point aimed for his breast. Then swiftly it happened. The flashing knife —

Graham flung himself aside, and a piercing cry arose as his hands were seen to strike out.

"Damn you!" shouted Graham, hurling himself at the girl.

One hand reached for her knife, the other was flung out to grab her about the middle. But somewhere there was a mistake. Graham found himself struggling like a man in the grip of a gorilla. Stark dismay gripped him as he realized now that he had underestimated the magic of Doctor Wong. His attempt to hurl the woman from him had failed completely.

Slowly, with despair gnawing at his heart, Dick Graham felt his own left arm being relentlessly forced downward. Closer and closer came the knife. Inches separated the point from his body.

Then-the impossible happened.

Ah Sin, prompted by the terrifying knowledge of the tortures of the living death, gained a swift, mad courage. A fierce cry was flung from his throat, and he wheeled upon Doctor Wong. Whipping up his knife he hurled himself toward the dais. Here was the Prince of Hell, alone, unprotected.

Pandemonium broke loose in the glittering palace chamber. Ah Sin was almost upon Wong. The knife sang through the air. With lightning move the wily Wong dodged, and leaped for a button. Click! Like magic the huge chest beside the dais sprang open. A beam of blinding light flashed on from a hidden source and there, blazing in the shaft of silver gleamed the most elaborately jeweled image of Confucius, fairly alive with diamonds and rubies.

"Thank God!" moaned Graham, snatching up the knife which fell from the limp hand of the girl. "Quick!"

Clutching at her wrist, he leaped away, dragging her with him, straight for the high panels of the outer door. Behind him he could hear the wild shouting of Doctor Wong, a cringing coward himself, but brave in the midst of his foolish slaves.

"Fools! Be quick. The infidel is loose!"

Graham and the girl had gained the door when Wong had managed to shut the glittering idol from view. With a roar that filled the chamber like the thunder of cannon fire the mob of Chinese sprang after the fleeing Secret Service man.

"Hurry," panted the girl at his side. "Get me free from this terrible place-and —"

There was no time for surprise at her words. Graham dragged, half flung her suddenly weakened body along toward the door, burst through before the panels could be closed.

He felt the whirring of a hatchet as it whizzed past his head and heard it strike-spang-into the brocade-covered wall panel. Before them loomed the door. But between them and that door stood a Chinese giant, bare to the waist and armed with a shining sword.

"Stop them!" came the voice of Doctor Wong. "By your life's blood, stop that white pig!"

The sword was raised, and a wild light sprang into the swordsman's slanting eyes. Graham saw it all in a flash, but did not pause. Instead, he lunged straight for the yellow devil and drove the knife he held deep into the other's chest. Right to the heart.

"Whew!" gasped Graham, gathering up the girl as the cool night air struck him full in the face. Only then did he realize that back in that hall a thrown knife blade had gouged into the flesh of his shoulder. Warm sticky blood was coursing down his arm, as up the street he turned and ran, stumbling, cursing angrily at his seeming weakness.

Behind him the maddened Chinese had halted before the doorway. Dared they follow him openly along the thoroughfare? He guessed not, but neither did he dare to slacken his pace, until the girl began to struggle again in his grip.

With a fierce jerk she was on her feet, glaring at him, tugging to break free. Graham fought with her but she was stubborn, defiant.

"Take your hands off me," screamed the girl. "I must go back to my master."

The announcement stunned Graham, and he tried to dissuade her, but she raved and tore at him until she broke free of his grip and turned on her heel to walk dazedly back straight toward the Oriental mob. Graham risking his life, waited, watching. He saw her swallowed up in the chattering crowd.

What was it? What wild craziness had turned her so quickly from a passive white woman to a fighting, determined slave of this yellow master mind of the criminal world? Should he turn back there, too, and charge the yellow men?

"I'd be seven kinds of a damn fool," he muttered as he reached a decision. "Nix!"

He could go back later, better equipped. Now he would be only walking to his death, and with no guarantee that he could release the girl from this powerful spell under which Doctor Wong must hold her. Now he was on his way.

Like a madman he raced along the street. A nauseating dizziness was coming over him as he turned a corner and discovered a uniform of familiar blue and brass.

"I'm Graham!" he managed to stammer out. "Federal agent. Ring alarm and-raid-Wong's house-number —"

Had he been able to tell it all? Graham did not know, for he sprawled inertly forward into the officer's arms.

Chapter VI
Cantonese Magic

Graham, with his arm bandaged and somewhat paler than he was when he started out to get Doctor Wong, sat in a deep armchair and listened with attentive interest. Professor Warren Carruthers, bearded and scholarly of mien, was talking of China and its people, their customs and the legends of the ancient republic. The professor was recognized as one of the world's foremost authorities on the subject.

"It is an odd thing, Graham, yes," Carruthers was saying. "Very odd. It's something I'd hesitate to discuss with any man who has not seen it himself. However, it is true. Just as the ancient Egyptians possessed secrets of nature such as the embalming process, so do the Chinese know strange things about the action of drugs, certain herbs for instance, upon the human system.

"Our medical profession has been far too much concerned with healing to delve into the mysteries of the black arts. Orientals have mastered what is almost sorcery to a white man's mind. For instance, this girl Ariadne now. I should say she'd been forced to take a drug so rare, so little known to modern science, that we have no name for it. I've never seen it myself, but my research has shown me that it has foundation in fact."

Graham frowned in astonishment. "You mean you believe she's been taking some drug that completely subjects her to the will of Doctor Wong?"

"Precisely," declared Carruthers. "She is robbed of her own will and becomes a ready victim to the hypnotic influence which this yellow man no doubt possesses. Under these spells she becomes a mere tool in his power."

Dick Graham sat wrapt in thought. The girl was indeed in a perilous position. Doubtless, when the Chinese devil had finished with her, when his uses for her were past, he would toss her like a helpless derelict into the streets.

"What of the drug?" urged Graham, "they gave to Raynor? It apparently killed him; I'll swear that he had no pulse at all. And his eyes-they turned yellow. To all appearances the man was dead-yet, as we now know, he did not die. How do you explain that, Professor?"

"Your Doctor Wong is a fiend of many talents," observed the man of science. "He has great knowledge. Such a drug, and by that I mean a drug producing such effects as you describe, is recorded in the archives of the third Ming Dynasty. Hundreds of years ago. It is there called the Drug of the Living Death. Evidently this fellow Wong has resurrected it from some hitherto unknown records."

For some time Graham and his friend Professor Carruthers sat in silence, smoking.

From Carruthers he had gathered sufficient information regarding the strange transformation of the girl Ariadne to explain the mysterious actions of the girl during the hectic struggle inside and outside of Doctor Wong's assembly chamber.

"And when we reached the street," argued Graham, "she turned on me like a spitfire."

"Exactly," nodded Carruthers. "Wong, you see, was rid of Ah Sin then and he was able to recast his spell over the fleeing girl. It has been done."

While Graham mulled this over it gave Carruthers a chance to review the scene as Graham had explained it. Suddenly he broke in on the Secret Service agent's dreams.

"I'm curious, Graham," confessed the scientist. "You seem to have been impressed with the idea that this fellow, Ah Sin, would surely have slain Doctor Wong, but for this ebony chest or coffin or whatever it was. Tell me, what was in it?"

Graham closed his eyes so that he might better see the chest again, the way he had caught a glimpse of it during his battle in Wong's palace. Little by little he pieced it together and told his companion of the jade idol set with jewels and the snakes winding about it.

"What?" Carruthers demanded.

Puzzled, Graham repeated his description of the idol.

"By God!" exclaimed the older man. "He's done it. But it can't be!"

"What?" demanded the law officer from Washington.

Carruthers became strangely preoccupied. "Please let's not discuss it now," he suggested. "I must look up something. This Wong person shall, perhaps, realize his mad dream yet, Graham. But don't ask me any more. Give me a ring in a couple of hours, will you?"

Dick Graham shrugged and got up. "Just as you say. I'll call you about dinner time."

As he let himself out he noted the figure of a police lieutenant who passed him and approached Carruther's apartment door.

Something odd about that man struck Graham and he was puzzling it over as he disappeared around a corner in the corridor. A moment more and he could hear voices. One was Carruthers' raised in irate altercation with his caller. The police officer protested.

Graham waited grimly. He had a hunch and was going to play it for everything it was worth.

Soon he saw the pair come into view around the corridor corner, Graham was waiting at the elevator door. He glanced up in what looked like surprise.

Or he hoped so.

"Thought you were going to be busy there," he greeted Carruthers.

"Me too," growled the professor. "Lieutenant Nolan here must have passed you in the hall." Graham nodded casually. "He has word from the commissioner who would like to have me sit in on some points of Chinese criminology."

Graham frowned, glancing from Carruthers to Lieutenant Nolan. The fact that the department wanted to consult the scientist was nothing new or startling.

But why did the commissioner have to send a police lieutenant. Why did he not telephone? Graham wondered as he looked frankly at Nolan, who, incidentally, had uttered no word. Nolan's stolid silence, be it known, was the real cause of Graham's sudden discovery.

A glance from the man's face to his uniform gave Graham an almost visible start.

"Steady there, Lieutenant," warned Graham, the service revolver covering Nolan's middle button. "I thought I noted something odd about you. Now, Professor," turning to his friend, "if you'll be so good as to go back and dig up that information you promised, I'll take care of Mr. Nolan. But before you leave let me point out," the gun muzzle indicated the lieutenant's badge, "that a lieutenant of the Metropolitan police wears a gold badge-not a nickel-plated one."

Carruthers' eyes widened and he chuckled. His footfalls faded away around the corner. Graham stepped closer to Nolan. "And you, my friend, if you happen ever to see Doctor Wong again, which I doubt right now, tell him to be more careful of his details. Even a Chinese master mind like the dirty Wong can muff one."

It was but a short while later that Dick Graham was entering police headquarters with Nolan in tow, and covered.

Inspector King was an old acquaintance of Dick Graham's. From behind his desk he recognized the G man entering, and beckoned to him. The pseudo police officer was hauled up to face the inspector.

"This fellow," explained Graham after greeting his friend, "is one of Doctor Wong's gangsters. Will you take a slant at the uniform he's been wearing right here in the city?"

"Cheap," commented the inspector in disgust. "The dirty louse."

"Well, Wong sent this mug up to Warren Carruthers' place to lure the prof away. Must've got wind of the fact that I'm depending on Carruthers for some mighty important dope on his native land. Since we raided the house where he held me in Chinatown and he was gone, the yellow devil has faded entirely. This bum is a lucky break for us, Inspector. He's our only chance to nail Wong."

"What do you want me to do?" inquired King, willing to go the limit for his friend Graham.

"I can't get a peep out of him. Make him talk. He's on Wong's payroll and he knows where the chink fiend is."

King considered this gravely. It was surely no time for dallying.

"Do you want to answer some questions," he tried the unwilling prisoner, "or-do you want to answer our questions?"

"If I squeal I die," he muttered.

"All rats squeal," cut in Graham, his anger rising every moment.

"He'll talk," declared Inspector King, decisively. "Sure McCarthy'll talk. I just got yuh, Mac, you dirty mug. Usin' the name o' Nolan, too. Hey, Lam!" he called to a heavy-set, red-faced man in plain clothes. "See this lad," indicating McCarthy, alias Nolan. "He's got some information we've got to have. Can you get it?"

"Sure thing, Inspector. Come wit' me, mister. Up those stairs."

Dick Graham watched them climb out of sight and began pacing the floor, explaining meanwhile the difficulties he had faced in his trail of Doctor Wong. Even while he waited now, the rat-eyed Chinese might be preparing his next move in the weird scheme for world conquest. When he could stand the strain no longer he rushed to one of the Headquarters telephone booths and rang Carruthers' number.

The professor's voice was excited.

"That you, Graham? —Sure. I was right! That's the Cantonese Confucius. This Wong has got it-or rather likely-it's a fake. But with even the fake, he'll rule all China within thirty days."

"My God!" groaned Graham. "How?"

"There's some legend," continued Warren Carruthers eagerly. "You know the Chinese are very superstitious people. Their lives are lived by their legends of the ancients. There's millions of the ignorant devils in that country who'll fall for it. It seems, listen now-about, well thousands of years ago, Confucius is supposed to have made his own image of jade and diamonds. Supposed to be eternal. Has immortal serpents to guard it. Now, this thing disappeared some way during the Third Dynasty, and it is written that whoever recovers it is destined by the gods of all China's forefathers to rule China."

"So —" Dick Graham managed to gasp his thanks, and hanging up with a reminder that he would see Carruthers very soon, turned to see McCarthy, alias Nolan, coming down the iron stairs with his guard.

"He talked," nodded the guard belligerently.

"And what did he say?" urged Graham. They were steering the prisoner toward Inspector King's desk.

"This Doctor Wong guy," the guard rumbled along while Graham and King listened, "he sails tonight for China. He's chartered his own ship. This guy here," —indicating the prisoner —"is supposed to meet some coolie at the Warren Street dock and the chink was to take him to Wong. That's where he gets paid off for knocking off your friend Carruthers. Says he don't know what boat it is."

Graham broke in swiftly.

"Thanks, Inspector. I can go it alone from here. Wouldn't be any sense sending a squad down there. The Chinese would never show us the ship. I'll play it solitary and I'll get on that ship whatever it is. Will you have the Harbor Police ready for action. I'll shoot a rocket from the deck."

Inspector King frowned.

"It's mighty dangerous business, Dick."

"Skip it," laughed Graham, grimly resolved. "If that chink gets loose with his fanatical dreams —"

Chapter VII
The Death Ship

Dick Graham sat in the stern of the little dory and watched the impassive coolie with narrowed eyes. It was a dark night, and, fortunately, starless. The water rolled blackly beneath the bow of the craft.

The Secret Service operative was well aware of the risk he was taking, of the dangers he faced. But he was inspired by the knowledge that he had Doctor Wong on the run and that this night would likely result in a clash that would be heard around the world.

The idea of this Chinese madman possessed of the power that his influence over his own race would give him, and secure in the grasp of the two most remarkable inventions in the history of the civilized world, gave Graham an added thrill with his realization of the part he was playing tonight.

Back along the shore the dock lights twinkled. Beyond, over the dark outline of the water-front glimmered the scattered lights of the great city itself. A metropolis such as this would be but a toy in the hands of Doctor Wong-if he was allowed to flee. And here he was. He'd fooled the stupid Chinese slave and was drawing nearer and nearer to his despised heathen enemy.

Graham wanted to speak, to say something. But he could not talk with this silent Oriental. And now, ahead of them, a blacker bulk in the darkness, loomed the huge hull of some ship. Was this the boat they were rowing for?

"This boat?" he leaned closer and motioned in the dark. "This Wong's battleship, China boy?"

"Yes," answered the yellow man, who was a mere blob in the night. "Boat of Plince Wong."

This was what Dick Graham was waiting for. The time had come. Sliding his service revolver from his pocket he moved up to the Chinese and shoved the gun into the yellow man's face.

"Good," he whispered. "Now, no blabber out of you, mister. Ship those oars, and put your hands up nice."

Awed by the weapon the yellow man did as he was bid. Graham watched cautiously. One oar came in. The Chinese shrugged resignedly and drew in the other. Then, swiftly, uttering no sound, he swung that long wooden blade.

Graham ducked, felt the oar swish over his head, and he leaped forward to smash the gun barrel down on the coolie's head with an audible crunch. The Chinese slumped soddenly into the bottom of the boat.

Slowly, alertly, Graham sculled the craft through the dark toward the steamer. Feeling his way along he came at last to a rope. And taking a firm hold of it, shoved the rowboat away into the tide. Then, hand over hand, listening as he went, Dick Graham climbed toward the deck. Crouching outside the rail, he halted, tense, but heard no sound.

"Funny," he mused, peering into the blackness of the night. "Don't seem to be a soul on deck."

Assured that this was possible he slid quietly over the rail and touched his feet on the firm deck. Here he crouched again and waited. Well, he was on Doctor Wong's boat anyway.

If he could get to the bridge and shoot a rocket from there he might be able to stand the yellow fiends off until the Harbor Squad arrived. This, then, was his job.

"Here she goes, boys," he told himself, and began to creep carefully along the deck. In the shadow of a lifeboat he paused to bring out his rocket pistol. This he examined and found ready for use. He now had the rocket pistol in his left hand and his service revolver in his right. He'd better be careful lest some speck of light find the metal on those weapons and mark him for some watchful eyes. Maybe they had already discovered him and were lying in wait. Well, it was his chance. He had to take it.

It took Graham many minutes of crawling to reach the bridge. There was no sign of life around him yet. His jaw was set in a hard outline as he stared about him. The shooting or the rocket might arouse the whole ship.

"The devil with them," decided Graham. "Let the yellow rats come!"

It might be his death warrant, but Dick Graham raised the rocket pistol, aimed it into the black sky and fired. Crack! A weird hiss marked the trail of the rocket as it went soaring upward, up, up into the dark, leaving a trail of whispers and a faint line of its passage that Graham could see for only a flash. Then, pop! it burst high up in the air.

A brilliant crimson flare blossomed aloft and the Secret Service agent flattened himself down in the shadows, watching, alert, ready for whatever broke.

For long moments he sprawled there, listening, watching the fluttering red glare above. The deadly quiet of the boat remained unbroken. No footfall reached his ear. Why? Graham rose and searched about, emboldened by the silence. Creeping back to the deck he began hunting the ship.

Somewhere back down the river there were police on their way to him now. They must be coming. If anything started it was up to him to fight the chattering yellow horde off.

Foot by foot he searched the deck, stalking along like a ghost, on tiptoe, more mystified with each step. Could it be that Wong and his henchmen were all below somewhere, in some private cabin waiting for the set time to sneak out of the big harbor?

The idea sent Graham groping about until he found a companionway leading below. To another deck. Here he took up his hunt again. At times he bumped into bulkheads and the dead ends of alleyways. Then, when he had about decided that he was either on the wrong ship and had been tricked by the coolie, or that Wong and his party had not yet arrived-he heard a soft heathen voice from somewhere ahead of him.

Crawling patiently toward the sound Graham came at last to a skylight. One of the ventilators was open and the Secret Service agent tiptoed to this. Peering over and down, he drew back with a smothered oath.

There in the saloon below, surrounded by a crowd of his yellow henchmen, stood Doctor Wong. Before him, held by a pair of grinning Orientals, was the girl, Ariadne. The would-be prince of the world wore a broad smile, and his eyes gleamed with a strange fanatical light. Close by him stood a half-nude yellow giant bearing a gleaming two-handed sword.

As Graham strained his ear to catch what Wong was saying he managed to get:

> " —and she has served us, but not of her own will. But her service is ended; we need her no more. Therefore she must die by the will that has guided her. It is mine!"

A rousing thunder of approval greeted his words and Graham gripped his revolver tighter, and listened as the Oriental murder master continued.

"Her fate is decreed, but she should know this fate and will die without my will to protect her from fear. Death to all white infidels." His eyes were fixed on those of the girl now and he spoke in clear, distinct English. "You are free, Ariadne. Go back to your own weak will."

Horror took hold of Graham as he watched the girl. Her expression changed. Slowly the glazed, dull eyes blinked. The hard, masklike face softened; the rigid tensity of her muscles relaxed.

Bewildered, she stared at Wong, at the yellow horde which surrounded her. Lastly her eyes fell on the gleaming sword, and a shrill, unearthly scream clamored from her throat.

It was more than the white man could stand and with a curse he leaped back from the skylight.

A running jump and he hit the glass feet first, plunging through amid the smash and clatter of the broken skylight. Bedlam broke out below him as he dropped. Thud! Graham scrambled to his feet amid scurrying Orientals who shouted and babbled like maniacs in fright and consternation. Blam! The brute with the sword was the first target for his revolver. The thunder of the shot echoed like a cannon in a tomb.

Right and left he fired, picking his enemies at random. For every cartridge he claimed a dead Chinese and gradually he fought and staggered across the saloon to the girl.

The voice of Wong filled the ship as the yellow beast strove to gather his clan about him, to urge them on to attack the wildly fighting Secret Service man. Even with a gun Graham could never hope to rout this horde, and as he reached the girl, and tried to sweep her up under one arm, he felt the vile grip of yellow hands.

Like the tentacles of a huge octopus the claws of the yellow men fastened on Graham, choking him, binding his arms, smothering him in a deluge of scrambling, floundering bodies. With empty gun, with fist and feet he fought and clubbed, kicking, jerking right and left, fighting more desperately than he had ever fought in his life-for his life.

But he was done for. The odds were too great. He was clamped in hands of steel at last and dragged bodily to where Doctor Wong, calm and confident, stood in judgment.

"You dog of an infidel," snarled the Chinese terror. "You come to me for death."

Dick Graham, panting and bleeding from a score of cuts and scratches, stiff and sore already from the terrific beating this mob had administered, hung in the grip of his captors and said nothing. He only glared defiantly at the grinning Wong. His brain was seething with fear, not alone for himself, but for this unfortunate white girl; fear that this was his last chance, that the police would be too late-or that they had never even seen the signal rocket.

"It is a thousand years since the Cantonese Confucius has tasted of a human sacrifice, my infidel friend. Tonight we shall go back through the centuries to the death of the snakes."

Wong spoke the words solemnly with all the dignity at his command, then he swung and swept his arms in a wide gesture. His jeweled hand pointed to where Dick Graham could see the ebony chest. That same chest with the inlaid ivory patterns. And in it-the glittering idol with the writhing white snakes.

"Bring the white fool to me," concluded Doctor Wong. "Here where we shall watch him feed the guardians of the jade Confucius."

Unresisting the Secret Service operative was dragged roughly across the ship's saloon.

Chapter VIII
The God That Was Eternal

Roaring like a pack of famished wolves, the Chinese crowded about the captured white man. The girl, too, was dragged up close where, as the fiend Wong declared, she might witness the feeding of her beaten rescuer to the reptiles.

Held there like a toy in the powerful grip of many hands Dick Graham, grated his jaws and resolved to put his brain to work quickly. A wild idea had come to him, come like a flash as he remembered Professor Carruthers and the things he had learned from the scientist about the jade idol.

"It's worth a fighting chance," mumbled Graham between his battered bleeding lips.

Standing there he saw Doctor Wong's long-nailed finger touch the magic button on the chest. The ebony panel slid back, and there-behold! —a king's ransom in jewels, a nest for the squirming, twisting adders the sight of which brought a terrified scream from the now conscious Ariadne's lips.

It was a ghastly sight. Graham shuddered in spite of himself. And he noted now that the whole ship seemed to have become strangely silent. Even Doctor Wong was motionless. But this was only stagecraft on the crime-mad Oriental's part. His lips moved again.

"Force the infidel's hand in there, Foo Ling," ordered Wong pointing toward the sinuous swaying heads of the serpents. "Feed him to the eternal guards of Confucius. Even the poison of this white blood cannot destroy them. Nothing can destroy them. Nothing can destroy the eternal image itself. There is no fire or steel can destroy what the Gods themselves have fashioned with their own hands. Bring him up and deliver him to the eager snakes."

Here was Graham's moment, his last chance for life. In the very face of death, a death he could smell with the stench of the reptiles, he made his play.

Like a steel spring he tore himself from the grip of his Chinese captors. With a single motion he wrested the huge sword from the headman's grasp and he swung.

Right and left-and left and right-he slashed furiously, driving the yellow mass backward.

Then, with a fierce battle-cry, he turned toward the idol and the serpents.

Swish, slash, crash!

The heavy, gleaming blade screamed through the fetid atmosphere of the steaming bodies. One snake, two, three. Graham worked like a man possessed, grunting with the effort, sweating, slashing heads from the eternal snakes, smashing the phoney idol to smithereens, scattering the cheap paste gems right and left, until the saloon was littered with plaster and paste.

Under the scurrying feet of the yellow men the fake idol and the jewels were crunched into powder. Chinese fell before his swinging scythe, and over it all hovered the fiendish cry of Doctor Wong, fear staring from his eyes, horror driving him backward from the path of the now berserk Secret Service agent.

"Slay him! Slay him!" bellowed Wong, beside himself. "Kill the infidel who destroys our gods!"

But it was a roar of wrath that sprang from a hundred throats. Egged on by the fear of this prince of evil, the yellow maniacs surged back, gathered, prepared to charge the white daredevil. And Graham, the dripping blade held ready, faced them.

"Fools!" he shouted. "You let him trick you. Wong is an impostor. He uses you to gain riches for himself. Is that eternal? Did I not destroy it with this ordinary sword? You poor pigs, to let this mad thief lead you into death without honor. He has played with you like pawns, bowed you down to a thing he pasted together of clay and imitation gems. He is your enemy. He is the enemy of your ancestors, betrayer of your gods!"

Slowly the truth sank home in the tortured brains of his listeners. Knives were raised in menacing hands, and the eyes of the mob swung from the white man to the figure of Doctor Wong.

A coolie touched it off with a shout of righteous rage. He started swiftly toward Wong, knife upraised. And with a rising roar for revenge, he closed in on the Emperor of Death.

It was a good time to retreat and Dick Graham snatched the wilting white girl in his arm and started for the companionway. The snarling, scrambling clash of bodies behind him told the story of the fierce onslaught. Doctor Wong was cornered by his own betrayed race.

As Graham reached the deck and the outer night air, he felt the bumping of smaller boats against the hulk of the steamer. Looking overside he saw the men of the Harbor Police squad coming swiftly up the ship's side. In a flash they were over the rail.

The lieutenant grabbed Graham. "What's happened?" he demanded hurriedly. "Lord, you're cut all to hell. Where's Wong?"

Graham left the girl with one of the police as guard and led the lieutenant with a group of officers below. From the doorway in the saloon he pointed to the mess. Over in one corner of the long saloon a tangled heap of writhing Orientals fought and clawed, their knives dripping, flashing.

"Wong is finished, I guess," said Graham. "He'll be under that heap somewhere, Lieutenant."

The police officer shot quickly over the crest of the squirming human heap. The bullet smashed into the bulkhead. But its message was plain. There was a swift unpiling of the fighting yellow men. Knives clattered to the floor. Hands were upraised in meek surrender. The sight of the sturdy bluecoats, the deadly looking pistols in their fists, calmed the place quickly.

When the mutineers had been backed to the wall and the room cleared Doctor Wong was found lying face down on the carpeted floor. He was a mass of wounds, and blood was spattered all about.

"Dead, huh?" muttered one of the policemen.

"No," grumbled the lieutenant. "Almost. These Chinese are a hard lot to kill, they tell me. Put the irons on him, Mike. We'll take him along."

Wong was promptly handcuffed. A pair of bracelets were also put on his ankles. Two burly lawmen lugged him away and up to the deck.

When Graham with his police friends and the chattering Chinese were again on the deck, the Secret Service man became aware that there were some strange police signals flashing across the water. Whistles were sounding, back and forth.

It was not long therefore, till another craft slid alongside the ship Doctor Wong had chartered for his world conquest. Over the side came Inspector King with a few more eager cops.

"Hello, Dick," greeted the inspector. "And"—he glanced at the girl, seated on a coil of rope—"this the woman in the case, eh? Well, I told you you'd get it. From the looks o' you, you damn near fed the fish."

"It wasn't fish this time, Inspector," grinned Graham. "But we had a close call with snakes."

"What about this girl?" demanded the police official. "Where does she fit in this?"

Dick Graham looked at her, then at King. The girl was weak, but it was a different girl entirely from the one he had known in his battles with the Chinese devil.

"She don't fit in at all, Inspector," replied Graham. "She was just another one of the madman's victims."

"Looks to me as if you were a couple of victims," laughed King heartily. "Suppose we get you patched up and write this thing off. Come on."

"But about Wong," added Dick Graham, as the party climbed down into the boats, and the yellow prisoners were herded into another. "I have got a little business with him in Washington, Inspector, and I'd like to see him in a Federal pen."

"You can have him, Dick," agreed the police official, "but I have an idea that when you've washed your hands of him in Washington you'll have enough. If he lives through the night I'll turn him over to you tomorrow and you can take him along."

"And if he don't live," chuckled Dick Graham, who had added another star to his record for the Secret Service, "you can have him. If there's anything I'd have no use for its a dead Chinaman."

Fangs of Murder

Chapter I
Underworld Elections

"You're wanted on the phone, Mr. Ricco. Long distance calling from New York City."

The big, scar-faced man in a flashy bathing suit turned with a scowl of annoyance on the pier where he sat sunning himself over the clear blue waters of Lake Arrowhead.

"Okay, bud," he growled. Getting up, he followed the white-jacketed attendant past other lolling guests of the quiet Adirondack summer resort to a chrome-studded, modernistic bathhouse. Here, in the indicated private booth, he lifted a waiting receiver.

"Yeah?" he demanded.

"This 'Scars' Ricco?" came a voice, at once coarse and yet seeming to hold an acrid, mocking tone.

"Yeah, go ahead!"

"I'm a pal of yours, Scars. Got a little tip for you. Somethin' about what's been doin' here in N.Y. while you're tannin' that beef of yours-somethin' about your mob."

Ricco scowled. But a crafty light showed in his eyes. "Mob?" he echoed naively. "I don't know what you're talking about."

"Cut the stall, Ricco. Just get this! Your mob's taken a powder on you! They've all sold out to Monk Gorman-every one of 'em!"

Ricco's fleshy body stiffened. The diagonal scar on his cheek suddenly stood out, livid. His voice roared.

"Monk Gorman? Why that cheap, nickel-dipping punk ain't got enough dough to buy out —" He broke off, seemed with an effort to steady himself. The scar went dull again as he gave a harsh laugh. "Well, now cut the kiddin'. Who're you and what do you want? You're talkin' to a busy man."

Unheeding this, the voice resumed, "Thought I'd get a rise outa you, Scars. I'm a pal of yours. And listen —"

When Ricco hung up, his scar was livid again. Eyes blazing, he stormed out of the bathhouse —only to burst in again, to grab his clothes.

Fifteen minutes later the stucco, gabled Arrowhead Hotel lost one of its best-paying guests-Scars Ricco, a guest who had been no trouble, kept to his own business, tipped generously. The answer to a management's prayer.

With luggage piled in the rumble seat of his canary-yellow Packard roadster, Ricco drove down the graveled road, out of the rustic gate, and onto the highway for New York.

The big roadster gathered speed as it hurled along with muffler open. It took a long hill, then shot along a level but curved road where white fencing and signposts warned of a sharp, steep embankment. Ricco, his scar livid, hunched over the wheel, mouthing oaths in tune to his fierce thoughts. Before repeal he had controlled the biggest bootleg racket in New York. And he was still a big shot! He still knew how to hold a mob together and-He broke off from his thoughts with a sudden exclamation of alarm. A shadowy shape had closed in swiftly, overtaking him under cover of his exhaust and was now crowding him toward the precipice. He had no time to distinguish it; it was like some Juggernaut bearing down on him.

Ricco's foot left the gas-pedal of his canary roadster. His hand tugged at the wheel. If he felt terror, his throat had no time to express it. For in the next instant there was a brief but jarring impact, the scrape of tortured fenders. There was a kaleidoscopic impression before Ricco's eyes of white fence-posts swinging towards him, parting crazily, flying to both sides.

The careening roadster crashed through the fence, toppled over the embankment. It rolled and rolled, while glass broke and metal snapped groaningly. With a resounding crash the car struck the jagged, stony foot of the cliff-like embankment. Debris mushroomed up, settled —

A pall of dreadful silence remained over the wreck.

In the twisted, broken mass which a moment ago had been a sleek yellow roadster, Scars Ricco sprawled, dead, with broken steering wheel crushed horribly against his ribs, blood drooling from his parted lips.

Above, on the highway to New York, that lunging shadow, a heavy, dark sedan, was shrinking speedily down the macadam, leaving the grim, broken fence far behind.

* * *

At Saratoga, the fifth race was well under way. Dutch Kaltz, comfortably settled in a grand tier box, grinned as he watched, his rubicund face wrinkled in satisfied folds around his Havana cigar.

The horses-thrilling blurs of flying hoofs and huddled jockeys-were coming around to the last stretch.

"Boy, oh boy, whatta race!" chortled Dutch Kaltz, his thick lips caressing the cigar. He turned to his companion, a bored-looking, faded blonde in a flashy green dress. She was stifling a wearied yawn.

"Listen, baby!" he said to her. "If 'Hot Foot' brings home the bacon, I'll get you that new mink coat for the winter."

The blonde came out of her trance with a snap that brought her to the very rail where she promptly shouted with the enthusiasm of a true turf-lover, "Come on, Hot Foot! Come on home-come on, Hot Foot!"

As the horses went into the finish stretch, an usher leaned over the box and slipped a note to Dutch Kaltz.

Annoyed, Kaltz opened it hastily. The cigar dropped from his suddenly gaping mouth. His eyes bulged at the bold, scrawled words:

> Your mob's run out to Monk Gorman. Someone's backing him with dough. Better take this tip from a pal and get busy.

Kaltz's rubicund face looked like a bloated moon. With a snarled oath, he leaped to his feet. Without a word of explanation to his companion, he began moving his shoulder-padded frame toward the exit of the box.

Simultaneously the crowd in the grandstand went wild with cheers. The human din drowned out all other sound. The blonde swept from her chair, yelling joyously as she turned.

"Hot Foot's in, Dutch!" she cried. "Oh Sugar, I can just see myself in that —"

She broke off as she saw Dutch Kaltz's vacated chair. Her eyes flashed with sudden anger across the box, to the exit gate. Then she screamed shrilly, wildly.

The rubicund figure of Dutch Kaltz lay slumped on the floor just beneath the exit. Blood lay in a pool around it. There was a blood-fringed hole in the front of Kaltz's sport coat where the single high-calibred slug had entered, and done its ghastly work. Dutch Kaltz had seen-and run-his last race.

* * *

Indian summer had come to New York City. The night was close and warm. The sky, dull and starless, reflected the bright lights of Manhattan in a vague, ruddy glow.

On a desolate, deserted side street on the lower west side stood a big brick garage which looked as if it had not done business for some time. Its slide-doors were closed, the glass panes covered up so that only dull chinks of light showed through.

But inside, there was sinister life. A crowd of men stood, smoking cigarettes, in various attitudes of attention. The light from naked electric bulbs starkly revealed their hard, coarse-featured faces, their shifty, ever-alert eyes.

"Okay, boys-the whole job's been done! An' without a hitch!"

The harsh voice rasped out in the confines of the garage, the voice of a burly, swart-faced man in a sport-belted slicker. Monk Gorman stood facing the crowd, his hand nestled smugly in a pocket which showed the protecting bulge of an automatic.

"You ain't workin', any of you, for your old bosses-because they just ain't going to be around any more!" he went on triumphantly. "All four of them are washed up, see. Kaltz! Ricco! Flowers Gorsh! And Big Boy Rinaldi!"

There was a grim but awed silence. Thugs who, until this night, had worked for one of those four big king-pins of New York City's underworld, looked impressed rather than regretful. In the unfeeling underworld there was little personal sentiment, especially when money flowed freely.

A broken-nosed man spoke then, with a self-important laugh. "Boy, did I finish Dutch in style! Nobody even heard that silenced gat when I clipped him from the aisle soon as he blew up over that note."

A pallid-faced, long-jawed thug put in, "Hell, Gus, you shoulda seen me sideswipe Ricco over that cliff—"

"Cut it, you mugs!" the big man in the slicker snapped out angrily. Again he addressed the hard-faced gathering.

"Them four babies all got just what was comin' to 'em, see? An' the same goes for anyone else who thinks he's big shot now! Why? Because you're workin' for a guy, bigger than any of these punks ever were! A right guy who won't keep you warmin' park benches while he goes off on vacations! They'll be dough, an' plenty of it! They'll be dough enough to buy the whole damn town! From now on we all got one boss-and we're doin' whatever he tells us, see?"

Eager eyes were fixed on the speaker.

Eager voices rose from the vast interior of the garage.

"Where's th' Big Shot, Monk?"

"Let's meet 'im! Th' dough you jes' passed out from him is like old times!"

"Is he comin' here, Monk?"

"Whadda we do next?"

Monk Gorman again held up his hand for silence.

"I've already told you guys that th' big shot's been-well, he's been sending me orders from where he's been hiding out. Yeah, he's coming to take personal charge tonight-about eleven, when the *Charlemagne* docks. But he ain't coming to this dump."

He paused and indicated the five bullet-riddled bodies which lay in a huddled heap in one corner.

"We've jes' finished our first job for him when we cleaned out Rinaldi's garage here, but we gotta scram. We got one more job to do, and then, if we do it right, we meet th' new Big Shot in person."

Chapter II
Murder by Appointment

Eleven p.m. the clock over the passenger gateway showed the time.

The huge, newly constructed pier on the Hudson River was jammed with people meeting the late docking S.S. *Charlemagne* which was nine hours ahead of its schedule. Private cars and taxis pulled up in turn outside the vast concrete and steel structure which was three city blocks in length.

In a rather small but handsomely finished office room of the big pier building which towered above cobblestoned Twelfth Avenue and the newly-built express highway which flowed north along the western edge of Manhattan, Inspector Thomas Gregg, chief of the Bureau of Detectives, spoke to seven elderly men.

"Without disrespect to you, gentlemen," he said gruffly, "I must say this sounds juvenile and screwy to me. The idea of a super-criminal staging a come-back after twenty years is ridiculous on the face of it. And there were no super-criminals twenty years ago. Why, I had one devil of a time even getting reports from the mid-west on this-er-Albert Millett. And look at the picture I got from Arizona —a smooth-faced kid with buck teeth. It's so faded you can scarcely decipher it."

"Inspector Gregg, you are making a grave mistake in taking this matter so lightly," said Carl Fenwick, the theatrical producer, in a solemn voice. "We were all young then, some younger than others, and photography was bad. You didn't know Al Millett. We did."

A sort of psychic shiver seemed to ripple around the group of seven at his words. Even Inspector Gregg felt it, and the hackles wanted to rise on his thick, red neck. This made the chief detective mad. He fairly scowled around the group which half-encircled him.

Seven elderly, influential, wealthy, distinguished men. He told them off mentally. Now that he thought of it, this was the first time Gregg had ever been in close contact with any of these prominent men-the very first time he had even heard of them appearing publicly together.

Clyde Dickson, gaunt-faced, with dark and brooding eyes, an unusually thick shock of grey hair on his oddly pointed head, was huddled deep in a leather armchair. He was the owner of the highly successful Palladium Club-one of New York's most luxurious night spots.

Stocky, broad of beam, heavy-jowled, but visibly short of legs despite their massiveness, Bernard J. Andrews leaned on a beautifully carved cane as rugged as himself as he stood there. Andrews was the president of a nationally known radio station.

Paul Corbin, owner and operator of a small chain of exclusive night clubs and cocktail bars, stood next. Corbin was small, slender, with an effeminate sort of face out of which looked large, tragic eyes which, in themselves, were beautiful. He wore loosely tailored tweeds which almost looked too bulky, too mannish for him.

John Gifford, massive-chested and craggy of features, with arms that were a trifle abnormal in length, sat beside Dickson and spoke to him in deep whispers. Gifford was a well-known operator of a huge amusement park at Coney Island and the designer of the breath-taking Leap-for-Life rocket ride.

Gordon Drake, a well known figure in the motion picture industry, stood looking out the window. Drake was the most handsomely proportioned man present. At fifty, his body was still classical in its lines. But he marred the sweep of his fine figure by wearing a light opera cape about his shoulders. And he always wore gloves.

Kenneth Meade, a renowned restaurateur, gaunt of feature and spare of frame, attired in evening clothes for his appearance at Milady's Salon, his newest and finest restaurant, was tapping on the desk and frowning anxiously.

Fenwick, the seventh man, was a tall, cadaverous individual clad in severe black and wearing a high, stiff collar which gave him a clerical air. Had he been funny instead of lugubrious, he could have walked right out on the stage in any one of his productions as the stage parson.

All of these men were prominent and respected. There was nothing particularly odd about them individually. But, together, they exerted a queer effect upon the inspector that was almost weird. It was an intangible feeling. Perhaps it was due to the fact that these men were noted for living so utterly alone. None of them were married. Their private lives were simple, retiring, exclusive. No two of them lived together, except the Marcy brothers, who had not arrived for this meeting.

Baffled, the inspector shook his head and scowled.

"All right, all right," he said. "Let's go over it again. This Al Millett was guilty of several minor crimes some twenty-odd years ago. The worst we can find is that train robbery in Utah, and he served a sentence for that. He called himself 'The Fang,' theatrically leaving a tiger tooth as a marker on the scenes of his depredations.

"The penitentiary sentence must have taken the starch out of him. He abandoned crime upon his release to become a showman. He joined Crowley and Buckill, the then-famous circus. That was the hey-day of circus business. They puffed him up as the 'Fang,' the man with the terrible and bloody history and the criminal mind which, if loosed, could wreck the country. And all he did was ride wild horses, shoot blank pistols, and generally exhibit himself as the madman from the gory West.

"That, gentlemen, may have gone over big in those days, but no hick town in the whole United States would give that sort of side-show attraction a second glance today.

"And, as for this Al Millett, the police of this day and time have never even heard of him. I am positive that you are needlessly alarmed over this twenty-year-old bugaboo —"

"But you don't understand!" broke in Gordon Drake, whirling about at the window. "We've explained that Millett disappeared suddenly just twenty years ago-right after his wife died. He blamed us for her death because we wouldn't back him in a venture of his own. He disappeared utterly, after swearing vengeance on us, individually and collectively. And, once a year, on the anniversary of his wife's death-for the past three years-he's been sending us grotesque warnings of hate and disaster. We showed them to you. They came from different parts of the world."

"We tried to trace these messages, but we couldn't," John Gifford spoke in his deep voice. "We thought at first like you are thinking now, but time has changed us. And this time we received this message which promises death to us, one at a time. We would have been foolish not to come to the police for aid."

Inspector Gregg picked up one of the seven copies of identical messages from "The Fang," and read it again.

In block-printed letters of red on black parchment paper, the words stared up at him.

MY TIME FOR REVENGE DRAWS NEAR AT LAST ON THIS TWENTIETH ANNIVERSARY OF BURNOOSE'S DEATH. WHEN THE *CHARLEMAGNE* DOCKS IN NEW YORK NEXT TRIP YOU SHALL FEEL THE FANG OF DOOM. ONE BY ONE NINE MEN SHALL DIE-IF I MAY CALL YOU MEN. WHO SHALL GO FIRST? I INVITE YUH TO MY DEBARKATION.

Inspector Gregg cleared his throat and glanced swiftly around the circle. He was surprised to find all seven men watching him in nervous intensity.

"This is theatrical hokum," he snorted. "It stinks of melodrama. I'm amazed that you let such a crank letter disturb you. And whoever heard of murder by appointment?"

"Inspector Gregg," said Carl Fenwick in a sepulchral voice, "please bear in mind that this Al Millett was a far more desperate and depraved character than you are giving him credit for, and that he hates the nine of us with a vindictiveness that fairly seethes in its intensity."

"It's too bad the Marcy brothers aren't here to talk to you, Inspector Gregg," added Paul Corbin in his queer, husky voice. "They knew Millett more intimately, and can give you fuller details."

"Anyway, we've increased the police guard for the *Charlemagne's* docking, and I have a cordon of plainclothes men on hand to apprehend this Millett guy for questioning and investigation. And you are here to point him out to us. So we'll pull his 'fangs' before he can even sink 'em in a piece of pie at the Automat."

"If we point him out," observed Kenneth Meade in his stilted, slow, hoarse manner of speech. "He may be in hiding—a stowaway. Perhaps he's changed his appearance-other men have. He was fiendishly clever with disguise. I wish—"

"The Marcy brothers!" ejaculated Gordon Drake from the window. "I see their car just pulling up. They're not getting out, of course."

"Why should they?" commented John Gifford quickly. "The boat's docking. We'd better get out of here ourselves."

"We'll see what the Marcys say, first," decided Inspector Gregg, leading the way swiftly out to the parking lanes, the others following him more slowly.

The Marcy car, resplendent with glittering nickel and liveried chauffeur, was parked in a little cleared space back from the front lines, as if shrinking from publicity.

In the rear seat, two brothers with faces startlingly similar, save that Benjamin wore a mustache, while Lyle was clean-shaven, looked out at the approaching detective. Famous as theatre owners, they shrank from notoriety.

"Well?" Benjamin Marcy's mustache bristled at the converging group, although his piercing eyes had the same brooding, world-weary, yet anxious look that all these worried men seemed to have. "You don't expect us to get out and jam into that crowd, do you? I'm tired."

"Just tell me in few words what you can about this guy Millett," Gregg spoke swiftly.

As one, the two brothers leaned forward.

"Al Millett must be a madman," Lyle Marcy stated, his lean face darkening. "We were all in the show business together many years ago.

"Millett got terribly angry when we wouldn't pool our money and back him in a crazy wild-west show of his own. His wife died, and he disappeared, after threatening us with revenge. As for his coming back now—"

"We don't believe it!" Benjamin Marcy broke in fiercely. "This whole thing is somebody's idea of a bad joke."

"Whose?" demanded Andrews, panting from his laborious exertions to arrive at the car in a group with the others, leaning heavily on his cane.

"You Marcys know you're as worried about this thing as any of the rest of us."

"The only thing I'm worried about is the publicity," denied Benjamin Marcy savagely. "Lyle and I hate publicity!"

The sound of a hoarse, bass siren shook the air around them. Growing commotion at the docks warned them.

"Come on, you men, and take your positions on the second level," cried Gregg. "All passengers disembark there. You can't miss your man, if he comes ashore."

Leaving the grimly waiting Marcy brothers, the group made its way to the spacious second level where alphabetical partitions awaited tourists and luggage.

Pulleys creaked, winches groaned, and the huge liner came gently to rest. In a moment the gangways came sliding down, and people were pouring along them like ants. A pair of plain-clothes officers stood by at each exit, watching for the chief inspector's signal. Gregg watched the faces of his companions who went to their appointed stations, staring nervously all along the side of the great ship and up and down the gangways.

Nothing happened. The stream of passengers dwindled, died away. And no alarm had been given.

"Well, gentlemen," grunted Inspector Gregg a bit peevishly an hour later. "After all your hullabaloo, your Nemesis doesn't seem to have even got off the boat. If you can wait another hour, I'll have the ship inspected from stem to stern to make sure your man is not aboard."

"Please," whispered Meade in his odd articulation. "We must be certain."

"Where's Andrews?" demanded Drake suddenly. "He's supposed to be watching the D to G section."

"There he is," Gregg pointed. "Guess he just went down to the washroom for a moment. You haven't seen this building until you tour it. It is conveniently arranged so that everything is accessible from almost any part of building or grounds. Well-engineered construction. Well, let's go on board and —"

The sudden wail of a police ambulance beat upon their eardrums and rose in a sharp crescendo of sound. Police whistles shrilled. Somewhere a woman screamed. A uniformed officer dashed up to Inspector Gregg and began murmuring in his ear. At once Gregg stiffened. He motioned brusquely for the policeman to lead the way. As they followed, very white of face, the seven elderly men who had been responsible for him being here tonight fell in line as he passed their posts, and streamed along after him.

Down in the parking area the night had turned into bedlam. Red-faced patrolmen were forming lines to keep back the surging crowd and divert traffic. Screaming sirens announced the arrival of radio and squad cars. Frantic terror clutched at the hearts of the men following the chief detective as they realized the direction they were heading.

The Marcy limousine, still in an area of shadows, but no longer avoiding publicity, was before them. The car itself was harshly outlined now in the concentrated glare of police hand torches. The first thing of significance that caught Inspector Gregg's eye was the liveried chauffeur, lolling over his wheel. The back of his skull was a bloody ruin, bashed in by some blunt instrument.

The inspector's eyes went to the rear of the car. He braced himself for this look. The uniformed man had told him what he would find. Even so, hardened to crime as he was, he recoiled. His usually placid face went grey, eyes widening in a shock of horror and revulsion.

Benjamin and Lyle Marcy were still together in the back seat, but they had slumped down. Where their abdomens should have been, there was a gaping hole in each corpse, in the back of which the very spinal columns were exposed. Blood and viscera splattered and fouled the seat, the sides, and the floor of the tonneau.

The faces of the two brothers were frozen in grimaces of agonized horror. Their sightless, staring eyes seemed still to be looking at the hideous, brutal death monster that had struck them down. A very bad joke, indeed, Messrs. Marcy!

Paul Corbin had pushed forward behind the chief detective. He saw, and a shrill, high-pitched scream left his lips.

"God!" he shrieked. "The Fang! He's killed the Marcys. We told you, Inspector Gregg-but you wouldn't believe —"

"Get a grip on yourself, man!" snapped Gregg curtly. "We'll see about this. There's been murder, yes; but shut up about this Fang business if you don't want publicity. You're as jittery as a woman."

He turned to the police captain near at hand. "Okay, Donaldson, boil it down for me-quick!"

"Very little, inspector," was the grimly terse answer. "No sound, nobody seen approaching or leaving the car because all eyes were on the docking *Charlemagne*. A late-arriving taxi driver noticed the slumped body of the chauffeur, took one look, and yelled for help. We are holding him for questioning. Rather weird, sir."

"Check," nodded Gregg. "I'll say it's weird. No clues?"

"Only this, sir," said the captain, and he held out a large saber tooth —a tiger fang. "I found this in the front seat by the chauffeur."

As he stared, Gregg's color drained out of his cheeks. Was it possible, after all, that Al Millett had come back after a lapse of twenty years to avenge himself for a fancied wrong?

His eyes went to the big, lighted liner with her rakishly slanted funnels still smoking at her berth. His men had watched every egress from that vessel. Seven anxious and determined men had gazed carefully at each disembarking passenger. After forewarning his victims, had some fantastic, theatrically inclined madman eluded all detection and slipped ashore to commit his first murder?

"All right, Donaldson," Gregg spoke. "You're in charge. Get pics, prints, suspects-everything you can. I'll go over it with you later. As for you seven gentlemen, I think, perhaps, you'd better go —"

A cop from a prowl car dashed up.

"Inspector," he saluted hurriedly, "there's been a near-riot at the Marcy Gold Slipper. Monk Gorman at the head of a big mob pulled a hijack stunt right under the noses of the theater crowds. Captain Waltham is over there hollering for you."

Marcy Gold Slipper! The finest, newest playhouse the Marcy brothers had built. And Monk Gorman-Monk Gorman, a muscle-man of no outstanding intelligence-had headed a successful robbery there! Robbery at their own theater while the Marcys themselves got murdered here! It didn't make sense, didn't tie in with the story of the nine alarmed men at all.

"On second thought," Gregg said to the white-lipped and shivering men behind him-towering figures in the entertainment world, but frightened children beside him now —"you men had better go home and stay there until you hear from me again. As soon as I look into both of these crimes closely, I'll get in touch with each of you. I'll furnish a police escort to see you home, a guard to stay all night, if you wish."

Paul Corbin, the excitable, laughed hysterically. He was assisted away by two uniformed officers. His wild cry came back over his shoulder.

"We'll need the whole police force to guard us now, Inspector Gregg," he shouted sobbingly. "For whoever heard of murder by appointment?"

Chapter III
Enter the Phantom

The towering, midtown *Clarion* Building, which housed the city's leading newspaper reared high in the night mists. Its windows glowed with lights; from its lower floors came the pounding of rotary presses-giving evidence that here activity went on perpetually, day and night.

It was well after midnight when a large but unobtrusive Cadillac sedan swung around the corner, its lights dim. It slowed near the chrome and glass doors which were the imposing front entrance of the *Clarion* Building.

Four slouch-hatted men peered from the open front and rear windows of the sedan. Their hat brims, snapped low, obscured their hard, brutal faces.

"Stop right here, Tony." A broken-nosed man leaned forward from the rear to tap a pallid, nervous driver.

"Okay, Gus!" Tony applied the brakes, but even when he had the car stopped at the curb, he kept the engine purring. "Hope this ain't gonna take long —"

"Don't be so jittery! This is a cinch!" Gus was leaning from the window, eyes covering the pavement. Every time a pedestrian neared the front doors of the building, especially when some hurrying newsman or other person connected with the paper entered those doors, Gus tensed a little, hand darting to his armpit holster. "Be ready, guys-we gotta pull this job smooth!"

"Say, who we gonna smoke?" the hatchet-faced man next to Gus demanded now. "This is the *Clarion's* joint, ain't it? Seems to me I heard somethin' special about this place —"

"You sure did, Choppy!" the fourth man, in the front, spoke through a gash of a mouth from which a cigarette dangled to bob with his words. "Hell, the *Clarion's* the rag that acts the contact for that bird called *the Phantom!*"

A strange awed dread followed the pronunciation of that sobriquet —a dread which seemed instantly to course through his companions, like a wave. Hate, the hate born of utter fear, gleamed from their eyes.

The Phantom! Throughout the underworld of the entire nation, that name had become a byword of fear. The Phantom, lone Nemesis of Crime, a living, elusive scourge who personified the antidote to crime!

"The Phantom!" Tony cried, hoarsely now. "Say, Gus-is *that* who we're waitin' for?"

Gus quickly shook his head. "Take it easy, guys! The Big Shot ain't interested in anyone unless he sticks his nose into this-which he won't if he's got brains! They say the Phantom made things pretty tough for us, sendin' so many of us up the river-but this boss is one guy he can't buck! Naw, we ain't after that slippery bird. We're just doin' a job on a punk named Eddie Collins, who draws them funnies you see in the papers."

"Funnies? You mean comic cartoons?" the gash-mouthed man said in surprise. "Hell, what do we want to bump a guy who draws *them* for?"

"Maybe the Big Shot don't like his funny pitchers, Pete," Tony put in, with sardonic mirth.

"You don't know how right you are!" Gus chortled, a purposeful look in his eyes. "But you just follow my lead —I'm runnin' this job. 'Course I'd rather be with Monk and the rest-they got another big heist job. The boss certainly knows how to get things movin' fast-why, he's only taken over the mobs last night, and we've done more than we did in years for our old big shots! The coppers'll never keep up with us now! Hell, there was hundreds of 'em down at that pier when the boat landed, and right under their noses —" he paused, as if realizing he was getting loquacious.

But the others broke in eagerly now. "You was there, Gus. Did you see him?"

The broken-nosed Gus swelled instinctively with a sense of importance. "Sure," his voice was unconvincingly casual. "Sure I seen him."

"What'd he look like, Gus? What kinda guy was he?"

"Well now-he was kinda muffled up in a coat. Couldn't spot his mug. But I seen his work-and that was enough! What he done to them two brothers, all by himself—" Despite himself he gave a shudder. "Don't know how the hell he done it. I'd sure hate to be on the wrong side o' that guy, and —"

Abruptly he broke off, body tensing, hand snaking from his armpit holster. A taxi had just pulled to the curb, ahead of the parked sedan. Out of it leaped a figure, turning in the gloom as the cab rolled on its way.

The figure strode down the pavement towards the *Clarion* entrance. Light from a street-lamp revealed him in the next instant. A stocky young man, hardly more than a grown kid-he was walking hurriedly, carrying a flat envelope under one arm.

"It's the Collins guy all right!" Gus spoke quick, low. "Okay, Tony! Step up that motor-he's comin' by! Me an' Pete'll use the rods."

Oblivious, the youth on the pavement walked on-coming diagonally abreast of the sedan in the next instant as two automatics trained their beads directly on his hurrying figure.

"Okay, Tony!"

The purring motor of the Cadillac rose abruptly to a vibrating clamor as Tony's foot jammed down the accelerator. The two guns leveled from the front and rear windows. Flame leaped livid in the night from their jerking muzzles!

The motor almost drowned completely the quick reports, so they were not heard by any passing motorists.

The four shots flamed in swift succession.

As if grabbed by some unseen giant hand in the dark, the youth on the pavement stopped in his tracks. His stocky frame whirled completely around. His hands clutched at his chest-and through his clawing fingers blood spurted darkly.

Slowly, his knees buckled. He dropped on them. In contrast to the darkness, his face showed white, agonized as it turned towards the roaring but immobile sedan.

Then a choking cry as of defiance came from the youngster. He still clutched the manila envelope-and some miracle of purpose seemed to spur his riddled body into motion again. Crablike, half-crawling in the gloom, he was moving forward.

The broken-nosed Gus saw that movement, gave vent to a livid oath. He yanked the rear door of the Cadillac open, his eyes peering up and down the street. It was dark, deserted. He leaped out, gun in hand. Pete and hatchet-faced Choppy followed.

Simultaneously the riddled youth, evidently seeing them coming, was suddenly, miraculously on wabbly legs-running, darting like a wild, wounded animal, instinctively trying to lose himself from his hunters.

Clutching the envelope he actually reached the corner, rounding the building as the others gained in their pursuit. They did not fire now-for their quarry was only a vague blur in the almost opaque gloom caused by the shadowy side of the building, near a railed areaway.

In that gloom, Gus, Pete, and Choppy closed in. Their hands groped. There was the sound of a scuffle-the ripping of paper-confusion.

The three gangsters became accustomed enough to the dark to regain vision. They found themselves in a tangle.

Gus cursed. "He went over the rail! He can't get far with them slugs in him-an' I don't know if we got all we want! Come on, guys, we gotta find him!"

They climbed over the rail, dropping into the lower areaway. Groping in the gloom, guns still in hand.

And at that same instant, Eddie Collins, youthful cartoonist, was swaying against the cage of a freight elevator which was speeding upwards inside the building. He heard his own blood dripping to the floor of the ascending lift. Torpor was dragging at his agonized body. Yet, like some stubborn spark, a fierce determination was keeping him alive and active.

Floors went by in a blur, painfully slow. Up through the building the elevator ascended. Then it stopped of its own accord, on the top floor, up in the tower.

Collins pulled his coat about his chest as if hoping to stem the flow of his own blood. He groaned with the effort of opening the gate, staggered out through a corridor, thence through swing service doors.

Somehow he found the frosted-glass doors he sought. He pushed into a lighted, well-appointed anteroom. He pushed on through, reached another door, marked private.

Eddie Collins grabbed the door handle-burst into the huge, private office whose French windows looked high over the Manhattan night.

At his rude entry, two men jerked up startled, surprised heads.

Frank Havens, elderly, rugged-faced owner of the *Clarion* and a string of other equally powerful papers throughout the nation, rose to his feet from the big desk where he had been sitting, proof-sheets bearing gruesome murder-news before him.

Richard Curtis Van Loan, wealthy young idler and man-about-town, who was here as Mr. Havens's friend and guest, lifted his bored, world-wearied grey eyes in questioning annoyance. Seated in a comfortable chair, Van Loan was puffing idly at a cigarette, his immaculately dress-trousered legs crossed.

Then, before anyone could speak, the bored Richard Curtis Van Loan suddenly leaped from his chair. His grey eyes lost their ennui, became sharp slits. It was he who saw the oozing, crimson trickle coming from beneath Collins's coat and dripping soundlessly to the soft carpet.

Collins's body swayed giddily as Van Loan leaped forward. The latter's strong arms reached out, caught the young cartoonist even as the youth went limp, collapsing.

"This man's been shot!" Van Loan said, his customary drawl sharp now.

Havens's momentary annoyance turned to quick alarm. The publisher grabbed an inter-office phone, called a downstairs office secretary, ordering that a doctor be summoned. Then he went over to where Van Loan had carried the riddled youth to a lounge and placed him on it.

"Collins!" he cried, all concern now. "What happened? Who —?"

The eyes of Eddie Collins, already going dull, flickered. His lips moved. A sighing rattle made the words which came from his throat difficult to hear.

"Envelope —" he gasped. "Envelope! Gangsters-probably still down in areaway cellar looking for me. Freight elevator-They got it-from me-but they aren't sure —"

"Got what, Collins? What do you mean?" Havens spoke with fierce bafflement. "How could you —a comic strip man-be mixed up with thugs, with shooting!"

"Envelope tells," Collins repeated. "Big case-Mr. Havens. I was doing it for a feature-when murder story broke. Bringing it for-the Phantom-now."

Even in his agony, he pronounced that name with reverent awe.

Havens stiffened. The publisher's eyes flashed to his worldly young friend, Richard Curtis Van Loan. And he got a fresh shock of surprise.

For Van Loan had suddenly gone into a whirl of swift action! He had peeled off his dress coat. In his hands was a flat leather kit, which was snapped open, to reveal a mirror and an array of tubes and jars.

Again Collins's gasping voice interrupted. "Case-for Phantom! God, if only you could-get him now, Mr. Havens." He sobbed. "Envelope-thugs got it —"

Havens administered to the riddled man as best he could while Van Loan worked away on his queer little kit.

When the publisher turned toward Van Loan, his jaw gaped.

Van, standing close, eyes darting from the man on the lounge to his own mirror, was still dabbing his face with a special charcoal. In seconds his handsome, world-weary features had almost completely vanished! In their place had grown another visage-the face of Eddie Collins!

It was not a semblance that could stand close inspection under bright light, being more an impressionistic sort of job, the likeness cleverly created by a few lines, by shading. Nor did Van Loan take any more precious time adding to it.

"Give me Collins's coat, Frank-quickly! It ought to be enough!"

Van Loan pulled on the coat and assumed a stoop. Though he was tall, he seemed by his posture to look even more like the bullet-riddled cartoonist.

So swiftly had he made the transformation that now, before the dying Collins saw what was happening, his own "double" was darting out of the office in a swift blur of motion which concealed both the incongruity of his dress, and his makeshift disguise.

Collins hadn't seen any of this. Nor had Collins dreamed that Richard Curtis Van Loan, the rich playboy he had seen so many times, was actually the mysterious and amazing sleuth whose fearsome name he had breathed, whose services he had demanded —the *Phantom Detective* whose perilous exploits in the dark byways of the underworld were known by the police the world over.

Only Frank Havens knew that Van Loan was the Phantom; only Havens knew how this seemingly bored young millionaire really gave his energies and lifeblood to the most exacting and dangerous task on earth-the tracking down of baffling and ruthless criminals.

Even to Havens, the Phantom was always a source of surprise and wonder. His quick-working brain was too fast to follow: his quick changes in disguise left the publisher gasping-as they had left him now.

Yet Van had acted with logic while acting with speed. Snatches of barely coherent speech from Eddie Collins had registered themselves indelibly on his mind: Freight elevator-thugs-still looking for Collins —

The Phantom scarcely knew Collins, only vaguely remembered seeing the youthful cartoonist around the *Clarion* Building. Certainly he had no idea what this was all about. As a matter of fact, his mind had been on other matters-on a bizarre, double murder which Frank Havens had called him down to discuss. But when Collins had come in, riddled-bringing crime flagrantly to this very building-Van had promptly dropped all other thoughts.

The Phantom reached the freight elevator, with its blood-stained floor, in the next instant. His lithe body pushed into the car-his long arm slammed the gate shut and started the elevator down. He reached into his pocket, into which he had transferred a fully loaded blue-steel Colt .45 automatic, U.S. Army, M-1911 —the favorite weapon of the Phantom.

Musty odors of the cellar rose to engulf the slow-descending cage. The Phantom tensed, adopting again the pose of Eddie Collins. His hand was on his gun, his thumb snapping back the safety catch. He knew he was deliberately playing with Death in his risky scheme.

The cellar loomed, dim and empty. Nobody in here. He hurried across it on soft-soled feet, eyes alert. Reaching the door of the areaway, he opened it softly. Night breeze, still carrying the heat of the Indian summer, met him.

He was out in the areaway like a drifting shadow. In the gloom his keen eyes, which had the cat-like gift of piercing darkness, glanced about. No one here. A surge of disappointment, a sense of anticlimax, narrowed his eyes. Despite his swiftness, had he been too long in coming?

He vaulted over the rail then, to the street. Cautiously, again emulating Collins-even staggering a little now-he moved down the block. The nearest street-lamp flecked his face. He caught a blur of movement and he dropped to the pavement like a deflating sack. Dropped as his every nerve combined in sixth sense to flash the warning to his alert brain!

Two guns flamed livid out of the dark, their reports shattering the quiet side street off Broadway. Bullets whined over the prone Phantom as he hugged the sidewalk. They ricocheted inches away, chipping the paving.

"Got him this time, Gus?"

"Better make sure!"

Van rolled as he heard the coarse voices. He saw three slouch-hatted figures charging from another dark doorway of the building, where they had been prowling.

His Colt snaked out. Eyes grim, he fired even as he rolled into position —a blind, snap shot at the charging trio.

One of the three, a gash-mouthed man, recoiled with a scream of pain. His hand clawed at his shoulder, blood spurting through the wound.

The other two also recoiled, amazed by the counter-attack. The broken-nosed man in their lead stared at the Phantom, who even now was leaping to his feet.

Madly he fired his automatic-fired as a suddenly panic-stricken man would fire.

Van ducked sideways, out of the lamp-light. The bullets went so far wide he didn't hear them. Not only was the man's apparent confusion spoiling his aim-in his left hand he was busily clutching a manila envelope! The Phantom grimly raised his Colt again. He drew a careful bead on the man with the envelope.

"Beat it, guys!" the third man was yelling. "The shootin's been heard-The cops're comin'!"

Crack!

It was Van's Colt that blazed in that split-second.

A hoarse cry burst from the broken-nosed thug. As if it suddenly burned him, he dropped the envelope. It fluttered to the pavement. The Phantom's well-aimed shot had creased his wrist-making his pained muscles release their grip.

Across Broadway now two bluecoats came into view —a traffic and a beat cop, blowing their whistles, reaching with free hands for guns. The scream of a prowl-car added to the clamor.

Van hurled forward. The broken-nosed thug, nursing his wrist with his mouth, hesitated. Then, leaving the envelope, dashed on around the corner.

The Phantom scooped the envelope up without stopping in his pace. Rounding the corner, he saw the trio piling into a dark Cadillac sedan which started rolling from the curb in the next split-second, gears grinding raucously. Van leaped after it, then ducked.

Glass in the rear window shattered as a gun smashed its muzzle through. A fusillade of lead came from the departing car as it careened around the next block, swiftly disappearing. An oncoming green prowl-car sped in pursuit.

The Phantom, already grimly certain the gang car had had enough of a start to make a safe getaway, whirled back toward the *Clarion* Building, envelope in hand. He moved so swiftly that the police did not see him.

Again he used the freight elevator, riding back to the tower. The Phantom had struck again and disappeared.

Chapter IV
Gargoyle Clue

Van Loan entered the private office. He saw Frank Havens standing, eyes filled with deep pain. A grave-faced man he recognized as the *Clarion's* doctor was turning away from the lounge where Eddie Collins lay very still, a glassy look in his eyes.

The doctor shook his head. Then started as he saw the dead man's double in the doorway.

"Don't be alarmed, Doctor," said Van in Collins's voice. "The Phantom-not a ghost. Will you leave us, please?"

The physician left and Van quickly shut the door. He glanced at Collins. "Too bad, Frank-he seemed a plucky kid," his voice came hushed.

Havens spoke huskily. "I can't understand it, Van! Collins was just a comic strip man, a hard ambitious worker. Why he should be murdered like this —" He broke off then, with new concern. "But you, Van! What have you been doing? Did you see his murderers?"

"I did, and drew a little blood," Van returned grimly, as he substituted Collins's coat for his own. His long arm scooped up Havens's phone. Matter-of-factly, he put in a call to the police. "My deception worked for a moment. The gangsters were lurking, thinking Collins was hidden somewhere down there. The police are after them now. I guess they'll be coming up here any minute. Before they come, let's see what we can make of this envelope."

Quickly he took it to Havens's desk. Its flap was loose. Evidently hands had already been rummaging in it. For a moment the Phantom thought, with a pang of disappointment, that it was empty. Then he drew out its only contents—a single torn piece of white paper. Black pen-sketching and lettering showed on it.

"Seems to be some sort of cartooning!" Van observed. "Collins's work, apparently."

He spread it on the desk, and Havens came over to peer at it with him. The first thing that met their eyes was a bizarre ink-sketch. It showed a skull, a lurid death's head, and beneath it a playing card—a joker.

Letters printed underneath read: *"Impossible but true is the Gargoyle Club, which sometimes meets secretly at —"*

Here the paper was torn, the rest of the sentence missing.

"Gargoyle Club?" Havens read aloud. "What can *that* be? And that joker and skull?"

The publisher broke off, the blood suddenly draining from his face. For now his eyes had fallen on three other ink sketches which comprised the remainder of the torn cartoon.

One of the three was torn, not clearly distinguishable. But the other two were full and clear. Two faces, both similar, save that one bristled with a mustache while the other was clean-shaven, stared up at them.

With one accord the eyes of Havens and Van Loan went from that cartoon to the wet front-page proof-sheet on Havens's desk.

There, in a photograph this time, those two same faces stared out of the front page, beneath the bold black headline:

TWO SHOWMEN BRUTALLY MURDERED

"Good grief!" Havens gasped, his face white now. "The Marcy brothers! Collins drew them here! That's the sensational case I was trying to persuade you to tackle, Van! The case involving all those big men of the amusement world-the nine who told the police of this criminal, Al Millett, the Fang-who apparently came to America on the *Charlemagne* tonight-last night. It's nearly morning."

Van's eyes narrowed to slits. His keen mind had absorbed the facts of the strange case. The shake-up of four mobs preceding the landing of the ship-the newly organized mob of four dead leaders suddenly cutting loose-the police baffled by a terrific outbreak of crime and violence. And now-this!

"It seems this case had landed on us personally, Frank," he said grimly. "It's reached out and hit the *Clarion*! But look here. The murder was just a few hours ago, correct? And until now these men involved had not come forward into the limelight."

"That's right! And for some reason, Collins drew a picture-maybe he hoped it would break into the news section —"

"That's the point, Frank," Van said slowly. "Collins did *not* just draw this picture. Or even last night! The ink on it indicates clearly that it's at least a week or so old!"

"But, Van!" Havens protested. "That means Collins must have known something of the Marcys before anyone dreamed —"

"Precisely. Can you suggest any way he might have worked on such a tack?"

"I can't even hazard a guess, Van. Collins stuck to his cartooning in the comic strip. True, I remember his saying something about changing his line-but as for this drawing, with its skull and joker, and that stuff about the Gargoyle Club —" Confused, his grim eyes went to the lounge-as if bitterly wishing for the death-sealed lips of Eddie Collins to speak the secret that they could never now reveal.

Van, meanwhile, looked at the third and torn face on the cartoon. Only the top of the head and the eyes showed.

"Look here, Frank. Something queer about this picture."

Havens, looking, noticed a blackish protrusion on top of the head, as though the cartoonist's pen had slipped. "An ink-blot probably," he said. "Makes it look as if something is sticking in the head there. Funny —"

He broke off, stiffening, as heavy feet sounded at the office door. Van Loan swiftly took a black silk domino from his pocket and slipped it on over his Collins make-up.

A bluecoat, followed by two men in plainclothes, entered. One of the latter spoke, eyes instantly going with recognition to the publisher.

"There's been some shooting in the street, Mr. Havens. Was that why you called Police Head —"

He stopped short as his eyes glimpsed the prone, inert body of Collins. That was his first surprise. His second came as he and the other two policemen saw the domino-masked Phantom, who now stepped forward, eyes gleaming through his mask-holes.

"It's all right, gentlemen. I called. I'm the Phantom-already on the case." As he spoke his palm flipped open.

The two detectives and the bluecoat stared in awe at the scintillating sparkle which was revealed. A sparkle of matchless diamond chips, forming the design of a domino mask against a badge of platinum.

The emblem of the Phantom! An emblem which every law-enforcement agent throughout the nation had been taught to respect.

Van gave crisp commands. "You can take over here. Conduct the usual investigation. Call Homicide and the Medical Examiner. This man is Edward Collins, who worked for Mr. Havens and —"

The shrill buzz of the inter-office telephone interrupted. Havens quickly snapped the key, picking up the instrument. "Hello-yes?" He turned. "Is one of you men Lieutenant Donovan? Patrolman downstairs is asking for you."

The larger of the two detectives grabbed the instrument with a gruff, "Thanks."

"Yes?" he said. "*What's that?* Okay-be right down!"

He whirled from the phone, his face beefy with excitement. "Radio flash! Signal 30! There's a stick-up at the Palladium Club!"

Van tensed even as Havens looked momentarily bewildered. In his social life, as a night-club habitue, he knew about the Palladium, the most popular of hot-spots. But his keen retentive mind was telling him something else.

"That's Clyde Dickson's club, Frank!" he crisped. "Dickson-one of the nine men involved in this case!"

He whirled on the detectives. "You two men stay here! Officer, you come with us. Is there a cruiser downstairs?"

The detectives nodded.

"All right, Mr. Havens and I will use it!"

It was the regular express elevator which took the Phantom, Havens, and the bluecoat down to the street level. Hurriedly they ran out to the curb. Two prowl-cars were pulling away, sirens screaming. The cruiser, a small sedan, stood purring, a police driver impatiently shifting at its wheel, the radio blaring repeatedly: "Signal 30! All cars in Division 1 —"

The bluecoat with Van explained. And it was unnecessary for the Phantom again to display his badge. An instant later, with Van and Havens in the rear, the cruiser sped screaming through the night, headed up Broadway.

As it approached the fifties, the scream of other sirens became audible ahead. The cruiser tore around Fifty-Second Street-agleam at this late hour with its line of nightclubs, all going full tilt.

The cruiser squealed on its tires, as it came before the vast neon sign: "Palladium Club." Prowl-cars here were banked two deep-but some were speeding off, hell-bent. From within the club came sounds of pandemonium.

"Better stay here awhile, Frank!" Van crisped, as he leaped from the cruiser.

The Phantom, together with police who were still rushing into the club, hurried through its palatial entrance.

Many times, as Richard Van Loan, bored socialite, he had gone into this lavish club. He knew its interior well. Yet as he rushed in now, he scarcely recognized it.

The well-appointed hall of the club looked as if a cyclone had struck it. Though wall lights illumined the place, the huge chandelier which had furnished the main light was shattered where it hung.

On the dance floor, tables and chairs were overturned. The band dais was a confusion of tumbled instruments, overturned music stands. Above, swinging crazily and incongruously, was a brilliant-studded but empty trapeze on ropes.

Van identified it at once; he remembered that the main attraction of this club was an aerial artiste —a young girl known only as "Queen Stella" who furnished a new thrill to jaded society crowds with her acrobatics.

All this Van's eyes took in with a swift comprehensive glance. Then his gaze went across the floor. He saw a huddling, terrified mass of people. Women in low-cut gowns; men in faultless dress suits. All jabbering with that hysterical excitement that comes after a crisis.

"My jewels-they took my jewels!" he heard a woman shrieking.

"They got away with my wallet, damn them!" a man cursed.

Police were listening sympathetically. Other police were scurrying about the floor, taking command of the exclusive club. Some Van saw at exit doors, shaking their heads.

The Phantom realized, even as Frank Havens now came up behind him, that he had come just after the end of the stick-up. The mobsters had obviously cleared out.

"Since we are here, let's look around," said the Phantom. "Where is Dickson?"

No one had seen the club owner since the excitement began.

Frank Havens saw the Phantom hurl suddenly forward-running toward Dickson's office.

Van's dash carried him to a rear door, so well shadowed behind drapes that as yet the police had not noticed it.

The door was closed. But as the Phantom neared it, sounds behind it grew louder. And then not only Van, but several nearby policemen, stiffened-eyes going wide.

From behind the closed door came a sudden, hoarse scream! A scream which rose, in blood-curdling agony and terror!

"You!" the scream came. "It's you! No!" Shrill now it rose, in a high, quavering pitch. "Don't —Oh, God —*don't* —"

Even as the Phantom yanked at the locked door, that agonized cry broke off with horrible abruptness. There was a ghastly thud —a shatter as of glass.

Eyes slitted in their mask-holes, the Phantom whirled to the men behind him. "Give me a hand!" he crisped. "Get this door open!"

Chapter V
The Fang Strikes Again

Brawny bluecoats promptly charged that door. Wood splintered with the successive impacts of their big shoulders. The door burst from its lock. The Phantom, gun whipping out, was the first to leap into the room, police following at his heels.

In one swift comprehensive glance, Van's eyes took in the scene. Three sights stood out at once. A safe, its door open and still swinging, its interior bare and gaping; a broken window, looking out into black gloom; and-on the floor —a prone heap, lying terribly still.

The Phantom rushed to the broken window. Outside was an alleyway, but it led to a high, dead-end wall. His keen eyes told him that no one was there, although as he backed away, policemen climbed through the window with flashlights and guns to investigate.

Van darted back through the room. He found two more doors. One, unlocked, gave upon the street in front of the night club with its milling confused throngs. The other seemed to lead to the orchestra dais. He turned back to the corpse.

Gasped, sickened exclamations rose as patrolmen and detectives looked down at the inert heap on the floor. Looking up, the Phantom saw the rugged face of Frank Havens. He had never seen the publisher so pale, so fraught with lines of utter horror and shock. Havens's eyes, stark and wide, were fixed in awful fascination on that inert heap.

The Phantom studied the body closely. His first brief glance had already determined that the man was Clyde Dickson, wealthy, gaunt owner of this club; and that Dickson was as dead as any man could be.

The corpse was sprawled on its back. The eyes stared up, sightless and glazed. The gaunt features of Clyde Dickson looked unreal, as if they were some frozen snapshot of a face caught in a moment of unutterable agony and terror. Beneath the disheveled mop of hair on the night club owner lay a small wet pool of crimson blood.

No bullet had killed Clyde Dickson. No knife had stabbed him. The Phantom saw now why the police were looking down sickened, and why, especially, Frank Havens was staring in such an uncanny, horrified manner.

For something dark and long was protruding from the top of the dead man's skull!

Van's own nerves went cold. His hand instinctively touched his pocket, where the torn drawing of the hapless Eddie Collins crackled. Incredibly, weirdly, a portion of that drawing had become accurately simulated by the corpse in this room! That one, torn face, with something blackish protruding from the head-something Havens had called an ink-stain!

Grim-eyed, the Phantom stepped forward, bent down. He saw the protruding thing for what it was. A broken length of iron crowbar. A crowbar, large and thick, had been driven somehow through the skull of Clyde Dickson-through scalp and bone, into the brains beneath!

"Good God!" Havens started to gasp in horror. The Phantom's mask flashed up blackly; through its holes his eyes darted a tacit command to the publisher. Havens quickly turned away, silent.

"Say, in all my time I never saw anything like this!" It was a square-jawed captain of detectives who spoke now, hoarsely. "Hell, we heard him being killed-but how could anyone drive a bar like that through a man's skull, all in seconds too! And what devil —"

Even as he voiced the chill question, the Phantom, eyes sharpening anew, quietly pointed to the floor, to a spot about a foot away from that gruesome, crowbar-riven head.

A small object lay there, hideously familiar to the police, though Van himself looked at it for the first time.

It was a white saber tooth!

"The Fang!" Several police voices chorused in grim unison. "The Fang again!"

Twice in one night, since the arrival of the *Charlemagne*, an elusive, diabolical murderer had struck-struck under the very noses of the police, leaving his flaunting mark of death! And his second crime outdid the first in sheer, bloody mutilation!

The detective captain bawled out, in fierce rage: "This Fang can't be far away, damn him! We've got his description! We must get him!"

His eyes swiveled to the broken window then, for, as if to answer his words, wearied bluecoats were climbing back in, shaking their heads. "No one in that dead-end alley," one reported. "And no one but a human fly could climb that wall."

"Or a human devil!" the captain added.

Van's voice, cool despite his inner tension, came like a sane note in the raw-nerved agitation. "The breaking window might well have been a bit of decoying," he suggested. "The criminal might have gone out that door to the street to mingle with the crowd. Or he might have re-entered the night club, using that other door concealed by the orchestra dais."

This sent the police hunting in new directions. Some went out to the street; others hurried into the night club proper, where the patrons and employees, here since the big holdup, still stood, huddled and frightened.

The Homicide Squad arrived in the next seconds, faces already wearied from the work of the first murder. The City Medical Examiner came with Inspector Gregg, detective chieftain, whose own placid face was now looking dull grey, his eyes bloodshot and haggard.

"So you're in the case, Phantom!" The inspector, after grimly viewing the corpse, faced the man in the domino mask. "Maybe you can help us out-though really this case seems open-and-shut. If only we can get our hands on Al Millett!" He swore harshly. "I've been getting headaches from reports from every precinct, and a lot of well-meaning cranks as well. Every Tom, Dick, and Harry has been taken for Millett-but the right man is still loose, running the big mob organized tonight. He seems to be getting a crazy revenge by robbing and killing in this mad way!"

Shaken, he glanced again towards the corpse. The Medical Examiner was kneeling over the dead man now, his face pale despite his familiar acquaintanceship with death. "Well, Doc?"

The examiner raised baffled eyes.

"Beats me!" he confessed, crisply. "The Marcy brothers case was bad enough-obviously killed with some sort of ax. But a crowbar —I never saw it used this way in a murder! Can't see how a man could be strong enough to smash it through the cranium!"

The Phantom spoke a quiet question. "Do you think the crowbar was driven in with one blow, Doctor?"

The doctor shook his head. "Can't tell how it was driven in, Phantom. The whole upper cranium is shattered; there was a bad internal hemorrhage."

Van turned to the inspector. "Can you offer any possible reason, inspector-from what those men told you at the pier-for the murderer killing in this fashion?"

The inspector wiped sick perspiration from his brow. "They claimed Millett had a grudge against them because they once refused to back him in a show. And that he had a criminal mind which ran amuck. That ballyhoo he used in his exhibitions twenty years ago, must be true-that he's a born criminal, a killer."

Van nodded, his eyes thoughtful as he listened to these theories.

Then, as fingerprint men and other experts of the Homicide took possession of the room, the Phantom, Havens, and the inspector strode out into the night club proper.

Here, other detectives had garnered a wealth of evidence from the frightened patrons and employees, who had not been informed of the murder so close at hand. They gave the inspector their reports.

The holdup itself had been quite orthodox. It had been led by a big man in a slicker with a tommy gun —a man identified by the police as Monk Gorman. The gangsters had shot out the chandelier and escaped through windows and doors when sirens sounded, someone having managed to summon the police.

No one had seen anybody go into the rear office, or out of it. The murder had apparently been an aftermath of the robbery in which jewels and money running into thousands, according to the claims of the victims, had been filched.

There was one queer element about the holdup, however. No one had seen the actual entrance of the gangsters. The reason was that all had been watching the girl on the trapeze.

Their eyes had literally been magnetized by that act, for at the moment the girl had been performing a daring somersault. Her grip on the trapeze had faltered, and it seemed she would fall.

Van's sharp eyes studied the dangling, studded trapeze he had noticed when he first entered.

"That was Queen Stella," the Phantom said aloud to the inspector. "The most remarkable aerialist of today, and rather a mystery herself. I wonder if she really faltered, or whether that wasn't just a clever part of her act."

The inspector had already quizzed the workers here. No one had seen Queen Stella since she was on the trapeze.

The inspector's eyes were narrowed. "Begins to look as if she sneaked out on us. And you say that losing her grip stuff might have been part of her act? Damned convenient if it was-it got everyone's eye when the holdup men came in."

The patrons of the night club were beginning to protest their detention. Presently one of them, a tall, dress-suited man, strode angrily forward to confront the inspector. Van's eyes went to him keenly. Tall, swarthy, with a short, but wide-spreading beard of black, bristly hair, he had a foreign aspect. His eyes were sharp and hard.

"May I ask permission to leave at once?" His English was flawless, the too-clear English which a well-educated foreigner speaks. "This detention is most distressing to me. To be robbed is enough."

The inspector eyed him in distaste. "Who are you?"

The man made a stiff little bow. "I am Count Karnov, formerly of the Russian Court —"

"Oh!" The inspector's smile was slightly depreciating, for ex-Russian counts, genuine and bogus, were all too prevalent on Broadway. "Well, I'm sorry, Count. We can't make any exceptions. Been in this country long?" he added, casually.

"Just long enough to learn," Count Karnov replied angrily, "that your customs are rather embarrassing."

Beard bristling, he bowed himself back to the other huddled guests.

The inspector sighed. "Guess I'll have to release 'em all soon now. Can't hold them all night-and we want to get the body out. We'll check up on them all as a matter of routine. What do you think, Phantom?"

"I think it's safe to let them go. But I'd keep tabs on Count Karnov if I were you."

The inspector cursed grimly. "Don't worry. We'll find out about him all right."

Minutes later the big night club was emptying. The patrons filed out like a mass of frightened sheep herded by bluecoat shepherds. The employees went home wearily.

Last to leave-only the Phantom, the police, and Havens remaining-was the gruesome, crowbar-riven corpse of Clyde Dickson. The body was carried out in a plain wicker basket, by two morgue attendants-carried humbly from the sumptuous club Clyde Dickson had owned.

Soon after, the detectives who still scoured the murder office emerged. They had found no significant clues-no prints save Dickson's own.

But the Phantom, though he fully trusted the efficiency of the police, was not satisfied with their reports. It was possible that with his own leads, leads known only to himself and Frank Havens, he might find something they had dismissed as insignificant.

Accompanied by Havens, Van stepped into the murder room. There was a single desk, full of papers which the detectives had obviously gone through. Nevertheless, Van proceeded to go through them again.

"Van!" Havens spoke freely now, as once more they were alone. "What do you make of all this? That cartoon of Collins has been haunting me ever since this murder! Why, Collins seemed to —"

" —prophesy this crowbar killing?" Van broke in, grimly, as he continued his search. "It almost seems so, doesn't it, Frank? Yes, Collins certainly was on to something vital to this whole devilish mystery. That's why I've got to see this case through to a finish, Frank." He spoke with gripping determination. "Collins took us in deep waters-and it's a case of sink or swim!"

"I can't make head or tail of it!" Havens confessed, baffled. "That weird story about Al Millett-the criminal of twenty years ago coming back and killing, robbing! It sounds mad!"

"It sounds theatrical," Van replied, his keen analytical mind showing its work now. "There's showmanship in these murders, if nothing else. The leaving of the fang-the sensational pulling of the crime right under the noses of the police. A devilish showman, this 'Fang.' And yet there must be a reason, Frank. The well-planned robberies, the organization of the gang by perfectly orthodox underworld tactics, shows cold-blooded planning! And something tells me that even the murder methods thus far used were based on sound, logical reason too."

"Reason!" Havens protested. "To rip the sides of two men out with an ax! To drive a crowbar through another man's skull! What reason could there be except what the men told the inspector-that Millett's mind is fiendishly warped, that he's been nursing a grudge and is now taking it out with homicidal fury."

"Perhaps," Van conceded. "Yet, somehow I'm not satisfied with that explanation. Frank, I want you to check up-in your news files and other sources-on all the men involved in this. See if you can bring anything to light."

He shook his head, still going through papers on the desk. "One thing else strikes me as strange. When I was trying to break into this room, I heard Dickson —I'm sure it was he-shriek out 'You! It's you!' in obvious recognition of the criminal."

"That isn't strange," Havens protested. "He simply recognized Al Millett."

"Yet, Frank, he sounded surprised-as well as terrified. Was he surprised to see Millett, knowing Millett was in town and at large? At any rate, did his recognition bring on his own murder?"

He broke off his grim musings as his fingers now thumbed through a small, frayed memorandum book he had found in Dickson's desk.

Its leather cover was peeling, worn at the edges. On its frayed pages, the Phantom saw scrawled names and addresses in faded ink, all of them business firms, mostly connected with entertainment. He thumbed on through the book. Suddenly, he paused at a fresh page-his eyes sharpening visibly in the holes of the domino mask.

"Look at this, Frank."

Havens looked. He saw what seemed at first a faint smudge of ink and alongside of it was an address, a number in the West Forties.

The faded ink showed it, too, had been jotted down long ago.

But Havens adjusted a pair of reading glasses and studied the item carefully under Van Loan's urging. He gave an exclamation. The smudge was a definite pattern, a clover-like outline.

"It's a design, Van! A sort of shamrock-no, not that —"

"Think of a deck of cards, Frank."

Havens eyes lighted with amazement. "Of course! It's the symbol for a club card! A card! And on that torn cartoon of Collins's there's a card, too: a joker under a skull. Do you think —"

"I think this symbol can be read as a word," Van's own voice held a gripping eagerness now. "What we have then is: Club, followed by an address." His body straightened now, eyes gleaming. "Club! And I've a hunch it might be the Gargoyle Club also mentioned in Collins's cartoon! It's pretty late-but I'm going there at once!"

Frank Havens wanted to go along, but Van, sensing danger now, feeling that the time had come to work undercover, insisted upon setting out alone. Turning over what evidence he had to Havens, and leaving instructions for Havens to check up on the men involved, also to try to obtain the murder-crowbar after the Medical Examiner finished his autopsy-the Phantom strode out of the Palladium Club.

A small but powerful coupe was already awaiting him at the side-street curb. Havens had phoned his chauffeur to speed that car here.

The Phantom moved like a shadow through the crowds that milled out here, keeping his mask low so the darkness virtually concealed it. Quickly, he slid into the coupe, stepped on the starter. The motor hummed.

The Phantom whirled in the seat in sudden alarm. Something whizzed in through the window of the car, falling upon his lap!

Grim-eyed, he now picked up the object that had been tossed in so surreptitiously. It was a note, wrapped around a small spoon from the Palladium. Delicate fine handwriting showed under the dashboard lights.

Phantom:

> *Anything you do will be a waste of time until you see me. If you really want to know of Al Millett, be at the corner of Bethune and Varick Streets tomorrow at six p.m. Come alone, or it will be useless. I knew you from your mask —*
>
> *Queen Stella.*

Queen Stella! The missing girl aerialist who had been drawing all eyes when the holdup began!

Van's eyes again went out to the crowd, looking for the girl. At that instant a taxi pulled up to the curb. The Phantom saw a tall man with a cane climbing stiffly into it; caught a brief glimpse of a heavy-jowled pale face. The taxi-door slammed, the cab shot off around a corner, at a breathless speed.

But the Phantom had recognized its passenger. That man was Bernard J. Andrews, the big radio station owner! One of the men who had come to Inspector Gregg with the story of Al Millett! What was he doing, lurking around the night club where the Fang had struck a second time?

The Phantom's own car hurled from the curb even with these thoughts. He drove rapidly around the corner, onto Broadway, scanning the still-heavy night traffic. Andrews's cab was lost in a maze of other cabs.

Nor did he try to find it now. He also shoved away the note signed with the name of Queen Stella, his eyes grim. Anything he did, the note said, would be a waste of time until tomorrow.

He smiled to himself as he set out for the address he had picked up in Dickson's office: the address marked only with the symbol of the club-suit from a deck of cards.

Chapter VI
The Gargoyle Club

Night was finally in its small, dying hours. Eerie tendrils of mist seeped down the street east of Sixth Avenue, cooling the deserted pavements which slowly relinquished the Indian summer heat of the previous day.

The side street had a lonely aspect. Yet, close by, was plenty of life and activity. From Sixth Avenue came sounds that drowned out the occasional rumble of the elevated trains-sounds of drilling and pumping-now and then the dull boom of a blast. A subway line was under construction, being rushed with three eight-hour shifts every twenty-four hours.

But the side street here was aloof from the clamor. At the moment, there was no visible sign of anyone on the entire block. Yet someone was there.

Blending with the shadows of the dark building fronts, yet moving hurriedly along the street, stole the Phantom. He had left his coupe parked on another street.

His keen eyes glanced at each passing house number. And then they found that which they sought, and his lithe body slowed in its pace. This building made a strange contrast to the tall, modern office skyscrapers that rose like canyon walls on either side of the street. It was small, squat, of ancient brownstone, and was squeezed between two of the skyscrapers, as if it had defiantly refused to heed the march of time-had stubbornly remained when its neighbors had been torn down to make way for architectural progress.

From every appearance it was a tenantless house. Though no For Sale signs hung on it, its windows were partially boarded, a few others showing broken age-begrimed panes. Its door, too, had boards over it.

The Phantom felt a sense of disappointment. This was the address, marked by the symbol of a club, which he had found in Dickson's ancient book. And from the looks of it, the place was long since fallen into disuse, as defunct as the rest of the addresses in that book.

The Phantom glanced up and down the block. It was empty, deserted. Moving to the worn stoop of the dilapidated house, he ascended the stone stairs, came to the boarded door. The boards, he saw now, were nailed to the door behind them, a hole cut through where the key-hole of the lock showed.

The Phantom's interest quickened. That key-hole looked new. Again he glanced up and down the street, eyes darting through his mask-holes. No one in sight.

From a pocket he now took out a slender piece of wire. It looked quite ordinary. Actually it was of specially tempered steel, malleable, yet always able to recover its original shape. Into the key-hole the Phantom inserted the wire. His deft fingers manipulated it. No burglar could have been more swift and expert at picking that lock.

In just a moment, with scarcely a sound, the Phantom had the lock picked. Cautiously he swung the big boarded door on its hinges, slipped into the house, closing the door softly behind him.

The gloom that met him at first seemed opaque. A musty odor clogged his sensitive nostrils. He moved cautiously, on his soft-soled shoes, eyes gradually accustoming themselves to the darkness.

The ancient interior of the house slowly came into view. Gaping doorways, a rickety flight of stairs. The whole place seemed desolate and dead, a decayed relic of the past. Once, no doubt, it had been a fashionable house-its ornate fixings indicated that. But now it was only an archaic shell, and as he groped his way through it, the desolate emptiness of it seemed to engulf the Phantom like a weird, evil spell.

He felt as if he had stepped out of all modern civilization and progress into a world that no longer existed, a world that could only hold ghosts of the past.

Ghosts! Certainly the *Phantom* could laugh at the idea of ghosts! Yet, even with the thought, a slight, scurrying sound came to his ears. He dismissed it quickly, with a little shiver. Rats, no doubt.

Then, all at once, he heard another sound. His lithe body jerked rigid.

As if welling up vaguely from some invisible source there came a sound of voices.

Nerves taut, the Phantom listened with ears acutely tuned, trying to reckon their direction. But they came only as vague murmurings, and Van half-wondered if his imagination was not playing tricks on him.

He moved about. Again came that ghostly murmur. But this time his ears told him it had come from above. The stairs, he had already seen, were covered with fully half an inch of undisturbed dust! Nevertheless, the Phantom ascended them, his soft-soles treading lightly on their creaking wood.

He reached the second and top floor of the house. A musty hall, again gaping rooms whose dirt-grimed windows hid the city outside, shutting this ghastly place off from civilization. Certainly, the floor was absolutely vacant, empty.

Yet, at that very instant, the voices sounded again closer now. He caught a snatch of words — *"I'll see you in hell first!"*

The speech came like a single, crackling explosion, then as instantly subsided, so that again Van couldn't be sure he had really heard them. Yet his every nerve told him something devilish was going on in this house.

The sound had come from close by, from the very top of the stair landing here. Yet there was no room here, just a wall, outside of which must be the street. He bent to the wall, fingers groping in the darkness-for he still dared show no light.

Suddenly his fingers touched metal, a small grille of oblong shape. In a flash he realized that it was one of the old-fashioned type of heat-grilles.

A slight draft came through it, but no light. Swiftly Van Loan comprehended. Those grilles made excellent sound conductors. The voices had come up between the walls from below.

Van moved again to the stairs, descended them. He came to the ground floor once more. His eyes, straining in the gloom, saw the side of the staircase now, saw how far outwards it extended. He hurried to it, Colt .45 whipping out, thumb snapping down the safety catch so that the weapon was ready for use.

He could hear nothing now, but his left hand groped along the wall of the staircase. A hunch had grown within him as he noticed the strange paneling here.

In the very next instant, near some coping, his hand was arrested by a small metal catch. With his other hand coming forward with his gun, the Phantom pressed that catch.

There was a click —a hissing swish.

Bright light momentarily dazzled the Phantom as it came flooding out toward him, grotesquely illumining the ancient, dusty hallway, throwing weird shadows.

Gun leveled, eyes slitted in the holes of his black domino mask, the Phantom hurled his body through the revealed doorway and to one side.

A large, strange chamber was before him. It was empty.

He was certain even before his eyes located a grille near the ceiling that this was where the voices had come from. But there was no one in the room! Had those voices come from invisible ghosts?

His eyes took in the chamber. Oak-paneled walls, windowless —a luxurious and well-kept room, pleasantly illumined by modern indirect lighting. An amazing contrast to the rest of the dilapidated house.

There was a table in the center of the room, a long oak table with several chairs around it. Two were pulled out from the rest, indicating that they might have been hastily vacated.

The Phantom's eyes went wider. He had come through the secret doorway to this room. He was sure it hadn't been used by anyone since his arrival in the house. Had those voices been imaginary then? Or was there another exit?

His eyes were drawn hypnotically to one wall and a chill shock went through him, tightening his every nerve.

Leering at him from that wall was a human skull. Beneath it, pinned to form a pattern with it, was a playing card —a joker! The strange symbol he had found in that torn cartoon by Eddie Collins!

He moved back to the table. Nothing on it. If only there were some clue as to who had been in here. He stiffened anew. There *was* something on the table. Or, rather, in the table's oak surface. A bronze plaque was inlaid at the head. Van bent over it.

Nine names were inscribed in that plaque, well known names that seemed to leap out like letters of blood before his eyes! Nine names he had heard at the very outset of this strange case.

Benjamin Marcy
Lyle Marcy
Gordon Drake
Bernard J. Andrews
Carl Fenwick
Clyde Dickson
Paul Corbin
Kenneth Meade
John Gifford

The mighty moguls of the amusement world, three of whom had just been killed! Here, in this room, under the symbol of the skull and joker, they apparently had held secret meetings. For what reason-if they had no past to hide, no secret?

Grim-eyed now, realizing that he had come to some vital core of the mystery if he could but interpret it, the Phantom proceeded to examine the secret room.

He found something else that caught his attention. On another wall, near the secret panel he had entered, had hung what had evidently been a large placard of some sort. Now just a corner of it remained, frayed and dusty. Printing, in an archaic type long since gone out of use, revealed three letters:

kil

The unfinished word seemed to blend with that leering skull across the room, and if ever Van felt the presence of menace, of death itself, he felt it at the very instant he gazed at that strange, mutilated sign.

At that instant the sixth sense which the Phantom possessed leaped once more to the fore. Certainly he had not heard the slight, cautious sound behind his back. He hadn't expected it, because he had already surveyed the entire room, and now he was facing the secret door through which he himself had come.

Only when his muscles were already whirling his body, his hand whipping up his gun, did he feel the draft of air from behind him, a draft which told him some other door must have opened. But even as he whirled, eyes sharp, the lights of the room went out!

The windowless chamber was plunged into Stygian darkness. The Phantom, though he could see nothing, was acutely aware of a shape charging toward him! His whole body braced. But, despite his forewarning of it, the Phantom was almost bowled completely over by the savage ferocity of the body which hurled against his own, knocking his gun from his fist. Hands reached for his throat, hands that were like vises of steel. In the darkness he struggled with his powerful antagonist, tugging at the hands which had closed on his wind-pipe and were choking the breath from his lungs.

Rallying his strength, the Phantom was matching his adversary with the strength and skill of self-defense he had practiced arduously. Something struck Van's back as his antagonist momentarily forced him against the wall. A light-switch, he was certain!

Gathering strength, he twisted his antagonist around. One hand had released the awful, choking pressure on his throat-he could breathe again. He gave a yank, freeing momentarily his left hand. Fiercely, he reached for the switch. Light would reveal that face. More than anything else, that was what Van wanted to see.

But even as his groping fingers touched the switch a sudden, rasping shout broke from his still-unseen attacker.

"Men! Over here! He's the Phantom!"

Almost simultaneously, Van heard a heavy rush of feet from the secret door he himself had entered. With a curse of alarm, he whirled as his antagonist now jerked away.

Now his eyes were able to discern several shadowy figures, groping for him. Rough hands reached out, grabbing at him. The Phantom struck out blindly with his own powerful fists, but there were too many for him now. Blows cuffed him. He heard an awful, swishing sound-the sound of a heavy black-jack arcing viciously through the air. His very brain seemed to explode, causing myriad colors to dance before his eyes.

Stunned, he fought to keep consciousness while hands frisked him in the dark-frisked him but failed to find one item that, by a secret legerdemain on Van's part, always defied ordinary search-the diamond-studded platinum badge of the Phantom!

In the next moment the lights went on. Blinking, the Phantom again took in the strange chamber.

There were five slouch-hatted men in the room. Three of them, yanking him to his feet and covering him with guns, he recognized at once as the thugs who had attacked him when he had posed as Collins. There was the broken-nosed thug called Gus with tape on his wrist which had been wounded. There was the hatchet-faced gunman, and the pallid one.

One more slouch-hatted figure was a stranger. The fifth, standing at the light switch, was a burly man in a sport-belted slicker. Van's eyes narrowed with swift recognition. Monk Gorman!

But where was the man who had originally attacked the Phantom single-handed, then given orders to this gang? Van was sure he was not one of these thugs.

As this thought flashed through the Phantom's mind, the big man in the slicker came striding over.

"So you're the Phantom," he sneered, glaring with hate at the masked man who had awed the underworld. "Well, this time you bucked something too big for you, pal."

Gus snarled then. "Say Monk-why waste time?" Despite his taped wrist he leveled his automatic toward Van, eyes alight with murder. "Let me give him a belly-full o' slugs, will ya, Monk? Hell, he's probably the guy who potted my wrist and wounded Pete when he got that envelope —"

Van stiffened as the automatic pointed its black muzzle towards him. Though his strength was not yet returned, he did not intend to die without a struggle.

"Hold it, hold it!" Monk commanded, pushing Gus aside. "We ain't doin' anythin' in here! Just one thing before we get goin' with this Phantom bird, let's have a good look at him!"

Van, menaced by guns, unarmed, did not try to make resistance, even though he saw Monk's intent!

Deliberately now, with evil satisfaction in his bead-like eyes, Monk's paw-like hand reached forward. It seized the edge of the domino mask. A savage rip-and the mask came off.

But it did not reveal the face of Richard Curtis Van Loan, a face that would have shown through the scant disguise of Eddie Collins. Before he had come to this building, Van, with keen precaution, had put on a new and strong make-up —a disguise which altered his features into those of a hard-looking man of indeterminate age.

"So that's what you really look like, Phantom?" Monk seemed disappointed, as if he expected to see some super-being. "Hell! I never seen your puss before. All right, we'll get goin'! Tony, bring that over!"

The pallid-faced thug came forward with a length of stout cord. In a matter of seconds the Phantom was bound hand and foot, arms pinioned behind him. His mouth was taped.

Monk barked a fresh order. They picked the bound Phantom up and started toward the secret panel.

"No, not that way, Choppy!" Monk rapped. "Might be coppers out front, an' I'm hot!" He moved to the opposite wall, where he pressed a catch.

Another secret panel, in that wall, slid open. The Phantom was carried through it into a dark, tunnel-like passage. The panel was closed behind as Monk followed.

A long journey through the dark passage which descended slightly and then rose. The faintly cool air of the misty outdoors engulfed the Phantom. He realized they had emerged on the next block downtown from the house. The passage, evidently some old drainage duct, afforded a direct route from the secret room to the street, leading out through the cellar of another house.

But who had been the man who cried: "I'll see you in hell first"? Who had been the powerful brute who had attacked Van Loan in the dark? Was the Phantom going to learn the answers to these questions?

Chapter VII
A Narrow Escape

Carried to a large sedan, the captive Phantom was tossed like a sack into the rear. Tony leaped into the front seat, got the motor going. Another thug slid alongside him. Monk, Gus, and the hatchet-faced man named Choppy climbed in roughly over Van's half-doubled figure, trampling him brutally down to the floorboards.

"Where we takin' this Phantom bird, Monk?" the broken-nosed Gus demanded, a note of awe in his tones. "Gonna take him to the new 'chateau' so the Boss can —"

"Shut up!" Monk snarled. "Tony, drive like I told you."

The Phantom, gathering strength to struggle as best he could against his bonds, relaxed, grim hope in his heart as the sedan rolled on. Helpless and bound though he was, he wished they would take him to that unknown destination, to the lair of the Fang!

And then the sedan rolled to a stop.

All this time, on the sides of the avenue, below the elevated, Van had been aware of the noisy clamor of the subway excavating. Now the din had reached a climax. The car had turned a little way into another dim side street. Monk alone climbed out.

He was gone several minutes. Then, hurriedly, his slouch-hatted head again poked into the car.

"Okay, guys! Bring him out. Follow me and be careful! If there's any trouble, use your rods!"

Again the Phantom was lifted bodily. Out of the car the four others took him, and trotted with him along the quiet street.

Bright arc-lights appeared on the avenue, where drills and compressors shattered the final hours of the night. There was a deep excavation, extending to a vacant lot here. Workmen swarmed in it. A huge derrick was steaming and straining in the center.

With a boldness that astonished the bound Phantom, his captors carried him down an incline into that excavation. Monk was signaling them on.

The workmen were all preoccupied, watching the derrick, whose great arm was lifting a dark, massive burden.

"Here-put him here! Hurry!"

They dragged the Phantom over rough, uneven, rocky ground. Suddenly, he was dropped violently. His bound body banged against the slanting surface of a heavy, sand-covered rock. Stunned again, his every bone shaken, he could not move.

As they dropped him, all five thugs scurried away like hasty fleeing rats.

Van, twisting up his head, saw —

The derrick arm was lowering. Its shadow was right above him. He saw the massive burden it was bringing down. A huge net of steel!

It was right on top of him, coming like a huge blanket. Somewhere to the right the workmen were guiding it by long ropes. They did not see him here in the gloom, nor could he shout to them with the tape over his mouth!

Down came the steel net. The Phantom braced his body, flattening as best he could against the rock, as his last effort to roll out of the way of the great expanse of net proved futile.

Then it was on him. Its crushing weight knocked the breath anew from his lungs. Steel links and cables bruised through his clothes, dug into his flesh. It was lucky he was not crushed to death.

Lucky? Even as the steel net flattened over him and the rock now, and the derrick swung away with empty jaws Van knew that he had not escaped death. This was but a grim preparation for it!

A vague figure out in the gloom, evidently a foreman, was yelling, "Clear away, men! This is gonna be a whopper!"

Simultaneously Van's eyes, jerking to one side, caught a faint outline of electric wires, going into the rock close beside him. There were two other rocks nearby, also covered with nets.

His blood chilled as he comprehended the diabolical intention of the murderous Monk Gorman. Instead of taking him to the "chateau," they had planned a ghastly doom for him! These three rocks were loaded with dynamite. They were about to be blasted. The nets that covered them were to keep the explosion as confined as possible, so the shattered rock would not erupt all over the place.

Three rocks to be blasted! And on the center one, pinned down by that steel net, lay the Phantom. In a moment now he would be blown to bits, his body torn beyond all means of identification! It was a devilishly clever means of getting rid of him, of removing him from the bizarre murder case without leaving a tangible clue.

"Come on, men, hurry up!" the foreman was shouting. Obviously he stood at the hand-detonator, ready to send the current through the wires to the fulminate caps packed in the dynamite. "Clear away, I say!"

Van had spent precious seconds trying to shout, but it was useless. The adhesive remained tight over his lips. Now, knowing that only seconds remained, he fought to keep calm in the face of the ghastly predicament!

In that swift moment, his muscles strained tentatively, feeling for any place where the pressure was not impossibly heavy. His left arm behind him was partially protected by the hollow of his back.

The Phantom had made a thorough study of escapes. He had analyzed the escapes of the late Houdini, until he had mastered similar tricks. Now he applied every bit of knowledge he could summon to this crisis.

His wrist twisted, muscles flexing and unflexing in his forearm.

"All clear?" The foreman was shouting.

The words spurred the Phantom's efforts. He gave a sudden peculiar jerk, with all his strength. His arm, with rope still clinging to it, came free.

Just one arm, his left, to work with at all-and the blast about to go off! But the Phantom had already gauged his one possible chance of escape from death.

The electric feed wires! With all his strength he pushed his arm out from behind him, his body heaving against the steel net, managing to push it upwards just a trifle, though the effort made every muscle groan in protest.

He couldn't see the foreman. Yet, as if his intuition had eyes, he could envision the man even now stooping to push the plunger.

An inch more! With one last effort he made it. His fingers seized both wires and yanked.

Br-r-rooooom!

The whole world seemed to detonate about his ears, leaving him deaf! Smoke and fire leaped about him. He felt the rock shiver under his spine.

But his rock had not been blasted! The two other rocks had disintegrated, gone up in that net-stifled upheaval! The wires to this rock, which he had ripped in that last split second from the fuse-caps, had not carried the current to the fatal dynamite sticks. A moment later cautious workmen appeared above Van's net carrying lanterns and coming to see why the dynamite had failed to detonate. Their cries of amazed surprise and alarm faintly sounded in Van's pained ears as their lamps revealed the pinned figure under the net.

They had to use the derrick to remove the heavy expanse of steel. Hands helped Van to his feet. Voices shouted questions at him. Someone ran to summon an ambulance.

But the Phantom was not there when the ambulance came. Bruised and shaken, he had paused only to recapture his lost wind, his ebbed strength.

Then, so quickly that the workmen were left gasping, he whirled from the group, darted across the gloom of the excavation, and disappeared in the misty dawn which was just breaking over the city.

* * *

"Yes, Frank, the criminal was at that Gargoyle Club or I miss my guess. And he knew I was the Phantom."

Morning sunlight slanted warmly through the French windows of Havens's office in the *Clarion* Building, as the Phantom, refreshed by clean clothes, medical treatment at the hands of his valet, and nourishment, sat beside the publisher's desk.

Havens's face showed the deep-lined strain of a sleepless night, mingled with the relief at seeing the Phantom safe and sound.

"The police went to that club, as you call it, as soon as you phoned, Van," he reported. "They found the secret room. But the name plaque you mentioned wasn't there; nor was that torn sign on the wall."

Van's eyes were grim. "Evidently they were removed by the criminal. Guess he attacked me because I saw them. I wonder what —" He broke off with a shrug, lit a cigarette thoughtfully. "Any other developments, Frank?"

"Yes. The police have been checking up on all the people present in the Palladium Club during that holdup. One of them, that man who called himself Count Karnov, seems to interest them. As far as they can make out, he arrived only recently in this country-and he's been moving fast from hotel to hotel. They're trying to check up on him. Queen Stella is still missing. And nothing known about her identity, either."

Van smiled grimly. He did not tell Havens about the note he had in his pocket, signed by the trapeze artist's sobriquet. He had left that note in the coupe when he had gone to the Gargoyle Club. Later, after his hectic adventure, he had found the coupe intact. But he kept the note to himself now, aware that it might still be a false lead, a red herring which might confuse the trail. But the memory of the wording of it —*"Anything you try to do will be a waste of time —"* brought a queer thrill to the Phantom. His visit to that strange house of the secret room had been far indeed from a waste of time.

"About this Al Millett, Frank," he spoke aloud. "Is it true he used to give some of his exhibitions for a circus-Crowley and Buckle's once-famous circus?"

"Yes, among other road shows. Why, Van?"

"I want you to get me all the data you can on that circus, Frank," the Phantom demanded without replying to the question. "Everything that might carry any information. I take it, you've already got some data on the men involved?"

Havens nodded. "A slew of stuff—I'm having it assembled. But I'm afraid it won't be of much value, Van. Those men have all been in the amusement business a long time. And as far as their careers go back publicly, there is nothing dark or hidden about them. Yet," he added, frowning thoughtfully, "they have one thing in common-their shunning of publicity. All are bachelors, living alone-except the murdered Marcys, who lived together. None of them seems to have any living relatives."

Van drew a puff of smoke, thinking as Havens spoke, of that mysterious room at the Gargoyle Club, the name plaque, those two voices-one heavy, and the other dry.

"If there are no relatives, who are the heirs of the estates of the murdered men?" he asked, interested.

"Their moneys are willed to charities, Van, institutions for the infirm-reputable places needing endowments. No one gains by their deaths except these institutions. Dickson and the Marcy brothers had practically all their wealth in their show places. But these are to be sold, the proceeds to be used in the settlement of their wills."

The publisher shook his head, sighed. "So you see, there isn't much to go by there. And I still can't see how Eddie Collins drew practically Dickson's murder before it happened." Grimly, his eyes went to the now empty lounge where the youthful cartoonist had died the night before.

"You looked through Collins's office stuff here? Checked up?" Van demanded.

"Yes. We found some scraps of comic cartoons-nothing much there. But I did find some peculiar scribblings, Van. They scarcely seem to make sense. I have them here."

He handed Van Loan some small pages, on which was bold handwriting. Van looked through them. His brows arched in surprise.

Bee doesn't die by sting-Red Sea is red as blood —

Van looked up, his eyes sharp, his mind racing.

"What is it, Van?" Havens demanded, noting the Phantom's absorption. "Do you see something there? It isn't, perhaps, some sort of code?"

"No, I don't think so," Van replied slowly. And slowly a light began to shine in his eyes. His voice was gripping now. "Frank —I'm beginning to see something! Something which is still without any definite pattern-but it's there-if only I can get a few more leads to it! And I'm pretty sure I know how Collins got mixed up in this!"

Havens stared at him, wide-eyed, accustomed though he was to the Phantom's often-amazing conclusions. "Van, what do you mean?"

"I'll tell you as soon as I'm a little more sure," Van returned. "And —" He broke off as the inter-office buzzer sounded.

"Beg pardon, Mr. Havens," the pleasant voice of the editor's secretary came from the speaker. "A Mr. Carl Fenwick wishes to see you. Says it is very urgent."

"Fenwick!" Havens repeated, glancing at Van Loan and observing his quick nod. "Send him in, please."

Van Loan swiftly turned up his collar and snapped a new domino over his face. Glancing swiftly around to be sure there were no traces of Richard Van Loan, he turned to study the newcomer.

Carl Fenwick, the man who looked almost like a clergyman because of his high, straight collar, came in with a nervous stride. His mild face was pale, fraught with agitation. His troubled eyes at first did not see the masked Phantom. "Mr. Havens," Fenwick said tensely. "Sorry if I've disturbed you. But I understand you can contact the man known as the Phantom! And —" He broke off, starting, as his glance now took in the domino-masked figure.

"You —I beg your pardon!" Fenwick stammered. "Are you —"

Van nodded grimly. "Yes, I'm the Phantom."

Fenwick gave a dry, mirthless, rather shaky laugh. "How-how fortunate, finding you here."

The Phantom said nothing to this; but inwardly he wondered if Fenwick meant those words. Was Fenwick surprised to see the Phantom alive? Had he perhaps come here to see if he *were* alive? Van had not forgotten that murderous attack in the secret room.

"Won't you sit down, Mr. Fenwick?" Havens invited now.

Fenwick nodded his thanks, took one of the comfortable chairs. He seemed to await a question from the Phantom. Van deliberately made none, coolly lighting another cigarette. He had already decided on his course of action: Carl Fenwick would have to take the initiative.

Fenwick tugged a little at his high collar. A moment of silence filled the room. Havens had already become a silent spectator, waiting at his desk. Then Fenwick leaned towards the Phantom. "I had to come to you, Phantom," he said, a haunting light in his eyes. His words came in a sudden rush, like a pent-up dam released. "I had heard, through the police, you were interested in this case. We went to the police, and they didn't help us. Now I'm coming to you. The others might not approve of it, but there's something I'm going to tell you."

Havens stiffened, scenting news. The Phantom remained cool, his eyes alone betraying his interest through the mask. Then he spoke dryly. "You mean," he said, "that you and others actually did do a real wrong to Millett."

Fenwick gasped and winced.

"No-no," he protested. "What we told Inspector Gregg was the truth. We simply refused to back Al Millett in a show of his own. As a result, he went broke. His wife died, and he disappeared. But there's more to the story. Millett and his wife had a child —a girl child who disappeared with Millett after the death of his wife."

The Phantom did not appear shocked or profoundly affected by this bit of information. He studied the theatrical producer thoughtfully for a moment. Then: "Very interesting, Mr. Fenwick," he said. "But just how, may I ask, does this item of personal history bear on this case?"

Fenwick tugged uncomfortably at his collar. "I—I don't know," he faltered. "I thought you ought to be told everything. Andrews, particularly, was opposed to my saying anything."

Van Loan remained thoughtful. Andrews was the radio company man, the chap the Phantom had seen walking away from the Palladium Club late last night after the murder of Dickson.

"Thank you, Mr. Fenwick," Van Loan acknowledged gravely. "I will remember what you have said."

The theatrical man, after a word of effusive thanks that the Phantom was on the case, took his leave.

"Well, Van?" The publisher asked. "What do you make of Fenwick's story?"

"Very little," Van admitted. "I believe him-certainly. But I still think there is a great deal more to this whole mess than any of them have told. Perhaps a talk with Bernard J. Andrews would be enlightening. Call Inspector Gregg on your private wire, Frank, and see where we can find the man right now. Gregg should know."

Havens quickly got the chief of detectives on the phone. His conversation with the inspector was brief. Turning back to the expectant Phantom, he exploded a bombshell.

"Van, Andrews has disappeared! He apparently slipped away from his home during the night. No signs of violence. He's just gone. There's an alarm out for him right now."

The Phantom stood erect. "Good-by, Frank. That means I've plenty of work to do. Get that information together for me and send it over to the lab as soon as you can."

And he was gone.

Chapter VIII
Queen Stella Again

Located in an old loft building was a queer business belonging to an eccentric recluse who went by the name of Dr. Bendix.

Neither the police nor the impoverished inhabitants of the lower East Side dreamed that, in the midst of the city's most squalid tenement section, there existed perhaps the finest and most fully equipped private crime-laboratory in the world.

The mysterious Dr. Bendix stood in that gleaming laboratory now, over a table full of retorts and test tubes.

Alone, he wore no mask or disguise. And friends of Richard Curtis Van Loan, the socialite, would have been amazed to see him hard at work here, in a stained smock, a cigarette dangling from his lips. That Richard Van Loan was "Dr. Bendix," that this was just another role of the Phantom, was a secret known only to Frank Havens.

Strange objects lay on the work-table before the Phantom. A broken iron crowbar. Two saber teeth. They had been sent here by Havens, who had obtained them from the Medical Examiner and the police department.

With a pair of tongs, Van heated the crowbar over the blue-white flame of a Bunsen burner. He dipped it, hissing, into a container of chemicals. His analysis was long and thorough. An analysis to get the blood of Clyde Dickson from the crowbar. To test the effect of the blood's oxygen content on the iron.

When at last he had finished, he had reached some strange conclusions. The crowbar was old-very many years old. Even the break in it did not look new. Why had the criminal who called himself the Fang taken an old, broken crowbar as a murder weapon? Van's eyes gleamed.

Of the Marcy brothers, whose sides had been ripped and mutilated, Van had no evidence of any weapon, but he had read the full, and baffled, autopsy report.

He gave his attention next to the saber teeth. He decided, by comparison with zoological books he had, that they were really the teeth of tigers. They could have been bought in any store selling trinkets of this sort.

The Phantom now moved from the work-table to a flat-topped desk. Here were the sheaves of newspaper clippings and other reports on the men involved in the case. Smoking thoughtfully, Van went through them.

The names of all the living men, with their corresponding dossiers, passed like a parade before the Phantom: Bernard J. Andrews, missing radio man-Gordon Drake-Carl Fenwick-Paul Corbin, night-club owner-John Gifford, amusement park manager.

The reports confirmed what Havens had already told him. But Havens had, in response to Van's request, sent one additional piece of information. Through his influence he had learned, from various law-firms, of the wills of all the rest of the men.

And like the murder victims, all of them were leaving their wealth to charities! Where the first victims had their money tied up in businesses that had to be liquidated, the rest had most of their fortune in sound Wall Street investments and in cash deposits.

It did not seem surprising. None had relatives, so it could be understood that they were leaving their wealth to public institutions. But it certainly seemed to offset any mercenary motive for their murder. They could have been robbed without being killed.

The Phantom rose, paced, brooding on his thoughts. It wasn't money that tied these men together. There was some bond which that mysterious club indicated. It didn't seem to be any dark or shady deed of the past. What, then? *What?*

Again that vague germ of light was in his brain. But it defied definition. Could the bond merely be a mutual fear of Al Millett-the Fang? No, for openly they had gone to the police confessing to such a bond while they had been darkly secretive about the Gargoyle Club. It was queer, the feeling Van had, the intangible feeling that as yet the right answer had not been found.

The Gargoyle Club-Van stopped on that thought, memory coming to him. He moved to a telephone, put in a call to the Department of Buildings. He asked for an official of high standing.

"This is Mr. Frank Havens," he said in the next moment, simulating perfectly the voice of the publisher who had given him full license to use this identity over the phone. "I called you before, if you remember, for a favor. Did you find out about the ownership of that old building on Forty-Fifth Street, near Sixth?"

"Yes, Mr. Havens," came the official's polite voice. "It belongs to a corporation-the Star Corporation. A Mr. John Gifford is president."

Gifford! The amusement park owner.

"That's a good piece of real estate, isn't it?" Van asked conversationally.

"Good indeed! You know how values have sky-rocketed in that section since Rockefeller Center was put up near there."

"Funny they don't develop the property."

"Yes, isn't it? I understand, too, they've had several juicy offers for it, but they refuse to sell."

When Van hung up, his eyes were keen, hard. Again he resumed his pacing. The ring of a bell at the end of the room brought him out of his musings. He waited a full moment, then went down the stairs to a foyer of the old loft. A package was waiting there, a big bundle of papers. Van knew that Havens's trusted office boy had delivered them, rung the bell, and quickly departed. His face eager, he carried the stuff upstairs, undid it on a table. It was the data he had been waiting for on the once famous Crowley and Buckill's circus.

Frank Havens, with his usual dependability, must have scoured the town to get such a mass of stuff. Some of the papers were frayed and decaying-their print archaic. In his preliminary examination, Van Loan pulled out of the stack an old three-sheet show bill.

He read the entire poster with careful attention.

Crowley & Buckill
GREATEST CIRCUS ON EARTH
Featuring the World's Largest
MUSEUM OF LIVING FREAKS!

Presenting the Famous Outlaw
AL MILLETT-THE FANG!

IN ADDITION
100 CLOWNS!
100 ACROBATS!
100 WILD ANIMALS
*SEE SIGNORINA BEATRICE,
THE WORLD'S GREATEST AERIALIST!*

Free Parade!

BAND OF 30 PIECES!

PLAYING HERE

There was a blank space for a dated streamer. But Van Loan's eyes went back to the first line-to the word "Buckill." With his hand he blocked off three letters-kil-and he knew what placard had been torn from the wall at the Gargoyle Club.

He spent the entire afternoon going through the stack of yellow and aging papers. He found individual posters on Al Millett's billing which described the fellow as a terror on wheels-followed by a thirty-piece band. There were single sheets on Signorina Beatrice, on the side shows, on the freak museum, on the animal tent, and so on. In their day Crowley and Buckill, like the Barnum who had preceded them, had been exploiting showmen. Van heaved a regretful sigh. This was like a trip back to childhood, to the sawdust paradise of the circus of yesteryear.

* * *

Dusk.

A tumble-down, desolate street near the Hudson River water-front. Just a few buildings and vacant lots. One lamp-post, its light having just gone on, was casting a dull glow in the thickening gloom.

The Phantom deliberately avoided that light.

In the shadows against the old buildings, he moved toward the corner of Bethune Street, domino mask once more on his face. His eyes were tense and alert; his right hand, which seemed to hang idly at the wrist, was ready to reach for his gun.

He was obeying the instructions in the note signed by the missing aerialist "Queen Stella." For there was a possibility the lead might prove bona-fide. He could not afford to pass it up.

The street, he saw, was empty. But it was not yet quite six-the hour of the rendezvous. Van neared the corner, saw that it formed the angles of an empty lot full of refuse-cans, garbage, wrecked autos.

It was then that a tension began to come over his nerves. A sense of danger.

He paused in the shadows, hesitating to step to the corner, where he would not only be revealed by the street-lamp, but also, with that open lot there, would be unshielded by any buildings. It was too perfect for a rub-out to suit the Phantom.

From where he stood, his eyes searched across the lot. Nothing in that refuse, he was sure. A slight movement that startled him proved to be a prowling alley cat.

Then his eyes went across the lot, to the rear of a dilapidated old building. It looked vacant, broken windowed. Because he was looking for it, he saw it then!

A broken lower window, something glinting over its sill —a round, dark muzzle! A gun ready to aim-and blast!

He sucked in a sharp breath, realizing that only his prescience had stopped him from walking out into the open before that waiting muzzle.

Then his eyes went to slits in their mask-holes. Grim purpose tightened his lips. He changed from the quarry to the hunter.

It was still a few minutes short of six.

The Phantom turned and went swiftly back from the corner. He slipped completely around the block, staying under cover, drifting like a dark mist to the front of that house on the next block.

Vacancy signs hung on it.

Half the front was torn down.

The brick walls were jagged and wrecked.

No one was in front of the house. There were no cars. No doorways where an ambusher could lurk unseen.

The Phantom approached the gaping front door of the house as stealthily as a cat.

The only sound he made was the slight click when his thumb pressed back the safety-catch on his Colt .45.

Like a wraith, he stole into the house. It was so ripped apart that he could see its emptiness. Toward the rear he saw that one door, on a single hinge, stood ajar. The Phantom peered in cautiously.

There in the twilight gloom a slouch-hatted figure crouched at that broken window over an automatic rifle which, Van saw by its extra coiled drum, had been converted into a machine gun.

From the portion of his sharp profile which the Phantom could see, Van knew that the would-be sniper was the hatchet-faced thug called Choppy.

The Phantom's slitted eyes narrowed in their purpose. He would get the truth from that felon in there, find out how this ambush had been pre-arranged. And why?

Cautiously, he moved the door. Then his breath sucked in. Despite his caution, the door creaked on its single hinge. There was nothing for it save to push on boldly in. He did so, whipping up his pistol.

Simultaneously, Choppy started. As he turned, his husky voice spoke:

"That you, Monk? That Phantom bird hasn't —"

He broke off in mid-sentence, hatchet-face blanching. For now he saw the domino-masked face coming toward him.

Coming like a grim Nemesis which every outlaw dreaded and secretly feared.

With a snarl of frightened rage, the thug snatched up the automatic rifle.

Desperation gave him almost superhuman speed. The barrel, sawed off in front, swung around and loomed blackly toward Van.

Crack!

It was the deep bark of the Phantom's Colt that shattered the empty, half-wrecked house. Van fired as he would at a desperate, dangerous beast.

The thug named Choppy seemed to freeze like a stone statue. Then the gun slanted crazily, clattered to the floor. And Choppy slowly slumped down after it, the life gone from his glazing eyes as he sprawled in a heap.

Grim-eyed, the Phantom moved forward. He glanced through the window. No one in sight. The shot evidently had not been heard-the rumble of trucks on West Street was enough to drown out more than one gun.

He looked down at the dead thug. He felt no sympathy for the felon, but he was sorry he had been forced to kill. Now his mind worked swiftly, to adjust to the grim situation. A glance at his wrist-watch showed it was just short of six o'clock. Outside the night was gathering.

Choppy had thought Van was Monk, the gang-leader, coming in here. Obviously he expected Monk, or others of the gang. But Van doubted that this old house could be the "chateau" the gunmen had mentioned last night. It was not a good hideout. It was only an ambush. Yet, perhaps any moment now, other gangsters would show up.

A grim decision came to Van then. It was six o'clock, and the fact that Queen Stella had not shown up made him feel the whole thing had been a trick to get him here.

He had turned the tables. Dared he go one step further, a step that might actually enable him to get directly on the trail of the criminal he sought?

His thoughts rapidly turned into swift action. He dragged the corpse of Choppy across the floor. It was still light enough to see, and he got more illumination when, once more, he drew out his flat make-up kit, snapped open the mirrored lid.

The corpse became his model, a model he now set out to reproduce on his own face with all his skill at disguise. Long, carefully drawn shadows gave his cheeks the hollows which made them look narrow and hatchet-like. A tiny bit of spring wire pinched his nostrils together, making them sharp and pointed like those of the thug. A cream-dye, rubbed into his hair, gave it Choppy's mousy color.

He took Choppy's clothes then, got into them. The blood-stain on the coat was small; he covered it with some more make-up. The clothes were tight, but he managed to pull them on, managed to put Choppy's slouch hat over his own head.

Hiding the corpse was his next problem. He solved it quickly. In the interior of the house, he found a corner piled with refuse. Minutes more, and he had Choppy's body screened behind it, hidden safely enough for the time being.

Again he slipped back to the rear room and peered out the window. His lips clamped back a sudden surprised exclamation.

Across the lot, under the lamp at the corner, apparently waiting, stood the slender figure of a girl! The aerialist had come to the rendezvous after all.

Van's mind raced. Was she actually intended as the bait for the trap, or was she innocent? In which case the gangsters must have learned of her rendezvous with the Phantom, and tried to turn it to their advantage.

In any event, the Phantom could not throw away this opportunity to meet the girl who had been missing since that murder at the Palladium Club.

Reaching a quick decision, he pulled his slouch hat a little lower, slipped out of the house the way he had come in. Again he circled the block warily, once more approaching the corner where the lamp-light cast its aura.

The girl was standing there, looking up and down the street anxiously. She wore a thin white summer coat, a halo hat. There was grace in every line of her slender body. But there was tension, too. Her white-gloved hands tugged at her purse.

The Phantom moved, unseen by her, until he was at the very fringe of the lighted corner-in the shadow of the last building there.

Then, low and soft, in a voice that was noncommittal, he called, "Queen Stella!"

Chapter IX
"Choppy" Investigates

Starting, the girl whirled. Her delicately featured, oval face showed whitely beneath auburn hair. For a moment she was confused, frightened.

Then she saw the vague figure standing in the gloom.

She stepped closer. But Van kept his slouch-hatted head down so she could not see him clearly.

"You came —" she almost questioned in a taut voice. It was impossible to tell from her tone whether she was grateful or not. But evidently she assumed he was the Phantom, for her words rushed on:

"You must not try to detain me. There is one thing I must tell you. It's about Al Millett —"

"Yes?" he prompted as she hesitated, his voice non-committal.

Her words came out passionately now; "Al Millett is not the fiend the police think! He was just a good actor-that's all! A charlatan, call him!"

Van's eyes narrowed. How did this girl-who could not be more than in her early twenties-talk so surely about Al Millett? And her voice was desperate, pleading, he noticed.

"You must believe me," she almost sobbed. "You must not hunt him down like a rat."

As she spoke she was shaking her purse, a white purse that gleamed in the light. It might have been purely nervousness, but on the other hand —"You and the police are wasting time seeking Al Millett. He isn't —"

The Phantom moved with the speed of lightning!

He had felt, rather than heard, the stealthy steps on the pavement. Now he saw dark shadowy figures, saw automatics whipping up toward his own figure.

Instantly he leaped past the girl, directly into the light of the street-lamp which shone upon his made-up face!

He knew that at that instant he was closer to death than he had ever been before. He knew that if his disguise were imperfect, if there were any flaw-Behind him now he heard the click-click of running high heels. The girl-running away! But he had no time for her now. Those revolvers were leveled right at him.

Then, "Hold it, guys! Hell, it's Choppy!" snarled the voice of Monk Gorman.

Van now turned around in feigned surprise which hid his relief. He saw the big, slickered gang leader coming forward with lowering gun. Saw the broken-nosed Gus, the pallid-faced Tony, and one other capped thug.

"Sure, it's me!" he answered, simulating perfectly the husky voice of Choppy, though he had heard it but briefly. "Who the hell did you think I was?"

The girl had vanished now. She was nowhere in sight.

Monk Gorman cursed. "What the devil you doin' out here, Choppy? Your orders was to wait in the house, so when that Phantom guy came —"

"Choppy was talkin' to the dame!" Gus put in.

"Sure, I was," Van returned. He knew he was on delicate, perilous ground now. For he still couldn't tell whether the girl had deliberately signaled these gunmen or not. "She stopped me and begun to talk. I'd come out-to see why the Phantom guy hadn't showed up," he said, with clever ambiguity.

"Okay, okay, forget it!" growled Monk Gorman. "So th' Phantom didn't fall for th' dame's gag, eh?"

"Maybe that blast really got him last night," Gus suggested.

"Nix!" Monk growled. "The boss said he's still alive."

Van's eyes narrowed imperceptibly. How could this "Boss" of theirs be sure that he was alive?

"Well, come on guys. No sense waitin' around-and cops might show." Monk Gorman gestured impatiently with his gun. "Jes' as well come, too, Choppy."

Choppy followed the rest obediently. He was grateful that they did not go back to the house. Either Gorman had forgotten or cared nothing about leaving Choppy's automatic rifle there.

The mob leader led the way hurriedly around a corner to the same dark sedan which had been used for Van's kidnaping the night before.

Once more the Phantom rode in that car, this time as a member of the gang, seated in the rear between Monk and Gus.

The ride proved a long one. The car worked eastward across the city as the night gathered. Again it rolled openly through traffic. Once it passed right by a police radio prowl-car —and Monk huddled back, gripping his gun. But the bluecoats did not suspect the sedan.

Van was silent-not risking any questions, lest he betray the fact he was an impostor. A grim hope sustained him as he played this perilous masquerade. If only it led him where he surmised it should.

The mists of another waterfront slowly engulfed the rolling car. The East River, this time. Up onto the ramp of the Queensborough Bridge. There was still no conversation, the gunmen evidently feeling tense while in traffic. The car followed the bridge traffic into Queens, and onto Vernon Boulevard.

Northward Tony now drove at a rapid clip through the deepening night. As the road grew more lonely, Monk Gorman sighed, leaned forward.

"We'll be plenty early tonight," he gruffed. "An' we ain't bringin' such good news. You sure you didn't see that Phantom guy, Choppy?"

"I tole you," retorted the man they thought was Choppy. "I was watchin' for him, all set to let him have it. Hell, you don't think I'd let that bird go if I got a chance to plug him, do ya?" Convincing underworld hatred of the Phantom threaded his tone.

"I guess you wouldn't." Gorman laughed evilly. "Not since the Boss fixed up that special medicine for crossers —the Ladle!"

As he pronounced those last words, Van saw the other thugs shudder perceptibly.

"The Ladle sure is a tough rap!" the broken-nosed Gus put in. "Maybe it wouldn't work in winter, but now —"

Tony gave a nervous laugh from the front seat:

"The Boss musta been in a hot country all right to think o' that one!"

Van made a pretense of joining their mingled awe and dread. What, he wondered, was this thing they called the Ladle? Why did they mention the "Boss" as having been in a hot country?

The gunmen fell silent again as lights and buildings loomed ahead. The sedan was rolling into Astoria. It passed on to the outskirts on to a road now where huge shed-like buildings, some of them having as many glass panes as greenhouses, reared in the night.

Motion picture studios! Here the big companies produced their small percentage of eastern-made pictures. Van's eyes narrowed in his disguised face. Gordon Drake owned some of those studios, he knew.

They passed the last of the line of sheds, rolled on a full mile more. And then, well-isolated from all the rest, another studio loomed. And here the car slowed.

This studio bore little resemblance to the modern structures they had passed. It looked small and old, deserted-with cracks in its many glass panes.

Obviously a relic of bygone days of the old silent movies which were thrown together hurriedly and cheaply, their casts composed of actors who were ashamed to be associated with the new show medium.

Even the grounds where it stood were deserted and isolated. The sedan turned into a side road and came to a stop before the dark building. In the gloom, Van saw other shadowy cars on the grounds.

"Okay, guys!" Gorman directed. "End of th' line."

The Phantom, his pulses throbbing, piled out of the car with the rest and followed Gorman to a boarded-up door. The leader gave a sharp rap, a timed signal and gruff challenge issued from within.

"Open up!" Monk growled.

The barrier opened. Past a shadowy, capped man who was evidently on guard, Monk led his companions. Through gloom, thence through another doorway, into the vast interior of the studio.

To Van's astonishment, there were lights here —a dim but ample illumination coming from bulbs strung on wires. His heart tightened with inner excitement. These lights were cleverly hidden despite the glass-paned building. For the glass was painted on the inside so it would be opaque. The paint looked fresh, recent.

Devilishly clever! From the outside this studio looked deserted, empty and dark. But inside it could teem with life.

The hum of many gruff, coarse voices filled the place. Standing or seated on packing boxes and other bits of equipment were a whole crowd of men, all of whom bore-in their manner, guise, or voice-the stamp of the underworld.

The Fang's gang! Assembled here, and members still coming in! Van recognized some of them. He saw the gash-mouthed man whose name was Pete, and whose shoulder was in a sling-Van had wounded him in that fight when he had posed as Eddie Collins. He saw others whom he recognized only by memory of rogue's gallery pictures.

Here in this old studio were gathered the co-ordinated mobsters of four former leaders who had been killed, their power usurped! The most powerful mob of desperadoes ever organized under one leadership! It was amazing.

They were all in attitudes of leisure. Some played cards, others smoked, others bent over a crap game. Van, still with Monk's crowd, walked into the midst of this devilish gathering, feeling like a man who has entered a den of beasts!

Inwardly, he prayed that his disguise was good enough to pass him by them all. That no one would suspect that he wasn't the real Choppy.

His eyes took in the strange surroundings. Piles of old sets in corners. Tarpaulin-covered shapes here and there on the floor. Part of the old equipment, presumably.

Monk swaggered through the gathering as voices greeted him.

"Okay, men, okay!" came his salutary reply. "We gotta wait here now, maybe some time. Meanwhile, let's see if we got everything ship-shape. Spike!"

A thug came forward.

"What'd you do with the bundle?" Monk asked, and Van saw the big man pale strangely.

"It's over there in the corner. I was afraid to get rid of it, Monk-until I got definite orders. Maybe somebody would find —"

"Okay. But hell, we don't want it around here. Well, leave it go."

Van had followed the speech closely, as well as the thug's pointing finger.

"Hey, Choppy-wanna come in?" one of the crap-shooters suddenly jerked up with the question.

"Naw," Van answered. Crap-shooting was something no two men did alike. He couldn't risk impersonating Choppy at rolling the dice. "Count me out tonight. I'm feelin' kinda low cause I didn't spot that Phantom guy."

"Well, can you beat that? First time Choppy ever dodged a crap game!" one of the others put in. And Van tensed. He must be careful, extremely careful.

Discreetly, he withdrew from the players. Moving unobtrusively, he threaded his way through the studio. He knew where he wanted to go, but he was taking his time getting there, making sure to attract no suspicion or attention.

Slowly, cautiously, he worked his way towards the corner of the studio to which the thug named Spike had pointed. As yet he saw nothing there but old refuse.

The atmosphere, he could feel now was getting tenser as the night deepened. There was a sense of expectancy among these thugs that made Van determined to stay here, to see this thing through. He had abandoned the idea of getting out while he still might manage it to call the police to surround the lair. For that would not catch the criminal he really sought.

Finally he drew close to that shadowy corner. He glanced around. No one looking this way. Monk had gone off to speak to others of the mob.

The Phantom moved swiftly, for a moment he was out of the role of Choppy, using his own lithe speed. The shadows of the corner engulfed him. His eyes darted around as he moved.

Suddenly his foot collided with something heavy, lumpy. He glanced down. There was a burlap bundle at his feet. It was not very large, yet Van felt a premonitory chill as he glanced at it. Something ugly and sinister about that bundle! He remembered Monk's paling face.

The Phantom stooped. His hands reached the burlap. He had to roll the bundle to get the covering off, so he gave a quick jerk. Then his blood went cold, as two bloody, gruesome shapes tumbled out of the wrapping.

A pair of human legs!

Legs hacked off above the knee, hideously amputated-with severed bone, bloody arteries and tendons showing raw and ghastly. But what filled the Phantom with a sense of horrified revulsion was the size of those legs.

They were small-spindly! The legs of a child!

For a moment all Van's conception of the case was thrown into a turmoil. Was this some new kind of crime of the devilish murderer who called himself the Fang? Was it possible that he had killed a helpless child?

Somewhere in the studio a bell clanged sharply.

It brought Van up rigid, made him whirl in alarm. Quick relief came as he saw that no eyes were turned in his direction. All were looking the other way, toward the other end of the studio.

Monk's voice rose then. "Get your places, everybody! Hurry! Choppy! Where the hell's Choppy?"

Chapter X
Klieg Lights

Just like that! Caught here at this moment, the Phantom knew suspicion would fasten upon him.

His mind raced. Then, deliberately, he raised his voice "Okay, okay, I'm comin'!"

But his voice did not seem to come from where he was hastily rewrapping the burlap around the gruesome, spindly legs. Instead, it seemed to come vaguely from the crowd of thugs. Ventriloquism was an art the Phantom had mastered along with all other arts of mimicry and disguise.

Quickly thrusting the gruesome bundle wrapped back into the shadows, he darted along the wall and came out in the center of the studio, presenting himself to Monk Gorman all in a breathless second.

"You stay by me," Monk ordered. "You gotta report on th' Phantom guy." As he spoke, others were busily removing the tarpaulin from the shapes Van had assumed to be old equipment. Black metal showed —a glimmer of glass. Then, a sudden hiss-and Van recoiled, his eyes suddenly blinded, dazzled.

A dozen super-powerful arc lights had suddenly gone on simultaneously. Kliegs! The modern, blazing lights of the movies! These were the shapes which the tarpaulins had hidden.

Their blinding flood blotted out the mild glow of other lights as though they had not been. Their heat permeated the studio almost like a blast.

The entire mob was thrown into vivid clearness, every face showing clear. Van felt trepidation about his make-up. He was glad he had spent some time putting on the disguise. For it must withstand that glare!

Monk seated himself on a packing case. Van followed suit. All others settled down facing the array of lights which, the Phantom saw, were grouped so that they came from one general direction-the opposite end of the studio. Blinking, the thugs must expose themselves to the full torture of the glare which was like a solid wall, beyond and behind which no human eye could possibly see.

As all voices ceased talking, and a hush fell over the assemblage, Van sensed a presence behind that wall of glaring light. An evil presence which intruded itself here in this strange studio hideout, making its horror felt even by the hardened crooks. Abruptly the silence was broken. A voice rang out from beyond the lights, a rasping, blighting voice: "This meeting is now in order! No one is to leave his place unless told to do so!"

Van listened carefully to the rasped tones, as his companions stiffened in mingled awe and dread. The Phantom could not identify the voice as any he had heard. He strained his eyes futilely to penetrate beyond the glare. Did he see a vague shape in that gloom beyond them? He could not tell-for the shape blurred into myriad dancing colors as his eyeballs ached from the sheer attempt.

"So far," the voice spoke again, "I have few complaints to make. You have proved yourself an obedient and efficient mob! Your former leaders must have trained you well! But they were small fry! You are working for a real Big Shot now! Already you have seen the returns! But that is what you, in your parlance, call chicken-feed! I have news for you tonight, good news!"

The men in the glaring light leaned forward with tense eagerness. Van's own eyes were narrowed now. His hand was close to the pocket where he had substituted Choppy's automatic pistol for his own.

He knew that the man who stood hidden behind that battery of light was indeed the criminal he sought, the brain behind this ghastly trail of death and robbery! But the criminal was well protected from any possible attack. Those lights made him an impossible target. He could see every face, every move, without being seen himself!

"I have news!" the voice rasped out. "Tomorrow the police of New York will see a robbery unparalleled! A robbery of millions-millions, which I shall share with you all! It is for this that I have prepared you, for this I have gathered you into one great mob!"

There was a tense, eager intake of breaths. Van's own lips tightened. A robbery! A climax to the crimes-tomorrow!

Monk suddenly rose now, spoke gruffly. "Listen, Boss! I'm in charge of it, ain't I? Have you changed your plans? Or are you gonna take care o' things at the office of that feller Drake?"

Even as Van pricked up his ears at the name, the voice of the master criminal snarled out with sudden menace that made Monk recoil. "That will do, Monk! I'll give you the proper orders at the right time."

Gordon Drake, the movie producer. And this was a studio! Why was the criminal so quick to suppress that name? Why had Monk mentioned it in connection with the robbery?

These questions raced through Van's mind while he listened. "Sometimes, Monk," the voice came like a purr now, "you are too impulsive! Perhaps Ricco, or one of those others, would have made a better lieutenant!"

"No, Boss!" Monk trembled. "Hell—I just sorta got excited, thinkin' of all that dough!"

"Very well. But be careful. Remember—*the Ladle* awaits bunglers as well as traitors!"

Again, this time from the criminal leader, came that peculiar name. And men shifted. Van saw several eyes glance upwards, towards the high ceiling. He saw nothing there but the cross-beams of a gallery and roof.

"I am impatient enough with you. You didn't get the Phantom tonight, did you?"

It was a statement rather than a question. The devilish Boss knew-somehow!

Monk spoke quickly, defensively. "He didn't show up, Boss. Only the dame showed. At least that's what Choppy says," he was quick to shift the blame. "He was talkin' to the dame when we come by to pick him up."

"Choppy!" Van's heart tightened as the criminal rasped out the name. "Step up front and let me have some words with you!"

The Phantom did not risk hesitation.

Rising, knowing that all eyes were on him, he strode forward before the gathering.

"Closer! I want to see you!"

Still Van dared not hesitate. He walked closer-until the array of lights met him, the heat of them engulfed him.

He felt sweat pop out beneath his make-up. Now he saw a dim, shadowy shape beyond the lights. But he could distinguish nothing. He could feel eyes probing him, scrutinizing him.

"Well, Choppy? Why did you talk to the girl?"

"It was like this, Boss," Van replied in the voice of Choppy. He told the same story he had told Gorman-that when the Phantom hadn't shown up he had gone out to look, the girl had accosted him, started talking to him, that he was trying to pump her when Monk startled her away.

"What did she say? Who did she think you were?" came the cross-examination from the gloom.

Van took the cue he read in that question. "She seemed to think I was the Phantom guy," he said, realizing how perilous was the implication of the words. "It was kinda dark, an'—"

"Oh—" There was a pause. Then, to Van's tense relief: "All right, Choppy." And Van turned to go from that hot glare which was searing his very flesh.

"Just a moment," the voice called him back, and he had to remain. "I want you to keep in mind, Choppy, and all the rest of you-that we must get the Phantom!" Hate threaded the rasping tones now. "He alone stands in my way, dares to cross my trail! He must be destroyed. Destroyed and—"

Abruptly, the voice broke off. Simultaneously, Van's heart stopped in its very beat! His every nerve flashed the frightful warning to his brain!

He felt it then! Something was oozing down his face, wet and sticky! Melting make-up!

The make-up of Choppy's features was changing, blurring and lengthening under the arch criminal's eyes. The Klieg lights! Van had not thought their heat was quite so strong! But they had done this deadly work!

There was a roar like that of a beast from the astounded leader.

The Phantom dropped to the floor, and began rolling to one side as a flash of flame leaped, just visible, from behind the lights. A flash of flame, and another!

He heard the bullets whine over his head, heard yells from the rest of the gang. He got out his own gun, whipped it around, fired two shots in the general direction whence those flashes had showed. But the uninterrupted roaring of that snarling voice told him he had missed.

"Grab him, you fools! He's an impostor! Hey, Rube!"

Van tried for another shot, this time in the direction of the voice, but, like a pack of sudden charging wolves, a score of thugs were upon him!

They, too, saw the running make-up now, and understood. For a moment Van thought they would tear him apart. Their feet kicked him so that his aching body doubled; their fists crashed to his sticky face, their revolvers swung like clubs at him. Disarmed, stunned, still blinded by the glare of lights, he could not resist capture.

He was yanked toward the front lights again. Monk's big paw, holding a handkerchief, was swabbing at his face. But the make-up, though smeared, was indelible enough to keep his real features covered-his only boon in this moment of trapped helplessness.

"So you thought to spy on us, did you?" the voice rasped out savagely. "I can guess who you are. You're the Phantom! What have you done to Choppy?"

Van neither denied nor affirmed anything. He was silent, inwardly fighting against a surge of despair. Those lights had betrayed him, and he had been neatly trapped!

"You won't talk? You'll regret that; you'll be raving for mercy!" came the savage voice. "Dawn is almost come, and the weather promises fair!" Van wondered at this poetic digression. "Whatever you may have learned here, Phantom, will never leave your lips!"

Van thought of what little he had learned. There was to be a robbery of tremendous magnitude. There was something connected with Gordon Drake's office. And there was-in a corner of this studio-the most jarring bizarre note in this whole mystery. A wrapped pair of childlike legs!

"Take him," the unseen criminal roared then, "to *the Ladle*!"

"Come on, guys!" Monk took up the command, in savage delight.

Chapter XI
A Trick with Mirrors

Helpless, the Phantom was dragged across the glare-lit floor of the studio, to one side, where there was a flight of ascending stairs.

The gangsters took him up to that gallery above. Then still further upwards, ascending a narrow steep stairs. The fresh air of outdoors suddenly smote the Phantom. He saw the sky above, the stars fading in the first grey flush of dawn.

They had taken him to the roof of the studio-to what seemed to be a huge pit in the otherwise slanted, glass-paned roof. At the edge of this sunken pit was a small, open-fronted shed. In it Van caught a momentary glimpse of gleaming levers.

He was lowered to this platform above the pit. Kept there by menacing guns and rough hands. He shifted his gaze to the pit itself.

Within the pit was a huge, globular affair. It had a peculiar sheen, reflecting off every trace of light, so that it seemed like an immense bowl of scintillating jewels, something like the mirror-set globes that twirled under the beam of a spot-light to reflect dots of light on a dance floor.

The Phantom knew at once what this was. That bowl was made of a collection of reflectors, the powerful concentrating reflectors used in motion picture making. It was a sun mirror of sinister and diabolical design.

Monk was talking to the broken-nosed Gus. "You'll stick here, Gus, an' take care o' this! You know how to move them levers! It's set now, by the Boss himself, for sunrise. You make the first change at six-thirty, an' every fifteen minutes after that. Here, I'm givin' you my watch-it keeps right time!"

Van, still twisting his head amid his captors, saw Monk handing over a large gold watch-saw Gus taking it.

At that moment, the Phantom noticed that his captors were momentarily relaxed.

Their eyes were on Monk and Gus.

A wave of grim desperation fired the Phantom's muscles with a sudden surge of strength. With a gritted oath, he leaped to his feet, his lithe body hurling upward in the very midst of his captors!

His feet crashed out before him like a ball of iron. It caught the heavy beefy face of the nearest thug and sent him sprawling. Before others could recover from their surprise, the Phantom hurled across the platform-against the broken-nosed Gus!

Gus snarled an oath. The rest, drawing their guns, dared not fire for fear of hitting their companions. Van's hand snaked down at Gus's wrists, one of which was still taped. He pushed Gus toward the shed while the latter wrestled furiously.

Even then the others closed in, raising revolver butts like vicious clubs. But the Phantom still fought with Gus in the faint, dim light of the open shed. His right hand was busy at Monk's watch while his left held Gus in a crushing head-lock.

A second more-give him a second more!

Myriad stars danced before his eyes as a gun-butt smashed against his skull. Hands, like talons, tore him away from the cursing, frightened Gus. The rain of blows left little consciousness in his body.

The next thing he knew, he was being taken down into that glittering, reflector-lined bowl. It swayed under gangster feet. In its very center was a metal shaft which rose vertically out of the base of the bowl like the stamen of a flower.

To this the Phantom was bound with steel wire! It seared through his clothes, through his very flesh.

He knew that he was trapped, was in the worst predicament that ever had overtaken him! Yet, even as the gangsters climbed out, leaving him here, there was a hope in his heart, even though it was a feeble hope.

"Okay, Gus! We gotta go," came Monk's voice. A moment later the big man's coarse face appeared, over the rim of the bowl. "So long, Phantom!" he gloated mockingly. "You'll be yellin' your head off soon enough! An' no one'll hear you! You may be a tough bird, but you'll jes' be a fried egg now. Sorry I can't wait to hear you sizzle."

The coarse face withdrew. There was a receding tramp of feet as the gang filed down from the roof. Only the broken-nosed Gus remained. He paced the platform above Van, glancing down now and then, first at the captive and then at his borrowed watch.

The Phantom had already begun to struggle carefully against his bonds. Thus far no bonds, or rope or wire, had ever been strong enough to hold him. He knew he could get out of these, but it would take time-too much time, he feared.

For now the sky was growing lighter. Dawn was on hand. And the wires were still searing deep into his flesh.

He heard sounds of motors-cars starting, gears shifting. He knew that the meeting was breaking up below. The mob was leaving to perpetrate that gigantic robbery while he remained here, helpless. The criminal leader, the murderer whom the police sought as Al Millett, the Fang, would be taking his secret departure while the Phantom was powerless to prevent him.

Going loose again, to commit more crimes! A murderer who had killed two men by brutally ripping out their sides, braining a third with a cudgel, leaving a fourth corpse with a broken crowbar in his skull and-Van thought of those childlike, spindly legs, and revulsion sickened him.

Gus swaggered above the rim of the Phantom's open-air prison, complete monarch of this domain by virtue of the departure of all the rest. He watched the sky eagerly.

The Phantom, struggling against the wire bonds at every opportunity, also watched the sky.

Slowly it began to redden in the East. The red turned to gold. The sun rose, bursting into slow but brilliant life. The bowl in which the Phantom stood bound glowed dazzlingly then in prismatic splendor. The rays of the sun hit the reflectors-and one and all, they awoke to life and magnified the rays, concentrated them upon the Phantom.

Even though the sun was as yet not in its full power, those intensified beams immediately seared through Van's clothes, began to warm, then blister his flesh! Sweat oozed down his face, down his body, in rivulets. *The Ladle* —diabolic invention of a devilish criminal-was beginning its fatal, ghastly work!

Van, with his knowledge of science had calculated that work on first glimpse of the device. It was simple-fiendishly simple. The bowl was so arranged that, by a mechanism, it could be turned with the moving sun at timed intervals, the levers in the shed motivating the turning. And each new angle would be calculated to cause the sunlight gathered by its concave-mirror walls to focus on the Phantom's bound body!

Van Loan understood now why the crooks had mentioned the likelihood of the Boss having come from a "hot country." They were right; he had come from Hell.

Even now the blinding, concentrated heat was growing. It was eddying upon the Phantom in waves. His eyes were unable to meet it, his flesh seemed to coil and wither. His sweat was drying now. And the wires that still held him were also growing unbearably hot!

To yell was futile-else he would not have been left ungagged. He must conserve his strength; he must keep cool. He had used his most consummate skill and science while wrestling with Gus. Had he miscalculated?

"Well, Phantom? How's the weather down there now?" The mocking tones of Gus floated down to him. Through his already heat-swollen eyes he saw the broken-nosed thug through a red haze. "At six-thirty I'll give you a little swing."

The Phantom worked desperately at his bonds. With the heat blaze that enveloped him growing ever hotter, he could not long withstand it. Death would be a matter of perhaps a half hour of such exposure —a long half-hour of torture, of blistering flesh, of blinded eyes! For the sun was shining at him through so many magnifying glasses; the bowl was hot as blazing fire.

He struggled coolly, systematically-knowing well that it would take him more than thirty minutes to get out of this wire. As it was, he knew he could not retain consciousness for many more minutes. His very stoicism was rebelling against the agony of the heat which had not yet begun to do its real damage.

Tropical death in Astoria! It seemed an ironical joke —a crazy paradox. Yet, it was coming if he had made an error. He gritted his teeth. He would know shortly, at least. And then, when he really felt his face beginning to blister, Gus's voice chortled again.

"Six-thirty —an' Monk's watch is always right!"

Gus's footsteps banged on the wooden platform beyond the rim. He went into the shed to the levers. There came a sound of meshing cogs, the hum of electricity. *The Ladle* began moving like a huge swing. And at that moment Van clung to the one hope that sustained him.

He waited breathlessly for the effect of the moving bowl. Timed properly, it would only bring the sun's shifting rays hotter upon him. But improperly timed, it would be out of focus.

His heart soared! The blaze of light that was meant to destroy him shifted just a little to one side of his bound body, as the wabbling bowl went still. Those rays were no longer directly upon him, though the bowl itself was still a fiery furnace.

Would Gus see this? Would his coarse faculties be shrewd enough to comprehend the truth? This had been the whole purpose of that desperate scuffle with Gus. Knowing he could not make any real break at that moment for liberty, he had managed to do the one thing that was now reprieving him temporarily.

He had managed deftly, while keeping Gus's attention distracted by the struggle, to reset Monk's watch-setting it forward by about eight minutes. Eight minutes, enough to upset this device which was as mathematical as a moving sundial. Gus had not been told what time the sun began its work. He had been told only to start working the lever at six-thirty and make an adjustment every fifteen minutes thereafter.

Hence the sun was now thrown off. Its blazing concentration point, unless Gus suspected, would stay where it was, to one side of the Phantom. And Van, no longer in the direct glare, began to recover his strength; his remarkable stamina quickly generating new energy.

Gus's head appeared again above the rim. He peered down, blinking. The brilliant reflectors defied detection of the actual concentration point.

Lest he look closer, Van now did the thing which his stoicism had repressed when he was in real agony. He opened his dry mouth, began to groan, to yell, to shout in cries of pain.

A cruel, mocking laugh rose above him. "Boy, oh boy, wish the gang was here!" Gus chortled. "They'd like this-seein' how the Phantom can't really take it after all! How he's just as human as the rest of us! Cripes! I wish I had a pair o' smoked glasses."

He turned away, chortling.

Van again worked at the wires, worked until another fifteen minutes had passed. Which he knew when again the bowl tilted and the motor hummed. Once more the sun-glare of concentration remained fixed to one side of his body.

And then one arm came wresting out of the wires. The wrist caught, the wire cutting into it excruciatingly. Van let the pain of it out in another deliberate yell. He twisted the wrist, deftly, carefully at the same time.

It came free. One arm free was all the Phantom needed. The rest was a matter of seconds.

The wires slid jerkily off his lithe body. He moved from the shaft, moved to the sloping side of the bowl just beneath the platform. When he tried to touch it, the heat of the mirrors seared his hands. He tore some of his own borrowed clothing off to use as protection.

There was purchase in the interstices between the reflectors, and he began to climb, the heat beating against his body. A little further now-almost to the rim —

A yell of enraged alarm greeted him. Gus, turning on the platform, had seen! With a snarl the thug leaped forward, gun whipping out. At the same instant, the Phantom's body literally catapulted over the rim, over and forward!

Leaping with all his strength, Van Loan caught the thug's gun arm as the frenzied man was taking aim! Instantly the two were struggling in a fierce conflict on the platform! Struggling against the very rail of the platform, beyond which the high studio roof inclined with its opaque panes of glass.

Gus, who was powerfully built, was fighting like a frightened beast … realizing he was up against the scourge of the underworld, a man he had twice seen make miraculous escapes from certain death. Snarling, he pushed Van with his whole body against the wooden rail.

It splintered, opening a gap. The Phantom's feet pulled him up as he swayed perilously. Then, both his hands caught the thug who was lurching against him. The thing he next did was instinctive.

A jiu jitsu hold, and Gus, heavy though he was, went flying through the air over the Phantom's head. Screaming, the thug landed on the slanted glass roof. The panes shattered, but the metal framework held. Gus fell forward from the impetus, his body rolling, rolling. Grim-eyed, Van saw it reach the roof's edge. Saw it topple off and go hurtling down through fully sixty feet of space, to the stone paving below. There was a ghastly thud. The body, a tiny heap down there, lay still The Phantom swore grimly. Gus, alive, might have told him where that big robbery was to take place. But again he had had no chance to take one of this desperate mob alive.

He walked tiredly to the roof entrance, into the studio, downward through its interior.

The place was empty. Even that burlap-wrapped bundle-and all other evidence was gone. The only thing left to do was to find where the big robbery was to be, and to prevent it if possible.

He stood, swaying, exhausted and dizzied from his ghastly experience. For a moment he felt too tired to go on-tired enough to drop right here. But then, remembering Monk Gorman's reference to Gordon Drake, his body straightened; a purposeful gleam leaped once more into his sun-dazzled eyes. He sprinted from the building.

Chapter XII
The Armored Truck Job

Morning activity to the average New Yorker, seemed the same as it did any other sunny morning-the usual bustle of traffic and scurrying workers.

But actually there was a difference. All over the city police patrols had been doubled. Extra prowl-cars were sweeping through every precinct. Squads of detectives, men who usually waited at station houses for their calls, were out on the streets, keen-eyed and alert.

For the police had received a tip from that Nemesis of Crime, the Phantom. Somewhere a big robbery was about to break! And, while they scoured the streets, Richard Curtis Van Loan himself stood, grim and expectant, in a closet in the empty office of Gordon Drake, motion picture producer.

Again the Phantom was masked, the domino covering the features of a slightly vacant-faced young Englishman in tweeds. He had slipped into this towering office building before it had opened. His pliable bit of wire had picked the lock of Gordon Drake's office. He was waiting for that which was supposed to break at Drake's office.

Van had come to New York from the abandoned studio in Astoria in a car. He had stopped off at his own penthouse apartment on Park Avenue for a shower, shave, breakfast, and fresh change of clothes. He was little the worse for his grueling experience-though his face was red with sunburn, under his make-up.

At his apartment, Van had phoned Inspector Gregg, and then called the New York Academy of Medicine, which had someone on duty night and day. He had requested a service of them, a service that required them to canvass, by their own swift means of communication, doctors throughout an entire nation!

"If you get any answers-kindly hold them for me," Van had finished. He had identified himself as the Phantom in that call, explaining that the evidence was vital to his case.

From Inspector Gregg he had learned of the progress of the case. The police were still investigating the mysterious Count Karnov. They were still rounding up any persons remotely resembling the Fang's description. Bernard J. Andrews was still missing. Also, Queen Stella.

Van had taken these facts, then given his instructions to the police.

Now, cramped in the closet of Drake's sumptuous office, he waited patiently.

Presently, as the morning sun slanted wider through the office windows, Van heard a key in the lock. He pulled the closet door to a chink, through which he could still command a view.

The frosted-glass door opened. Gordon Drake, the heavy-set movie producer, strode in alone. He took off his cap stiffly, but left on his cape-like topcoat.

He glanced about the office. Then, scowling, he began to pace back and forth as if waiting. Van remained motionless in the closet.

Came a knock on the door. "Come," growled Drake, as though he expected it.

Into the room strode two more of the men involved in the Fang case, men Van recognized as Drake pronounced their names.

"Hello, Corbin-good morning, Meade!"

Paul Corbin, slender and effeminate night-club owner. Kenneth Meade, the eccentric restaurateur who wore a long, tight buttoned coat and articulated with difficulty.

Somehow, seeing the three of them together, Van sensed again that queer feeling all the men involved gave everybody-something strange, intangible, they had in common.

The three stood looking at each other. It was Corbin who spoke. The little man seemed agitated.

"Drake, are you going to give your consent to this foolish plan!" he asked in his high voice.

Drake shrugged. "It's out of my hands," came his reply. "I don't care a hoot, to tell you the truth."

Meade shifted his heavy-coated frame. "I told Corbin he is on the wrong track," he said in a hard labored voice.

"All right!" Corbin shrilled. He waved an angry hand at them. "You're going to regret this, both of you. Mark my words!" Despite its shrillness, there was menace in his tones. "You all think you're clever-but you're fools, see! Fools!"

He whirled angrily, started for the door.

"Where are you going?" Drake demanded. "What are you up to now, Corbin?"

Carbon's eyes blazed with a light that seemed almost fanatical to the watching Phantom.

"I'm going out to prove," he said, as if too impulsive to weigh his words, "that the police can still be fools, as well as you! That vast amount of money —"

He broke off and stalked through the door. Meade started uncertainly after him.

"Sit down, Meade," Drake said dryly. "There's really nothing we can do now. The Gargoyles must trust each other. Corbin can do nothing."

The closet door swung open, revealing a masked man with leveled automatic.

"But there's a great deal that I can do," Van's voice clipped, cold as the steel of his own Colt automatic. "Do not move, gentlemen, if you value your lives!"

Drake and Meade recoiled, violently startled.

"The Phantom!" exclaimed Drake, face paling.

"Right," snapped Van Loan. "I'll talk with you men later. Just now I've an engagement with Mr. Corbin. Remain quietly here, if you value your lives."

He heard an elevator door closing even then. Corbin going down! Leaving the two speechless and immobile, he darted out of the office and sprinted for the elevator bank. He was not followed.

As he reached the elevator doors, pressing the down button, the Phantom took off his mask. To his satisfaction, an express elevator stopped for him in the next instant.

"Go straight down, buddy," he directed the operator.

"But I —" the capped man's protests ceased at the sight of the bill extended towards him. The elevator didn't even make its express stops.

As it reached the main floor, its doors sliding open, Van saw that the other elevator which had preceded it more slowly was just coming to a stop. The slender figure of Corbin, hatless, walked hurriedly through the foyer and out the main glass doors. Behind him walked a pleasant looking but vacant-faced Englishman.

Van Loan saw Corbin climb into a small, expensive roadster. The motor started with a hasty grind of the self-starter. The car slid from the curb, quickly gathered speed as it headed across town.

Van hurried down the pavement, climbed into the coupe which he had left parked there. It was a coupe he had borrowed from the Police Department-one with special equipment with which the police were recently experimenting.

The Phantom's eyes flashed through the windshield even as he got the coupe going. Corbin's car was shrinking across the next intersection. Van stepped on the gas, maneuvered the coupe deftly through traffic, and when he was not far behind the roadster, he settled down grimly to the trail.

Across town his quarry led him, then onto Broadway, headed down-town. Corbin drove faster now, almost recklessly in the morning traffic. Once he passed a red light. Van passed it, too.

Broadway narrowed as the two cars finally reached its lower extremities, coming into the financial district with its tall skyscrapers and narrow, canyon-like streets. The roadster swung east, went onto Broad Street. It turned south again. Then, so suddenly that Van scarcely had time to follow suit, the roadster skidded to an abrupt stop.

It had stopped almost opposite a square stone building on the corner —a prominent bank which had its own truck entrance.

Out of that entrance now, a green-turreted armored truck was rolling, obviously leaving the bank on some errand. The truck turned onto Broad Street.

Van was still pressing down his own brake pedal, eyes on Corbin's roadster which had stopped almost in front of the truck. And now, astonishingly, Corbin's slender figure leaned out of its open door. Corbin was waving at the armored truck-commanding it to stop.

In the next instant, even as a chill premonition flashed through Van, several things happened at once, all with the breathless rapidity of a speeded-up motion picture.

The armored truck slowed momentarily. Its green turret swung warningly. Two sedans, a Buick and a Cadillac, suddenly curved clear across the street from the other side, their gears meshing. From two angles they converged towards the armored truck, which Corbin's car had already partially blocked.

The Phantom's foot left the brake pedal, going to the accelerator. His hand was on the gear-shift, his eyes tense and grim. He sent the coupe hurtling forward.

Above his engine he heard a spurt of fire. It came from the turret of the armored truck. A repeating rifle-shooting warningly.

The Cadillac sedan suddenly swung straight in then, to one side of the green truck. Van gave a cry. He saw something dark and heavy come hurtling out of the Cadillac's rear window, arc through the air and —A most deafening explosion shattered the morning air! A great blinding sheet of flame which quickly turned into smoke blotted out the entire armored truck from view.

The Phantom felt his coupe shiver with that reverberating concussion which shook his very teeth. The shatter-proof windshield in front of him became a mass of spider-webs. He heard screams as the explosion died-saw people on the pavement who had been hurled several feet, some of them badly hurt.

He was still driving the shaken coupe towards the scene. The billowing smoke was just dissipating. He caught a glimpse of the armored truck-and his heart chilled. The heavy vehicle was overturned, its wheels kicking around like some wounded animal's. Its armor plate was dented, broken.

Slouch-hatted figures were leaping upon it like human vultures. Van saw a big, slicker-clad form amid them. Monk Gorman! He saw them jerking open the shattered door of the armored truck.

As he continued to drive towards the scene, eyes grim as death, his hand moved to the dashboard of his coupe where there was an unusual array of dials. He turned a switch. He yanked out a microphone hanging by its wire to the dash. Driving with one hand, he spoke into the microphone in crisp tones: "Calling all cars —1st Division!" he bit out. "All cars-Signal 30! Signal 30! Armored car hold-up in progress at Broad Street and Fourth Street. Signal 30!"

He knew that his every word went through the powerful transmission set in this car. Tuned to the short-wavelength of every prowl-car in the city, it went out through the ether from the antenna atop Van's coupe. For this car was one of the only two cars in the Department that could send out radio calls even as the Voice at Headquarters sent them out.

Now the Phantom was at the scene. He saw the slouch-hatted mobsters snatching bags and packages out of the armored truck, working with speed and efficiency. In mere seconds they had evidently taken their loot-were scurrying back to the two waiting sedans, ignoring the damaged roadster of Corbin and the coupe of Van Loan.

The Cadillac started in the next instant. It swung away, bearing off its part of the loot.

The Phantom dropped the microphone, took the wheel in both hands, his lips a tight line of fierce purpose. He sent the little coupe careening around the scene in a spurt of speed to head them off-at least delay them!

The Cadillac was gathering speed. The Phantom pushed his accelerator to the floorboard. The coupe arced past the Cadillac, then diagonaled in on the big, fleeing car.

A tommy gun began its snarling chatter. Van heard bullets pelt like hail against the coupe's sides. One slug whined through the open window past his face. He glanced to one side and back-saw Monk's coarse features in the rear open window of the Cadillac behind the gibbering tommy.

The Cadillac, heavier and larger than the coupe, tried to threaten it out of the way with heavy iron fenders. Van swerved out. The Cadillac started to pass him. He saw it would get away.

He pulled his wheel hard around, his lithe body bracing simultaneously as he floor-boarded his accelerator. Like a startled deer, the coupe leaped into the side of the heavy Cadillac at an angle he thought should enable it to take the crash without completely telescoping.

There was a frightful impact of metal against metal. The coupe shivered, shaking every bone in the Phantom's body. Water spurted from the radiator, steamily. Then, with a shrieking of tortured metal, the coupe was dragged sideways. The Cadillac, locked by its running board with the coupe's fenders, tried desperately to pull the lighter car with it.

Monk's face leaned out-murderous, livid, Van ducked as he saw the tommy swinging to hose down the police car. Then, even as he thought the tommy would blast his stanch little coupe to ribbons, he saw Monk and the others start to abandon the Cadillac like frightened rats.

Only then did he hear the scream of sirens, scores of sirens, filling the already noise-shattered street. Police cars! Green coupes! Hurtling dark cruisers! Coming from two directions, turning in from every side street! Blockading the whole vicinity!

The Phantom's radio call had brought a response. Those cars had been waiting for just such a signal. "Signal 30—come quickly with drawn guns!"

Van leaped out of his wrecked, tangled coupe. The street was full of fresh sounds of gunfire now. Police positives roared. Smoke curled insidiously in the sun. Flame flashed. And thugs from both bandit cars were going down, riddled bodies hurling, bloody, to the street.

It was over by the time the Phantom limped out of his wreck. Grim-jawed cops were sheathing their guns. Others were trying to gather the bundles of currency, the bags, which were strewn amid the dead and in the two sedans. And other policemen began pulling out what was left of the men of the armored truck crew. Two had apparently died from the explosion; a third had been riddled by the gangsters. The fourth and fifth were badly maimed and unconscious.

* * *

"Well, we got a good part of the mob, anyway-even if Monk Gorman and two other of his men escaped!"

Five minutes later, in the ornate office of the bank, Inspector Gregg, who had also answered the radio call, spoke these words as he mopped his placid but heavy face with a handkerchief. "And from the looks of it, Phantom, you enabled us to save a large portion of the swag! How much did you say, Mister?"

This to the shaken, grey-haired president of the bank who was stacking piles of currency and bonds, some of them stained with blood, on his desk.

"Over two million dollars here." He announced the staggering sum, then shook his head. "The audacity of those thieves! It's lucky the money was saved. Certainly the bonding company would think there was something queer about the truck being robbed at our very doors! They'd say we didn't give it proper protection-or that there was some sort of inside work."

The Phantom having identified himself in his present disguise to the chief of detectives, glanced across the office. In a chair, attended by two policemen, sat Paul Corbin. The man's face was cut, and he seemed dazed, but he had refused ambulance attention.

"You say the original sum was almost three million," the Phantom then spoke to the bank president. "Isn't it unusual to send out such a sum? And on the face of it, don't you think you should tell us who authorized it, and where it was to go?"

The bank president hesitated. Then he made a gesture as if laying cards on the table. "The securities and money belonged to the Star Corporation," he announced. "They were being shipped to one of its authorized officers over in Brooklyn."

Van's eyes narrowed. The Star Corporation! The corporation which owned the building of the Gargoyle Club! He turned to the dazed Corbin.

"Well, Corbin, do you feel ready yet to offer an explanation?" he asked crisply.

"Explanation?" Corbin echoed. "What for? What have I done?"

"Why did you rush down here, and wave that armored truck to stop?"

The inspector, to whom this was news, turned with an exclamation. "What's that? He stopped the truck?"

Corbin was on his feet then, shakily.

"Yes —I tried to stop this fool move! And I'll tell you why!" he cried, a wild note in his voice. "Some of that money, a good part of it, belongs to *me!* And I didn't want it taken out of the vaults here! The others wouldn't listen to me. I told them it was dangerous. I told them that Gifford was making a stupid, blundering move —"

"Gifford?" the inspector echoed, while Van showed no surprise, remembering that John Gifford, amusement park owner, was president of the Star Corporation.

"Yes, Gifford! He sent the order. He was going to store our securities in his new big vault at Coney Island. The others refused to interfere! They said Gifford had the best business brain-if he made a move like this he must know it was the only move!"

Van turned with tacit inquiry to the bank president. Slowly that official nodded. "Yes, the order was authorized by John Gifford," he said.

The inspector's brow screwed into deep lines. "That's funny. Gifford ordering the movement of a lot of dough when he knows this Al Millett is on the loose with his gang, plundering and robbing all the men involved!"

The Phantom nodded. "I think," he suggested, "that it might pay to have an interview with Mr. Gifford about now."

Chapter XIII
The Fang Claims Another Victim

Driving rapidly, the Phantom sat beside the inspector in the latter's shield-fronted limousine a few minutes later as they headed into Brooklyn, and onto the highway to Coney Island to interview Gifford.

They had allowed Paul Corbin, still shaken and dazed, to go home from the bank, intending to grill him plenty a bit later.

With screaming siren giving it a clear road, the inspector's car made the trip to Coney Island in record time. Nevertheless it was well past noon when the maze of Ferris wheels, scenic railway tracks, carousels, and other amusement machines in which millions found thrills and pleasure loomed before the inspector's car, then engulfed it on Surf Avenue.

Gifford's Park was doing only a modest business now, at the tail end of the season. Most of the attractions were closed, although others were just opening up. Uniformed attendants guided the inspector's car to a small, but massive concrete building-Gifford's new offices and vault.

Getting out of the limousine, the Phantom and the inspector strode in. A man was pacing the office floor-agitated, worried looking. It was not Gifford! It was Carl Fenwick.

The clerical looking producer looked up with startled eyes which widened quickly at sight of Van Loan's innocuous face.

"Police?" he breathed. "Here?"

"Yes. What brought you out here, Mr. Fenwick?" Van asked casually.

"Gifford phoned for me to come!" Fenwick answered. "Said he had some news to tell me. I'm waiting for him now."

"He isn't here?" the inspector demanded.

"He was here. Just said 'hello' to me, then bolted out in a hurry-said he had to attend to something, and for me to wait."

The Phantom's eyes were suddenly tense. "When was that?"

"About three minutes ago, perhaps even less."

The inspector scowled. "That was just about the time we were coming into the Park! Wonder if he got word we were here?"

The Phantom, who had already considered that possibility, hurried to the door, out onto the Park grounds. The tension was still in his eyes; a strange apprehension was tightening around his heart.

He crisped a question at a special Park policeman standing on the pavement. The latter replied, "Yes, I saw Mr. Gifford. He went over that way-toward the Leap-for-Life."

He pointed toward the maze of spiraling tracks of the big rocket railway designed by the owner. It had evidently just started running. Two streamlined cars, half-filled with patrons, were beginning the ascent on one side, being dragged by the moving cable up the incline.

The Phantom quickened his fast stride, the somewhat confused inspector at his heels. They hurried toward the gigantic, futuristic railway.

At that instant, above the faint clatter of the climbing cars, there sounded a hoarse cry! A cry of terror —a feeble but blood-curdling sound drifting from far above!

Galvanized by the sound, the Phantom catapulted forward, his eyes darting upwards. Through the lattice-like, open trackwork, just in the middle of the arc of the first long and steepest hill of the railway, he glimpsed a vague, dark bulk!

The Phantom jerked his head back, crisped out with fierce haste, "Get them to turn off the power! Hurry, before those cars reach the top of the hill!"

He did not wait to see his command carried out. Never before had he moved with more lightning rapidity. He leaped for a ladder-one of the many ascending the framework of the tracks. The Phantom scrambled up like a monkey.

In seconds he was nearing the top. Simultaneously, his ears told him the cable had stopped moving. The power had been shut off. But then-His heart went chill!

On top of the long steep incline, he heard a rumble, a clattering rumble which grew rapidly louder. One of those cars had reached the hill crest before the power had been turned off. It was going over that crest! Like a rocket, it was coasting down the hill, hurtling earthward with its passengers!

The Phantom spurred his body up with a terrific lunge, climbed over the open track-work. He glanced up the converging rails of the steep ascent, saw the car coming down now, swaying and rocking with its roaring speed!

In the center of the tracks before him writhing weakly, huddled the corpulent figure of John Gifford.

He was not bound, seeming merely to have been stunned, and thus unable to move.

"Gifford!" Van yelled above the roaring, downcoming rocket car. "Gifford!"

Gifford raised his head, stirring a little clumsily, but remaining on the track. The Phantom got his footing on a tie, caught hold of a metal strut, and leaned out over the track as he saw the car growing huge-coming on like a juggernaut! A juggernaut that threatened to mangle and kill both Gifford and him-and perhaps wreck and kill its own passengers as well!

He swooped down in that instant, got the man by the collar and heaved. Despite his corpulent appearance, Gifford proved such a surprisingly light burden, that Van nearly jerked him over the outside of the track-edge.

He recovered his balance and held Gifford against the framework just as the massive car whizzed by like a rocket.

Then, hands of park workers who had come up the ladder reached out. They got Gifford down and the Phantom lowered himself over the edge.

One of his hands was skinned where the rushing car had lightly touched it.

Fenwick and the inspector were on hand below when the dazed Gifford was brought down. He stood, shaken and pale, looking confusedly at the masked Phantom.

"You-you saved my life, sir," he gasped weakly. "I couldn't move!" Stark terror was growing in his eyes. "I was called out by phone-told there was some trouble under the scenic track. I went there-and never knew what hit me! The next thing I knew I was on the track and the car was coming down."

The inspector, listening, dispatched policemen who had arrived at the scene to search the grounds. "It's the Fang again or I miss my guess!" he cursed. "Lord, will he never end this reign of terror?"

Fenwick, standing by white-faced, blurted out. "If only *you* would end it! Gifford, why wouldn't you and the others —"

Gifford jerked up his head fiercely. "No! Drake was right. I wanted to see you about that, Fenwick!" He seemed now to have made an almost remarkable recovery; his voice was strong now-the dominant voice of a hard-fisted, successful business man. "I took certain measures to protect our interests."

"If you mean that you ordered three million dollars shipped to you in an armored car," Van put in sharply, "those measures were not sufficient. We've just come from the attempted hijacking of that fortune!"

"What?" Both Gifford and Fenwick stared with bulging, horrified eyes, chorusing the exclamation in unison.

Then Fenwick almost screamed, "You ordered out that truck! Damn you, Gifford, you had no right —"

"Wait!" Gifford put in. His voice shook now with a horror that seemed greater than he had shown before. "I didn't give such an order!" he cried. "I was considering it-but I didn't give it! That's what I wanted to talk about. I was merely going to have the bank put an extra guard on the money-God! *Someone forged my name to that order!* No wonder they tried to kill me! To cover up —"

The inspector spoke grimly. "This Al Millett did go in for some forging," he said slowly. "I wonder —"

The Phantom, too, was wondering. There was something strangely pat about Gifford's alibi. At the same time, Van felt a sense as of anticlimax. As if, despite the hectic rescue he had just made, his nerves had been braced for something that hadn't happened, yet which he felt was still in the air.

He turned to Gifford, started to frame more questions. At that instant an attendant came running from the concrete office building.

"Inspector! Call from your Headquarters! Urgent!"

The inspector's heavy frame charged across the ground. The Phantom, nerves going tense again, followed.

A waiting hand-set phone was ready for the inspector. He scooped it up. "Inspector Gregg talking. What?" An invisible spring seemed to straighten his whole body. "Okay-okay —"

He slammed down the instrument, whirled to the Phantom, who knew even before the inspector spoke that the climax he had missed had come after all.

Nevertheless, the inspector's shaken voice rang out like a knell.

"Kenneth Meade has just been murdered!" he announced. "Let's go!"

Leaving Fenwick and Gifford at the amusement park, guarded by uniformed police, the Phantom and Inspector Gregg sped back to Manhattan. The inspector's car rolled up Seventh Avenue and came to a stop before a huge restaurant facade-Milady's Salon.

Prowl-cars, cruisers, and riot squad trucks were already at the scene. The police were herding back a crushing mob-roping them off. The restaurant was empty of patrons-it functioned only at night.

The inspector and the Phantom strode through gaps in the saluting bluecoats, entered the premises. They found men with cameras already at work, the Homicide Squad busy at the scene.

Threading their way through tables piled with napkins but unset, they came to a spot at one end of the floor where the knot of detectives was thickest, and where the stocky Medical Examiner was at work.

Kenneth Meade, restaurateur, was sprawled with arms and legs rigidly outstretched. He lay on his back, but his body had a half-doubled aspect. His face was contorted in a grimace of agony, the lips horribly bluish, the sightless eyes protruding from their sockets as if they must pop out.

The clothes of the dead man had been ripped from his upper torso, exposing his neck and chest nakedly. In the naked flesh, in the lower part of the neck, just under his Adam's apple, was a hideous gash —a deep cut from which blood still slowly oozed.

"What is it, Doc?" the inspector demanded hoarsely. "Was he stabbed in the neck?"

The doctor rose slowly. If ever a man looked shaken, thrown entirely out of his professional equilibrium, this stocky city medical examiner did. "Yes, he was stabbed, but that didn't kill him," he said in a small, dazed voice. "The gash you see missed the trachea and went directly into the *esophagus* —the canal which takes food to the stomach. A man will live with such a wound."

"Then what —?" the inspector demanded, bewildered. The Phantom said nothing as he noted the rigid aspect of the corpse.

"Poison!" the doctor pronounced then, his voice shaking. "Bichloride of mercury, from the symptoms. Poison which was fed to Meade through that gash in his esophagus-which carried it to his stomach!" He shook his head. "This is a death unparalleled in all my career as a doctor. Evidently the criminal decided he wanted to poison Meade-but why he put it through a gash in the esophagus instead of through the mouth, I can't understand."

Sickened, the inspector turned away from the gruesome sight. Turned away only to stare with fresh horror at the tiny but familiar object a homicide officer now held out to him on a handkerchief.

"Found this next to the body, inspector," he said.

The inspector's eyes blazed. "I thought so! The Fang again! The same saber-tooth guy! At least he couldn't have been at Coney Island this afternoon to put Gifford on the track! He's making a laughing stock of us! With our whole department after him, he still goes right on, killing, plundering-He's getting in my hair."

"I wouldn't be too sure of that, inspector," observed Van Loan thoughtfully. "Meade could have been wounded, poisoned, and left unconscious to die slowly while the Fang went out to do other devilment. Just because Meade has just died doesn't mean the crime was just committed. It could have happened any time since I left him in Drake's office this morning."

A sudden commotion interrupted the conversation. Into the restaurant came a group of plainclothes men, dragging a struggling figure in their midst.

Van's eyes went sharp. The figure was the bearded, saturnine Count Karnov, the mysterious foreigner who had been at the Palladium the other night!

"We found this bird sneakin' around outside!" one of the detectives said. "And I think we found something on him that might answer a lot of questions!"

Karnov scowled, still struggling silently. The detective handed a paper to the inspector. "This was in his pocket, sir! Take a look. And get ready for a shock!"

The Phantom was at the inspector's shoulder as the latter lifted the paper. It was torn. There was a hasty scrawl in ink across it.

Even the Phantom gasped as he read it.

—so I've decided to send you a last warning.
—Al.

"Did you write this?" the inspector's voice was sharp as a knife as he faced the Count belligerently.

Karnov's dark eyes glowered.

"I refuse to answer any questions," he said in his flawless English.

"Oh, you do?" the inspector's hulk looked ominously menacing. "Well, do you deny that you're Al Millett?"

At the mention of that name, Karnov gave a perceptible start. He smiled then —a nasty, venomous smile. "You'll have a difficult time proving that, inspector." But there was desperation in his eyes.

The Phantom, with his keen knowledge of psychology, could see that the man wanted to get away quickly. Those glowering eyes were looking about furtively, like those of a trapped animal who would take the first possible loophole of escape.

"I'd like to really see the face you've got under that beard!" the inspector grated now. "Wait until we get you down to Headquarters! I think we'll have the end of these crimes!"

Karnov wet his lips, but was still silent. Van's mind was racing now. He moved across the floor. In the center of the big restaurant stood an immense porcelain vase, its top, about three feet above the floor, gaped dark and empty.

Van looked at the vase. It signified more than a vase to him. It was here for a purpose, a common thing in prominent European restaurants.

The Phantom picked up a napkin idly from a table. "I think I'd like to ask Count Karnov a few questions," he smiled. "Bring him here, please."

The detectives pushed the prisoner, whose eyes now were fixed darkly on the Phantom, across the floor. They stood back, a confident circle surrounding the man.

Van, standing at the vase, spoke carefully. "You're in a pretty tough spot, Karnov, as we say in police parlance." He dropped the napkin idly into the vase. It disappeared completely in the gaping interior. "The evidence is stacked pretty strongly against you. The police have ways of making men talk, when they get them down to Headquarters. So —"

A sudden, animal-like cry of desperation burst from Count Karnov's lips. He dived head first into the huge vase. So swiftly did he move that his guards were taken unawares. The inspector and others rushed to the vase while Van Loan stood quietly by.

"Come out of there, Karnov," rapped Gregg. "You fool, what good will that move do you?"

He broke off, face going bewildered, eyes filling with uncanny incredulity as he reached into the depths of the vase. "Why, he's gone! He's not in there at all! There's no bottom to this damned thing!"

The Phantom smiled and spoke. "I wanted him to think he was escaping, inspector. You carry on here. I'll find him all right." He whirled and hurried out of the premises. Out on the street Van slipped past the police-lined front of the restaurant, around the corner on which it stood, to the side of it. He was not surprised to glimpse a furtive figure crawling from a cellar exit of the building. The disheveled but desperate figure of Count Karnov!

No police were watching this side of the restaurant at the moment. When Karnov's eyes darted around furtively, the Phantom's lithe shape quickly flattened against the building. Count Karnov turned, dashed the opposite way up the block, running on legs obviously guided by sheer desperation.

The Phantom, slipping out, followed him.

On Sixth Avenue, Karnov hailed a taxi, leaped into it, slamming the door. The cab turned around, sped uptown. The Phantom hailed another taxi. He displayed a bill to the driver.

"Follow that cab!" he commanded. "But keep well behind it."

Chapter XIV
Trapped in the Penthouse

Affably the cabby nodded. Like most cabbies, he knew that kind of work. The trail did not prove difficult to follow, though it was a devious one.

It led uptown, through the oasis-like green of Central Park, out through Seventy-Second, thence over to West End Avenue.

The afternoon was already lengthening into dusk when Karnov's taxi came to a stop, in the upper eighties. The Phantom's cab stopped at a discreet distance behind. Van leaned forward. He saw the figure of Count Karnov alight to the curb, pay off his driver, then stride beneath the canopy of a towering apartment building.

Swiftly, Van paid off his own cabby and moved to the canopy of the apartment. Karnov's figure had already disappeared into the building.

The Phantom pushed in through the glass-paned doors. His alert eyes flashed around a large, ornate foyer. Three elevators stood with gates open, but a smaller bronze door was closed. From behind it the Phantom's keen ears heard the sound of mechanical motion. A private elevator in such a building invariably led to a penthouse.

That was where the desperate Count Karnov was apparently going.

The Phantom paused a moment in a manner which befitted his vacuous expression before he walked into one of the regular elevators-first glancing up at the last number on the indicator.

"Twenty-eight," he said to the operator, as the gates slid smoothly shut and the car began its swift ascent.

The elevator took him to the top floor of the apartment. He sauntered out, in a leisurely manner. But as soon as the gates had closed behind him, his leisure dropped away like a cloak. Moving swiftly, he found the fire-stairs, and ascended to the penthouse floor. As he climbed, he slipped on his domino mask.

Emerging on a landing, a skylight overhead showing the gathering twilight, he saw the closed bronzed door of the private elevator, the door opposite to the only apartment up here.

He slipped to it on soundless feet. He put his face close to it, listened. He heard a vague sound within. Then a voice. He could only catch a few words, but those were enough to sharpen the gleam in his eyes.

" —a transatlantic call-to London, England-reverse the charges-hurry —"

Karnov's voice!

A tight, grim smile flecked Van's lips. The pieces of this mighty, bloody puzzle were clicking into place; he knew that he was close now to the end of the gruesome trail. But many threads were still loose, many questions still to answer.

The penthouse lock was difficult, especially difficult to open without sound. His wire twisted, curved, wriggled in and out, as his deft hand guided it.

At last it clicked. The Phantom turned the handle slowly. Cautiously, he pushed the door open. Its well-oiled hinges made no sound. Wraith-like, he slipped into the apartment. A wide stucco-walled hall, deep in unlit twilight gloom, engulfed his stealthy figure. His keen eyes flashed down the hall. Two doors, one on either side of the wall opposite the entrance door. Which?

A sharp ring of a telephone answered his question in the next second. He heard a quick, leaping step in the phone room. Karnov's voice was speaking.

"Hello? Yes-my party? Yes, I'm holding on —"

The Phantom moved to the door, peered in, cautiously. The room was in gloom, no lights having been lit. Twilight showed outside a single open window that evidently was flush, on this side, with the building—a sheer drop into space. The room itself, a living room, looked strangely feminine in its appearance. Soft, silky covered furniture. And a faint perfumed scent.

At a taboret to one side, Count Karnov crouched over a white-enameled telephone. His voice came again in its flawless English.

"Hello-This is Karnov!" Anger threaded that voice now. "Listen to me! I have reached the end of my rope! I intend to leave this country at once." He laughed harshly. "Oh, I got enough money. I have done as much of my work as I could —"

The Phantom, his ears taking in every word, had slipped into the room behind Count Karnov.

Like a panther, the Phantom leaped! His right hand closed on Karnov's hand holding the telephone. His left hand stifled the amazed out-cry on the Count's lips.

He twisted the phone out of Karnov's fingers, managed to place the instrument down-still out of its cradle.

His right hand, now free, doubled into a balled fist. It did not move far; but it moved with timed precision and judgment. The blow landed on the Count's bristle-bearded jaw. The foreigner staggered backwards, his mouth open now and unhampered, but only an expelling sigh coming from it. He slumped in the shadowy gloom of the far wall.

The Phantom, deciding he was out for the time being, did not delay another instant. He grabbed up the phone. Immediately an angry voice came to his ears.

"Are you there, Karnov? Confound you! Why don't you answer?"

Van felt a thrill in that hectic moment. He was listening to a voice that was coming from three thousand miles-across the Atlantic Ocean-from England.

"Yes, I am here," Van said into the mouthpiece, speaking in the flawless voice of Count Karnov. "Listen to me. You have read, doubtless, the newspapers. The detective called the Phantom is working upon this case. He is ready, almost, to bring it to a close!" Though he spoke in Karnov's voice, his words rang with grim sincerity now, for they were true words. "He needs but one more proof! You must act swiftly if you wish to save yourself! I have already told you what I am going to do! But you must make a sacrifice!"

"Karnov!" the English-accented voice rose harshly. "What do you mean? What do you dare to —?"

"You must come to America, to New York, at once!" Van went on. "Take now the fastest boat! One perhaps with a mail-service plane-charter it if you can! That will bring you in the more swiftly!"

"Karnov, are you mad? Are you trying to make me put my head into a noose? Here I am, safe with a perfect alibi —" As if realizing he had said too much over the public wire, the speaker broke off with a gasp. "You are mad!" he finished weakly.

"I warn you for your own good. It is a matter of life and death," Van said, with difficulty keeping the voice of Karnov. "The Phantom will get to you, regardless —" He went on speaking, rapidly, persuasively.

He heard a movement behind him then. He jerked back his head quickly, expecting to see Karnov getting to his feet. His eyes went wide then, as he stifled a surprised exclamation. Karnov was not in the twilight room at all! He had vanished! And instead —

"Put down that telephone!" came a steady, low feminine voice.

In the doorway of the room stood the slender, white-faced figure of the missing Queen Stella! A small but deadly automatic gleamed dully in her hand.

Her eyes gleaming with a determined light, the girl aerialist advanced towards the telephone as she spoke.

The Phantom spoke three hurried words more into the mouthpiece in that split second. "Get here quick!" Then he banged the phone down in its cradle, and leaped upright, whirling toward the girl. He saw her finger tighten on the trigger-and his body sprang as if from a catapult.

His long right arm snaked out, catching the gun as flame spat from it, twisting it so the bullet was deflected to one side. Simultaneously he saw the girl's eyes widen with horror and astonishment, realized she was staring in the gloom at his domino mask.

A cry of relief came to her lips, but even as she opened her mouth to speak, there was a rush of heavy feet from the hall. Like a flood, slouch-hatted figures burst into the room with leveled guns!

The remainder of the Fang's mob! Led by the slicker-clad Monk Gorman!

The girl screamed. Van grabbed her by the arm, half flung her across the room, where she dropped under the window. He still had the automatic he had twisted out of her hand. He pivoted, swinging it upon the charging mob of gunmen and jerking the trigger.

Crack! A thug dropped in his tracks—a pimply-faced man whose life blood spurted from his chest as he fell. Monk Gorman, moving rapidly despite his size, reached the light switch.

The room became dazzling with the sudden flood of illumination. Before the blinking Van could fire again, the thugs were upon him. There were enough of them to make resistance futile. He was pummeled, cuffed, kicked, by hate-glaring felons of the underworld!

Stunned, he was pushed back across the floor. As he fought to keep his balance, he heard a faint moan beside him. Queen Stella standing there, all blood drained from her face.

Both of them, unarmed, were facing a line of thugs who stood between them and the door. Guns were leveling at the two captives. Monk, in their center, holding the deadliest weapon of all, a blue-steel tommy gun, at which he had already proved himself adept!

"Well, well!" he chortled above its barrel. "This time we really got you where we want you, Phantom! Got you lined up, an' you, too, Sister!" His evil eyes swiveled to the girl.

Outside in the hall, beyond the closed door of this room, sounded a step. Another person had entered the apartment, was walking down that hall!

The steps came forward decisively, entered the room next to the living room where all were listening breathlessly.

The connecting door opened just a few inches. Blackness only showed from within. But once more, as he had felt in that ghastly studio at Astoria, Van was aware in every nerve of a blighting evil Presence!

The menace he knew as the Fang had followed to this penthouse apartment, trapping him there. The next instant a familiar, rasping voice sounded from that chinked door.

"So, Mr. Phantom, you have crossed my trail again!" A diabolical chortle rose from the darkness beyond the ajar door. "We have caught two birds, as it were! One who is just a foolish young woman. The other devilishly clever-and of many lives, it seems. I suppose, if I were to have Monk remove your silly domino, I would see the features of Al Millett this time. Bah! Your childish disguises weary me. But your escapes annoy me. This time I'll watch you die with my own eyes!"

Van was silent, eyes fixed on the door. The girl stood just behind him at the window, pale, yet with a certain defiance on her delicate, oval face. From her lips came a low whisper which barely reached the Phantom's ears.

"I'm sorry," she murmured. "I didn't know it was you. I sent Karnov for the police while you were talking over the phone. I thought you were the Fang. And all I've done was to help trap you—"

Van broke in quickly. "I know, Miss Millett," he said simply, sympathy and understanding in his tone.

"What are you saying, Phantom?" came the evil voice from the other room where the terrible genius behind this whole bloody reign of crime stood in darkness. "You speak? You had better finish swiftly. The boys are waiting."

Which was unpleasantly true. Monk's blue-steel tommy gun was raised, ready. The other thugs formed a line of dark, hungry automatic muzzles. The Phantom remained stoically silent. He was thinking furiously.

"Come, come," mocked the arch criminal. "Do you not wish to talk before you die? It is a boon I grant you-both of you. You aren't gagged. You seem to know so much, to be so astute. Talk your way out of this impasse, Mr. Phantom."

"You fiend!" exclaimed the girl vehemently. "You inhuman—"

"Steady," counseled the Phantom, flashing a glance at her.

She fell silent. And Van Loan's eyes continued to rove swiftly about the room. If it were not for the girl, he might have found some means of escape. But at the first move, even if he managed to win clear, those guns would blast, and the girl would die. And it was very essential now that this girl did not die. If only he could stall until the police came!

The window! A sheer drop, with nothing but flimsy ledges to hold to. It would take an acrobat-Into his mind flashed the swinging trapeze at the Palladium Club. He reached in that moment the most desperate decision of his career.

He glanced quickly at the girl and then let his gaze dart toward the open window behind her.

"Dare you?" he whispered tersely out of the corner of his mouth.

She understood instantly. Her eyes widened, sparkled.

"Yes," she formed with her lips.

"So you won't talk, eh?" grated the voice from the other room, mockingly imitating a third-grade detective. "Well, too bad you won't live to file this case —"

"Wait!" said Van Loan sharply. "I'll talk."

"I'm listening," agreed the unseen man amiably. "What have you to say?"

"This!" shot out the Phantom, without warning hurling himself down and sideways straight at the waiting line of gangsters.

Before they could react, before they could train their weapons upon him, he was tangled against the legs of three of them. With a mighty sweep, he gathered legs and all within reach to himself, and brought the amazed thugs to the floor in a mad scramble with him.

"Sit down on him!" barked the vindictive voice of the hidden leader. "Fools! The girl! Grab her!"

But it was too late. Like a sleek jungle cat, Queen Stella had swung herself up into the window at the Phantom's first move, and out into the nothingness of space. Guns roared futilely, hot lead smacking into the window frame, shattering the upper sash, and drumming out into the open air.

Monk Gorman and two of his muscle men yanked the Phantom savagely to his feet, while others darted over to the window and gawked out into the night, seeing nothing but the myriad winking lights of New York skyscrapers.

"Gawd! She's gone, Chief!" gasped one. "She did a Brodie!"

"Her body'll attract attention, Boss!" shouted Gorman. "We better finish this guy an' lam."

"Wait!" snarled the leader. "This building is recessed. She didn't fall to the street. We'll have time. I want you to search this place."

"Anyway, this guy ain't gonna die like that," grunted Monk Gorman viciously, and he crashed the muzzle of his tommy gun against the head of the Phantom.

The world exploded for Van Loan, and he went out like a light. Went out, crumpling to the floor, just as the entrance door of the apartment crashed back against the wall, and the charging rush of heavy feet surged like a wave into the penthouse.

"Th' cops!" howled a panic-stricken thug. "Scram, everybody!"

"You can't scram," snarled the unseen leader. "Fight it out, you scum! You're trapped and done for if you don't!"

Pandemonium reigned. Through the hallway door came the charge of bluecoats. Guns barked their snarls of defiance. Smoke filled the room with the reek of cordite. Men bowled over like ten-pins, screaming in agony. Gangsters and policemen in one mad carnage of hell!

The end was inevitable. Monk Gorman, his machine gun chattering like an enraged ape, took a slug over the heart just as his stream of leaden hail cut an officer almost in two. His gun went silent as he grunted once and dropped to the floor, his career of crime over forever. The remnants of four mobs had met their Waterloo.

The police were busily mopping up when Queen Stella and Count Karnov pushed their way in. The girl uttered a cry of alarm at sight of the Phantom on the floor, and rushed to his side. He was already stirring, conscious again as she raised his head.

A plainclothes detective rushed in from the recently darkened room and reported to Inspector Gregg who was in charge of this raid, having been found at Milady's Salon by the frenzied Karnov.

"Inspector," he babbled, "there was a murdered man in that bedroom as I went through a minute ago-lying on the floor in the dark with his neck broken. I saw it! Head twisted nastily to one side, tongue hanging out. I went on to the kitchen with the harness bulls to make sure everything was mopped up, and then I came back to examine the corpse-and it was gone!"

"You're nuts, O'Brien," snapped Inspector Gregg curtly. "If—"

The Phantom pushed away Queen Stella's fluttering hands and staggered erect. He reeled his dizzy way into the room in question. It was empty!

He came back to the living room doorway, catching on to the casing for support. A bitter smile twisted his mouth beneath his awry mask.

"On the contrary, inspector," he said wearily, "O'Brien is not nuts."

"Then, maybe I am," growled Gregg acidly. "I found out, too late, about that tricky vase at the restaurant. It's rigged up like lots of those European places —a blind for a clothes chute to the cellar for soiled napkins and tablecloths."

Had he not been so intensely disappointed, Van Loan could have laughed.

"I know," he articulated wearily. "But this dead man with the broken neck was a better trick. That was no dead man. *He was the master criminal!* And we've let him get away!"

Chapter XV
The Phantom Speaks

Five days later the big room on the third floor of Police Headquarters on Centre Street held a queer group of people. Besides the commissioner, Inspector Gregg, and half a dozen uniformed officers, there were numerous visitors.

Frank Havens, the publisher, was there at the desk with a mass of papers before him. Seated in a semi-circle facing the desk were four well-known figures of the amusement world-Paul Corbin, Gordon Drake, John Gifford, and Carl Fenwick.

"I don't understand," said Paul Corbin nervously, "why we are all gathered here like this. We've been waiting half an hour. And for what?" He seemed more womanish than ever in his pettish annoyance.

Gordon Drake clasped his gloved hands stiffly, a tolerant smile about his handsome lips. "Contain yourself, my dear Corbin," he advised.

"Nobody's been killed during the past five days, anyhow. That's something."

John Gifford merely grunted. His big frame seemed more huddled than usual, his craggy, gnarled features more grotesque than ever.

Fenwick said nothing. He merely tapped on the arms of his chair, tugged at his high collar, tweaked at his ear, and went back to his drumming.

Inspector Gregg shuffled through some papers at his own desk, scowled at his assorted company, and squinted at the calm and composed publisher of the *Clarion*.

"I'm getting a bit impatient, myself," he said gruffly. "The Phantom asked for this meeting, promising to break this Fang case for us today. And he isn't even here. What's the answer, Mr. Havens?"

The grey-haired publisher smiled as he looked up from the papers he was carefully arranging.

"I can't explain, inspector," he admitted frankly. "All I can tell you is that the Phantom has promised to meet us here and surprise us. And he never breaks a promise. As for these papers, he'll have to tell us exactly what they mean."

An orderly came in and spoke to the police commissioner. The latter cleared his throat and glanced around the group. Then "Send him in," he said.

All eyes turned to the door as the orderly went out. In an instant another figure appeared on the threshold. And four men gasped in amazement. A young man with buck teeth, thick lips, and attired in the quaint garb of the first decade of the twentieth century looked over the company, smiled, and came forward.

"Hello, Gordon, Carl, Paul, John," he greeted. "You remember me?"

Paul Corbin half-rose out of his chair with a stifled scream.

"Al Millett!" he choked, eyes bulging in terror.

"Don't be a fool!" growled John Gifford. "Al Millett looks as old as we do today."

"True," smiled Gordon Drake. "This is the ghost of Al Millett of yesterday. Hello, Al."

"This is crazy!" snorted Fenwick, tugging at his collar.

Inspector Gregg was on his feet, hesitating in pardonable uncertainty.

"You are all correct and all wrong, gentlemen," smiled the newcomer, approaching the desk and taking up a position beside the publisher and the pile of papers. "I am neither Al Millett, nor the bloody criminal called the Fang. This was just a screwy idea of my own. A great many people know me as-the Phantom. I'm sorry to have kept you waiting, but I had to meet a boat —a different one from the *Charlemagne*. Allow me to present the real Albert Millett!"

At his words, almost before the various gasps of surprise died away, another man crossed the threshold, a middle-aged man on whose arm came the aerialist known as Queen Stella.

The newcomer, a pleasant-faced man with greying hair and thick lips about which there were deep lines, came forward hesitantly and bowed stiffly in English fashion.

For a full moment there was a stunned silence. Then Inspector Gregg started forward with a growl.

"Wait, please!" crisped the Phantom. "Albert Millett, where have you been for the past twenty years?"

"I have been in the wine business in London," answered Millett. "I was a fool as a young man out West, and, after my wife died, I went away with my daughter to start life anew. This is my daughter, Estella Millett. She has been in America for more than a year. She inherited her mother's ability as an aerialist, and that has become her chosen calling."

"When, Mr. Millett, did you arrive in America?" inquired the Phantom, making no effort to conceal the fact that this was a rehearsed inquiry.

"I set foot on my native land for the first time in twenty years just an hour ago when the *Queen Mary* docked," replied Millett in a firm voice.

"You can establish this fact?" went on the Phantom coolly.

"Without question. I left England but four days ago."

"Then you couldn't possibly have landed from the *Charlemagne* a week ago in New York?"

"I could not, sir."

"Then you could not be this fiendish murderer who has terrorized New York for the past week under the name of the Fang?"

"Most certainly not!" said Millett emphatically.

"Then this," cut in Inspector Gregg succinctly, "shoots our case all to hell, and we're back where we started from. I thought you were going to break it, Phantom."

"I'll have to go into it methodically," answered the Phantom. "I'll try to be brief, inspector. By the way, Count Karnov-as you have already ascertained-is Mr. Millett's representative in the United States. He is exactly what he purports to be, and no more. As for breaking the Fang case-let me explain that Mr. Havens and I have had to dig back into a lot of ancient history. For one thing, the Academy of Medicine had to canvass a great part of the United States for us in search of certain knowledge. We have dug up a number of interesting family skeletons.

"First, I might touch on the once famous circus of Crowley and Buckill wherewith Al Millett got his bad exploitation as a fanged monster. There are handbills and circus posters here that will interest you, Inspector Gregg. But the private life of Al Millett has little bearing on this case. He was just a red herring dragged across this trail. The real criminal is not Millett, nor his daughter, nor Karnov, nor anybody imported into this country. He is one of the very men, inspector, who came to you with that wild tale about the Fang."

The inspector gasped. "You mean that yarn was made out of whole cloth? One of them was the maniac? Andrews! By God, it is Andrews! The missing man!"

"Not so fast, inspector," the Phantom calmed him. "I'll tell you. But first —" He turned toward the tense and alert four tycoons of the entertainment world. " —before I can clear up the matter, I must ask your permission, gentlemen, to reveal jealously guarded secrets of your intimate life. It pains me to embarrass you, but the truth will have to come out. You know what I refer to-the Gargoyle Club."

All four men winced. Paul Corbin, unaccountably, began to sob. Gifford seemed to shrink in his chair, growing more crag-like than ever. Fenwick turned deadly pale. Gordon Drake was the first to recover. He laughed bitterly and stood erect, stretching his manly figure to its full, symmetric height.

"After all," he said wearily, "why not? Nature made us what we are. It's nothing to be personally ashamed of."

"Thank you," said the Phantom softly. "I respect you, Mr. Drake. These brutal and revolting murders, each different, were not the haphazard affairs that you may think, Inspector Gregg-Commissioner. They were perfectly logical when one knows the reason. Had they continued, they would have woven the same grotesque pattern of startling individuality. For instance, Drake-had he been killed-would have been found with his arms amputated at the shoulders. Paul Corbin's body would have been split in half.

"Gifford would have been horribly mangled-as he so nearly was by his own Leap-for-Life railway. And Carl Fenwick *—would have been found with a broken neck!*"

At these last emphatic words, Fenwick leaped to his feet with a strangled cry. In a flash Van Loan had him covered with a pistol, his face set in hard, uncompromising lines which almost revealed the clean-cut contour of the face of Richard Van Loan.

"Hold it, Fenwick!" he said, cold steel in his voice. "Take him, Inspector Gregg! He is your man!"

The inspector, though dumbfounded, was a good policeman. Without question he leaped forward and snapped a pair of manacles about the theatrical producer's wrists. Two uniformed officers converged on the accused man and gripped his arms. Fenwick wilted.

"But-but just what does this all mean?" demanded the confused commissioner.

"Just this, sir," answered the Phantom. "Nine men, today wealthy and famous, were once freaks in the show of Crowley and Buckill. In those days when hokum was king, these genuine freaks were featured attractions. They laid the foundations of their own fortunes while they made Crowley and Buckill rich.

"The Marcy brothers were Siamese twins, joined together by a cartilage and a spinal structure. An operation might have severed them, but both were afraid to chance it. When they retired from circus life they became recluses, exhibiting themselves only behind a double desk or in their limousine. They were always together, of course, hampered by their natal tie, but remarkable business men for all of that."

Van Loan drew a breath and continued.

"Clyde Dickson was a different sort of oddity. He was not born with his affliction. As a young man on a construction job a flying crowbar was driven into his skull. By some queer accident it didn't kill him. So it was sawed off and left in his head. There is another case of this nature on record at the Harvard Medical School. They have the skull of a man whose name was Gage. He was injured like Dickson, and lived to die normally at an old age.

"I have the record here of Dickson's case, the report of the son of the doctor who waited on him. That was why Dickson wore a mop of long hair over the protuberance from his skull.

"Meade, the fourth man to die, was another extraordinary case. At some time in his early life he developed a stricture of his esophagus which prevented him from taking food. He was operated on, an artificial opening was made at the front of his throat, and he lived. He exhibited this second mouth as a freak in the circus.

"Andrews has not run away. He is dead. His case is one where his torso developed normally, but his legs from the hips down atrophied as a child. I saw those severed legs in that abandoned studio out in Astoria. He wore special braces and used a cane, if you will remember.

"You see, each murder had to be different in order to obliterate the fact that the victims were abnormal or subnormal. Gifford would have been mutilated because he is a hunch-back. I found that out when I saved him from his own rocket car. He was phenomenally light; his padded clothes partially hiding his deformity and giving him a portly appearance.

"Paul Corbin is half man and half woman, a genuine hermaphrodite. Gordon Drake was born without any forearms, the upper arms ending in stubs about the elbow, stubs that he learned to handle so dexterously that he was one of the most interesting attractions of the circus."

"I did better with them than I ever have with these artificial arms," admitted Drake ruefully.

"Fenwick was another queer experiment of nature," went on the Phantom. "One vertebra in his neck is missing. Instead, he has a section of limber cartilage. He is able to dislocate his neck and assume the appearance of a man with a broken neck at will. That is why he always wears a high, stiff collar.

"And that completes our group of unusual men, men so bizarre that they felt they had no place in normal life. So they remained banded together, forming a little club of their own which they called the Gargoyle Club and where they could be at ease and at rest, where nobody stared or commented on the infirmity or deformity of another."

"But why did Fenwick go berserk?" demanded Gregg.

"All their holdings were pooled," explained the Phantom. "All their wealth was in a holding corporation which was licensed under the name of the Star Corporation. They supported charitable institutions for afflicted persons. Upon their several deaths, the estate was to go into such endowments.

"But Fenwick was the exception. Instead of pitying others, he was intensely bitter and he was the least afflicted of the lot. Since he couldn't inherit from the others, he undertook to murder and rob them.

"The thwarted armored truck holdup would have been his sweetest haul. He must have planned his bloody crimes for years. I doubt if he knew Al Millett was still alive until Dickson gave Estella Millett a job at the Palladium Club. And that only intensified matters, because Fenwick was a disappointed suitor for the hand of Estella's mother.

"I think I was about the last person to hear Andrews's voice. I surprised Fenwick with him at the Gargoyle Club the night he was killed, and when I so nearly was. And, gentlemen, I think that about winds up the most bizarre case I have ever had the pleasure of assisting the Homicide Bureau with. We all owe a great deal of thanks to Mr. Frank Havens for his painstaking research and finding of old records."

"Which reminds me of one thing," spoke up the publisher. "How did my cartoonist, Collins, get mixed up in this business?"

"That was an unfortunate accident," said the Phantom. "He was a very inquisitive and aggressive young chap. He was acquainted with Estella Millett, who knew of these men from her father. One night in an unguarded moment, she let something slip about fact being stranger than fiction. She mentioned the names of Dickson and Marcy, and that was all Collins needed. He ferreted out enough to seal his own doom.

"What puzzled me for a long time was how the leader of the crime gang always knew I escaped from his death traps before he should have known. That was the first clue which led to Fenwick. Fenwick kept in touch with the Phantom through Mr. Havens, and that smartness was finally instrumental in bringing about his downfall."

Carl Fenwick raised his head and stared at the Phantom with hate-glazed eyes. Then, uttering a mad cry of bafflement, he tore free from the laxly guarding officers and rushed straight toward the nearest window. Heedless of the shouts behind him, he dove head first through the glass.

When those with sufficient hardihood gained the window and looked down, they saw uniformed police running to surround the ghastly remains of the most horrible Gargoyle.

By an irony of fate, Carl Fenwick had actually broken his neck in his fall.

"I am truly sorry for you all," said the Phantom wearily. "I only hope you who are left are able to pick up your lives and go on bravely from here. As for me —" His broad shoulders drooped with fatigue. " —I think I'll retire to the shades and sleep for a week."

They watched him depart in awed silence. Only Frank Havens knew the full extent of the suffering the Phantom had borne, and his heart swelled at the thought of the man who had dedicated his wealth and his life to protect and safeguard his fellow men from crime while the careless world little suspected that the rich idler, Richard Curtis Van Loan, was the Phantom who troubled the dreams of criminals.

Tycoon of Crime

Chapter I
Maiden Flight

The lonely shack stood in the chill night gloom, its windows faint squares of light. Thin mist, driven by a wind which shook the dark branches of surrounding heavy trees, swirled coldly about the small, solitary building. Within it, under the glare of a single naked ceiling bulb, two men stood with their backs to the bolted oak door. They were watching a third man who crouched across the room before the gleaming dials of a small but full equipped short-wave radio apparatus.

His hands-slender, nervous hands-were turning the dials with swift, jerky motions. The back of his hatless head was a shiny black knob, plastered-down hair glistening like patent leather in the light. His slender, crouched body swayed as he worked, graceful except for its slight jerkiness. His flashy top-coat trailed on the boarded floor.

Harsh, raucous static coughed abruptly from a loudspeaker, rising and diminishing as the man turned the dials.

"What's the matter, Slick? Can'tcha get it?" came the coarse, deep voice of one of the two, a huge, barrel-chested hulk of a man who seemed almost to fill the cramped little shack. His fedora hat seemed pygmy-sized over his wide, swart face with its small, glinting eyes, flattened nose, and wide gash of mouth.

He took a step forward as he spoke, moving with a loping, almost simian gait, one arm swinging at his side, the other nestled with snug ease around a blue steel Thompson submachine gun.

"Me," he snarled, "I'm gettin' tired of waitin' around here like this."

"Shut up!"

The authoritative command came in a harsh, jerky staccato from the man at the radio. He turned from the set. The light fell on his face-olive skinned, its darkly handsome features marred by a livid, zigzag scar which ran across his left cheek from chin to ear.

"I'll get it any minute now if you keep quiet."

He turned to the third man who was standing immobile as a statue, a faint wisp of smoke from the cigarette in his lips alone giving him semblance of movement. Tall, lean, he had an angular face with pale, expressionless eyes.

"Luke!" he snapped. "You sure you tipped off the others?"

Without moving the man Luke answered: "They'll be around on the dot, Slick."

The patent-leather hair of the man called Slick showed again as once more he bent to the dials. The static continued, grating in the silent shack.

Then, suddenly, Slick's crouching figure tensed as through the cloud of that static a voice began to materialize.

"Listen, guys!"

Slick turned the dials more. The static diminished, the voice grew in volume and clarity. A crisp, incisive voice speaking rapidly, with clear enunciation.

"—Plane Number One from Chicago, calling Newark Airport-Pat Bentley, pilot, speaking-Plane Number One —"

Out of the night, out of the dark ether, came that call. And as the three men in the shack listened with tense interest, there was a swift answering voice.

"Newark Airport. Go ahead, Bentley."

"We're still over the Pennsylvania, nearing Balesville. Visibility getting bad up here at fifteen thousand. Been keeping altitude to cross the Alleghenies and to get best speed, but clouds are too thick. Don't worry, though. We're smack on the radio beam. Ought to make Newark in another hour."

Slick rose to his feet. His dark eyes glinted, and there was a crooked, evil smile on his lips as he looked at his two companions.

"Newark in another hour, eh?" he chortled. "That's what he thinks!"

"Number One going off," said the voice in the loudspeaker. "I'm taking the controls again. Stand by."

Slick glanced at his wrist-watch. His slender body had gone tense again.

"We've got to be all set, guys! Luke-you keep your ears on that radio. Ape, you just keep that mug of yours closed."

The burly man with the tommy gun at once broke that command.

"Listen," came his coarse-toned protest, and there was a baffled look in his small, wide-set eyes. "I don't savvy this business, honest! What are we gonna do? I thought we was bein' paid to mess around with that railroad-wreckin' them trains an'—"

"If you was bein' paid to think, you'd sure be out of luck!" Slick cut in with his harsh staccato. "Stop worryin'. The guy who gives us our orders knows his stuff, an' I don't mean maybe. You ain't workin' for no mobster, punk. You're workin' for the Tycoon!"

Awe threaded his voice as he pronounced that title-and the awe communicated itself at once to the burly Ape, who winced and was silent. Luke remained immobile, but the dangling cigarette in his thin lips bobbed slightly, as if to express his own feeling of respect.

"Yes, an' the Tycoon knows his stuff," repeated Slick. "Maybe it's the swag on that plane." His eyes narrowed. "But I ain't trying to figure it. Whatever it is, it's gonna put dough in our pockets."

He broke off as once more the loudspeaker came to life.

"Pat Bentley calling-Visibility worse —I think I'll go down a ways—"

"He thinks he'll go down," Luke echoed, his words significant despite his expressionless tone.

"Yeah." Slick's malignant smile flickered again. "He don't know the half of it!" He moved hurriedly across the floor. "Got to be ready now! Any minute the time'll come. Any minute!"

* * *

Through the high-swirling cloud banks piled seemingly against the very stars, the huge-winged Douglas transport sliced downward, twin motors thundering, propellers churning the mists.

At times those mists swallowed the big plane completely. Then it would reappear, a great, silvery, birdlike shape, with lights showing from its cabin, and green and red running lights on its wing tips.

Below, through gaps in the mist, mountains showed dark, jutting peaks, gaping valleys. Presently, as the heavier clouds were left drifting above, the big monoplane leveled in its flight, straightened to roar ahead.

In the cozy, lighted cabin, ultramodern in its appointments, the dozen passengers gratefully unstrapped the belts they had been cautioned to fasten during the descent. They settled back comfortably, secure in the knowledge that this plane was in capable hands, and that even through mist the invisible but complicated network of radios and beacons which had made sky-travel as fully developed as any railroad on signal-marked tracks, helped guide the ship safely through the night.

"Coffee?"

A trim-uniformed stewardess, her cap set jauntily over her copper-tinted hair, emerged from her compartment to pass down the corridor with her tray. She was pretty in an efficient, capable-looking way. As if she regarded all the passengers as helpless patients as long as they were in the air, she treated them with firm solicitude.

"Now, Madame —" She was speaking to the rather stout but mink-coated wife of a big Chicago business man, who had fought for tickets on this first, new run of the airline. " —do take coffee. It will steady your nerves."

She passed the cup over, continuing her journey. Most of the passengers were men-men of wealth and position.

Two had brought wives; another a daughter. The cabin had the air of an exclusive, privileged society.

But not all of its occupants were so comfortably blase. In Seat Number 1, directly behind the closed-off pilot's compartment, a thin man in a black Homburg hat leaned out across the aisle. He had a scrawny, pallid face, its leanness accentuated by the tension that etched it. The cords of his neck stood out like whipcord. His eyes, in which all the personality of the man seemed concentrated, were dark, burning. He clutched a black briefcase in his arm as he spoke.

"I tell you, Garth, I feel nervous," came his low whisper, lost in the vibration of the motors. "Why did you insist on our taking this plane?"

Max Garth, a chunky man, muffled in a great-coat, from which his hatless head, large, square, and with a shock of greying, reddish hair spoke without leaning from the opposite seat. He wore thick-lensed glasses which gave his eyes a hard, concentrated stare.

"Cool down, Truesdale!" His low voice had a hard, brittle terseness, as if emotions were something he neither understood nor tolerated. Those who knew Max Garth-and he was famous in his profession of geology-knew him to be one of those cold men of science whose brains work only in cold logic, without sentiment. "You know it was a break-getting on this plane! Now nothing can go wrong. The whole affair will turn out as we expected. Why, the trip's almost over." He was reasoning as if with a child. "What is there to worry about?"

And like a child, David Truesdale relaxed a trifle. He, too, was a scientist: one of the country's foremost mining engineers, who had done noteworthy work in ventilating mines. But his work had become a shell into which he retired from worldly life, and he displayed that naivete which is so bewildering in men otherwise brilliant.

"Guess you're right, Garth. It's just nerves." He passed a blue-veined hand nervously over his pallid face.

"And don't hug that briefcase so," Garth said sourly. "Maybe you'd better give it to me!" His voice had an edge in it as it dropped still lower. "You don't want to attract attention."

Truesdale's clutch tightened on the briefcase as these words seemed instantly to bring back his fear. His eyes were burning, bright. "What's the use?" he began fearfully. "If someone knows-and he must know —"

"Are you going to bring up those threats again?" Garth's glasses seemed to glare. "Are you going to take the phone call of some crank seriously?"

"But if you had heard that voice over the phone!" Truesdale said shakily.

"I did," Garth returned coolly.

"What?" The eyes of David Truesdale went wide. "You mean, he-he threatened you too, this person who calls himself —" His voice was a frightened whisper. " —the Tycoon?"

Garth stiffened a little at that title; but his voice was contemptuous.

"Yes," he conceded. "He called. And gave me the same time limit. Nine o'clock tonight."

"But you never said a word about it."

"Because there's nothing to say, except to the police, when we get to New York."

Abruptly Garth broke off. He had turned in his seat, and his glare-glassed eyes caught sudden sight of pretty Nancy Clay, the stewardess, standing directly behind the two seats with her coffee tray. She was staring at them both, her lips half parted.

Garth darted a warning look at Truesdale who seemed oblivious of her presence. He spoke to Truesdale in a tone momentarily harsh:

"Well, forget about it! It's all a joke of no importance."

But the stark, haunted fear in Truesdale's eyes did not lessen. He started to speak again, then gulped and shut his lips tightly. Only then did he seem to become aware of the stewardess, as she came forward.

"Coffee, gentlemen?"

Garth shook his head. Truesdale growled a shaky: "No thank you, Miss."

"Come, come," she insisted. "It will warm you up. Make you feel fit for the landing."

"When do we land, stewardess?" Garth demanded.

She flicked around the wrist of the hand gripping the tray to look at her watch.

"Little more than three-quarters of an hour now," she said. "We're scheduled to land at nine-forty-five. It's now exactly two minutes to nine." She smiled, glancing at the closed partition in front of the two seats. "And if I know our pilot, we'll make that schedule!"

On the other side of the partition, his strong young hands gripping the Dep-wheel, Pat Bentley turned to his co-pilot.

"You can take over soon, Bill. I want to tell Newark now that everything's okay."

His eyes glanced through the oblique windows in the nose of the ship, at the dim mountains growing less precipitous ahead and below. Visibility was fairly good now. Not far ahead, Bentley saw the Balesville beacon funneling upwards, blinking like a white tentacle in the sky.

Yet, in the light from the myriad-instrumented dashboard, the young ace pilot's rugged, wind-swept face was etched tense. His broad shoulders were braced as if against some invisible foe. Veteran of thousands of flying hours, the big Douglas was a placid baby in his skilled hands-and yet, somehow, he did not feel right tonight.

A grim responsibility weighed him down. This was a maiden flight-for a big airline. Important people were in this plane; and there was important cargo too. Bentley had seen the armored truck come up on the Chicago field, seen the strong boxes being loaded into the great plane. Exactly what they contained he didn't know. But he did know he was carrying a fortune of some kind.

His keen eyes narrowed, thinking about the passengers. Two of them had acted queerly when they went aboard. The pilot had overheard a few words, tense words. Now that he thought of it, he realized that was what had created the uneasiness in him.

Garth and Truesdale. Two big scientists. Working, just now, Bentley knew for the Empire and Southwest Railway line. He grinned crookedly. That railway was in a slump: the growth of airline travel hadn't helped it any-Why had Truesdale looked so frightened when he climbed into the plane?

And why had Garth looked so icily cold?

Bentley cursed himself inwardly. He well knew just what part of his nature made him so curious about things like this. Once a newspaper man —

Yes, he had worked for a paper, a big New York paper. For several years he had been a flying reporter, and a radio news commentator. His voice had become as famous for its rapid-fire reports as Floyd Gibbons. He had covered many "exclusives," but now his real love, flying, had claimed him again and he had welcomed the job of piloting this new transport.

"It's just nine, Pat. Better call in Newark." The voice of the young co-pilot held the proper amount of respect for his "skipper."

"Right!" Quickly Pat Bentley snapped out of his reverie. "Take her, Bill." And added, listening to the neutral sound of the radio compass. "She's right smack on the beam now."

He released the Dep-wheel and rudder bars in precise synchronization with the moment that his co-pilot took them in control. Adjusting earphones under his trim visor-cap, he picked up the radio microphone.

" —Number One calling Newark-Number One calling Newark."

"This is Newark," came the prompt answer. "Go ahead, Number One."

"We're passing Balesville now. Visibility okay at eight thousand. How's the weather ahead?"

"Ceiling nine thousand. Visibility good."

"We may still beat the schedule," Bentley stated, hopefully, then broke off.

A buzzer had sounded in the little glass-windowed compartment in the nose of the big ship. It rang once, then again-imperatively. The co-pilot jerked up his head.

"Someone ringing, Pat."

"Just a minute," Bentley clipped into the microphone.

He reached back with annoyance, to unlock the partition door. And then his annoyance changed to sudden surprise.

His eyes went wide, stark, with horrified amazement!

Chapter II
One Did Not Die

"Just a minute."

In the modernistic, gleaming radio cupola of Newark Airport, those words of Pat Bentley's had emanated from the loudspeaker.

Two uniformed operators sat at tables in the brightly lighted room, handling two microphones. Two more stood at the big sets, with earphones glued on, their eyes watching the great, humming transmitters, the many tubes and condensers. From this room planes in the sky and on the field were guided; and though the atmosphere was tense, the work was performed with smooth efficiency.

Tonight, attention had been focused chiefly on the new flight from Chicago. While no other planes had been neglected, the men in the airport cupola had given their utmost cooperation to the big Douglas to see that the trip was smooth and successful.

The confident, incisive voice of Bentley had kept them reassured, even when the Douglas had been flying in the high clouds of fog. They had followed its every move, knew the exact position with which it should correspond with the big map on the wall.

As Bentley's voice said "Just a moment," the radio man at the microphone who had conducted the conversation with the plane relaxed, smiling.

"Two to one he beats the schedule!" he offered, and had no comers. "This is going to boost the Harvey Airlines all right. It's the fastest Chicago run in the air! And with Bentley the safest —"

He broke off, suddenly jerking up his head. From the loudspeaker came a low exclamation. Then —

"Wait!" Bentley's voice, no longer crisp but suddenly sharp, agitated. "Something's the matter! Something's wrong!"

The four men in the room stiffened, their confidence changing to quick alarm. The man at the microphone jerked forward.

"What's the matter, Bentley?" he snapped. "What —"

Then it came!

Of a sudden the loudspeaker seemed to burst into a din of raucous sound, which filled the cupola and brought a cry of alarm from every throat.

The first sound was like some rumbling detonation, brief yet reverberating. It was followed by a terrible, rending crackle! Horrified, the men in the cupola froze into rigid immobility, aware that something dreadful had just happened out in the night sky. And then, curdling their blood, came the hoarse scream:

"She's burning! She's burning!"

Pat Bentley had screamed those ghastly words! Screamed them more, it seemed, with horrified amazement than fright. Screamed them above that horrible, crackling roar.

"Fire!" Bentley shrieked, "It's broken out! The whole ship's burning like so much paper!"

"Bentley!" Helpless, the radio operator was wringing his hands at the microphone. "Good God, Bentley, what are you saying? What —"

The dreadful sounds from the night grew to a crescendo in the loud speaker. The crackling roar filled the room, And now, faint but horrifying, came other sounds-human cries. Cries of terror, of panic, of agony.

"God, she's going down! She's going to crash!" Bentley's frenzied voice came again. "The fire's creeping up — I can feel the heat-getting worse-worse! No hope! Going to crash —"

Abruptly the voice and the sounds ceased.

The radio went dead. In that awful moment, the aviation men's eyes showed the vivid horror of their air-trained imaginations. As if they could see a flaming Douglas plane, crashing like a fiery torch somewhere out in the night miles away. The fire consuming it, its radio crumpling, its passengers and its pilot caught helpless, without a chance of escape!

196

Then came swift reaction. The radio men hurled into a simultaneous rush of action. All other work was momentarily suspended. Both microphones carried frantic messages as their operators spoke in rapid fire.

"Trenton! Calling Trenton! Any more signals from Number One?"

"Balesville, Pennsylvania! Any reports of Number One in that vicinity?"

One of the operators picked up a phone. "Hangar Five! Send out planes to locate Number One!" He gave details, then: "Get me the commanding officer of Miller Field-Hello! Can you send out some flyers to aid in reported burning of transport?"

The continued calls set into motion every available machinery. As always, an air disaster brought swift cooperation from the Army Air Force, as well as from all commercial units.

The chief operator, having set such machinery in motion, spoke with gripping tension.

"We've got to get hold of Mr. Harvey! He must be informed of this at once. What a ghastly blow to the new line!"

Even as he spoke, out in the night, scores of searching planes were already taking the air. The hunt for the huge transport which had disappeared in the night was in full, feverish swing —

* * *

And meanwhile, outside a small shack rearing near heavy, wind-swaying trees, a group of shifting, shadowy figures, most of them in slouch hats with low-pulled brims, were gathering tensely.

There was a stench in the air —a burning, smoking stench. There was a dying, ruddy glow which flickered over coarse faces, over malignant, furtive eyes.

But the eyes of the group were all drawn hypnotically to a small closed coupe which had just emerged out of the night, come to a stop before them.

At first glance that coupe looked like the usual model of a well-known high-priced make of car. But closer inspection would have revealed the unusual heaviness of its metal body, the thickness of its glass windows. The window opposite the tense, dark figures was not quite completely closed; a crack showed on top. But glass protected the head of the car's lone occupant.

A face looked out through that glass —a strange, grotesquerie of a face whose features seemed to shimmer as if made of jelly. It was a ghastly sight, even though the men watching knew it was caused by some imperfection in the thick, bullet-proof glass.

Impossible to tell the true features of that distorted face. It remained, by virtue of the glass, a vague blur; frightening, yet malignantly compelling.

"And so everything has come off exactly as I planned!"

The voice came from the crack of the coupe's window. It was a ghastly voice, a sort of harsh whisper which eddied out into the silent night. It spoke in blighting malice.

"It has gone off like clockwork! And they will hunt in vain for the wreck! I commend you-all of you! Especially you three who were in the shack."

Slick, his head a dark shiny knob in the night, stepped forward with his nimble, jerky grace. Ape, still gripping the blue-steel tommy gun, stood grinning, while the man named Luke quietly lit a new cigarette.

"Hell, it was a cinch, Boss!" Slick spoke towards the car. "You had it figgered just right!"

An eerie chuckle sounded from the coupe, as the distorted face shimmered behind the glass.

"I always have things figured! And now we must prepare for my next enterprise! My work has only begun. The night is still young, and by midnight I strike again-this time in New York! There another enemy, perhaps even two, will pay for opposing me!" Harshly the whisper rose, with fanatical triumph. "Soon everyone will know the power of the Tycoon!

"And you, who are only one part of my mob, will see that you are not working for any small stakes. Before I am through, there will be millions-millions!" He repeated that word with avaricious greed which swiftly communicated itself to his listeners, to show in their evil faces. "Just obey my orders and nothing can stop us! Midnight tonight-remember, that is the time I have set. And I want you all to check your watches and synchronize them with my own now."

Watches came out or were turned up on wrists. The Tycoon gave the minute, and the watches were set.

"At midnight then," came the eerie voice. It lowered, giving further orders. Then the self-starter of the coupe whined; the engine purred.

"So I will go. And you will all hurry, too. I trust you checked up, as I said-on the dead?" he pronounced the phrase with grim mirth. "Did you take all the effects of Truesdale and Garth?" Hate threaded his tone as those names were spoken. There were gruff assents. "Good! And the pilot? You made sure of the pilot?"

As he spoke eyes shifted to the ruddy, dying glow. A few faces paled a little sickly.

"Yeah, I made sure he's dead," a squatly-built man stepped forward to answer. The ruddy glow revealed his squarish head, set low on wide shoulders. His face was crooked-featured, as if one-half of it had slid beneath the other. "I seen his brass buttons."

"You mean," the Tycoon said bitingly, "that there were two such men with brass buttons, don't you, Maxie? There was a co-pilot too."

Maxie's crooked face showed surprise. "But there was only one, Boss. I —"

"You bungling fool." The whisper lashed out like a whip, in sudden, frenzied rage. "Slick, count those bodies! Tell me the count!"

Slick hurried forward. He was quick to return with an answering number, but when he told it a snarl of enraged conviction came from the coupe.

"It's true then! One of them escaped! He's loose! That must be Bentley, the pilot, from what I know of his stubborn character. But he can't be far! He must be found-he must be killed!" The voice fairly crackled. "He must die before he can menace my plans!"

His fierce words lashed the whole crowd to action. Automatics glinted as they were whipped out. Ape gripped his tommy gun. Breaking up into smaller groups, thugs were scouring the vicinity-with murder in their eyes.

"He can't escape!" The voice of the Tycoon spurred them on. "There is only one way he could have headed. Get him! Get him no matter how far you have to follow him!"

* * *

Yes, Pat Bentley was alive!

He was disheveled, his face smoke-blackened, his eyes wild with horror and shock-but he was very much alive as he ran furtively through a sleepy little village-the village of Mulford, New York. A long, long way from where he had last radioed a message from his doomed plane.

His brain was a rioting tumult of rage, of horror, of anguished realization. Now he knew the reason for all his presentiments. And those two men he had felt queerly about at the outset of the flight. Garth and Truesdale.

He knew now the meaning of the frightened words he had heard in their conversation. But what about those strong boxes on the plane? Had they melted, burned? Their valuable un-known contents been destroyed? Conjectures raced through his mind as the question rose: What to do!

Then his wild eyes caught the light window of an all-night drug store. A telephone!

The lone clerk on duty in the store was dozing in a corner and did not even see Bentley. The disheveled, smoke-blackened pilot lurched across the floor to a single booth. His eyes glanced wildly around, then he entered, closing the door, change jangling as his hand reached into his pockets.

"Long-distance-New York City —" his voice came in a gasping croak. "I want New York City Police Headquarters. The number is Spring Seven Three One Hundred. Hurry-emergency!"

He was crazily putting in coins as he spoke, the toll-bells clanging. The urgency of his voice evidently brought swift cooperation from the telephone office.

The connection was made.

"Police Headquarters," boomed a stentorian voice.

"Let me speak to the commissioner: This is a matter of life and death. I've important information."

There was a pause at the other end. Faint words there; then a click of switches.

"Hello!" came a gruff voice. "This is Chief Deputy Inspector Gregg. Who's calling?"

"I want the commissioner."

"You can tell me what you have to say. I'm in charge of the Detective Division." And the man on the New York end of the line repeated: "Who's calling?"

"Listen!" Again Bentley ignored the question. His voice came rapid-fire, with crisp incisiveness, with the clear yet rapid enunciation that had made him famous as a news commentator. "Something's going to happen in New York at midnight at Grand Central! A murder —a devilish murder! There's a fiend behind it! I heard him talking! You police must stop him! You must —"

Abruptly Pat Bentley whirled. Was that a movement outside the drug store? Or just a shadow? The voice of the Manhattan inspector was barking questions in the receiver-but suddenly reaching a new decision, Bentley hung up without another word, without telling who he was.

He sneaked across the floor past the dozing clerk, glancing out. No one in sight. His imagination? Or perhaps a premonition. For the trail he had left would be wide open. They'd be after him.

He had done what had to be done immediately. Even as he had been talking he had realized he could not chance further information to any phone, nor tell what he knew to any police inspector. He must get to New York City, in person. He had phoned because he knew that not even a miracle could get him there before midnight, and at least he had warned the police, though they had no idea whose murder they were to prevent or who had given the information. But now —

As he hurried through the dark village streets, Bentley's eyes gleamed; those far-sighted eyes of the born flyer. There was one man to whom he could tell the whole ghastly story-the incredible story. The man who had been his boss when he was a newspaperman. Frank Havens, owner of the New York *Clarion*!

Havens would know what to do with this dynamite news that would be too inflammable for the police! For Havens knew how to contact the one person who could cope with such a thing; the great unknown detective who had unraveled other baffling and bloody enigmas.

"The Phantom!" Bentley's dry lips whispered, as they twisted in a crooked grin of hope. "The Phantom-must be-called!"

Chapter III
Murder on the Balcony

Night in Manhattan. In Times Square, the city was wide awake and gay, the bright lights glaring. Crowds from the theaters were hurrying to nightclubs and restaurants. From the waterfront fog-horns tooted, factories still ground out their work, smoke belching from their chimneys. To the east, cars streamed like illuminated, linked chains across the bridges.

Other cars streamed west, too, to enter the Holland Tunnel, to whisk over the George Washington Bridge. There were but few lonely streets in the teeming metropolis.

Wall Street and the surrounding financial district were deserted, the office buildings rising like dark canyon walls. But its streets were still pounded by alert patrolmen.

The poverty-stricken tenement sections where evil figures stalked-drunks and derelicts, shifty underworld characters-also lay in sleepy gloom. And police were watchful, knowing that no night passed in these districts without some violence and bloodshed.

Police Inspector Thomas Gregg's bulking form sat in the cushioned shield-bearing limousine which was whisking him and a hard-eyed subordinate uptown, toward Grand Central, its short-wave radio bringing every police call that went out from Headquarters.

"I suppose that anonymous call from Mulford, New York, was from a crank," the inspector grumbled "But I guess it's just as well not to take chances. That voice I heard on the phone-There was something about it-something familiar. Kinda made me sure feel the tip was hot!" He pulled out his watch. "Pretty close to midnight. Get on up to Grand Central. If anybody thinks he's going to pull any murder there —"

* * *

In a huge, brightly lighted room six tense men sat at a long conference table, talking in low voices as they watched a wall-clock which showed that the hour of midnight was approaching.

A more diverse-looking group could not have been found. Yet these six men were all linked by mutual reputations in the field of science and engineering. All were famous throughout the country for their work in these lines.

Nor was that all that linked them.

There was another bond which seemed to hold them together as with some hidden magnet. A strange, furtive bond-one of conflicting fear and hope.

Near the unoccupied head of the table Vincent Brooks, one of the country's leading electrical engineers, ran a gaunt hand over his long, rugged face, his dark, hard eyes narrowing beneath beetling brows.

Next to him a wiry man with a shock of grey hair that kept getting into his eyes, hunched tensely forward. Leland Sprague, a surveyor.

Beside those two sat Joseph Ware and Paul Talbert. Ware was a quiet, well-built, grey-haired man who was a specialist in waterways and dams. Paul Talbert, a shoring engineer, was broad-shouldered, with a wind-burned face, a military mustache, blond hair and clear, far-seeing eyes.

The fifth man of the group, solid-built but pallid-faced, with crow's-feet under his eyes, toyed nervously with a pencil. He was a geologist named Donald Vaughan.

Finally, running his hand over his high, thin-haired skull, was John Eldridge, another surveyor.

"Well, gentlemen?" Paul Talbert spoke, sitting erect, his mustache bristling. "I still say the time is opportune! Everything has worked out as we planned it! We have only to go ahead." His eyes gleamed.

"What about the threats?" Joseph Ware demurred. The quiet-looking waterways man's voice was low and tense, and only his eyes showed the panic he kept from his quiet face, "Remember, I've been getting them. And now that we've learned what happened to Truesdale and Garth —"

"You're jumping to conclusions, Ware!" Sprague broke in, a little shrilly, pushing back his shock of grey hair. "They haven't found that plane yet! We don't know for sure."

"Besides, it was undoubtedly an accident, that disaster!"

"Undoubtedly." Talbert agreed. "And while it means a delay, we can still go ahead as we planned! This is no time for faint heartedness! Don't forget what's in this for all of us if it works out!"

There was a slight stir around the table. Greed, that dark driving urge which at times can overcome the best of men, flashed in several eyes. Greed-and fear!

"I agree with Talbert!" Vincent Brooks, the rugged-faced electrical engineer, clipped. He laughed harshly. "And I have been warned myself by these strange phone messages! But whoever this Tycoon is, he can't know our secret. Only we know it at this present moment! And no one but ourselves will ever know it fully!"

"Lord, if it ever leaked out!" Donald Vaughan strained forward, the crows-feet twitching under his eyes. "If this Tycoon suspected it he could ruin us all!" He shook his head. "And if the Government ever knew —"

He broke off abruptly, as if not daring to finish. And again the current of invisible fear coursed about the table.

"We've got to keep our heads!" Eldridge said, his thin-haired head bobbing. "We're in this thing together no matter what happens."

Like an invisible curtain a hush closed down on the group. Lips clamped suddenly tight. Eyes hid the emotions which a moment before had shown stark and clear.

The frosted glass door leading from an anteroom had opened unceremoniously. Three more men came in.

The one in advance, a heavy-set man, florid of face, his head bald save for a fringe of iron-grey hair, strode toward the table.

"Good evening, gentlemen! Glad to see all of you got here early. I hope you have made yourselves at home here in our executive office."

In the sudden silence, the six scientists heard the muffled but continuous bustle of sound outside the offices; the movement of hundreds of feet; and, further away, an occasional clang of bells, a hiss of air-brakes.

This big room, the New York office of the Empire and Southwest Railway, was situated on the gallery floor of Manhattan's biggest railway terminal, the Grand Central, famous throughout a continent.

Talbert was the first to speak, in a quiet, hard voice, to the rugged man who had strode forward.

"Hello, Strickland! We've been waiting for you!"

James Strickland, vice-president of the Empire and Southwest Railway, moved to the head of the table and took the chair there.

The second newcomer, Charles Jenson, secretary of the railway company, a thin-haired, bespectacled man with a mild, timid manner, also joined the gathering.

And if these two high railway officials seemed almost like aliens in the conclave of scientists, the third man who had entered at their heels was out of place with both groups.

He stood alone near the door —a big, broad man with grizzled, grey-peppered hair. A man who gave the impression of dominant strength.

"Oh, sit down, Mr. Harvey!" Strickland said to him, gesturing as if just remembering the amenities. "You gentlemen must know Mr. Andrew Harvey, president of the Harvey Airlines!"

Tensing again, the eyes of the six scientists swiveled to the visitor.

He grinned —a hard, tight grin-meeting their glances levelly.

"I'll stand," he said in a booming voice. "What I have to say won't take long. I'm here on business-cold, plain business! I'm here to make a cash offer for this railway! While Strickland and Jenson have given me little encouragement, I thought I might find the rest of you more interested!"

No electric shock could have caused a more startled reaction. Their eyes widening, for a moment the six scientists seemed speechless.

Then Strickland spoke, as if for the startled men.

"This is most irregular, Mr. Harvey! In the absence of the line's president, Mr. Garrison, who as you know, is in St. Louis —"

"I'll deal with Garrison when he gets back!" Andrew Harvey snapped. "Right now I'm dealing with all of you here. That's enough!"

A mirthless smile curved Talbert's lips beneath his mustache. "You seem to be laboring under a misconception, Mr. Harvey," he said. "We are merely technicians working for the Empire and Southwest Railway."

Harvey's laugh was harsh, contemptuous. "You're wasting your breath! I know you're the chief stockholders of this railroad, all of you! You've all acquired big blocks of shares! And I'm here to buy you out-to take those shares at better than their present market value!"

The silence was ominous. The six men, rigid now, turned fierce glances to Strickland and Jenson. Strickland blurted something. The mild Jenson spoke in a meek voice.

"I'm sure Mr. Harvey didn't learn that from us." The secretary's tone was conciliating. "These things leak out, you know."

"I make it my business to know such things!" Harvey said shortly. "And I know you men, with your technical skill, are trying to put this railway on its feet! But it isn't worth the effort. The only use for it now is if it can be run in conjunction, as an auxiliary, to my own airline! That's why I want it. If you think you can run it in competition, you're sadly mistaken!" His eyes narrowed to slits, his face grew grim. "Even the sabotaging of my new Chicago transport plane isn't going to cripple my growing airline!"

There was a gasped intake of breath; and indignant scrape of chairs.

Joseph Sprague, the wiry surveyor, was on his feet then, his shock of grey hair dancing.

"Are you daring to insinuate that we had any connection with that plane disaster?" he demanded shrilly.

"Take it that way if you want," said the blunt Harvey. His lips curled. "Of course, all of you will begin to produce alibis showing you were in New York City at the time of the disaster; but you men do get around, don't you? And there are more ways than one of cooking a goose, especially if you're a technician!"

Talbert leaped up. "If this is a joke, Harvey," he said with cold fury, "it's in pretty bad taste."

Sprague leaned forward, fuming.

"It's outrageous! I refuse to listen to it! You can have my answer to your offer right now, Mr. Harvey! I'll see you in Hell before I'll make any deal with you!"

For a moment it seemed he would spring bodily upon the weathered-faced airline president, smaller though he was. Instead, however, he pushed back his chair and, his face flaming, strode out of the conference room, slamming the door behind him.

Strickland's eyes showed haggard worry. "You shouldn't have said that, Harvey! After all, a knife can have two edges. Sprague was a close friend of both Truesdale and Garth-also of our company, and passengers on that plane. Truesdale and Garth were valuable men," he added significantly, "very valuable men."

"And also," Joseph Ware put in grimly, "don't forget that there has been a lot of sabotage of the railway itself. Especially in the Southwest."

It was the airline man's turn to stiffen indignantly. Glaring, he seemed about to voice an angry retort when Vincent Brooks, the gaunt electric wizard, suddenly rose to his feet, pointing at the clock-whose hands were converging to midnight!

"It's time for the new electric sign to go on!" Brooks announced. "Inasmuch as I constructed it, I'd like to be out there to see it!"

Strickland nodded hastily. "Of course. We all want to see it." He turned to Harvey. "You'll join us, Mr. Harvey? You noticed the preliminaries as you came in. Perhaps you'll be interested to see how modern we, too, can be in our methods."

The whole group were hurriedly rising. With a scowling Harvey accompanying them, they passed through an anteroom, emerged upon a gallery, then descended marble-bannistered steps which led them directly upon the immense, dome-ceilinged concourse.

An unusually large throng milled on the floor; a throng much larger than the usual flow of travelers who always streamed through the big terminal. Huge banners, all proclaiming A New Era in Railroading, gave the huge place a festive air.

Over the noise of the crowds sounded the blare of trumpeting music. A band composed of dusky Pullman porters in gaudy uniforms, led by a busby-hatted drum-major, was playing "Casey Jones."

"What is this anyhow?" Harvey snorted. "A circus in a railroad station?"

Strickland glared at him, but the mild-eyed secretary, Jensen, said, in an explanatory tone:

> "In just one minute now, you will see that sign go on." With a moving forefinger he signified a continuous dark oblong strip of metal, dotted with electric bulbs, which ran around the four walls of the great concourse. "In St. Louis, Mr. Garrison, our president, will press a button. The impulse will be carried over our own wires to the device on the gallery which operates the sign."

"Very elaborate!" sneered Harvey. "But nothing can put this line on its feet, I'm warning you."

Nevertheless, he displayed interest as the Pullman band ended its number with a martial roll of drums. An expectant hush fell over the crowd. All eyes went to the strip of dark bulbs.

A second went by, then —

Abruptly, a flickering blaze of light leaped into life at the beginning of the strip, coursed jaggedly along the sign, forming bold letters-words:

GREETINGS TO THE PUBLIC-WE TAKE PLEASURE IN ANNOUNCING
OUR MODERNIZED RAILROAD POLICY-OUR MANY NEW
INNOVATIONS —

The words, with their smooth advertising, continued. The crowd watched.

—AND NOW IT IS TIME FOR THE MESSAGE OF THE TYCOON OF CRIME —

So smoothly did these words follow on the wake of the others that at first their utter strangeness was unnoticed by the crowd. But instantly sharply indrawn breaths of amazement issued from the group of men who had rushed down from the executive offices. Their eyes bulged as they followed those bold words, carried unerringly around the strip of bulbs.

—THE TYCOON OF CRIME HEREBY WARNS ALL THOSE WHO HAVE
FLOUTED HIM —

The crowd had begun to murmur, to laugh as if believing this some deliberately humorous part of the ballyhoo, not yet understood.

"What's the meaning of those crazy words?" Strickland burst out.

"Meaning?" screamed a voice. "Good Lord, don't you realize? The Tycoon! The criminal we all laughed at!"

No one had noticed that Leland Sprague, the shock-haired surveyor who had so angrily left the conference room, had joined them. It was he who had made this outburst. His agitation seemed to have driven away all remembrance of his anger; his face was ashen. Madly he waved towards the coursing, illuminated words.

"The sign!" he choked. "He must have got at the box that makes the sign go!"

But while Jenson and Harvey both looked as bewildered as Strickland, the scientists in the group had all jerked rigid, their faces blanching.

Even the hard-featured Paul Talbert looked shaken.

Then Vincent Brooks, who had made the sign, suddenly dashed toward the gallery stair. John Eldridge, the thin-haired surveyor, also broke away at a run.

The bold words which thousands read continued to leap into view, and run around the sign like letters of fire.

—SOME HAVE LEARNED THIS VERY NIGHT OF MY POWER-OTHERS WILL SOON LEARN-MORE BLOOD WILL BE SPILLED-MORE WILL DIE-TAKE THIS LAST WARNING—

The explosion was deafening!

It crashed thunderously in the spacious interior of the dome-ceilinged concourse, the sheer concussion hurling many of the gaping crowd off balance.

From the center of the balcony, above the coursing sign, had leaped a blinding, hissing sheet of flame! The sign went dark even as the detonation followed. And at the same instant—

A scream of horror burst from scores of throats as, whisked off the balcony like some mere feather, a human shape came hurtling straight down —a shape of limp but flailing arms and legs.

That the body didn't fall on the panic-stricken crowd seemed sheer luck. With a ghastly thud it crashed to the tiled flooring beneath the balcony.

Strickland, Jenson, and the rest of their group rushed over as the din rose higher, though railway police were struggling to restore order.

They reached the inert heap on the floor, looked down. A scream broke from Charles Sprague, who pointed.

"It's Eldridge! Good God-Eldridge!"

John Eldridge was a gruesome sight. His body was a maimed, bloody heap which stained crimson the white-tiled floor. A whole portion of his chest had been blown out. A gaping hole showed the broken bones, ripped flesh, tatters of clothes. His face was frozen in a grimace of contorted agony, the eyes glazed and protruding like marbles.

Strickland cried out hoarsely. "And he was blown off the balcony-just when the sign went off! Where's Brooks? Brooks should know about the sign!"

His question was quickly answered by Donald Vaughan. The geologist had rushed up to the balcony, and his voice called down shakily. The rest hurried up there, oblivious that Andrew Harvey was no longer with them.

They found what was left of Vincent Brooks piled against the balcony wall. His head had almost been severed from his torso by the explosion. The chin was blown away, leaving a broken bulge of bloody jaw-bone. The features, bloated in death, were barely recognizable.

Opposite the corpse, on the stone balcony construction, was a shattered box of metal, its parts strewn about.

Strickland stared at it.

"That's where the strip that controlled the sign was running!" he burst out hoarsely. "It's blown to hell! This is ghastly-ghastly!"

Quick glances were shot up and down the balcony. It was empty. But the crowds from below, in mingled panic and morbid curiosity, were already surging up the stairs. Railway police fought them back. Then came the shrill whistles of regular city police on duty in this precinct.

And outside in the night, in the next moment, rose the scream of sirens.

The law was coming swiftly. And a certain shield-bearing limousine carrying a worried inspector was now hurtling straight to the terminal.

Chapter IV
The Corpse on the Pavement

Richard Curtis Van Loan, debonair young society man and *bon vivant,* turned his sixteen-cylindered Cadillac roadster onto upper Park Avenue and headed downtown through a neighborhood-which, in this section, was shabby and unkempt.

A slender, dark-haired girl in a pert, Buddhistic hat sat beside Van Loan, her dark, liquid eyes wistfully stealing now and then to his well-cut profile, etched in the dashboard lights.

In the spacious rumble seat, another couple sat, in each other's arms, and it could have been seen at a glance that they were newlyweds. The girl, blond and hatless, clung possessively to the young groom who had been one of the social register's most eligible bachelors until he had looked into her blue eyes.

"Say, where are you taking us, Dick?" the man suddenly leaned forward to ask.

"To my apartment," drawled Van Loan, without turning from the wheel, "where we will do justice, with champagne, to your marriage, then let you go off on your honeymoon in peace. Do you agree, Muriel?"

Muriel Havens smiled up at him.

"If you ask me, I have a sneaking suspicion the newlyweds are just dying to get rid of us!"

"Now Muriel!" the girl in the back protested. "We're not leaving until tomorrow. We even hoped to get your father's blessing before we went. Do you suppose we'll get a chance to see him?"

Muriel sighed. "I don't know. The paper's been keeping him pretty busy. He's in his office night and day."

"Isn't it extraordinary," Van Loan drawled languidly, "how some men will bury themselves in work? Why doesn't your dad let the *Clarion* run merrily along, Muriel, and step out for a good time?"

Muriel Havens's small but firm chin lifted. A momentary anger swept her eyes.

"Some people wouldn't understand it, I guess," she said pointedly. "But Dad feels he's doing something useful in this world."

Van Loan made a sad, clucking sound with his tongue.

"Ouch!" he said. "That remark has a vaguely personal tinge. But really, can you imagine me getting up the energy to indulge in hard labor?" He stifled a yawn.

On Muriel's lovely, intelligent face was disappointment. She could not have felt surprised.

Richard Curtis Van Loan was hardly a man of action. Good-natured, lazy, he fitted only into the social set, whiling away the hours with his select friends in pleasure and amusement. Because he was handsome and too wealthy for any one man, he was one whom doting mothers longed to have their daughters ensnare.

Yet, oddly, Muriel Havens had never accepted Van Loan as a mere lazy, social parasite, an idler who gayly flung to the winds the wealth his father had slaved to attain.

Again she glanced at the well-built young man beside her; at his strong hands, gripping the wheel with steady ease. And she shook her head, her lips pressed against any words of protest she might have felt like uttering.

As the roadster continued downtown the avenue changed in aspect. The shabby district suddenly gave way to Manhattan's most exclusive and wealthy residential section. They were riding down past the green-parked "islands" under which trains rumbled.

"Why so silent, Newlyweds?" Van drawled. "This is a celebration, not a funeral."

"Oh, don't mind us!" the young bridegroom laughed. "We're just sitting here smugly enjoying the idea of being married. And let me tell you, Dick, it's great! Why don't you try it sometime?"

"It is a thought," Van Loan grinned-and looked at Muriel Havens. For a moment, she saw in his eyes something that was seldom there; and so briefly now that she might have only imagined it. It was so totally out of gear with the languid, idling Van Loan.

Van saw her dark eyes glow-for that one moment. And turned back to the wheel, covering his expression with another suppressed ostentatious yawn.

Dick Van Loan knew Muriel was hurt by that gesture; wounded deeply. Yet it had been necessary. His hand had covered more than the yawn. It had covered an implacable bitterness which had tightened his lips and narrowed his eyes.

Had Muriel or the others had any inkling of the thoughts that were going through Van's brain at that instant, they would have been more than amazed.

They were stern, fierce thoughts. Thoughts sealed by a long-kept pledge within his mind. Thoughts that cruelly drove the human feelings of Dick Van Loan to some dull recess where he could only keep them for the distant future.

In his mind, Richard Van Loan was seeing vividly remembered sights, alien to his social life. He was seeing dark byways, where shadowy, evil figures stalked; he was seeing gruesome bodies, riddled, knifed, killed in other heinous fashions. He saw, too, the terrible implements of justice. The inexorable electric chair-the noose-the lethal chamber. And cowering, convicted criminals ensnared by them.

A grim parade of diabolical murderers who had thought they could cheat justice! Sometimes they had foiled the law, made a laughingstock of the police. But, like a relentless Nemesis, a single unknown had proved their undoing. The mysterious scourge of crime known as the Phantom Detective.

The Phantom! Throughout the world, in every law-enforcing agency, in Scotland Yard, in the *Surete,* to the Berlin Police that sobriquet had become a synonym of perfect crime detection. Just as, in the underworld, it had become a byword of fear and dread.

Richard Curtis Van Loan, sitting next to Muriel Havens, wished he could have turned to her now and driven the reproach and disappointment from her eyes by telling her the great secret. He wished he could have said:

> "Muriel, I am the Phantom Detective! Yes, I—Richard Curtis Van Loan, whom you hold in contempt and yet love. Your own father, Frank Havens, was responsible. It was he who told me years ago, that I was wasting my life and energy; he who suggested that I anonymously try to fight crime. Since then my life is no longer my own. I have to forego all that every normal man takes for granted as a part of his life. My lazy social life is just a pose-to enable me to gather energy for the next case, which can come at any moment. My real time is spent in study-the study of criminology, disguise, delving into realms you would never dream interest me. But perhaps some day, some time, when my case book is full, I can come to you, free and unshackled."

Aloud, however, Van Loan said with a lazy drawl as the car picked up speed, "Well, here we come. Now to negotiate a turn, get to the other side of the block-and home sweet home."

He did not look at Muriel Havens as he spoke, as he nodded toward the "island" beneath which sounded a dull rumble. The sidewalk opposite, dim in the street lights, was empty. On the corner toward the palatial apartment atop which was Van's luxurious penthouse residence. Van guided the purring roadster down to the intersection, thence around, waiting for the lights to make the complete turn before heading the car uptown on the other side of the block.

Steering towards the curb, he slowed the roadster. That was when his ever keen eyes-eyes trained to alertness by night as well as day-suddenly sharpened. Without giving thought to it, he had observed that the sidewalk had been empty as the roadster passed down the block, on the downtown side.

But now, coming up on this side, he saw that the pavement was no longer empty.

In the very middle of the block, a shadowy heap lay on the sidewalk.

A huddled, bulgy heap from which came no sign of movement.

"What is it, Dick?" Muriel had noticed his sudden stiffening.

Without replying, Van braked the roadster to an instant stop, apprehension tightening his lips.

Ignoring the questions of Muriel and the others, he slid quickly from behind the wheel, alighted in the street on his long legs, and hurried around the car to the sidewalk.

Only the dim light of the nearest street-lamp illumined the bulgy heap.

But it was sufficient to bring out a gruesome sight.

The corpse of a well-built man lay at Van's feet. It lay half on its side, legs drawn up grotesquely to the stomach, hands clutching out like frozen claws.

The clothes of the man were so disheveled, torn, and begrimed with dirt and blood and what appeared to be soot, that they were scarcely distinguishable.

The man was hatless. His light-colored hair looked like a wet, flat mat-wet with crimson blood.

But it was to the face of the man, full of bruises that Van's eyes were drawn so grimly. Or rather, to what had once been a face.

On first glimpse it looked like some horrible smear of blood and dirt and torn flesh so that the outlines of the skull showed through. Near the lower right jaw was a huge, uneven hole; obviously made by a heavy-calibered bullet. Once, in Chicago, during a gang war, Van had seen a man shot in this fashion. Shot in the face at close range, so that the bullet had completely disfigured him.

Something of this face remained however. Though not enough to offer any clear picture. Grim-eyed, Van stared at the bloody, revolting face, at the glazed, blood-stained eyes which peered out stark and sightless. In the full moment he studied that face Van decided the man had been fairly young, had probably had well-formed features.

A gasped cry-he recognized Muriel Havens's voice-jerked him about. Quickly Van stepped around the corpse as he saw Muriel and the newlyweds standing, white-faced, on the pavement. With his tall, broad-shouldered figure he screened the gruesome corpse from them as best he could.

"Dick-that man! He's dead, isn't he?" In Muriel's choked-cry —a statement, rather than question, was horror.

"Yes, so it seems."

Van's languid drawl was slightly constricted. His mind was racing. Something was prodding it, hammering at it like some stray waif of memory trying to gain admittance.

"Better not come any closer," he said. "It's rather a nasty sight." He turned to the groom. "Listen. This has rather upset my night, but there's no sense in letting it spoil your party. Take my car, take Muriel with you. Continue your celebration without me. Just take the time to summon the first policeman you see and send him here. Better not tell him what's here or he might make you come back. I'll remain with-this."

Despite the fact that he still clung to his drawl, there was something so decisive and commanding in his manner that all three stared, unable to comprehend this change in the idle Van Loan. Again Muriel Havens's dark eyes swept to him with that strange, probing look: half hope, half unbelief.

She came forward, a brave look on her firm, finely chiseled features, "I'll stay here with you, Dick. Maybe I can help."

"Help? My dear girl, this is a matter for the police. I myself do not intend to stay any longer than I have to. Until the law takes over.

"By the way, don't mention my name when you call the policeman. I don't wish to be dragged into this. After the law comes, I shall discreetly retire; and because I feel a bit upset, take out a nice bottle to enjoy in solitude."

His drawl, forced back, was cold again. Once more Muriel's eyes went dull with disappointment and hurt.

But his words, as he had calculated, had the desired effect.

Chapter V
Clarion Call

Muriel Turned, gesturing to the others. In a moment they were piling back into Van's car, the bridegroom taking the wheel. Rolling from the curb, the big roadster moved up the avenue. Van caught a glimpse of Muriel Havens's white, hurt face, looking back through the darkness. But he thrust aside any emotion that face disturbed in him. For already his brain had turned into a cold, methodical machine, functioning in full power.

All languor had dropped from his athletic body. His movements had become dynamic, purposeful.

Again his gaze riveted to the mutilated face of the corpse on the sidewalk. Though the features were gone, there was something there that struck a reminiscent chord in the Phantom's brain. Something-what was it? What was that elusive identifying mark?

That vague memory in the back of his brain tugged at Van. He felt certain of one thing, however. Somewhere he had seen this man. But where? Under what circumstances?

He studied the clothes as his fingers swiftly searched through them. All the pockets were empty. Even the buttons of trousers and coat were missing. The material was blue serge, and though ripped, the suit still retained a certain trimness. A uniform, perhaps? Not a police uniform, but —

Then a sudden light flashed through Van's brain as he moved so that the street light fell more directly on the corpse. Though it was so deeply bloodied that at first it had not been distinguishable, the white streak in the dead man's hair was now plain to Van's keen, observant eyes. A peculiarly formed streak.

He had it! His eyes went narrow as his lips spoke a name.

"Pat Bentley!"

The young flyer who had once worked as a news commentator for Frank Havens!

In his role of idler, Van Loan had met Pat Bentley in the *Clarion* offices. He had noticed that streak in young Bentley's black hair, even as he had been admiring the nerve of the adventurous youngster. He had known then he would never forget that peculiarly distinguishing mark of the young flyer's. And Havens had told Van, later, that Bentley had become a crack transport pilot.

That blue serge material was used for the uniform of such a pilot. It plainly was a uniform, even though the telltale brass buttons were gone.

But-and bafflement came to Dick Van Loan's face-how had Bentley come to be killed in this horrible fashion here on Park Avenue?

Naturally Van did not know of the air disaster. It had occurred too recently, too far upstate, for any news of it to have reached farther than the newspaper offices yet, where the presses were even now whirling off the details of the air tragedy.

But he did know that finding Pat Bentley dead-killed in this vicious manner-and practically on his own doorstep, was a challenge to the Phantom, though there had been no such intention.

He had to find Pat Bentley's murderer!

He bent over the awful, mutilated face. The bullet, he saw, had entered the lower jaw, had come out behind the opposite ear. It had passed partially through the brain.

Death, then, would not have been instantaneous. A man might even live for awhile, manage to move for awhile, with such a wound.

Again he went through the clothes for some possible clue. This time he found something as his fingers turned back one of the trouser cuffs. Within it lay a few tiny bits of paper; like confetti.

Puzzled, Van straightened. Where had the dead man come from? The sidewalk had been empty when Van had driven past. No cars had passed before he had discovered the body, he was sure. His eyes scanned buildings, including his own apartment house. One of them, perhaps?

Suddenly his eyes sharpened, centering on the street itself. Little jagged smears of red showed on the concrete sidewalk, extending to the curb, out onto the asphalt of the street to the rail of one of the midstreet "islands." Blood! A brief trail of it.

The jigsaw-like clues clicked into place in Van's razor-sharp brain. The blood trail-the confetti-like bits in the trouser cuffs-the "island," beneath which he had heard a train rumbling a few minutes before his discovery of the corpse.

A train! That was the only possible answer. The "confetti" clinched it. The little paper bits were undoubtedly the punchings from a railway ticket.

That-and one other thing-clinched it. For as Van glanced toward the "island" he saw that the big iron ventilating grille in the center of the grass and shrubbery was undisturbed-but the smaller grille that usually covered the manhole-like square at one end of the "island" was off, tilted against the iron fence.

One of the workmen must have forgotten to replace it and bolt it from the under side. And Bentley had found the open grille. Some instinct must have guided him even in his blinded, mortally wounded condition.

Van's mind was racing. Pat Bentley, then, had been on a train, though in which direction it had passed Van couldn't tell. Doubtless the pilot had been shot on that train. Then he must have jumped, or fallen from it. The last ounce of his dying energy had been spent in climbing to the street level; getting as far as the Park Avenue sidewalk.

It was almost as if Fate had thrown Pat Bentley upon Van's doorstep, bringing him this case. For certainly Bentley could not have known that Van lived here, much less dreamed that Richard Van Loan was the Phantom! The fact that the man *had* fallen so near Van's own home was one of those bizarre coincidences at which the Phantom no longer scoffed.

Van prodded himself to haste. He must follow up his hunch-and quickly. There was need for haste otherwise, too, for glancing down the deserted block, he glimpsed a burly figure coming at a run, with a swinging night-stick. A beat patrolman. Muriel and the others must have sent him.

Richard Van Loan was in no mood to tarry and face inquiries now. His lithe body whisked into the dark shadow of building walls, streaking to the door of his apartment house.

No doorman was on duty at this late hour, and before the night elevator operator could see him, Van had slipped into his private elevator, closed its door, and pressed the starting button.

It took but a brief moment for him to reach his penthouse floor, high above the city. His key admitted him to his luxurious, French-windowed apartment. He strode through the foyer, into a living room, pressing on light-switches as he walked. Modernistic-globed lights flooded the place.

Flinging his coat to a chair, Van stepped beside a taboret on which stood two telephones and the phone directories. He flipped the Manhattan book open, found his number. Scooping up one phone he dialed swiftly.

"Grand Central Terminal Information," came a smooth, clerical voice.

Van's own voice was crisp, incisive; totally unlike his customary drawl.

"Will you tell me when the last train left from your terminal-and also the last train that arrived there?"

"Just a moment." The clerk, accustomed to answering even stranger questions, replied politely, yet with a certain tenseness of tone which made Van wonder. There seemed to be a lot of noise at that end of the wire, too, as if something were wrong.

Van was using one hand to get off his jacket, ripping open buttons of his shirt as the clerk's voice came again.

"Last train to depart was the Rochester Special. That was at eleven fifty. The last to arrive here was the Toledo Limited, at eleven thirty-eight."

Van glanced at his watch. It was twelve thirty-three now. Neither of those trains could be the right one. The run between the terminal and here was only a matter of some ten minutes either way.

"When is the next arriving train due?"

The answer brought a thrill of conviction to him.

"It's due now, sir. It's a few minutes late, but should be in any minute. The Buffalo Local-on Track Forty-one."

"Thanks!" Van hung up, eyes glittering.

That must be the train. Swiftly, he scooped up the second telephone.

This was a private line, one which connected him, as soon as he lifted the receiver, directly with the executive office of the New York *Clarion,* automatically causing the phone at that end to ring.

"Van!" The familiar voice of Frank Havens came instantly, a voice oddly threaded with gladness and surprise. "Why, I was just about to call *you!*"

"Listen, Frank!" Van spoke tersely, hurriedly. "I have no time to talk long! But I want you to use your influence to have a train, the Buffalo Local, due any minute at Grand Central Terminal, immediately searched by the railway and regular police. All passengers and crew to be held for the time being. No one is to be allowed to get away! It's important, Frank —I'll explain later. Can you do it quickly?"

"I can do it this instant!" came the reply, to Van's surprise. "As a matter of fact I have the railway officials on another wire even now! I was just about to call you after what they told me. But evidently you already know, though I don't see how —" the publisher broke off sharply. "I'll carry out your instructions-at once!"

"Good!" Van clipped, and hurriedly slammed down the hand-set, his ears echoing with Frank Havens's strange words!

So Havens had been about to call the Phantom-had railway officials on another wire. Certainly it could not be about this corpse Van had only moments ago discovered and identified. The train whence it had come was not yet in!

With conjectures whirling in his brain, Van was already hurrying into his bedroom now, closing the door behind him, turning the key in the lock for safety's sake. His shirt was off in a jiffy, his lithe arm muscles revealed in the bright light.

Quickly, he moved to a dressing table. In appearance it was a usual, though expensive piece of furniture. The maid who came in to clean had dusted it every day without suspecting that there was anything out of the ordinary about it, save perhaps the fact that, unlike most men's dressing tables, it had three extremely good mirrors.

Van pulled open a bottom drawer. He tossed out a layer of clothing. The false bottom was so neatly fitted that it defied detection, even with the drawer empty. By a secret catch, Van opened it like a hinged door.

The first object he took out was a flat leather kit. The lid snapped open at his pressure, revealing a small but complete array of vials and tubes. Enough of a variety of makeup here to supply any character actor, for any part. This was all he kept in his apartment. When the supply gave out he replenished it from another, more fully stocked source.

Van's well-formed features stared out at him as he adjusted the mirrors. But not for long! For his fingers began to dab stuff from the makeup kit onto his face. A cream dye to change his complexion to a lighter shade. An Oriental preparation, rubbed into his scalp, turned his chestnut hair into sandy color. Tiny bits of hard rubber cartilage in his nostrils changed their shape. A bit of putty on the end of his nose completed the change, making the nose long, pointed.

He was not attempting to make up as any particular person; he was merely creating a face totally different from the face of Richard Curtis Van Loan. There was no time to do more.

In less than five minutes a sharp-nosed face of indeterminate age, topped by sandy hair, stared out at Van from the mirror. Satisfied, he turned away to dress himself in a modest business suit.

He took a battered hat from his closet, then, from the secret compartment of the dressing table took three more objects. The first was a glistening blue-steel Colt .45 automatic, which he shoved into his coat pocket. The second was a black silk domino mask, with elastic attached.

It went carefully up his sleeve, concealed there. The third he had to take from a small plush-lined box. As the box was opened, a scintillating flash of matchless diamonds sparkled in the bright light.

It was a platinum badge, and the diamond studs on it formed a replica, in design, of that black domino mask.

As Van tucked that badge within a vest pocket he ceased to be Richard Curtis Van Loan. It was as if the badge were some magic charm which erased his personality as a society man.

In that moment he flung off all last thoughts of Muriel Havens, of friends, of human feelings and cravings.

He became truly the Phantom. The Phantom, whose only mark of identity was the diamond-studded platinum badge which, throughout the entire world, could bring obedience and respect from any law-enforcement officer.

Yet it was a badge few had seen. Van used it sparingly. Indeed only when dire necessity made its showing necessary.

He straightened, eyes grim, purposeful, in his disguised face. He was ready-prepared to take up the trail to wherever Pat Bentley's dead body might lead him.

Chapter VI
In the Elevator

Short minutes later, Van Loan emerged from a side door of the big apartment house, having descended in another private elevator that let him out that way unseen.

He walked out on the side street, and even his walk was totally unlike that of Richard Curtis Van Loan. It was a shuffling gait which was at the same time rapid. Hurriedly, yet unobtrusively, he moved to the corner, glanced down the Park Avenue block.

He saw two police radio coupes and a detective cruiser. On the sidewalk, surrounded by a crowd which had materialized out of the night, was a little knot of bluecoats and plainclothes men hovering over the corpse. A sudden flash for a Homicide photographer's camera threw them all into relief. The routine investigation was under way.

Avoiding that block, the Phantom walked up the avenue and hailed the first cab that passed.

A five-dollar bill, waved at the taxi man, resulted in a speedy, light-defying ride all the way down to Grand Central.

But as Van alighted from his taxi he saw with frowning surprise that a whole array of police cars were lined before the stone facade of the huge railway terminal. What was more, when he entered the terminal and walked down a ramp into the immense dome-ceilinged concourse, he found himself in the midst of a grim, tumultuous scene.

Crowds, fearful yet curious, were being herded back by perspiring bluecoats. A whole area of the concourse floor, under one gallery, was being roped off by the police. There and in the gallery itself, flash-bulbs were going off at spasmodic, lightning intervals.

Even as Van Loan looked, two pairs of dark-uniformed men hurried across the tiled floor, each pair carrying between them a large wicker basket. Morgue attendants! Evidently coming for two bodies!

This, whatever it was, must be the reason Havens had been about to call him. Something big had happened here. Yet the Phantom did not stop to investigate it now. He must stick to his trail which had begun with the body on the sidewalk-the body he believed to be that of Pat Bentley. After that he could return to whatever was going on here.

He crossed the wide, marble floor, passing train-gates and noting their numbers. Track 41. He was approaching it now.

A group of railway police, some bluecoats and plainclothes men, stood grouped around the gate, all looking confused and worried.

Van Loan approached the gate with the manner of a man who knows where he is going. He hoped he would not have to use his platinum badge to get through.

In a businesslike way he strode directly to the gate, banking only on his knowledge of psychology. His whole air was so completely that of a man who had a definite right to go through that gate, that the group gathered there scarcely gave him a glance.

Walking down the ramp to the platform of Track 41, his eyes peered keenly into the dim, wide tunnel where bells clanged and trains moved in two directions.

The platform was crowded. On the track alongside, with sounds of compressed air still issuing from its brakes, stood the train he sought, its big electric engine humming at the bumper.

The passengers, standing by their baggage, were making loud protests. Railway police and bluecoats who were guarding them were giving weak answers to the protests.

So Havens had carried out his instructions.

Van's keen eyes searched the crowd. All looked like average people —a smattering of business men, a few families, sleepy-eyed, crying children, buxom mothers. And denim-clad men of the train crew and angry-looking conductors.

"Is everybody off the train?" Van asked one of the railway police, his tone officious.

"Yes, sir," the man replied without hesitation, evidently assuming that this sandy-haired stranger had authority. "We have everybody from the train right here."

The Phantom wasn't satisfied. He was not even remotely suspicious of anyone in this crowd. Turning on his heel even as a bluecoat started to move toward him half challengingly, Van slipped aboard the train, hurried through empty Pullmans toward the rear, which he had noted was unguarded, his hand close to the pocket where his .45 nestled.

The last car was not a Pullman, but a coach. It was empty, he saw at a glance through its corridor. He hurried through it hastily, glancing at each seat. Nothing there.

When he had reached the open rear doorway where chains swung to form a gate leading to the train's rear platform, suddenly Van's eyes sharpened. Near the closed-off door of one side of the platform, the side overlooking the tracks, he saw a streaky splatter of red on the glass. Blood!

The Phantom's deductions had been grimly corroborated. This, no doubt, was where Pat Bentley had been shot! Then the pilot had fallen or jumped off the rear of the train.

Van glanced out of the rear, down the darkening tracks. Were the rest of his deductions correct? The train had not been here long. It had been searched, all passengers seen getting off stopped. But there were no police behind this rear, open door!

Yet the tracks behind the car were obviously deserted and —

Again Van's eyes focused narrowly, keenly.

Behind the train, cut through the terminal platform, was an immense steel structure. A freight elevator shaft, open on all sides, running up to the next level.

The elevator in that cage was moving! Slowly it was moving upward-yet it contained no baggage. But Van could glimpse shadowy figures in its open but dim interior. Shadowy figures who seemed to be shrinking there, blending with the gloom.

With swift suspicion firing his muscles, the Phantom dashed from the train, hurled himself toward the ascending elevator. It was already halfway up.

The Colt whipped from his pocket as he ran. His thumb snapped back the safety-catch which guarded its hair-tuned trigger.

"Stop that car!"

His voice cracked out in the crisp command as he raised the gun.

The answer was swift. So swift that, had it not been for his alert intuition, Van would not have ducked so swiftly, leaping behind one of the concrete pillars.

Three livid spurts of red leaped from the darkness of the open-fronted car. Three shattering reports of heavy-calibered automatics crashed through the tunnel. Two of the bullets ricocheted from the post where the Phantom stood, chipping concrete.

The elevator kept rising.

Van waited, even as he heard a commotion at the other end of the platform, where the railway police and bluecoats were whirling toward the sound of the shots.

But the elevator was disappearing into the gloom of another level. The Phantom, savage determination in his eyes, darted from his hiding place as he saw that the occupants of the cage no longer could get a good shot at him.

He saw no access to the floor above immediately at hand. The bottom of the elevator was well over his head. The well of the shaft gaped deep below, with its cable-wheels turning down there.

The Phantom braced his lithe muscles, timed his distance. Then deliberately he leaped into the open shaft, leaped upward, both arms flinging overhead.

His right hand caught supports on the bottom of the ascending elevator. His left hand followed-and he dangled there, momentarily over space, being hoisted up with the car.

Some common sense portion of his brain told him the folly of the risk he was taking. But some stronger feeling spurred him on.

Police were running down the platform, but Van knew they could give him little help now. Clinging desperately to the ascending elevator, he looked upward.

The square of the next floor was looming. It would soon cut off the open front of the elevator. Unless he hurried —

With painful effort Van squirmed his way to the very edge of the shaft's open fronting, fervently hoping that the occupants of the elevator were unaware of their extra passenger. Again he measured distance, judged time.

If he failed to make that landing his body would be crushed like so much pulp!

With his legs doubled up beneath him he reached up with one hand, up past the open fronting, until he had hold of the floor of the elevator. With a grunting heave, he got the other hand around and up, so that he was now clinging to the floor's edge.

The square outline of the next floor was coming down like some grim guillotine. Gathering all his strength then, with one mighty heave, Van chinned himself up past his hands, scrambled onto the elevator floor, was in the cage just as the beams of the oncoming floor closed off the front.

His gun, momentarily pocketed, was out with lightning speed. Even as he got his balance he was training it on four shadowy figures who were shouting in hoarse surprise. Flickering terminal lights from the floor suddenly lighted their faces, under their low, slouch hats.

The smallest of them seemed to be the quickest. He moved with a sort of jerky nimbleness. Flashily dressed, hatless, with patent leather black hair, and an olive-skinned face, he would have been handsome save for the livid zigzag scar on one cheek.

"Watch it, guys!" he snapped in a quick, jerky staccato of authority. "Ape —*your* job!"

A huge, barrel-chested thug, with a flat-nosed face and gash of a mouth, and something simian in the way he swung his arms suddenly charged across the car. One of those arms rose. A blackjack in the huge hand arced back.

On the balls of his feet, the Phantom sidestepped the big man's unexpected lunge. The blackjack whistled viciously through space-missing his head by scant inches. But he was still unable to bring his gun to bear before the thug fell upon him bodily.

"Okay, Slick! Okay!" Ape's coarse voice yelled. "I got him! Leave him to me!"

The big thug's left arm encircled Van's head in a crushing grip as the elevator came to a stop. A dim floor, filled mostly with baggage and piping, lay beyond its open front. The Phantom struggled fiercely, gasping for breath in the viselike hold of his burly antagonist. With his right hand, the thug was trying desperately to swing the blackjack again.

The flashy, scarred man called Slick was making a gesture with his gun at the other two men whom Van had barely glimpsed in the flickering light. One was tall, with an angular, immobile face. He seemed to move without animation, holding his gun behind an unbuttoned overcoat.

The other man, who was holding a cloth-wrapped bundle, was squat, his head low on wide shoulders, his features crooked, as if each half of his face had lifted or lowered a little.

"Come on, guys!" Slick's staccato snapped. "Gotta scram before the coppers come. Finish that bird, Ape, whoever he is."

As if assuming that Ape could well handle the job, the others started scrambling off the stalled elevator.

Van's head was swimming from the pressure of the big, flat-nosed thug's grip. But inwardly he rallied his own strength, remained cool even though his gun-arm was twisted out of reach.

He spread his feet a little to give him support on the flooring. Then suddenly his whole body, including his gripped head, moved like a springing bow, arcing swiftly with strength and skill.

With a surprised yell the huge, burly thug, heavy though he was, went flying off his feet. The force of the hurtling motion had made him relinquish his terrible head-lock hold.

He sprawled heavily to the floor, dazed surprise on his flat, gash-mouthed face. A clever trick of jiu-jitsu, an art which the Phantom had mastered from the Japanese champion, Soji Kamuri, had come to Van's aid.

With camera-click speed, the Phantom brought his gun around, started for the big thug on the flooring.

Just as quickly he leaped back, ducked behind a protruding steel support of the elevator. Slick and the tall, angular thug had whirled. Their automatics blazed simultaneously, the tall thug firing from the hip.

Van snaked out two shots in return, but he was ducking ricocheting lead and could not properly aim.

Before he could aim, Ape had rolled off the elevator. With the alacrity of desperation, the big man catapulted to his feet to join his companions. All four, with the squat, wide-shouldered one carrying that cloth-wrapped bundle, dashed away in full flight now.

Chapter VII
In Terror's Grip

Quickly the reason for that hasty flight was apparent. Bluecoats and railway police were surging from the top of a stairway, with guns drawn. With the instinct of rats the four thugs were scattering for the dark labyrinths of the pipe-filled rooms beyond.

And only the Phantom, recovering his breath after his brief but hectic encounter with Ape, saw that murderous quartet disappearing. The bluecoats and railway men were merely milling about confusedly.

Bitterly sensing that the thugs had made their getaway, Van moved across the elevator floor. Something caught his eye, stopped him momentarily. From the floor he picked up a torn bit of cardboard.

In the dim light he saw that it was part of a torn railway ticket. On it was the name: Mulford, New York.

It had lain close to the spot where he had hurled the big thug. Had it fallen from Ape's pockets? "Hey, *you!*"

The gruff, challenging shout jerked him up. As he had walked off the elevator, quickly thrusting away the piece of ticket, several police and railway officers suddenly confronted him in an ominous, blocking group, hands on guns.

The four thugs had eluded them and now they glared at this fifth, sharp-nosed man with suspicious hostility.

"Who are you?" a plainclothes detective demanded. "You came in and started giving orders- then we find you mixed up in a gun-fight! Keep your hands still!" he warned, as Van's arms started to move.

The Phantom's eyes hardened, then he relaxed as his decision came to him. He did not offer resistance when the detective strode forward, frisked him hastily, and took away his gun. He drew a breath of relief that the search had been too hasty for the officer to discover the hidden domino mask, the platinum badge and the ticket he had just tucked away.

"My advice to you," Van said, in a cool, level voice, "is to scour the Terminal for four thugs."

Quickly, tersely, he described the four from his brief but retentive glimpses of the quartet. Something in his tone evidently impressed the big detective in charge. He sent bluecoats on the search, told them to get help.

But then his hard eyes swiveled again to the sharp-nosed, mysterious man before him.

"Well, I'm still asking you-who are you? What's your business here? How do we know those guys you described are gunsters? Maybe it's you who're in the wrong!"

"I suggest," Van said in the same level tone, "that you let me see whoever is in full charge down here, at present. I believe I can identify myself properly then."

The detective, eyes narrowed, reluctantly agreed. At his orders, Van was ushered by two of the bluecoats and the detective himself across the floor, through a doorway, down another ramp, up marble stairways.

Quite suddenly, the party emerged onto the gallery surrounding the huge, domed terminal concourse. Van's eyes went with interest around the balcony where he had seen that police activity. But, though police were still there, the commotion had quieted.

Then on the floor below, Van saw the same pair of morgue attendants. They were leaving with the two wicker baskets, heavy now. The bodies were being taken away!

The big, square-faced detective ordered Van taken to the north end of the gallery. Entering a lavishly furnished suite of offices through a frosted glass door, the Phantom realized he was in the executive offices of the Empire and Southwest Railway.

He was brought to a halt in a large anteroom, brightly illuminated, modernistically furnished. Two other doors led to inner offices. One was closed. On its wood panel was lettered:

PRIVATE

The other door was open and through it came a hum of tense voices. Van caught a glimpse of several shifting figures, bobbing heads.

Then, at the big detective's call, a familiar figure emerged from that office-and Inspector Thomas Gregg, head of Manhattan's Bureau of Detectives, confronted Richard Van Loan.

Well Van knew this hard-faced detective chief, whose fleshy, placid face belied the grim alertness in his keen eyes. But there was no recognition in Inspector Gregg's eyes now as, listening to the detective's hurried explanation, he narrowed his gaze on the disguised Phantom.

"Well?" he demanded, in the gruff, barking voice that had broken down the reserve of many a hardened criminal. "What have you got to say for yourself? Talk fast! If you're mixed up in this affair it's not going to be so good for you! What were you doing down at that train?"

Van Loan hesitated. All he would have to do would be to let the inspector catch a brief glimpse of his diamond-studded badge, and no more questions would be asked. But that meant openly coming into the case as the Phantom. Coming into a case which already he saw was full of baneful ramifications he had not foreseen. If he were to allow it to become known that he was the Phantom, might that not prevent his having a free hand?

Yet there seemed no other way, if he was to pursue an immediate course of investigation. His platinum badge was his only means of identification, his only proof. And so, reluctantly, he reached into his vest pocket, his fingers closing on the valuable emblem.

Then, with a sudden thrill of gladness, he released the badge-let it drop back unseen.

For at that moment a newcomer came striding hurriedly into the anteroom. A rugged, elderly man with keen, alert eyes. Frank Havens, owner of the *Clarion*!

The inspector, recognizing the influential publisher, gave a respectful greeting. Nodding, Havens's keen gaze darted about the room. His eyes swept Van, passed the Phantom-unrecognizing. Then quickly, Van spoke:

"Say, Mr. Havens, will you tell the inspector that I'm working for you? That you sent me here?"

As Havens's eyes swiveled to the sandy-haired, sharp-nosed man, Van quickly made a strange move. With a gesture that seemed merely nervous habit, he reached up and tugged at the lobe of his left ear.

A gleam of comprehension lighted Havens's eyes. He stepped forward.

"What's the matter, inspector?" he asked crisply. "This man is one of my crime reporters-Elwood Mason." He was quick to invent a name. "I sent him to get facts on this case."

Instantly the inspector's attitude changed. Van's gun was handed back. The Phantom's eyes veiled his satisfaction. Havens, the one man who knew his true identity, could always be depended upon. The ear-lobe tugging, a signal arranged between them, always told Havens what Van's ingenious disguises so often hid.

"Glad to see you, Mr. Havens," the inspector said, and he was. The *Clarion* had always given the police department the breaks. "As for the facts here-Well, I've been trying to get 'em myself. Come along in. You too, Mason."

The inspector ushered them into that inner office. Havens and Van were introduced to the tense gathering whose voices Van had heard from outside.

Some of them, James Strickland for instance, Van recognized on sight. Others he placed by their names.

Strickland, the railway vice-president, was standing behind the long conference table, his florid face a picture of dejection and horror. Next to him stood Charles Jenson, mild-eyed, spectacled secretary of the line.

Four other men completed the group. Men whose names and reputations in the field of science were well-known to Van.

Leland Sprague, wiry, shock-headed surveyor. Donald Vaughan, solidly built but weary-eyed geologist. Paul Talbert, the tall, military-mustached shoring engineer. And finally, quiet-faced, but with dark, frightened eyes, Joseph Ware-the waterways expert.

If Strickland and Jenson looked shaken, these other four seemed to be in an almost paralyzing grip of terror and horror! Van could see it in their haunted eyes, their pale features. Only Talbert seemed to maintain a certain calm; but his hands worked nervously at his sides, giving him away.

James Strickland stepped forward, recognizing Frank Havens.

"Mr. Havens! I've been waiting to hear from you! That order you gave over the phone to hold the passengers of the Buffalo train! We can't hold them much longer or we'll have lawsuits on our hands!"

Havens's eyes flashed a worried glance toward the Phantom. Van spoke quickly. "That tip we had about the train, Mr. Havens, was *bona fide.*" He compounded fact with prevarication smoothly. "There were some gunmen aboard, but they got away. So I guess it's no sense holding the passengers any longer."

"Gunmen?" Strickland blurted. "Damn! Has something else happened on this railway?"

Shaken, the vice-president phoned down to the track, ordering the release of the passengers. He also learned, and told the listening group with him, that the thugs Van had described had vanished without any trace.

"Well," Inspector Gregg clipped. "Let's get back to the case in hand."

He began speaking and, bit by bit, aided by an occasional word from Havens who had been acquainted with the matter through his efficient news organization, Van learned the staggering facts of what had happened in Grand Central Terminal.

Chapter VIII
An Empty Glass

Inspector Gregg told Van of the anonymous phone call from Mulford, New York, prophesying a crime in New York at midnight. Mulford! Van touched his pocket where he had a railway ticket from that place. Facts were beginning to dovetail.

The story of the tragedy in the balcony of the concourse followed quickly, Van learned of the huge electric sign, motivated by a device here in the terminal-but started by Garrison, president of the railway, from St. Louis, over the railway's own wires.

The sign had suddenly gone haywire, and a macabre message from the Tycoon had flashed across its flickering lights. A ghoulish prophecy, hideously carried out when an explosion had occurred, killing Brooks, the sign's maker, and Eldridge, a surveyor.

"Brooks and Eldridge must have gone to the box which worked the sign," the inspector said. "We found bits of a bomb of the 'pineapple' type in the shattered box —a planted bomb which went off there and killed these two men."

An effort had been made, Van learned, to contact the railway president, Garrison, in St. Louis. But he had already left the office where the button had been pressed, had rushed in and out of the place so quickly that few had seen him.

Meanwhile, Death had struck down two scientists who were connected with the Empire and Southwest Railway. Nor had they been the first victims! Two others of the same scientific group-Max Garth, geologist, and David Truesdale, mining engineer-had also been doomed. In as horrible, if different fashion.

And not until then did Van know of the airplane disaster.

Pat Bentley, pilot of the doomed transport, he learned, had radioed his frenzied message that the ship was burning, somewhere over Pennsylvania. Andrew Harvey, president of the airline that owned the burned airplane, could have known nothing of the tragedy up to a short time ago, for he had been down at this terminal. Though on what business, the inspector had not been able to learn.

Pat Bentley! Even as the flyer's name was mentioned, Van saw Havens's eyes go hard; saw grief on the publisher's face.

But Havens did not know, nor did the police even dream that Van himself had found Pat Bentley on Park Avenue; that it was Bentley's corpse that had led the Phantom into this diabolical web of mystery and murder!

During the next minutes the inspector received a call from Headquarters, reporting that a body had been found on Park Avenue. It had not been identified. The inspector dismissed that information as something to be attended to later, with no slightest suspicion that it might be connected with this case.

But Van knew now that it was one of the most devilish affairs he had ever encountered. Out of a maze of violence and intrigue, a mysterious, unknown criminal personality had emerged, had imperially taken the center of stage. The Tycoon!

Van's eyes swiveled to the men in the room, to the quartet of frightened scientists. Knowing that he was backed by Havens's influence and authority, he began to ask crisp questions.

"Have any of you others been warned by this so-called Tycoon?"

The men shifted, exchanging quick glances. Then Joseph Ware gave a weary sigh.

"Yes, I've been warned!" he said hoarsely. "This criminal called me up tonight-said I would die tomorrow! And he means it! After what has happened to the others —"

"The police will give you adequate protection," Van assured, and Inspector Gregg nodded grimly. "But these warnings," Van persisted. "What does this criminal want? It seems he is making some sort of demands —"

Before he had even finished this question, he saw the lips of all four men tighten. Their eyes became veiled, secretive. But, a good psychologist, Van saw that Ware-the man who admitted he had been threatened-was weaker in his resistance than the rest.

He concentrated his probing gaze on Ware.

"With your life at stake, Mr. Ware, don't you think you ought to confide what you know to the police? As the best way of enabling them to safeguard you? For it's clear —" he repeated Ware's own words, " —that this means business!"

"Yes! You're right, Mr. Mason!" the distraught Ware cried.

Sprague started to interrupt, but Ware waved him off with an agitated hand.

"What's the difference? Even Andrew Harvey knew that we all are stockholders in this railway!" He looked at Van, jaw tightening firmly. "The Tycoon has been trying to extort the stock we own. Warning us to turn over the shares, which are negotiable, to him or else die!"

Havens, as well as Van, showed interest at the news that these technicians were stock owners.

"But that can't be the answer-extortion!" Strickland broke in, hoarsely. "It's more that someone is trying to ruin this railway! There's been sabotaging of our lines-looting of trains! And Garth and Truesdale, technicians, who were valuable to the railway, were killed. That further cripples the line and its progress!"

"There was some sort of loot on that airplane, too!" the inspector agreed. "That might be the real reason some way was found to crash it."

Strickland spoke again. "Yes, extortion must just be a blind! Why, the very sabotaging that's been going on has been lowering the value of the stock. The criminal would be a fool to do that-if stock is what he wants."

Talbert laughed harshly. "Maybe not such a fool!" he offered, though he had been tight-lipped until now. "Why, didn't Harvey want to buy out this railway, just to get rid of any competition? I didn't swallow his talk about running it in conjunction with his airlines! Extortion is one way of getting stock. Lowering its value by sabotage is a way to get it for a song!"

Both Strickland and Talbert were vehement in their arguments. But the Phantom sensed that there was something else beneath the surface. What it could be, however, baffled him.

"Just how does this Tycoon demand delivery of the stock?" he asked.

Again the four scientists shifted uneasily. Then Ware, who seemed to have recovered his quiet manner, spoke in a calmer tone.

"I was simply told to be ready to give the stock over. I would receive future instructions, I was told."

"We'll be there if you do!" Inspector Gregg promised firmly.

The Phantom keenly eyed the four scientists. Strange, but he was certain that they were all hiding something-that some dark, secret bond lay between them.

However, he knew he could get no more out of them now. He decided to make the next move in his investigation.

Throughout the quizzing and unsatisfactory answers Van had taken cognizance that the name of Garrison, the railway's president who was in St. Louis, had been frequently mentioned. Where did that important official figure in the maze of mystery?

Eyes thoughtful, Van casually remarked that he'd like to look into Garrison's private office; the room with the closed door on the other side of the anteroom.

The door of that office, which Strickland said had remained unopened since Garrison's departure for St. Louis, proved to be unlocked.

Leaving the inspector talking with the harassed men, Van strode into the railway president's private office. Unobtrusively Frank Havens followed him, closing the big door partially behind him.

"Van!" For a brief moment the publisher dropped the pretense of masquerade, spoke in low tones, emotion gripping him. "What do you make of all this business? And how did you happen to get into it, before I called you?"

The Phantom had switched on lights, which flooded the modernly appointed office. "I'll explain that when we have more time, Frank," he said hurriedly. "Right now I want to get what clues I can together."

After a swift glance about the room, he had moved over to give his attention to a flat-topped desk.

"Pat Bentley was pilot of that plane," Havens reminded. "Maybe you remember him. He used to be my ace news commentator." Grief was in his flat tones.

"Yes, I remember him," Van said, with no word about that corpse on Park Avenue. And then a sudden exclamation of interest broke from his lips.

On one side of Garrison's desk, partially hidden by papers, he had found a drinking glass. It was empty, but moisture-and some peculiar whitish substance-clung to its inner surface.

"If I remember correctly, Frank," the Phantom said, after briefly examining the glass, "all those men in the other room claim that nobody entered this office since Mr. Garrison left for St. Louis the other day. Feel this glass, Frank. Touch it carefully. I don't want to spoil any prints that might be on it."

Havens touched the glass surface cautiously.

"Why it's cold-almost ice-cold!" he exclaimed.

"Colder than it should be in this warm room-unless it recently held cold water," said Van, glancing at the electric water-cooler in the corner.

He smelled the glass, studied the whitish particles clinging to it, then carefully wrapped it in a handkerchief and put it in his side pocket.

"Well," he said, "I guess we've got all we can here. Let's go to your office and tackle this affair from every angle together. Then I'll see if there's anything in what I've found here; if they are clues."

Havens nodded and both men moved to the door, out through the anteroom, and into the other office.

The men there were still talking to Inspector Gregg. Joseph Ware was arranging to have police protection because of the threats he had received.

"I don't see why we should be detained any longer!" Talbert was growling, his mustache bristling. "We've been here most of the night now!"

"We'll be getting along right away," the inspector said gruffly. His beetling eyebrows raised as he saw Havens and 'Mason.' "Well, gentlemen? Any fresh ideas? Looks like straight extortion to me. What do *you* think?"

Havens gestured to Van. A smile flickered across the Phantom's disguised, sharp-nosed face.

"I'm afraid I have little to offer," he said deprecatingly. But his hand was unconsciously touching the pocket where reposed the glass he had confiscated, and that torn railway ticket.

As the inspector was starting to dismiss the rest of the group, Van and Havens left the executive offices. With no suggestion of the tight bond of intimacy between them they walked down the balcony steps, across the great concourse.

"My car is opposite the main entrance," Havens remarked.

Van nodded, and they took the long ramp which led out to the crosstown street which usually teemed with traffic at this hour of the night, or rather morning; however, but few vehicles traversed it.

Across the street, near several parked police cars, stood Havens's coupe. The two men stepped off the curb, walking toward it.

They had taken perhaps five steps when apparently without reason, Van gritted a sharp warning. Grabbing Havens with one powerful hand, he yanked the publisher off his feet.

Havens's first natural thought was that a car he hadn't seen was bearing down. But even as Van rapped: "Down, Frank!" the publisher saw that no car was in sight.

The quiet night was suddenly shattered and rent! A blurred but raucous staccato, as if from some demon invisible typewriter, chattered shrilly.

The staccato of a tommy gun!

Chapter IX
Machine Guns

Van, who had seemed miraculously to divine that sudden menace, had Frank Havens down on the pavement now, with his own lithe motions, and was forcing the publisher to roll toward the curb.

A dancing line of flying bits of lead flew as if magically toward the two men, missing them by scant inches. The rain of slugs lifted them-for all tommy guns have the uncontrollable tendency to fly upwards as they are fired-and the bullets whistled over the heads of Van and Frank Havens.

Even in his predicament Frank Havens saw Van twisting out his own Colt. The automatic roared, spitting livid flame. The Phantom was firing, it seemed, at the empty gloom out in the middle of the street. Havens had not seen the two heads and shoulders that for a moment had appeared out there, and then sunk from view, as Van had seen.

Across the street bluecoats sprang from their prowl-cars, started running with drawn guns. But as suddenly as it had set up its chatter, the tommy gun had ceased its blasting.

As Havens struggled to his feet, Van was already up, had catapulted halfway across the street, gun gripped, eyes narrowed to slits.

Van's strong fingers were scooping at a manhole in the middle of the street. He yanked it partially up, pointed his gun downward, fired two shots into the gloomy well below. Almost with the same motion, he was climbing down into the place himself-to the tunnel close below, on top of one of the city's water mains.

His eyes scanned the gloom. Nothing. Again that sense of frustration, though, even as he searched, careful to keep his body flat against the sides of the tunnel wall. He could see that in one direction the tunnel led toward Grand Central Terminal.

"They got away again!" he said. As he climbed out to rejoin Havens his thoughts were savage; and within his pulses surged a fierce anger, a luxury his cool mind seldom allowed.

It had been a clever, a diabolically clever attack! Only because his alert eyes had seen a suspicious movement of that manhole cover had Van been able to anticipate it.

But from whom had it come?

From those four thugs who had first clashed with him in the freight elevator?

That manhole could easily have been reached through the tunnel from the terminal. But those men had not had a tommy gun-unless it had been wrapped in that cloth-wrapped package the one crooked-faced thug had carried.

Of one thing, however, the Phantom was grimly certain. The brain behind that previous attack on himself was that of the criminal behind this whole intrigue of blood and murder!

The reason for this last attack seemed plain enough. Though no one could have guessed that he was the Phantom, it was known-or reasonably suspected-that he had picked up some clues. Doubtless the criminal had ordered the attack to keep him from making use of them.

Those six railway and technical men had known he had something, must have known from the way he had spoken to the inspector. Van had watched them for some reaction, but seen none. But now he wondered. Right after he and Havens had left, that group had broken up. Could one of them have been behind the attack?

At least, Van decided, as he climbed to the street, where the dazed Havens was ringed by questioning police, this proved to him that he had discovered vital clues. The glass in his pocket had not been broken; the handkerchief wrapping had protected it.

He made no explanation to the police.

"Mr. Havens," he said hurriedly, "I have an errand-uptown. I'll meet you at your office later. Can you wait for me there?"

But before Havens could answer, could ask questions, the Phantom's lithe figure had slid off into the night.

* * *

Day had broken over the city, and the morning sun was beginning to slant through the high windows of the mid-town *Clarion* Building, in whose depths the pounding rotary presses made a steady vibration.

Seated at his great mahogany desk in his luxurious office, his eyes red-rimmed from sleeplessness, Frank Havens had just turned off the electric lights when the frosted glass door opened discreetly-and Richard Curtis Van Loan strode in, smiling a tight greeting.

Van no longer wore a disguise. Once more he was the impeccable, handsome socialite.

"Morning, Frank," he drawled. "Now we can get down to cases. Sorry if I kept you waiting. Had to make a trip to my laboratory to set things going."

He lighted a cigarette, took a chair near Havens's desk without really relaxing. Though he had been up all night, he showed no signs of fatigue. His eyes were alert, keen.

"Any fresh news, Frank?"

Havens told what he knew. The police had furnished protection for Joseph Ware, the threatened waterways man. And upstate the army was helping search for the wrecked transport plane on which Garth and Truesdale had been passengers.

"They've covered hundreds of miles in a scouring circle from where that plane was when last heard from," Havens said, shaking his head. "They even tried to carry on the search by night, with flares. But they can't find a trace of the wreck."

Van nodded, grimly. Then he reached into his pocket, drew out a large folded aviation map. He arose and laid it down on Havens's desk.

The publisher saw that it was a detailed map which included the states of New Jersey, Pennsylvania, and New York. On it, was a large circle, drawn in ink.

"I suggest, Frank," Van said very quietly, "that you get in touch with all aviation search units, and tell them to move their search to this area that I've marked here in New York!"

Havens's eyes went wide. "But Van!" he protested, checking over the circle. "That's fully a hundred miles from the terrain they've been searching. It's in the Catskill Mountains! What on earth makes you think that a plane flying over Pennsylvania —"

"A hunch," Van said simply, as Havens, despite the fact he was accustomed to these uncanny tips from the Phantom, stared at him amazed. "Of course it may be wrong, but it's worth a try."

Havens did not hesitate. Reaching for a phone, he called Miller Field and the Newark Airport. He repeated Van's suggestions.

When he had completed the calls, he shook his head.

"They can't understand it, Van. Say that would be way off the beacon-But they're desperate enough to try anything."

Van had already dismissed the subject, turned to another. "Any word about Garrison, the man they couldn't contact in St. Louis?"

"No, Van. None that I know of."

Van's eyes half closed. "I'm rather interested in both Garrison and that railway-in which technicians own stock. Suppose you dig up all the data you can on that subject. Perhaps it will tell us some more about these crimes."

Havens smiled, and shrugged. "I've already ordered the men in charge of the *Clarion* morgue to look into the files." He switched on an interoffice phone, spoke briefly. "Hurry up with that data. Send it up to my office as soon as it's ready."

He turned back to the Phantom. "I've also checked up on those scientists, Van. And I learned something odd. Before they came to work for this railway-quite recently-all of them were working for the Government! They were mapping out a Government airport which is to be built in Nevada next year. When they finished that job, they resigned from the Government service and took their present positions."

Van's eyes flickered slightly at this news.

"That *is* peculiar! And now they are stockholders in the railway." He considered a moment, blew out a thoughtful puff of smoke. "Frank, I'd like to get full details on their former work.

The Department of Commerce must have the maps they made of the Nevada field. See if you can get them for me."

"I'll do my best. It will take some time though, I'm afraid."

The publisher broke off as a knock came at the door. Instantly Van Loan relaxed, assumed the languid manner associated with him in his character of wealthy socialite. A man wearing a green eye-shade entered with a great sheaf of papers, clippings, books. He deposited them on Havens's desk and unobtrusively departed.

Both Van and Havens were expert at swiftly gleaning the gist of such data, of reading between the lines. For some time they pored over the mass of printed matter dealing with the Empire and Southwest Railway.

Stories of the line's various operations. Stock quotations. Diagram maps. The lines operated most extensively, of course, in the Southwest.

"It's in the Southwest, too," Havens commented, studying some data, "that most of the sabotage of the railway-looting of trains, even wrecks-has been occurring."

Van nodded. "And you could add, Frank, that the Southwest is the one part of the line that seems best to have withstood the Depression. But from these stock quotations the whole railway was in a slump before any sabotage began. The stocks have been absurdly low. Those technicians certainly cannot consider themselves wealthy in owning their shares!"

He paused, brow furrowed as, turning the clipping, he came to a photograph. A strong, hard face peered out of the picture —a face with bushy brows, black eyes, hard, thin lips, iron-grey hair brushed tightly back.

Beneath was the caption:

Winston B. Garrison

"And here's the elusive president," Van said musingly.

"Yes, I've met him," Havens remarked. "A hard-fisted man, Van. Something of a penny-pincher. He inherited the railway from his father who built it across a wilderness, fighting Indians, going through all the vicissitudes of a pioneer. His son took over, and began expanding the whole line in boom times. Naturally, when the depression came, he had too many tracks-too many trains."

"Yes, that's easily seen. He has many spurs in the Southwest-in several states." The Phantom crushed out his cigarette in an ash-tray. "Frank, everything I've learned so far has told me the criminal behind this mystery is after something big-bigger than we can guess! I've got to find out what it is." Carefully he scooped up the clippings. "I'm going back to my laboratory now. I'm convinced I'm on the right trail-but there's one other thing I want you to do." He hesitated, then said brusquely: "Get all the stuff you have on Pat Bentley!"

"Bentley?" Havens echoed, as a fresh pang of grief plainly stabbed him. "Where does he fit into the picture? It was just his misfortune that he happened to be piloting that transport."

Van's lips drew tight. But still he did not tell Havens yet about that corpse. Though he could trust Havens with any secret, he felt that he should first corroborate all he had deduced. The corpse had not been yet identified. If it had been the police would have informed Havens immediately.

"I'm particularly interested in Bentley's work," Van said. "Get me anything you can on that."

And then, not wanting to draw attention to his keen interest in the hapless pilot: "Don't forget that Department of Commerce map, Frank. Also, on another map, I wish you'd have some one on your staff mark out-and keep marking-the exact locales where the railway is being sabotaged or looted. Keep it going as a sort of running reference."

Having given these instructions, Van once more left the anxious Frank Havens-strode out of the office.

After riding down in the elevator, he emerged on the ground floor lobby as the morning shift were coming to work, some of them glancing at this wealthy young socialite as if surprised to see him up so early.

Suddenly Van drew in a sharp breath.

A slender, dark-eyed girl in a sports dress had entered the foyer. Muriel Havens! Here, doubtless, to see her father.

Another moment and she would have seen Van. But in that moment, changing his very walk, he blended quickly with the throng, avoiding her-and stifling again the quick ache in his heart.

Chapter X
Laboratory Test

On a squalid east side section of the Bronx reared a ramshackle brick loft which no one gave a second glance.

The real estate agent who had formerly had it on his hands had felt that manna had dropped from heaven when an old, stooped-shouldered, grey-haired man, giving his name as Dr. Bendix, had bought the building for a modest sum.

And only Frank Havens knew that Dr. Bendix was—the Phantom! That this was another of the varied roles which Richard Curtis Van Loan lived.

Arriving there quietly and making his way to a back door of the old loft off the street, Van pulled out a ring of keys. Keys which opened a multiple lock that made the house virtually impregnable.

Entering, he walked up one flight of dusty stairs into a large chamber where he had left lights burning. And it was like stepping from some dead past into a modernistic future of scientific marvels. A crime laboratory that rivaled the famous one at the French *Surete,* and that had as many instruments as the Berlin police laboratory, was nested in that deceptive building. Retorts, rows of bottles holding varied chemicals, reposed on the many shelves of the room. Gleaming microscopes and bullet-testing apparatus stood on tables. One entire wall was lined with an immense bookcase, in which were books on crime-detection, on chemistry, physics, and every other conceivable subject. Books written in five languages. From those books the Phantom, poring over pages through many a night, had acquired a knowledge of criminology second only to that of the great Lombroso himself.

Bubbling, hissing chemicals greeted Van with sounds like that of some modern witches' sabbath as, entering, he took off his coat and put on a stained smock. Eagerly he moved to a table where, before his visit to the *Clarion* office, he had left a retort simmering over the flame of a Bunsen burner. Within that retort were the whitish particles he had taken from the drinking glass he had found in Garrison's office. Aside from that powdery white stuff the glass had been a disappointment to Van. It had yielded only smudgy, unidentifiable prints.

Putting on insulated gloves, Van lifted the retort, glanced at it. Tiny, segregated crystals danced in it, having assumed definite shape.

Carefully he poured off the hot liquid chemical and captured the crystals in a small steel strainer. Thence some of them were transferred to a glass slide, placed under a 500-power microscope. The Phantom put his eye to the tube, turned the focusing handles. The crystals became immense patterns; with a clear structure. From the bookcase he drew out a volume on chemistry, flipped its pages. He read:

> "In cold water, will effervesce violently and briefly, throwing off the tartrates and citrates."

He dropped the crystals in a test-tube. Another test-tube he filled with cold, filtered water. Quickly he poured half of it into the first, then just as quickly screwed the mixture tube beneath a large, pyrex-glass retort, turned upside down. Already a bubbling had begun in the test-tube. The water became a boiling froth, rose rapidly. In seconds a wet mist accumulated in the retort above as the effervescence ceased.

Van seized the retort, unscrewed it, turning it right-side up. He poured a fresh chemical into it, and a muggy, bluish liquid appeared.

He gave a sigh of satisfaction. The experiment was finished. He had discovered beyond doubt what those white particles were.

They were a peculiar bromide substance, with a strong morphine and acetylene content. A depressant drug of unusual strength. It was known under the trade name of "Morphomine."

Because of its strong narcotic content it was rarely prescribed by physicians. Indeed, as Van knew, it could be procured only at five specially licensed drug concerns which he found listed in a directory. And in each case the doctor procuring it had to use his regulation slip supplied by the Federal Bureau of Narcotics, registering the traffic of the stuff.

Morphomine! This was the stuff that had been in the glass recently used in Garrison's allegedly unentered office! The tartrates and citrates had been released in gas when the water was mixed with the powdery remnant, but by adding those chemicals he had selected to the few clinging particles Van had recreated the crystals in their original form.

Van picked up a telephone-another phone with a private wire to the *Clarion* office. He told Havens what information he wanted; and in minutes Havens called him back.

"The Narcotic Bureau got it for me," the publisher stated. "Only one of the druggists you mentioned sold any morphomine of recent date. It was requisitioned by a Dr. Carl Ferris, delivered to his private sanitarium-wait, here's the address." He gave a West End Avenue number. "What's this all about, Van?"

The Phantom's eyes gleamed. "Just following up a clue, Frank. You'll hear from me later." Terminating the conversation, he stood considering a moment.

Then, from a secret, small vault hidden in the wall, he drew out a large black ledger.

The Case-Book of Richard Curtis Van Loan!

In those pages were written the full facts of every case the Phantom had ever tackled. Step by step, his progress and deductions were recorded. It was a book replete with the factual stories of bizarre crime and mystery. Detailed reports which not even Frank Havens had read.

Placing it on a desk Van turned to a blank page. With his fountain pen he wrote swiftly, jotting down what facts he knew; especially the facts about Pat Bentley.

Placing the ledger back into its hiding place, the Phantom strode purposefully across the laboratory to a curtained alcove. He swished the curtain aside, entered.

No actor's dressing room could have approached this alcove in the completeness of its makeup equipment.

There were full length mirrors in which one could see himself at every possible angle. There were shelves of jars and tubes containing makeup. There were floodlights, and a special sun-lamp to create artificial daylight. On a long rack hung clothes of every description, of every nationality-from the rags of a derelict to the turban and robe of a sheik.

The Phantom had discarded the role of Mason, Havens's investigator, because the criminals who had attacked him could identify him in that role. So once more, he did a quick and temporary job with his face. Though, as previously, he was not trying to create the replica of any particular man's face. He merely wanted to surely disguise his own features —

It was near noon when a tall, businesslike individual climbed out of a cab on upper West End Avenue —a man of apparent middle-age, with greying hair and sharp, intelligent features.

The Phantom had reached his destination.

Before him reared a granite, modernized house which looked like a private dwelling, but over whose doorway was engraved:

FERRIS SANITARIUM

Van scanned the building. It had a quiet, subdued air. For a moment he hesitated, then deliberately walked up the few steps to the closed front door that resembled any private house entrance and rang the bell.

He heard its muffled ring, then heard clicking, rapid steps.

The door opened. A blond young woman in a nurse's starched, white uniform peered out. Though her face was attractive enough, under the starched cap which topped her mass of wavy blond hair, there was something hostile in it, too. "What is it?" she demanded crisply.

"I want to see Dr. Ferris about one of his patients," Van said with equal crispness.

"Dr. Ferris isn't here. This sanitarium is closed. We are not keeping any patients at this time."

The words came just a little too glibly to suit Van. She started to push the door closed. But Van moved faster.

Firmly, yet unobtrusively, he put his weight to the door, pushed the nurse back with it. And as she reluctantly retreated, he strode into a foyer smelling of disinfectant, and giving onto a corridor. At its far end of which Van glimpsed, through an open door, part of a white room-apparently an operating room.

The nurse had stepped behind an information desk. Her eyes were angry.

"This is a private place," she snapped. "You have no right to force your way in. Who are you?" She was reaching threateningly for a telephone.

Obviously she was not afraid of him. Yet she seemed in a desperate hurry to get rid of him. The peculiar look in her eyes betrayed furtive haste which the Phantom didn't miss.

And then, Van's whole body went suddenly rigid.

From the other end of the corridor came a sharp, unearthly cry! A man's cry-raised in mortal, blood-curdling agony! A scream which resolved itself into one frenzied word.

"You!"

And on that word the scream stopped-gurgled off in a ghastly, sighing gasp.

The nurse had leaped to her feet, her face going starkly white under her makeup, her eyes bulging with fright. As she stood rooted to the spot, and with the echoes of that scream still ringing, Van's lithe body catapulted past her, his hand yanking out his .45. All pretense was dropped now.

His ears had told him the direction of that scream. He dashed to the end of the corridor, where it turned at right angles. The Phantom did not turn with it, but, gun out, dashed straight into the open door of the operating room.

And even though he was on his guard, he was almost taken completely unaware. The room had seemed empty, and Van had not been prepared for the appearance of the tall figure, with a handkerchief drawn over the face, that suddenly darted out the opposite door.

Two reverberating reports crashed out in swift succession, from the gun in the disappearing man's hand. The Phantom ducked, even as he whirled to glimpse the flash of pistol shots. He heard the slugs whistle over his head; heard the splintering of glass as an instrument case flew to bits.

Van's own gun blazed the moment before the man was out the door, slamming it behind him. Van realized that the glimpse he had had of the fellow had been too brief for him even to take note of the attacker's clothes. And the handkerchief had completely hidden his features.

But Van Loan had seen something else in that brief moment. He saw it as he leaped across the room toward the slammed door. Something bulky and limp in the center of the floor.

Seizing the door and shielding his body by its frame, he opened it. The empty turn of the corridor, with closed doors opposite him, alone met his view. Not a sign of anyone there.

For just a moment he hesitated, deliberating pursuit which he sensed would be futile. Then he turned from the door, crossed the operating room to the thing he had seen on the floor.

Spreadeagled there lay a tall man. His overcoat had been thrown back, and protruding from his chest was the metal hilt of a long bone-handled knife, such as might have come from the sanitarium kitchen. It had been driven into the victim's heart. Blood, a ghastly stain of it, surrounded the knife, and more blood lay in a crimson pool on the floor.

That the man was dead was at once apparent. His eyes were glazed; his face was frozen in a distorted grimace.

Van's own eyes bulged as instant recognition of the man came to him. Joseph Ware, waterways expert of the Empire and Southwest Railway! The man who had asked the police department to protect his life from the Tycoon!

Ware, stabbed to death in this private sanitarium!

Suddenly Van stooped over the corpse. A bit of paper, crumpled in the dead man's outstretched right hand, had caught his eye.

He pried it loose, glanced at it. It was a check, dated this day. It was made out to Joseph Ware for the sum of twenty-five thousand dollars. But what made Van's eyes widen with slow amazement, even in this tense moment, was the signature.

The check was signed by *Max Garth*.

Max Garth, the geologist! One of the passengers on that ill-fated airplane transport. And here was a check, dated this day, made out to a man who could never cash it now.

A sudden hoarse exclamation made the Phantom whirl, gun whipping up.

In the doorway stood a tall, white-coated man. His eyes were two dark pools of horror and amazement as they swiveled from the knifed corpse to Van.

"God!" he gasped. "What —" He stared at Van with suspicious fear.

Van spoke crisply. "Dr. Ferris, I believe?" It was more a statement than a question.

The tall man nodded dazedly. "Yes! But who are you? Who is that dead man?"

But before Van could reply, a fresh sound came to his alert ears.

Muffled, yet distinct, rose a woman's voice-the voice of the nurse. It came from somewhere beyond the second closed door of the operating room.

"No, I tell you, you must stay in bed! You can't get up!"

Chapter XI
Missing Man

Paying no attention to the dazed, horrified doctor, once more Van yanked open the door. The corridor was still empty. The voice must have come from beyond the door across the little hall.

He leaped to open it, plunging into a small white bedroom.

In the middle of the floor, the blond nurse was trying to force a struggling man back onto a cot. Even as Van entered, the man ceased his struggles and slumped onto the bed. He lay there unmoving, as if only half conscious, though he was fully clothed.

The nurse whirled, frightened, to face Van whose eyes roved from the man on the bed to a table nearby, where he saw a bottle of whitish powder. Morphomine!

"He-he's too sick to get up!" the nurse stammered. "Oh, what am I going to do with him! He insists he's going out-has business. He even got into his clothes during the few minutes I left him!"

Van did not answer her jittering.

"Call the police!" he rapped at her. "And don't leave these premises!"

She stared at him, confused. Then Dr. Ferris, in the doorway, broke in hoarsely:

"Yes, Miss Keenan. Call the police at once!" As she ran out, he glowered at Van. "I must ask you to come out of this room, whoever you are!" he said indignantly. "This patient has a bad heart. Any excitement —"

"If he has a bad heart." Van said levelly, "you, Dr. Ferris, will find yourself arrested for malpractice-for giving him morphomine, which no man with a bad heart could safely take!"

A hoarse, croaking cry suddenly came from the cot. The man in the bed was sitting bolt upright, staring at Van.

His face was worn, pallid. His eyes held a burning, bright-pupiled glare. Now and then his whole body —a firmly knit, well-built body, seemed to tremble as if with ague.

No mistaking the identity of that man. Van had recognized him immediately, from a photograph he had seen. He had identified the hard, dominant features, the strong chin which now so incongruously was quivering with weakness.

"What's happened?" croaked the man. "What's going on here?"

"A great deal is going on here —*Mr. Garrison,*" Van answered levelly.

And Winston B. Garrison, president of the Empire and Southwest Railway, sagged back on the pillow, eyes fearful.

"You know me?" he croaked. "Who are you!"

Van did not quibble. He had already decided on his next move. The time had come.

"I am known," he said crisply, "as the Phantom Detective."

"The Phantom?" echoed Garrison hoarsely, while Dr. Ferris, too, stared at the disguised Nemesis of crime. Both seemed amazed to find the famous detective so prosaic-looking.

"Yes," Van said shortly. He turned to the doctor. "I should like to speak to Mr. Garrison privately-before the police come."

The doctor's dark eyes showed hostility, but he went out, closing the door.

"Mr. Garrison," Van clipped to the patient, "I appreciate that you're ill, but the police will be asking you some questions. I thought you might rather talk to me-first. I might be of help to you." As Garrison stared at him wordlessly he said: "Joseph Ware has just been murdered in the operating room. His murderer either escaped or is someone here. The police will certainly notice that your door here is opposite the door of the operating room-and that the nurse discovered you out of your bed!"

Garrison's jaw dropped; his eyes continued to stare in horrified alarm.

"I'm sorry to have to speak so bluntly, but you're in a tight spot," the Phantom pursued grimly. "Especially since you were supposed to be in St. Louis! That alibi is completely shattered! I happen to know you were in Grand Central Terminal last night, where two men were murdered, though none of your associates saw you."

Garrison was straining forward from the bed now, the muscles in his neck bulging like heavy cord.

"Wait," he cried hoarsely. "If you think I had anything to do with these murders, I can explain all that! I'm a sick man. Bad business has wrecked my nerves! But I couldn't let my associates know it. That would have ruined what morale they have left. I sent my secretary to St. Louis. He went into the office there wearing my upturned coat, and pressed the button to motivate the electric sign. I cleared up some papers at my own New York office, then came here, where I've engaged the entire sanitarium-my own nurse, and Dr. Ferris. You can see from my condition —" He paused, gasping, his eyes a plea.

But Van was not forgetting that vigorous struggle with the nurse.

"Tell me, Mr. Garrison, how come that group of scientists acquired shares of stock in your railroad?"

Garrison leaned back on the pillows. "I'll be frank with you, Phantom. This railway has been my life —I promised my father on his death-bed I would always keep it going. But the depression hit the line hard, and it didn't recover. Still I held onto it-didn't want to sell out. My last cent of capital went into it, but it was like pouring water into a sieve.

"Then Garth and the others came to me with a proposition. They offered me plans to modernize the railway, to put new life into it with modern inventions, as streamlined trains. They knew I had no money to hire them-so they demanded shares of stock for their work.

"What did I have to lose?" He gave a harsh laugh, and for a moment Van saw the hard-fisted, penny-pinching business man Havens had described. "The stock was worth little. If their modernization saves the railway it will be their gain. Otherwise nothing is lost. A fair bargain, as you can see."

"Yes," Van nodded, his glance keen. "That is, if on second thought you didn't regret giving them the stock."

"I hardly care any more," Garrison sighed. "For now, with this sabotage and murder, my railway faces ruin! Whatever work they are doing is being undone by enemies! Someone is trying to ruin me-that is certain."

"Have you any particular person in mind?"

"No. Perhaps a rival company, though I can't think of any." Garrison's eyes narrowed, and he seemed less ill. "Of course, Andrew Harvey's been after me to sell out to him for a long time, but —"

He broke off, as the wail of sirens, the squeal of brakes, sounded outside.

Van hastened to the door.

The police were in the place the next instant-detectives from Homicide coming close on the heels of the precinct bluecoats who had responded to the nurse's call.

And this time Van flashed into view the scintillating diamond-studded badge which was his identity.

The Phantom had come into the open!

Inspector Gregg, among the first to arrive, studied the Phantom, whom he had seen in other disguises, or masked.

"So you're working with us, Phantom," he said gruffly, and as always, it was hard to tell whether he was grateful or whether he resented the idea because of official pride. "This whole business is getting under my skin, I don't mind saying. Ware had two precinct detectives with him. What happened? He gets a phone call-and gives them both the slip. They couldn't trace the call, either. And now —"

He pointed to the corpse, the silent chief actor in a drama of flash-bulbs and fingerprinting activity. The quiet sanitarium was a bedlam now inside and out. For reporters from various papers were already showing up, waving press cards and demanding entrance.

Gregg questioned Garrison, the blond nurse and the doctor. All were tight-lipped, but denied any part in the tragedy. The nurse said she had seen no stranger on the premises outside of the

Phantom. She gave her name as Shirley Keenan, and said Garrison had engaged her to work in both night and day shifts.

Garrison said nothing about his faking the trip to St. Louis. Nor did Van mention it. For Gregg was beginning to look at the railway president suspiciously, and Van wanted to withhold that vital bit of evidence until he could satisfy his own mind.

The phone in the office rang as Gregg and the Phantom stood in the corridor. The inspector was called to the instrument.

"Hello-Yes, Mr. Havens," he said with quick respect, and Van's ears pricked up. "Yes, it's true-another murder. And we've found Garrison here! Glad you decided to send the Phantom on the case. He's here now." He nodded to Van. "Mr. Havens wants to speak to you."

Van took the phone, spoke crisply, impersonally, "Hello, Mr. Havens."

"Phantom!" Realizing that Van wasn't alone, Havens used the sobriquet. "I have urgent news for you! They've found the wreck of the transport plane!"

A gleam leaped to Van's eyes. "Yes? Where?"

"In the very area you suggested they search-up in the Catskills, two miles north of Mulford! Two army flyers spotted it, and though it crashed on a sort of plateau, they didn't chance a landing. They report no sign of life. Andrew Harvey, at Newark, is trying to arrange search parties to go up there from Mulford."

Van spoke with quick, sharp decision.

"No-we don't want any bungling there! Have those search parties called off, Mr. Havens. Let the authorities wait until they hear from me. I want to see that scene firsthand!"

Vital clues at that wreck might be obliterated if there was a public search of any sort-obliterated accidentally, or by design.

With Havens's brief, though anxious assent, Van hung up the phone. He did not delay a moment. Even as the stocky medical examiner came striding into the sanitarium with his bag the Phantom dashed out, eyes grim with the knowledge that the biggest break of this baffling case had come!

Chapter XII
Gun Girl

A dull afternoon sun was slanting in the western sky. In its greyish light, the lonely Catskill mountain top looked very desolate and funereal, with all its timber.

Death lay on this mountain.

On a grassy plateau of ground was one charred, ugly swath. Metal, twisted and bent and fire-blackened, lay strewn about it. Two immense Douglas engines, with propellers grotesquely twisted, lay at absurd angles; reduced to so much twisted junk.

And amid this wreckage, which was their only grave, lay the gruesome bodies.

All were burned, charred, and blackened, and in some cases featureless. Skeleton bones showed in some, and even these bones were fire-blackened. Eyes, like baked marbles, stared sightless but as if to call the heavens to their hideous plight.

But among the dead, one living being moved on that mountain top; one man who had used every facility to rush to this scene.

A cab had sped the Phantom to Mitchell Field. Thence he had been flown to the town of Mulford, where there was a small airport. There he had hired a small, serviceable Ford coupe, driven it up the steep mountain road, and cached it just below the plateau.

Now, face stern, he moved among the dead. He was counting those dead. There were twelve of those charred bodies. And aboard that plane had been fifteen persons, including its stewardess and two pilots.

One of the missing, of course, was Pat Bentley, whose corpse still lay officially unidentified in New York. But what of the other two?

Had their bodies perhaps been completely consumed in the holocaust?

Suddenly the Phantom paused in his grim search among the scattered corpses.

A glimmer had caught his eye. It came from the burned, almost skeleton hand of one charred corpse. A ring, platinum.

Gingerly he removed it from the burned hand, lifted it in the greyish afternoon light.

On the inside of the band fine, engraved script met his eye. A name.

David Truesdale!

The famous mining and ventilating engineer, working on the railway staff, who had been on this plane.

Then Van saw something else a little distance from the corpse. A smoke-blackened briefcase, open. He scooped it up, saw that it was made of fireproof material. At first examination it seemed quite empty. But then the Phantom, delving into it, drew out a small, jagged bit of hard, ore-like substance.

He looked at it curiously, then shoved it into an inner pocket; dropping the briefcase for the time being.

He continued his examination of the dead. Brass buttons identified the co-pilot's corpse. Doubtless others would be identifiable. But he could not identify any of them definitely as the stewardess, or as Max Garth. Garth, whose check for twenty-five thousand dollars, dated today, he had found on the murdered Joseph Ware.

Next Van came across some half-melted, broken boxes of metal. Strong boxes. Empty! But on one of them he found an aluminum tag that read:

1500 shares, Empire and Southwest.

Stock! Stock, which Ware had claimed was the Tycoon's extortion demand, had been on this plane!

Van straightened. He gave his mind to the most baffling part of this enigma now. How had this plane, which Bentley, ace flyer, had reported as being over Pennsylvania, crashed here in New York, a hundred miles off the radio beam?

Havens had been astonished that Van deduced it *had* crashed somewhere in this vicinity. But the Phantom had reached that conclusion from two dovetailing clues. The railway ticket he had found on one of the thugs, and the inspector's mention of the anonymous phone call he had received from Mulford.

He had deduced that Bentley, escaping from the plane, had somehow reached Mulford. From there, after calling the police, he had taken that train to Manhattan. Thugs had followed him, killed him. With that as a premise it had been plain enough to Van that the big airplane must have fallen somewhere near Mulford.

But how —

He gave his attention to the plateau then. One edge was fringed with trees. Through them Van could see that the mountain dropped rockily, in a sheer, precipitous cliff.

On the other side the slope was more gradual. The plateau was small, yet —

Van walked over the stubbled ground, pursuing a will-o'-the-wisp thought. And suddenly that thought materialized. He had found twin swathes through the stubble. Two long, even tracks.

His eyes went to slits. The discovery, strangely, brought a surge of fierce anger leaping through his veins.

"The devils!" he gritted.

It was only then that he saw the shack.

Perhaps he would have seen it before except that he had not been looking for any such thing. Besides, the trees screened it well. He strode hurriedly through those trees, gun in hand.

The shack was small but stoutly built, of heavy timber. It had small, dust-grimed windows. The rear of it was backed against the very edge of the steep, precipitous cliff, the top of which was grassy.

The house looked deserted. Van's eyes scanned the grass to either side. He saw two huge metal drums among nearby trees. Gasoline drums!

He did not stop to examine them now, but moved to the shack, tried the door. Locked. He studied the lock as from his pocket he drew a pliable bit of specially tempered steel wire-equipment he seldom failed to carry.

Deftly the Phantom twisted the steel bit into the lock, letting it assume the shape of the notches. It took him less than three minutes to pick that lock.

He swung the heavy oak door of the shack outwards with one hand, covering the dim interior with the gun in his other hand.

But no one was inside. There was not even any furniture. Stepping in, the Phantom's keen eyes roved about the interior. A glint in one corner of the room attracted his glance. Moving toward it he looked down at a tangled mass of wires, broken coils, and large, jutting bits of broken glass tubes, still screwed into sockets. His glance went upward. He saw a hole in the roof, wire coming through it, dangling loose and twisted.

As he moved about, absorbing this evidence, Van's foot kicked something, sent it skittering across the floor. Quickly his eye followed it, and in another moment he picked up a flat small bit of hard rubber. One edge was arced smooth; the others formed jagged sides of a triangle, giving the effect of a flat cut of pie. Parallel grooves ran through the piece.

He looked about but saw nothing else. He pocketed the rubber piece. His eyes were gleaming with grim comprehension. He was ready to turn this place over to the authorities now.

He strode out of the shack; out once more upon the lonely, desolate plateau with its strewn, charred dead and —

A sudden snarled shout froze his blood!

Even as he stiffened in the greying afternoon light he saw diving figures materializing on that plateau.

Over the slope, and from trees they appeared-slouch-hatted, charging men, guns glinting in their hands. One and all, they were charging toward Van!

And even as they plunged forward Van recognized familiar faces. The olive, white-scarred face of the man he had not long ago heard called "Slick," a flashy, sport-coated, nimble figure who was giving jerky commands. The square, crooked face of the squat, wide-shouldered man-and that of the tall, angular thug. The three who had mixed it with the Phantom in that railway terminal conflict.

Van ducked back in a defensive crouch. The sight of a mob of thugs charging upon him roused him to reckless rage. His Colt, at his hip, jerked in his hand. Two quick, blind shots crashed on the mountain top, as his automatic blazed.

A ratty-looking gunman in the charging group screamed, clawing at a shoulder while blood spurted out between his fingers. Others momentarily fell back. The Phantom darted for the nearest tree-trunk, as Slick's voice ripped:

"Let him have it, boys!"

Guns blazed. A whole fusillade of bullets smashed through the trees, chipping bark. Van's lithe body slid all the way behind a tree trunk. He must find some means of retreat or they'd have him! His Colt snaked out, firing again-and again the gunmen felt the grim wrath of the Phantom, as another fell, wounded.

A crunch of underbrush behind him made Van whirl. Just in time to glimpse a huge, burly figure leaping upon him with a snarled cry. The flat-nosed, gash-mouthed thug called Ape!

In his loping, simian-like attack, the big mobster was upon the Phantom before the latter could bring his gun to bear. Van went down under the sheer weight of the man. Down, struggling, to the grassy turf, with Ape's murderous face above him.

With a gritted oath, Van tried to roll the big man off. But instantly the others were rushing to the scene. More of them fell upon the prone Phantom. Blows from revolver butts banged against his head and body. Kicks jarred his ribs, brought agonizing gasps from his lungs.

Half stunned, he felt Ape's weight lifting as the big man rose. He himself was yanked to his feet, to find himself ringed by some dozen thugs, with the two he had wounded groaning on the ground beyond.

Rough hands frisked him. His Colt was already gone. But helpless though he was, the Phantom, by a secret legerdemain which he had never revealed to anyone, managed to keep other articles undiscovered. A diamond-studded badge, a black domino mask, as well as the bit of hard rubber he had found, were concealed on his person.

The quiet, crooked-faced gangster was leveling a gun at him.

"Let me give him a bellyful right now, Slick," he begged with evil eagerness, finger tightening on the trigger.

"Hold it, Maxie, hold it!"

The jerky command came from Slick who stepped forward authoritatively, a nervous hand toying with his gun. He was hatless, as usual, his plastered-down hair making a familiar black, shiny knob of his head. He came forward to the Phantom, dark eyes flashing. And Van was thankful that his disguise could stand the late afternoon dimness.

"Yes." A quick nod from the appraising Slick. "This is him all right. Same feller we mixed it with in Grand Central. I got a good gander at him if the rest of you didn't. Probably a private 'tec somebody's hired to horn in, but anyway the boss'll be wantin' to know about it, wantin' to have a little talk with this guy. I'm just figuring what we can do with —"

"You can stop figuring right now, Slick!"

The sudden new voice made Van start as violently as it did the others. It was a woman's voice!

Through the crowd came a slender, shapely girl. She was hatless, and in the dimming light her hair was a wavy mass of red. She was heavily rouged, too. She carried a small revolver, and her grip on it was one of confidence and experience.

Van stared at her as she came to Slick's side. Who was she? What did her words mean? A reprieve?

"Kitty!" Slick's voice was an annoyed rasp. "What the hell did you come up here for? This ain't no place for a moll right now!"

"No?"

Van saw how hard her face was; saw the peculiar icy glint in her eyes. He had seen the type before; the type of gun moll who could be more vicious, more cold blooded, than men who followed the same calling.

"No?" she repeated, her eyes flashing. "Well, I didn't come up here just to look at your dirty mug!" She spoke with heat, and the look she gave Slick told Van more than her words did. "Not that I ever get a chance to see you lately. I don't, if you can steer clear of me!"

"Aw, lay off, Kitty!" Slick complained. "We got business here. This bird's somebody the boss'll be wantin' to see. He's been follerin' us, tryin' to mess things up. We got to do something with him —"

Her eyes flashed to Van, hate flaming in them. Then she gave a shrill laugh.

"You're telling *me* he's been messing things up! That's rich. Listen, Slick —"

She pulled the gang lieutenant to one side, and for moments spoke swiftly, eagerly. Van saw the deep frown that settled on Slick's face, saw the hate that filled the gangster's eyes as they flashed to the Phantom. But there was exultation in those eyes as Slick turned from Kitty and faced the gang.

"Fellers," he announced, with staccato triumph, "this ain't no cheap mug we've grabbed! He ain't no snoopin' private 'tec. Boys, *we've got the Phantom!*"

A growl of animal-like fury and vengeance rose from every man there, as Van's heart went cold. So they knew! This girl had told Slick who he was, but how in heaven's name had she known? Only those in the sanitarium had seen him identify himself as the Phantom, in this particular guise. Had the tip-off come from someone *there?* Who could have given this girl the information?

"The Phantom! So that's what he looks like!" It was the tall, angular thug who held his gun under his overcoat as he had in the terminal elevator who thus expressed his disappointment. "Not so hot, if you ask me."

"Luke's right," put in the crooked-faced Maxie. "He's just a mug!"

Van hid his one surge of relief. At least they didn't suspect he was disguised. They wouldn't remove that disguise and reveal his true identity.

"The Phantom!" Slick danced up close before him. "Thought you'd pull a fast one, didn't you? Lucky we got here when we did-and that you were sap enough to come alone."

Van was silent. It was true that he had not expected the arrival of the thugs; not so soon anyway. Certainly not the sudden appearance of the red-headed girl with her startling information. Yet he still felt that had he not come alone to view the evidence he wouldn't have learned all that he had. Not that it would do much good now, it was beginning to look like.

He could see his death warrant in every face around him. Yet he remained cool, his mind working, and he was fighting to recover the strength that had been beaten from his body.

"Well, you're finished now, Phantom, see?" Slick announced, more triumphantly. "You won't be sendin' any more boys up the river!" His dark eyes flashed. "The question is now, just how we're gonna give it to you-give it right!"

The girl came forward quickly, grabbing Slick by the arm.

"Wait, Slick!" she commanded. "Listen to what I've got to tell you before you gun him!" Her voice was shrill. "I've got new orders-from the Tycoon! I just had time to bring them. Have to get back right away."

"Thought you had another job scheduled." Slick had drawn her swiftly aside and was speaking to her in a low voice, one that did not reach to the men who were guarding the Phantom. But Van's keen ears caught the gang lieutenant's words.

"That date's for tomorrow, at dawn," the girl answered. Her voice warned. "Gee, Slick, it's good to see you. Even like this. If it wasn't for the way I feel about you, I wouldn't be doing all this."

"Cut it, cut it! What's the Tycoon want?"

To reply, she lowered her voice so greatly that Van could catch but few snatches of what she said.

" —like the others-And then stick these there —" From a handbag she drew out some shiny brass buttons, handed them over with some other articles.

Van saw Slick's olive face pale a little. "Say, I don't like that. Why can't we just plug —"

"I'm telling you what the Tycoon ordered." Her voice was hard. "You think I like it any more than you do? But we've done worse for the Tycoon. What's one thing more?"

Slick looked at her hard features, her cold eyes. "Cripes, Kitty, for a dame you sure got nerves like ice."

His own face hardened, the scar showing livid, evil, as he turned from her. "Okay, boys!"

He jerked out orders.

Chapter XIII
Flaming Death

Cold Apprehension Tightening about his heart, the Phantom still could offer no resistance as once more rough hands seized him. Rope was now produced. While the hard-eyed girl looked on, Van was bound hand and foot, the cords digging into his flesh.

Helpless, he was lifted bodily, carried to the shack. They tossed him in as if he were a heavy sack of meal. He crashed to the floor bruised. The door closed on him, was locked from the outside.

Even as that door closed, though, Van was already trying to struggle against the bonds that held him, using all his skill and strength.

Outside he heard the gang moving about busily. He heard Slick's voice.

"Two of you'll stay here to attend to them brass buttons and stick him with the other stiffs. The rest will scram. Okay, Ape. Let her fly."

There was a grunting sound of effort, apparently from Ape. Then a swish of liquid. A pungent, sweetish odor assailed Van's nostrils.

His blood went cold. Gasoline! From one of those drums he had seen! They were saturating the wooden shack with it. Full comprehension came.

He was going to be burned alive, converted into a charred corpse like those many others! And only too clearly now did he see the criminal's clever, devilish purport.

Those brass buttons would be planted on his corpse. So would the other stuff the girl had brought. Van had no doubt they were effects taken from Bentley! And his corpse would be found and identified as Bentley's.

The criminal was covering his tracks. If the police should learn that Bentley had actually been murdered in New York, the investigation of this whole disaster would be carried to a feverish pitch. If "Bentley" were found here, the crash might still seem an unfortunate accident. The investigation would doubtless die out, especially without the Phantom to carry it on.

Van cursed himself for not having told Havens about Bentley's body. True, if anything happened to him Havens would eventually find his case-book and learn the truth, but by then it would be too late. The criminal would have had further time to cover his tracks.

This thought spurred Van to a desperate frenzy. With all his skill and strength he struggled against the ropes that bound him, battling with every last ounce of power in his body for a way out of his predicament.

The gas fumes choked him. Some of the stuff was already dripping through the small window.

In spite of all his efforts his bonds were as tight as ever. Groaning he managed to roll partially across the floor. By force of will as much as strength, somehow he managed to reach the corner where that broken tangle of wires still lay. Promptly he rolled on his back, working his bound wrists to the broken, jagged glass tube screwed rigidly in a socket near the floor.

"Go on, Slick." That was the gun moll's voice. "Get it over. We don't want to hang around here."

Fiercely, the Phantom's wrist sawed at the broken glass. Shards cut his flesh —

Then —a snap. The cords suddenly parted; his hands jerked loose. In the space of a breath he extricated his feet. Free!

But even as he leaped to his feet there came a hissing roar. The window on the front of the shack became a square of blinding, livid flame.

"Now burn, Phantom!" Slick's high-pitched voice taunted.

Van was lurching toward the door. But, as instantly as he recoiled from it, the wood walls seemed to turn into transparent flaming paper.

The heat seared his flesh, sent makeup rolling down his face, drove him back. The front of the shack was a solid sheet of flame. Black, billowing smoke eddied in, filling his eyes and his lungs at the moment he heard the mobsters breaking up, heard the woman's receding voice.

No possible escape on the front side of the shack. And the windows were all too small for him to get through. Blindly Van stumbled to the opposite wall; the wall that overlooked the steep cliff. His body lurched against it, trying to split the wood. Flame-tongues, yellow gasoline flame, reached for him like fingers of incandescent death.

The rear wall shivered at the impact of Van's hurled body, a large loose board rattling a trifle. Van kicked at it, flung his body at it again and again, ignoring the bruising pain.

And the board split, falling outward. A gaping space, shadowy in the dusk, was revealed-the drop of the cliff. And at the instant that board splintered the flames literally came cascading across the shack interior with a surging roar.

Desperately the Phantom squirmed through the aperture which had helped the flames with its draft. To hesitate for even a split instant now would mean to be instantly engulfed in the roasting fire.

He dropped, his hands clutching the very edge of the cliff. Pendulant, he swung there between flames that seared his knuckles and a drop to sheer, jagged rocks below.

Clinging with one hand, with the other Van started to work his way along the cliff's edge. The shack was a roaring bonfire now, with smoke swirling like a black pall. Suddenly the shack began to topple toward the cliff, threatening to crash down on the Phantom's hanging body.

He doubled his efforts, working his way hand over hand along the cliff, with the heat of the flames scorching him.

Then, even as half the shack tumbled crazily off into space, dropping in a flaming mass, Van was out of the way of it. With his almost exhausted strength he was chinning up a free portion of the cliff edge.

His body rolled onto the plateau, livid in the night from the flames of the half of shack still burning. And the first thing Van did was to reach into his hidden pocket for his black silk domino mask and snap it on over his face, on which the makeup had melted and run.

Two slouch-hatted figures whirled towards him even as he got that mask on.

The two of the mob who had been left to finish this job!

Both cried out in incredulous alarm, as they saw this domino-masked man whom they still could recognize in the flickering glow of the fire as the victim they had thought doomed.

One, a man with a pallid, expressionless face, leaped forward with a snarled curse, whipping up his gun. His companion, tall, with a flat-cheeked face that looked hatchet-like, was slower, because his hands were full. But he dropped the objects he held; reached for his own gun.

A wrench-and Van had the weapon, pushing its owner aside. The second thug leaped, his own gun only half-drawn, grabbing for the Phantom's revolver.

The unexpected bodily attack sent Van hurling backward to the very edge of the cliff. And then the Phantom acted out of sheer desperation.

With a lurch, he swung his attacker full about. His fist doubled into a ball that had iron power, crashed out in a short, but powerful jab.

It crunched against flesh and bone. With a stunned gasp, the hatchet-faced man staggered backward. And before he could stop himself, his swaying body pulled him over the edge of the cliff.

Screaming, the thug hurtled down through space. A ghastly thud below proclaimed his doom on the jagged rocks there.

Breathless, Van was already swinging about to bring his gun to bear on the remaining gun-man.

But the latter, unarmed, had had enough! He was already streaking through the trees, down the slope side of the plateau. He had lost himself before Van could even start pursuit.

Savagely panting, his body aching with bruises and burns, the Phantom nevertheless prodded himself to action. That one live gangster now escaping might bring the others back when he reported that the criminals' Nemesis had broken free, had killed the hatchet-faced thug.

Suddenly the Phantom stooped to the ground, illumined by the burning shack. Those objects the hatchet-man had dropped! Quickly he retrieved them. The brass buttons —a watch.

Pat Bentley's watch.

Just as he was about to make his way off the gruesome plateau, a throbbing roar overhead jerked his eyes up. A large Boeing plane swooped low in the sky, wings shimmering. The eagle and star of the United States Army showed on its wings and fuselage.

Army flyers had been attracted by the fire; a fire where the wreck had previously been discovered.

Relieved, Van ran out in the ebbing light of the flames, even as the plane circled low. He waved with both arms, caught an answering wave from the open cockpit. With his thorough knowledge of flying, (he himself had done plenty of it) Van signified that there was room on the plateau for a landing.

The army plane negotiated that landing with ease, by firelight and moonlight. Moaning, it glided in and the Phantom rushed up in his domino-mask, pulling out his platinum, diamond-studded badge —

* * *

Little over an hour later, a tense group of men were gathered in the brightly lighted administrative office at Newark Airport. Andrew Harvey, grizzled airline chief, stood in grim, questioning silence next to the four radio men who had been on duty the night of the big disaster.

At a table Frank Havens, his rugged face tense, was opening a large suitcase, exploring through it.

And before them all, dominating the scene, stood the Phantom in his domino-mask, his eyes gleaming keenly through the holes of the black silk.

The army plane had flown him here, after first circling in an effort to locate the escaped gang. Van had regretted losing track of the mob, yet he was clinging to a conviction he had formed during that macabre experience; a hunch he felt would later put him back on the trail not only of the gang but, what was more important, would lead him to the devilish unknown who was their leader.

The man who called himself the Tycoon!

On his arrival here Van had phoned Havens, asked tense questions to which he had received an assent.

And now —

"This must be it!"

Havens broke the silence, and from the suitcase he pulled out a phonograph record. Van took it silently. The Phantom pulled from his own pocket the bit of hard rubber surface he had found on the shack floor.

Fortunately the heat of the fire had not melted it.

The Phantom compared it with the record Havens gave him. He nodded with quick satisfaction.

There was no doubt in his mind now.

His eyes swiveled to the radio men.

"All of you heard Pat Bentley's message that night," he said. "Undoubtedly you remember it in detail. Now I want your attention —"

He took the record, moved to a portable phonograph which Havens had also set up. Placing the disc on it, he wound the machine.

"Bentley," Van said, his voice grim, "was a news commentator for Mr. Havens before he became a transport pilot. He covered important air news, mostly. Because he was in great demand, many of his news broadcasts were recorded by the studio, as a matter of course. This is one such record which was sold to a limited public. Bentley had drawn the assignment to cover the arrival of the dirigible *Hindenburg*. As usual, his broadcast from Lakehurst was recorded, without any inkling of how sensational it was to become."

He placed the needle on the whirling record. Immediately a youthful, crisp voice-the voice of Pat Bentley-filled the silent office.

"Well, folks, Germany's pride of the air is just coming into sight now. In the twilight she's been maneuvering around to avoid storms-But they're nosing her down now—"

The voice went on, calm and crisp, giving a routine news broadcast. Describing the crowds. The big ship coming down. Guy-ropes dropping as she maneuvered towards the mooring mast and —

It came then! The phonograph itself seemed to shake with a sudden reverberating sound, followed by a roaring crackle. And then, suddenly frenzied with amazement and horror, came Bentley's voice:

"She's burning! She's burning!" Hysterically came the blurted words. "Fire-it's broken out-the whole ship's burning like so much paper!" The crackle of flames, the scream now of trapped passengers so close overhead.

"God, she's going down! She's going to crash! The fire's creeping up —I can feel the heat now-getting worse-worse! No hope! Going to crash!" A rending, terrific impact. "She's hit-Folks, forgive me if I can hardly speak-This is the most ghastly thing I've ever witnessed-Wait, I must go and see if I can help in the rescue —"

Van stopped the record there.

The four radio men were standing frozen, stupefied. At the words, "She's burning!" all had gone rigid, as if again they were back in the radio room where they had heard those words before. But at the concluding phrases they were apparently feeling the shock of realization.

"Why," one of them blurted, "those are the same words-that one part there! The same, exactly!"

"What can this mean?" Harvey demanded hoarsely.

"It means," the Phantom clipped, "that the plane that cracked on the plateau did not catch fire in the sky at all. In some way-how I do not yet know-Bentley and his co-pilot were persuaded to leave the radio beam, and to land on that Catskill plateau, where I found wheel-tracks that proved the ship had landed intact.

"The message you heard from Bentley was this phonograph record, played by the criminal or his henchmen in the shack, when somehow Bentley himself was cut off from the air. The record was literally made to order for the criminal's scheme. Or rather it probably inspired the basic idea for the whole thing!"

"But," Harvey cried, "the plane did burn!"

"Yes." Van's eyes were slits. "After it had landed, the criminals *burned it on the ground* — deliberately cremating its occupants, who must have been first rendered helpless or perhaps they might have been drugged into total unconsciousness."

"Good God!" Havens gave that horrified exclamation. "Of all the fiendish —"

"Yes, it's fiendish," Van agreed. "And we're dealing with a criminal who hasn't stopped there, one who is violating every code of law and humaneness. I intend to find that criminal —"

He turned to Harvey. "Mr. Harvey, there's one point about that airplane crash that I haven't yet brought to light. I happen to know that the plane was carrying a great deal of Empire and Southwest stock as well as Garth and Truesdale, two of the railway's most valuable technicians.

"That, as you can readily see, virtually makes that plane more valuable to the railway than to your own lines. So that its doom and the looting of the stock further helped cripple the Empire and Southwest."

Harvey had gone rigid, his eyes flaming.

"What do you mean? What are you getting at?"

"According to Garrison and the rest, you have long been trying to buy out that railway at the cheapest possible price. I am not accusing you. I am just stating your rather delicate position in this matter."

Harvey had abruptly paled. "I don't deny I've tried to buy them out-but I wanted to run the railroad in conjunction with my planes, not wipe it out! Good Lord, how can you think that I —Why, no man is more anxious than I am to see the guilty party behind this horrible crime brought to justice."

Chapter XIV
Rendezvous

Frank Havens drove the Phantom back to New York. "Van," Havens demanded, as they went through the Holland Tunnel, "there's one thing I still can't understand about that air wreck. How did you know where to have them locate it?"

"Through Pat Bentley," Van said simply, and at last gave the information he had withheld. As Havens's knuckles went white on the steering wheel, he told the story of that unidentified corpse he had found in the street.

"And, so that this wouldn't be learned," he concluded, "they were going to put Bentley's buttons and watch on me when they burned me!"

"But why did Bentley come to New York, Van, after calling the inspector at Mulford?" Havens demanded. "Why didn't he tell what he knew when he did call?"

"Because," said Van, his face set and hard, "he probably knew this was something of staggering momentousness. Frank, I'm convinced he wanted to come to you, his old boss who he knew could get the Phantom. And because I happen to live on Park Avenue, the irony of Fate brought him to my door."

His eyes went grim with a fierce purpose which drove the fatigue, the pain of the burns he still felt from his lithe body.

"I'm going to see that he didn't come to my door in vain, Frank!" he promised.

The two men finished the journey in silence —

It was close to another dawn.

Once more disguised, the Phantom paced in the shadow of buildings on West End Avenue, directly opposite the private sanitarium where he had learned Garrison was still staying, despite the murder of Ware that had occurred there.

Before coming here, Van had been busy at his laboratory. That bit of ore-like substance he had found in the fireproof briefcase at the plane had gone through an intensive analysis. The results had not been definite, because the piece was too small to prove what Van suspected. Later he meant to make further tests.

As he paced, his eyes gleamed with hope. He flicked up his wrist-watch. A few minutes more, now, according to the discreet inquiries he had made previously.

He passed those minutes patiently with that unflagging patience that he could muster in his grim investigations.

Then, suddenly, his muscles rippled with quick preparation for movement.

An oblong of light slanted down the small stoop as the front door of the sanitarium opened. Nurse Shirley Keenan, a dark cape thrown over her white uniform, came out on her serviceable-heeled white shoes. It was the hour when she was off her night shift, permitted to go home or stay at the sanitarium for sleep.

No sooner had she appeared than Van moved like a shadow. Down the block to a small parked Chevrolet coupe on his own side of the street.

He had already made sure, by checking the license, that the coupe was owned by Shirley Keenan. And he had also picked open the lock of its rumble seat.

He had waited only to make sure the nurse was heading for the car. Before she or any passers-by could possibly have seen the movement, Van lifted the rumble seat, and climbed in, doubling his lithe body on the floor, pulling the cover over him.

As he settled in the cramped space, he heard her climb in. The door slammed. There came the whine of the self-starter, the cold bark of the motor.

The car was moving. Once or twice Van dared to raise the lid a little. Not so far that she might see it in the rear-view mirror, but far enough to watch the progress of the car.

It was heading down West End Avenue.

Nurse Keenan drove fast, though she heeded the few traffic lights still on at this hour. Quickly West End Avenue changed from an exclusive residential section to a gloomy street where freight trains ran, Eleventh Avenue or, as it was called because of all the accidents that had occurred here, "Death Avenue."

Presently, near the freight yards where many parallel tracks crossed the avenue, the Chevrolet came to a stop, was parked at the curb.

His body cramped from the ride, Van waited until he heard the nurse getting out, heard her heels clicking across cobblestones.

Then quickly he lifted the rumble seat, his body gratefully uncoiling, and leaped soundlessly to the pavement.

The caped figure of the nurse was moving straight into the freight yard, unnoticed by a watchman some distance away. A strange place for a private nurse on her off hour to be going, Van thought tightly.

Strange, yet not irrelevant. This was also part of the Empire and Southwest's spur. Its freight division.

To a desolately dark portion of the tracks the girl moved, to freight cars obviously long since abandoned, and left here on rusty tracks to decay.

Then, incredibly, she climbed into the open, slide door of one of those abandoned cars!

Van did not follow her to that door.

Instead he slipped around to the one which was also open. Cautiously he peered into the car.

A dim light flickered inside the musty, empty car interior. The nurse stood by that light, as if waiting. And a change seemed to have come over her. Her face was hard, her eyes cold, calculating.

She reached beneath her cape, pulled out a small flat automatic; held it, as if prepared.

Van ducked low as he heard a heavy step, a low whistle, thrice repeated.

He lifted his head again when he realized the step came from the other side of the car. From his door he peered through, to see a shadowy, capped figure climbing into the train.

The girl, gripping her gun, stood tense, challenging, as the man came into the light. Van could not see his face. All he could see was that the man was large of build, and moved agilely. Also he could see that the man's clothes were dusty.

The Phantom knew, however, that he hadn't seen this man before.

"Hello, Frenchy," the nurse greeted.

The man, whose hands were in his pockets as he swaggered toward her, barked challengingly, with a Gallic accent:

"What is zis? You I do not know!"

"Sure you do."

The nurse stepped forward. She swept off her cap. And then, as she removed hairpins, her blond hair also came off!

Wavy red locks were revealed. That alone changed her whole aspect.

Crouched at the door, a comprehensive light was in the Phantom's slitted eyes. His keen deductions had again been correct.

"Ah, it is indeed Mademoiselle Keety," came in relieved tones from Frenchy.

Kitty! The gun moll who had brought orders from the criminal for the Phantom's death! Kitty, leading a dual life, playing a female Jekyll-Hyde role, showing a mastery of disguise which almost rivaled the Phantom's own.

But clever women could do that sort of thing. Makeup was part of their everyday routine. Rouge, lipstick of varying shades, artfully applied to suit varying chosen roles could change almost any woman into another personality, totally different from her natural self.

She had almost completely fooled the Phantom. He had not recognized her as Nurse Keenan at the plateau. Not until he had seen her hands had he even guessed her identity.

He glanced at the shoes she wore-nurse's shoes she had to keep whitened. Some of that stuff must have clung to her fingers despite a thorough hand washing. She had brought it on her fingers to the plateau.

A nurse? This cold, criminal-minded woman? Garrison's private nurse. Now it was clear who had tipped off the criminal Tycoon about the Phantom's identity!

But that still did not answer the question-was the murderer one of the people in the hospital, or an outsider?

But though these thoughts flitted instantaneously through Van's brain, primarily his attention was on the gun moll and "Frenchy." He could only see the man's dust-covered back now.

"Well, I am arrive," Frenchy was saying. "An' I think I should receive, yes, more cut of ze money. Ze boss he does not know eet is difficul'. More and more police they send against us down there."

Kitty flung back her head and laughed contemptuously.

"And I thought you were a tough egg-you, claiming to be an apache! Listen, Frenchy! You better not beef to the Tycoon! He might get sore, and then he could sort of tip off the French coppers that he knows where they can nab Jacques Barac, who ran away from the-What d'you call that meat-chopper?"

"The guillotine!" Deadly fear was in the words. Van could see the broad back tremble. "Dieu, he would not squeal on me, ze Tycoon?"

"Not if you play ball! But I ain't talkin' for him! I got a message for you, that's all! Tonight, at six o'clock, you go to the corner of West Broadway and Bleecker Street, uptown side, and —" Rapidly she described the spot. "You'll be picked up there."

The girl made a gesture to show that she had finished the interview. She was replacing her wig and cap, powdering her face as she held a small compact.

"Go the way you came," she instructed Frenchy.

She extinguished the lamp. Then Van crouched suddenly back from the doorway, for she came to his side of the freight car, jumped agilely to the ground.

She passed within feet of the Phantom, unconscious of his nearness. She headed for her car, as Frenchy who had climbed out the other side of the freight car started away in a different direction.

The Phantom reached a quick decision. He had the girl spotted now; knew her role of nurse in the sanitarium. He was more interested, just now, in Frenchy!

Stealthily he slid around the freight car. The back of the French apache was disappearing across the yards.

Van followed. His plan was formulating swiftly. Capture Frenchy-secretly. Make up as the French thug and take his place at that West Broadway rendezvous.

Glancing back to Eleventh Avenue as he gained on his quarry now, the Phantom saw a car moving off. The girl was probably returning to the hospital.

Van drew out his Colt —a new one replacing that he had lost to the gangsters. No one was in sight, though a train of freight cars was backing slowly out of the yard, on a track close ahead.

In the darkness, the Phantom swiftly closed behind Frenchy.

And then some sixth sense-for certainly Van made no sound on his soft-soled shoes-must have warned the foreign thug. Of a sudden he whirled. In the darkness Van only saw his eyes-glowing dark eyes.

"All right!" Van said crisply, his voice low but menacing. "Put your hands up, Frenchy!"

With a shrill cry, the Frenchman leaped wildly at Van.

The Phantom could have shot him dead then, but he wanted the man alive. He brought his gun down on the capped head, hoping to stun Frenchy. But the cap was heavily padded, and evidently the apache's skull was thick!

The next instant a human cyclone struck Van. He knew how the apaches fought-with hands, feet, teeth-anything that could punish and do damage! And here was a taste of it.

The Phantom managed to shove his gun into his coat freeing both hands to grapple with the desperate thug. Then his powerful arms were getting a grip on Frenchy, tying up that windmill of fists and feet.

Frenchy suddenly lurched away. Something glittered in his hand. A knife! With desperate skill, he was maneuvering its deadly point toward Van's chest.

Both were wrestling across the tracks now. With fresh alarm, Van saw a glowing red light moving towards them-the freight train that was backing out! He grabbed at the knife, twisting it aside. Even as he was doubling his fist to hurl a blow at Frenchy's jaw the apache, in his effort to retrieve the knife, gave a mighty backward lurch.

It pulled both man and knife from Van's grip, sent him staggering to the middle of the track. "Look out!" Van cried, his heart stopping.

But it happened before he could prevent it; before the brakeman on the rear car could stop it either.

Though moving with fairly slow speed the train loomed over Frenchy like a Juggernaut. Half off balance, he was struck down by the push of the freight car bumper.

He screamed once as he fell —a short, horrible scream, cut off like a phonograph record. Then the train was rolling over him, the heavy steel wheels rumbling.

Minutes later, the Phantom saw police gathering around a mangled, bloody mass of flesh and bone and torn clothing. All that was left of Frenchy. The steel wheels had ground his body to a pulp before they could be stopped.

And Van's eyes were grim.

Frenchy had died despite his efforts to keep him alive-and Van had not even seen his face; would never see it now!

It was already daybreak. In less than twelve hours, Frenchy's rendezvous was scheduled.

Chapter XV
A Perilous Chance

Half of those hours had passed when the Phantom, once more in the great laboratory of "Doctor Bendix," was making ready for the most perilous experiment of his entire career in crime-detection.

On a table, he had laid sheaves of paper. One was a cablegram. The others were still-damp pictures which had been sent by the Bartlane wireless photo process.

Both had come from France, from the headquarters of the famous *Surete,* in Paris. Havens had handled the telephoto with the facilities of his papers.

During his visit to Havens, however, the Phantom had received another set-back in his plans.

He had ordered the police to go quietly to the Ferris Sanitarium, and secretly arrest Nurse Keenan. But evidently some woman's intuition had told her that the law was on her trail, for she had vanished completely, leaving Garrison without a nurse. Van had given a description of her as Kitty, the gun moll, and a general alarm was out for her.

Grim-eyed, the Phantom gave his attention now to the wireless photos. A vague, smudgy face peered from them. It had not taken him long to decide the pictures were useless to him. Evidently they had not been good pictures, to begin with. The transmission had made them more vague.

He picked up the long cablegram. It read:

TO THE PHANTOM

JACQUES BARAC ALIAS L'APACHE MORT ALIAS FRENCHY WANTED AS FUGITIVE FROM JUSTICE CONDEMNED TO GUILLO-TINE STOP THE BERTILLON MEASUREMENTS OF THIS CRIMINAL FOLLOW

Then followed detailed numbers and signifying letters. The anthropometric system of French criminal identifications.

Van drew out an immense drawing board, on which paper was fastened with thumb tacks. He divided it, by rule and T-square, into several squares, all numbered.

Then he set to work. His long study of the methods of the French Secret Police gave him a full understanding of the system by which, from bone measurements which could not change, they reproduced likenesses of wanted criminals.

Every bone structure of the face, from forehead to chin, was identified as a "type," marked by a number, which Van found in his book on the subject. The face itself was divided into numbered squares, representing these parts.

From the guiding numbers of the cable, and his own book on the subjects, Van began to fill in those squares.

Slowly, parts of a face took life-size shape. A cruel face with high cheek bones, small, wide-apart eyes, a sharp, hooked nose, a thick-lipped but evil mouth, and a receding chin.

Van looked at the cable:

COMPLEXION SWARTHY STOP HAIR CHESTNUT COARSELY THICK

Finished with his work at the drawing board, Van carried the drawing with its measurements into the alcove dressing room. Here he arranged not the daylight lamp, but a powerful flood-light, for he was making up for night, not for day. Then, with only the drawing he had made, with bone structure measurements as his model, he set to work.

The high cheek bones first. Bits of rubber, shoved under his gums, upward, held by small wire clamps. The sharp nose then. A wire pincer over his own nose; flesh-colored clay added.

Then a cream dye to give the swarthy complexion; a special preparation to coarsen his own hair before he used another dye to bring it to the right color.

In his mirror a replica of the face in the drawing was slowly but definitely taking shape.

Was it the face of Frenchy? Despite his faith in the Bertillon method, Van could not be certain.

"But I've got to chance it!" he gritted.

With a swift movement he swept aside the curtain of his replete clothes wardrobe. He had at least seen Frenchy's suit. It was not difficult to find a suit of somewhat similar material. He put it on.

FRENCHY HAD CARRIED A KNIFE-no gun had been found on him. Van moved to a closet, unlocked it. A small arsenal containing every conceivable weapon from a Malay *kris* to a Western derringer gleamed before him. He selected a knife of the type Frenchy had drawn, shoved it into his belt. But he also pocketed a .38 automatic.

Nor was he finished yet.

Moving to his full length mirrors he walked up and down, imitating the way he had seen Frenchy walk. He made gestures that Frenchy had made while the apache had been talking.

He moved to a Dictaphone, he began to speak into it, phrases that Frenchy had spoken; mimicking the man's accents. "Ah, Mademoiselle Keety-Well I am arrive —*Dieu,* he would not squeal on me, ze Tycoon!"

He played the record back, listened to it with critical appraisal. For a full hour he practiced before he was satisfied.

Then, over the private wire which ran straight from here to the *Clarion* Building, he called Frank Havens.

"Any new developments?" he demanded.

"Yes, Van!" the publisher announced tensely. "You remember Leland Sprague? The surveyor who found the body of Brooks the other night? Well, Strickland has reported him missing from his home. Fears something happened to him!"

Van's eyes went grim. Had the Tycoon struck again?

"And another thing, Van. The first autopsies on some of those airplane victims were made. There was a heavy morphine content in the stomach of each as well as food and caffeine. It begins to look as if they were drugged before being killed!"

"Have any of the bodies been identified as Max Garth's?" Van asked.

"No, though most of them have been identified. No sign of Garth's body, nor that of Nancy Clay, the stewardess-By the way, Van, I have those maps you asked for from the Department of Commerce. The maps of the air-field in Nevada that group of scientists drew up for the Government."

"Good! Send them over here to my laboratory any time, though I don't know just when I'll get at them."

"What are you doing now?" Havens asked anxiously.

Van spoke grimly. "I'm about to experiment with the late Monsieur Bertillon's famous system. An experiment by which I hope to get still closer to this Tycoon!"

* * *

West Broadway and Bleecker Street at its least crowded hour.

Elevated trains rumbling overhead. And, on the northwest corner, moving about furtively as if he had an eye out for the police, a swarthy-faced, sharp-nosed man, plainly Gallic.

The Phantom had come on the dot at the scheduled time. Now he waited, his heart pounding with cold suspense.

So smoothly did the dark sedan slide up to the curb that at first, even alert, he scarcely noticed it. Then he saw the rear door open, heard a low whistle.

The crucial moment had come.

With a swaggering walk, Van approached the car. He climbed in confidently.

He found himself sitting down next to the burly Ape. At the other window, Slick, now wearing his pearl-grey slouch hat over his patent-leather hair, leaned forward. The movement showed that distinguishing scar.

"Okay, Luke!" Slick ordered.

The thin, angular-faced thug was at the wheel. He promptly started the car, sent it back into traffic.

"How's your eye-sight, Frenchy?" Slick asked the question sharply.

For a brief moment he pondered that. Then he laughed shrilly, speaking for the first time. "Eet is ver' good. Why?"

"Because," said Slick, "you ain't gonna be using it for a little while-Now hold still, I got my gat on you, and Ape here is handy with his mitts!"

For a moment Van felt his arduously built-up plans crumbling about him. Then, as a heavy cloth was brought roughly over his eyes by Ape and securely fastened, the moment passed.

For Slick said: "You savvy, we ain't taken any chances. You're still a new guy to us, even if you have been workin' in the other territory, and we've all seen you."

Van sat still. The blindfold, which Slick himself reached over to adjust, fully obliterated his vision. He did not try to maneuver it. He was playing a precarious enough part and must do nothing suspicious.

Thus far he seemed to be getting by. They had seen the real Frenchy whom he had never seen, yet his disguise seemed to have passed their inspection.

The car rolled on. Now and then Van could tell that it was stopping in traffic, or turning, but he could not gauge its course. Once he heard a sound in the rushing wind as of the sides of a bridge passing; he could sense water. But he wasn't sure what bridge it was.

Then the car suddenly gathered speed, rolled smoothly, rapidly. An open road now, doubtless.

For a long period the journey continued. Another turn, then the car began to jounce roughly, violently, making slower progress.

Then at last it came to a stop.

Instantly the blindfold was taken from Van's face, and he was glad his makeup had been put on solidly enough not to be affected by it.

With the others he climbed out of the car, in night which was pitch dark. But with his blindfold accustomed eyes he could see clearly.

The trees of a heavy woods rose darkly on every side. The Phantom and his underworld companions were standing on a clearing amid those trees, on a lawn where reared a dark, stone mansion.

What was the location of this house Van could not guess. Nor did he have much opportunity to study its exterior.

"Come on, Frenchy," Slick said. "We ain't got much time."

With Ape walking behind in his loping gait, all moved to the front door of the house. Slick pressed a bell-button, but apparently the bell gave no sound. Waiting only a moment he took out a key and opened the front door.

They came directly into a large foyer. A heavy oak door was opposite them, closed. The foyer was dimly lighted, the furniture covered with shrouding cloth.

And at once Van became aware of an evil atmosphere in this place —a sense of chill menace. "Wait!" commanded Slick.

He walked across the foyer to that heavy door; rapped on it three times.

There was a click, as of a lock being turned. Slick opened the door, slid quickly through it, closing it before Van could glimpse the room beyond.

Minutes passed. No sound came from the closed-off room. Ape stood patiently, rolling a cigarette with his pawlike hands. Luke paced the floor. Another gangster came in then and Van recognized the twisty-faced man as Maxie.

"Say! Look who's here!" Maxie exclaimed. "If it ain't Frenchy! Hope you brought good news."

"Stow it!" Luke said gruffly. "No questions or talking here. You know the rules, Maxie." Silence again in the foyer.

Then once more the oak door opened. Slick came out. He looked awed, yet a trifle disappointed, and he wheezed as if he were cold. His eyes flashed to Maxie.

"Come on, you! We ain't gonna go on this job. The boss wants us to wait around for orders." He nodded to "Frenchy."

"Go in-Ape, you stay with Luke. Both o' you wait for Frenchy."

Chapter XVI
The Ice Chamber

As Slick and Maxie moved for the front door, Van walked unhesitatingly to the door of oak and the inner room. He tried the knob. The door was unlocked. His nerves steeled, he pulled it open, entered.

On its own spring the door closed behind him.

He found himself in a large, brightly lighted oblong chamber, with bare walls. Though there were no visible signs of ventilation, the air seemed fresh. Also it was strangely cold, bringing an instant chill to his body.

Though his senses registered these things, his real attention was immediately drawn, as if magnetically, to the far end of this strange room.

In the metal wall was a small square window of heavy glass. And as Van walked forward in the bright light which was challenging every line of his makeup, he discerned a face in that window.

A crazy grotesquerie of a face. Distorted as some face in an amusement park's sideshow mirror. Shimmery features which had a ghastly aspect.

But the Phantom realized, as he looked at that grotesque visage, that the glass of the window had probably been made with some deliberate imperfection to cause that distortion.

"All right, Frenchy! Stand where you are!"

From a camouflaged microphone in the glass the voice, a strange ghostly whisper which nevertheless filled the bare-walled room, rapped out the command. At the same time, the air seemed to grow colder-uncomfortably colder.

The Phantom came to a stop some twelve feet from that window.

"Well, Frenchy, now you meet me personally." The distorted features shimmered eerily. "I am your boss-the Tycoon!"

Van had all he could do to conceal the surge of hate and rage that flamed through his every fiber. His hand itched to whip out his gun. Behind that distorting window stood the master criminal he had sought on a trail of blood and slaughter.

Twelve feet apart that criminal and the greatest living detective faced one another. But the Phantom knew that as far as coming to vital grips with the criminal went, that distance might as well have been miles instead of feet.

He had seen the invulnerable position of the Tycoon. Not only was the wall metal, the glass undoubtedly bullet-proof, but the criminal had another, even better protection.

This big, bare chamber outside the window was obviously air-conditioned. And from behind that window, the criminal himself operated the air-conditioning power. His making the room colder when he had wanted "Frenchy" to halt had been a warning.

Cleverly hidden vents near the ceiling were letting that cold air in. Unquestionably, if the criminal willed, he could turn that air to freezing point, could make it fatal for any human, while in his segregated chamber the Tycoon could remain comfortable and safe.

But who was he? In his Gallic pose, Van peered hard at that shimmery, grotesque face in the window.

An eerie chuckle sounded from the microphone then.

"I am sorry you cannot see me as clearly as I can see you," came the voice of the Tycoon.

Van was glad then that he had not relaxed playing his role to perfection, in every posture. That glass must have clear places in it, through which the criminal peered, saw him out here in the bright light, watched his every move.

"And now, Frenchy, to business. My time is valuable. It is not often I give it to anyone. Soon all will realize my position!" The whisper rose in gloating triumph. "They will pay tribute to me in millions-millions. You know that, do you not, Frenchy?"

"*But* oui, I know eet!"

It was the first time Van had spoken in this eerie place. And even as he spoke, he was grimly wondering what mad scheme of power and wealth this diabolical criminal had. There was a ghastly confidence in the man's egotistical boasting.

"And that brings me to your work, Frenchy." The eerie, whispery voice changed in tone. "I am not completely satisfied with the results you and your mob have been getting in-your territory. Up here, my men have worked smoothly and tirelessly. You used to give me more action! What is the matter?"

Even as he puzzled over this speech, the Phantom's retentive memory leaped suddenly into the gap of his unconnected thoughts. He took a long shot, and quoted almost verbatim words he had heard the real Frenchy speak. Even though he knew they were perilous words, he had to make his role convincing.

"Eet is ver' difficult, *Monsieur* Tycoon. Ze police zey make theengs hot. I do not weesh to complain, but ze cut of ze money —"

"Ah, so that's it?"

The whisper had become a tigerish purr. And significantly, the air in the room grew still colder. With alarming rapidity. Van felt goose-flesh pimple his body as almost Arctic air came rushing through the vents.

"Oh, eet ees cold! Please, *Monsieur* Boss —I do not mean to offend."

"No, you could not be that foolish. That is why I shall pass over your words, and forget them. And perhaps you will yet redeem yourself. I am going to send you back now, along with two of the boys who will show you how we operate up here! If you can help them, so much the better. This is an important job, and I am taking no chances!"

As he spoke, Van noticed the temperature of the room was no longer dropping. But the air remained uncomfortably cold, refrigerated. And it was at that very moment that Van became aware of a sensation that filled him with sudden alarm. The skin of his face, under his makeup, was becoming rigid, painfully taut!

He knew, with a sharp clutch at his heart, what was happening. His makeup could have stood heat; even blistering heat. But he had not expected to find himself in icy coldness!

His makeup was stiffening in that cold. The cream dyes were shrinking as they congealed! The fixed temperature was doing its work! As he stood there he could feel that artificial face changing, contracting, beginning to pull out of shape!

He knew the criminal's eyes were watching that face. In another moment the would Tycoon see. Van would be betrayed! And something told him that if he were, he would never get as far as that oak-paneled, air-tight door with its lock apparently operated from behind the criminal's window.

In that perilous instant, with the contraction starting to distort his face, Van's mind raced. Some loophole, some escape —

Then swift inspiration came.

With a feigned gasp the Phantom let his knees go limp. He dropped to the floor of the icy room as if passing out from the effects of the icy air. It had, indeed, brought lassitude to his body.

He fell forward, so that he could put one hand to his face to shield it and warm it at the same time.

"Ah-too much for my warmblooded apache friend?" The criminal behind the glass chuckled. And the air suddenly grew warmer. Van stirred. If only he could get a chance to come to grips with that fiend!

A bell clanged, somewhere outside the oaken door. The lock clicked and Ape, with the tall, angular-faced Luke came in, with drawn guns.

"Take Frenchy out of here-and go on with the job!" came the eerie whisper. It seemed to recede as if sinking.

And the moment after Ape had "helped" Van to his feet, the grotesque face disappeared from the window.

"Come on!" Luke said, shivering. "It's damn cold in here. An' we just about got time to make it."

They were pulling Van along to the open oak door. The Phantom did not resist, nor try any false moves. The criminal leader was still safely out of reach, and this mission to which the Tycoon had assigned him was going to be vital. It seemed his best lead now.

His companions led him through the empty foyer, thence out into the tree-shrouded grounds, into the dark night. Van heard the muffled purr of a high-powered auto motor, somewhere in the rear of the house. The Tycoon-driving away?

In vain the Phantom tried to guess his surroundings as they moved across the soggy, muddy grass. At least it didn't seem they were going to blindfold him now. He should find out before long where this eerie house was located.

Then, suddenly, he suppressed a sharp intake of breath.

They had reached a turn. And, nestled in a bay of trees, a silvery cabin monoplane loomed into view, squatting like a huge bird with outspread wings.

A modern Fairchild it was, Van saw at once. Luke stepped forward with an authoritative air. The tall gunman opened the cabin door, stepped in, reaching for the dashboard. Then he hurried around to the self-starter.

The starter moaned. Its moan was drowned in the sudden staccato burst of the Wright engine coming to life, as the propeller whirled.

Luke, obviously a trained pilot, was already in the front seat, at the stick. He had turned on the cabin lights.

Ape's huge figure climbed in next, then Van followed. There were two seats behind the pilot, opposite one another. Ape took one. Van took the other, pulling the door closed at a command.

The motor scaled up and down, warming. Then the plane lurched forward. Expertly, Luke taxied the ship across the wide clearing, headed it into the wind. A rush of gathering speed, then the sudden smooth lift as the monoplane took the air.

The Phantom looked covertly from his window as the dark ground dropped away.

He saw the dark mansion, the woods, but they looked vague because the lights in the cabin lessened visibility outside.

The plane was climbing in a slow circular course. And before Van's keen eyes could get a clearer view of the mysterious locale they had left the place behind and low-hanging cloud-wisps engulfed the ship. Luke was watching his dashboard instruments, flying by them. Nor could Van see them clearly from his seat, though he could hear the buzz of the radio compass.

Vaporish mists wisped past the windows. Then clear starlight. Luke was above the clouds.

Chapter XVII
Sky Ride

Unquestionably, a full hour went by with no conversation in the throbbing, coursing plane. Luke silently guided the controls. Ape settled back in his seat, in an attitude of relaxation. The Phantom was still wondering from where they had taken off, and where they were headed.

Once his glance had gone down covertly to his shoes. He noted that they were caked with mud from the grounds over which he had walked. Peculiar, greyish mud.

Unobtrusively Van managed to scrape some of that mud off with a bit of match-box from his pocket, and to shove the folded cardboard away. Once before a pair of shoes had aided him-the white shoes of "Nurse Keenan."

A sudden gap appeared in the cloud-vapors through which the ship was coursing and, glancing through the window, Van caught a glimpse of the dark relief-map earth below. Rough terrain, with dark hillocks that were growing to mountain ranges! Somewhere off to the right the faint tentacle of a beacon-light darted into the sky.

"Where are we, Luke?" Ape asked gruffly. "Jersey?"

Luke spoke without turning. "Cripes, we passed outa Jersey ten minutes ago. We're crossin' Pennsy now. And I hope the Tycoon gave us plenty of fuel for this trip so's we can make it on the exact time he planned!"

As time went on, Van Loan learned that he was being taken on no small "hop." The plane was racing across the continent! Flying on a steady, southwesterly course while Luke, who Van realized was not only an expert pilot but a tireless one, guided it by the regular air-beacons and radio beams.

The darkness of the night deepened as the ship winged in and out of clouds. Once it "detoured" to avoid a storm area which showed black in the sky, an area that was being announced by the radio operator of the Pittsburgh airport.

Ape's big head was lolled back now. The huge thug dozed off, and his snores rose beneath the engine's throb. But Luke continued to guide the controls in silence.

The Phantom's mind was working at top speed. With each hour he was being flown further from New York; from the scene of his investigations. Should he try to wrest control of this ship-capture these two thugs and fly back? He could do it, with Ape snoring, and with Luke concentrating on the controls.

But he didn't make such a move. The Tycoon had said, "an important job," and the Phantom must learn what that job was. He must know why this plane was making such a long trip.

And so he, too, pretended to relax while the night dragged on. Actually, though, he was wide awake, alert to every change in their course, to every buzz of the radio compass.

He knew when they were passing over Ohio. The winding silver ribbon that was the Ohio River gave him his bearings. Ohio-then Indiana, stretching its flat plains below.

Ape woke up as they winged over Illinois. The big thug reached into a compartment and produced sandwiches and a thermos bottle of coffee. He took a greedy share of both, passed them next to Luke who used one hand to drink and eat. "Frenchy" was then offered his share-and the Phantom partook of this felon's meal, knowing his body must have nourishment to maintain its energy.

When the grey dawn seeped across the sky, and the sun rose red behind the speeding plane, Missouri was spread out below.

Full morning found them flying over Kansas, over dusty flatlands.

Then, just as Van was wondering whether this flight was going to cross the whole continent, Luke twisted his expressionless face over his shoulder and spoke. In his tone was the triumph lacking in his features.

"We've hit the schedule to the dot, guys! Now if the boss was right —"

As he spoke he was easing the joy-stick forward. The plane dipped, began a long descent over the Kansas landscape-over the Southwest state to which Van had flown so far in company with two underworld thugs.

The earth loomed beneath the descending ship. Dusty fields, meadows, trees. And then Van saw twin, glistening lines growing into distinctness-lines which cut across that landscape.

Railroad tracks!

Luke was following them with the speeding plane, having leveled it at low altitude. For a long period the Fairchild sped on a parallel over those glistening lines.

Again Luke twisted his head around to speak.

"Be ready, Ape. Ought to be comin' in sight now!"

Instantly Ape was fully awake, his eyes gleaming with evil anticipation. He reached beneath his seat and Van, heart tightening, watched him pull out a wooden box he had already noticed there.

Pear-shaped, steel-encased missiles gleamed in that box. Grenades!

"You can help with the pineapples, Frenchy!" Ape said, grinning ghoulishly. "You oughta know the lay down these parts!"

A shout suddenly broke from Luke. The Fairchild abruptly slanted steeply, rushing down a hill of space with roaring speed.

"There she is!" Luke cried.

Van looked. His eyes widened.

On the track below and ahead, a long, glistening train had loomed. A streamlined train, racing along those rails like a graceful, silvery bullet! Obviously one of the latest Diesel-engined trains. It moved effortlessly, smokelessly. Ape had opened the window beside him, ignoring the rush of wind. The big thug lifted one of the "pineapples."

Closer loomed the train which, despite its speed, was far slower than the down-rushing airplane.

So this was the grim objective which had brought these thugs way to Kansas! They were diving on a streamlined train —a train full of people! Diving with murderous intent!

Ape was taking aim with the bomb now as the plane, swooping low over the rounded roof of the train, banked to give him a perfect throwing range.

And in that instant, Van knew that he must act. Role or no role, he could not sit idly by and watch an act of such devilish destruction! Though for almost twelve hours he had withheld himself from any action, he could do so no longer.

Ape's arm came back to take aim with the bomb-and the Phantom pushed out of his seat, sideward. He lunged with his shoulders against Ape's arm, cleverly blocking it in its poised position.

Ape cursed. "Hey, what the hell's the matter with you, Frenchy?"

"Ze lurch, it threw me," Van explained quickly.

The plane had slithered on past the gleaming, streamlined train, was banking vertically to swoop anew.

"Get over it, Luke!" Ape growled. "I'll finish it right!"

Again the train was beneath them. Ape once more aimed the pineapple. And again the Phantom deliberately lurched. This time he could not block the throw but he delayed it. The plane had slithered past the train and over a field before Ape could let go with the grenade.

A geyser of brief flame, followed by the slower-traveling concussion, shot out of the empty field-safely to one side and behind the train.

Ape growled a curse at this second apparent clumsiness which had spoiled his aim. But another cold voice suddenly snapped out like a whip. Luke's voice.

"I saw that, Frenchy! You did it on purpose! Trying to ball up the works, eh?" The pilot, holding the plane in a climb, was looking back, his hard, expressionless eyes giving his face a deadly aspect. "Say, no wonder the boss didn't trust you too much! If you think you're gonna pull a doublecross —"

With a snarl, with that quickness by which an underworld felon could change at once from comrade to deadly foe, Luke whipped out an automatic, snaked it around.

The Phantom threw all pretense aside then. Gritting an oath, he catapulted forward. His hand caught the pilot's gun arm. His other hand, balled into a fist, swung in a short but terrific jab to Luke's angular jaw.

The pilot gasped, slumped; out for the instant. The plane leveled into neutral by its own stabilizer.

A growl of enraged comprehension came from Ape then. The big man had turned from the window, was lurching forward, his head low to avoid the ceiling. And his big hands scooped up a tommy gun. Its muzzle swung like a dark cannon-maw at the Phantom.

"You doublecrossin' rat!"

Van had no time to draw his own secreted automatic. The tommy was right in front of his face, ready to blow his head off!

He made one rapid movement-swooped one long arm for the joystick, gave it a crazy yank.

The Fairchild see-sawed drunkenly, standing on one wing tip in midair. Cursing, Ape was thrown off balance, even as the tommy blasted three shots into the cabin ceiling. The plane sideslipped; began to wabble and to lose flying speed.

Its nose dropped sickeningly as the earth came up in a spinning rush. The tracks to one side; the train far ahead.

Ape yelled in alarm as his huge frame slid down the flooring of the steeply tilted ship. Van ignored him now, for the earth was spinning up closer. A fatal crash was imminent.

The Phantom yanked at the stunned pilot to move him from the controls.

And at that very instant Luke came to, began to struggle fiercely, flaying out with both arms, kicking, squirming.

Cramped between chairs, Ape again had the tommy. Somehow, despite the sickening drop of the plane, the huge thug was again aiming that gun at Van.

The Phantom let go of the weak but struggling pilot. This time he managed to get his automatic out. It blazed once in the giddy plane.

Ape's big body slumped over the chairs —a bullet in his brain.

Jagged green trees seemed to leap up at the plane like mammoth teeth. With a mighty heave, Van yanked at the pilot in a final, desperate effort. Even as the ground loomed right below, the Phantom at last cleared the control space, pushing the cursing Luke aside. He slid into the seat, grabbed the stick, found the rubber bars with his feet.

With the skill of an expert flyer, Van struggled with those controls, knowing how slim his chances were of righting the ship. He used the throttle and stick, trying to bring up nose and drooping wing, at the very moment the tree-tops slanted right beneath.

At the last instant he did succeed in getting the plane over a wide road which ran parallel to the railroad tracks. But that was all he could do. He could not get the ship on even keel, nor could he get it to the flatlands on the other side of the tracks. The road came up at a menacing, swinging angle.

Van sat tight, flinging his arms in front of his face, after flicking off the ignition switch. He saw Luke trying to rise, yelled a warning at the thug. Then the crash came!

A rending impact —a shivering moan of twisting metal. Its nose telescoping, the monoplane settled in a wing-buckling heap.

Fortunately, there was no fire, due to Van's quick thought of turning off the ignition. Nor did the "pineapples" aboard explode. By crashing on the road and getting the nose of the plane up as far as possible, Van had avoided an impact that would have blown the whole wrecked plane to bits.

Chapter XVIII
Looted Train

Dazed, shaken, but otherwise unhurt, the Phantom crept through the wrecked cabin. Ape lay on the floor, dead from Van's own bullet. But he was not the only corpse!

With the top of his head horribly crushed, Luke, the angular-faced thug, lay in a gruesome heap. He had made the mistake (an ironic mistake for such a skilled pilot) of trying to stand up when the crash came. A metal roof support had done the rest.

Van got out of the cabin as quickly as he could; out on the road, where he pulled the two corpses. He searched both with lightning speed, took all their possessions.

One article, found on Luke, interested him as he glanced at it quickly. It was a tagged key, marked Piedmont Hotel. Van knew that hotel in New York. It was one of the flashy type of places which gangsters often used as hide-outs, posing as respectable business men.

As Van hastily pocketed the key, a scream of sirens, a raucous roar, came to his ears. Coming down the road were motorcycles, tan-uniformed figures astride them. Kansas State troops —a whole squadron of them! Someone who had seen the plane crash must already have reported it.

Van stood up quickly. Over makeup which, though somewhat marred now, nevertheless still clung to his face, he placed his black silk domino mask.

And then he realized the troopers couldn't have known about the plane. For though none could have failed to see it in the middle of the sunny road, the majority of them did not even stop, but sped past in frantic haste.

The few who braked their machines to a standstill and dismounted were soon staring with surprise at Van's platinum, diamond-studded badge.

"The Phantom!" came husky, ejaculations.

For like the police in every part of this nation, and in every other nation as well, their regulations had reminded them to be on the lookout for that scintillating emblem and its anonymous owner, wherever found.

But the Phantom wasted no time in formalities. Those other motorcycles had sped ahead—something must have —

"What's happened, Sergeant?" he asked one of the troopers. "What were you called out on?"

"Big train wreck-about two miles up, near Emporia," the sergeant answered quickly. "News just phoned in."

The Phantom's heart turned to ice.

A moment later, with one trooper remaining at the crashed plane with its two New York gangster corpses, the remaining motorcycles roared again down the road. And the Phantom sat astride the fender of the careful but speedy-driving sergeant.

Ambulances and local police from Emporia had already reached the wreck when they arrived. In the full morning sun it lay like a ghastly blight upon the landscape.

The streamlined train which Van had saved from an airplane bombing lay toppled over an embankment, its engine telescoped, its silvery cars twisted and bent.

The crew had died, all of them. Most of the passengers still lived, but many of them were horribly maimed, bleeding and groaning as interns rushed with stretchers to pick them up.

From horrified survivors the Phantom learned the facts, and the first thing he learned came with the impact of a blow, though he had already surmised it.

The train belonged to the Empire and Southwest Railway. It had just inaugurated this run, from Topeka to Salt Lake City, Utah.

When the airplane had appeared, no one had known its intent. Its one exploded bomb, well behind and to the side of the train, had not been seen. But as the train proceeded, two closed automobiles had appeared on the parallel road beside it, having turned in from some branch road ahead.

There had been a terrific explosion coming with cataclysmic suddenness. Tracks upturned, and the train derailed. And thugs from those automobiles had looted the baggage car, taking everything of value.

Grim comprehension narrowed the Phantom's eyes. Even in his fierce anger and grief over this ruthless vandalism, he paid unwitting tribute to the devilish cunning of the Tycoon.

In the east, somewhere in or near New York, the criminal leader had planned this crime with utmost thoroughness. It was natural that he could not entirely rely on the plane making the trip on schedule, and doing its work. Out here he must have another mob in contact with him, the mob from which Frenchy had originally come!

They had been on hand, in cars. Even if the plane had succeeded in bombing the train, the local gangsters would still have been needed to loot the wrecked train. They had simply carried out both jobs.

And Van could only console his bitter feelings with the thought that, had he not thwarted the men in the plane the wreck might have taken a greater toll.

In Emporia, where a police chief turned over a private telephone to him, the Phantom put through a long distance call to Frank Havens. The publisher was astounded to hear the Phantom's voice talking from Kansas, when little over twelve hours ago Van had been in New York. But the train wreck was no news to him.

"Yes," he said briefly, "I got it from my correspondent over the wires. I phoned it to Garrison at the sanitarium. It threw him almost into a raving state. He's in debt now, it seems, for backing that streamlined train and its fast run. He relied on it strongly to pull the railroad out of its slump." Havens hesitated for a breath. "But there's something else I have to tell you, Phantom. About Leland Sprague."

Van's heart tightened. "You told me he was missing from his home," he said quickly. "Has anything —"

Havens spoke rapidly. "No-and that's just the point! Sprague showed up at my office about midnight last night. He seemed in a state of utter terror-actually ill, acting wild and queer. Said he felt he needed protection and had come to me in the hope of finding the Phantom. At the same time he denied-pretty vehemently, I thought-that he had been missing at all. Said he'd been home, buried in work, all the hours the police were looking for him. Because he seemed so ill, I insisted on calling my own physician. He took Sprague to the Polyclinic Hospital, saying the man obviously needed rest, if nothing else. Sprague's still there."

The Phantom had listened to this report with narrowing eyes. His apprehension had changed to a sudden sober conjecture. Sprague's absence and return-the timing of them included the hour when Van had seen the mysterious Tycoon at that unknown hide-out.

"Listen, Frank," Van ordered crisply. "Have your doctor make sure that none of Sprague's clothes or other belongings are touched or lost. I want to look into this matter personally when I get back to New York. I'm taking the first plane I can."

* * *

It was not yet midnight when the Phantom opened the multiple-locked door to his secret laboratory in New York's Bronx.

He had already made two visits since his return.

The first he had made with the police-to the Piedmont Hotel. The key he had found on the dead Luke gave him entrance to a room on the twentieth floor. It was deserted, but evidently had been quite recently occupied, not only by Luke, but by others. Clothing was strewn about. So were empty whiskey bottles, glasses, cigarettes.

Van had made a thorough search, taking every item that seemed possible evidence. He had brought them now to his laboratory. Police had been left to guard the hotel room, which had been rented under fictitious names. The Phantom doubted, however, whether any thugs would show up there again.

Before returning to his laboratory Van had hurried to the Polyclinic Hospital. He had seen Leland Sprague there-seen the shock-headed surveyor in a wild, agitated state, his face flushed and feverish, his eyes small-pupiled in their glaring. Talbert, the tall, mustached shoring man, another of the scientists, had also been present, trying to persuade Sprague to remain in the hospital, for Sprague was demanding to go.

Both men had been tight-lipped in the Phantom's presence. Van had learned nothing from them. But he had learned something of significance when he had examined Sprague's clothing, in the privacy of an office. On Sprague's shoes had been two layers of caked, clayish mud. The same mud, Van had seen at once, that he had scraped from his own shoes in the plane, just after leaving the Tycoon's hide-out. Sprague, who had sworn he was not "missing," had been on those grounds!

Havens's doctor, who had attended Sprague, had then said he was unable to tell just what was wrong with the man, but suspected he had recently taken narcotics-cocaine, in all likelihood. Since arriving at the hospital, Sprague had steadfastly refused to submit to thorough examination; above all, he had refused to have a blood test taken.

But the Phantom had come away with some of Sprague's blood nevertheless. The scientist had been scratched on his wrist, which the doctor had bandaged. The bandage was changed, and Van took prompt possession of the old, blood-soaked gauze.

Now, in his laboratory, Van once more put on his smock and set to work.

He gave first attention to the mud he had scraped from his own shoes, and from Sprague's. From his great crime library, came every book on soil he possessed. The dab of mud went under a special geologist's glass, thence through strainers to segregate clay, humus and sand. The Phantom soon analyzed it. He took out a map then, giving in various colors the different types of soil in every locale. He limited himself to a small area of the map, for he knew from the length of that auto journey he had taken blindfolded that the mysterious house couldn't be far out of Manhattan.

At first he saw no green in this area at all.

Then his eyes sharpened. Yes, there was one emerald dab.

Long Island. The only place where soil of this peculiar clayish substance was to be found close to New York City. The clay was present because of the marshy banks of the nearby Sound.

Recalling the immense woods that had surrounded the house, Van took out a map of Long Island, pored over it. When he was finished he had limited the locale to three possible points. Filing this temporarily away in his retentive mind, the Phantom proceeded to his next work.

One of the outstanding features of his laboratory was his collection of equipment for the testing of blood-blood, which figured in almost every crime case. He had apparatus for testing hemoglobin content, after the method of the late Dr. Zangemeister of Munich, as well as data and material to make the group tests of Beam and Freak.

Sprague's blood, transferred from bandage to a glass slide, went through several tests, each viewed under a microscope.

That blood told a story—a grim story.

And strangely, it brought a fresh memory to the Phantom. He hurried downstairs to the entrance of the loft where there was a big box affixed under a slot in the metal door, like the night-vault box of a bank.

In it Van found a wrapped package. Havens, he knew, had left it here some time previously. He took it upstairs to his desk.

And when he unwrapped the package he was gazing at more maps. All marked "Department of Commerce, U. S." Except for the map which had been made by Havens's staff men-one showing the locales of the Empire and Southwestern Railway sabotage outrages.

Searching through the lot Van found what must have been the original map of the planned airport in Nevada, work on which the scientists had engaged for the Government before re-signing their posts.

It was a large map, and property on it was marked off according to ownership. The first words Van saw were: "Empire and Southwest Railway."

So the railroad's right of way ran right through this section of Nevada! It extended out pretty far, too; to the boundary of government-owned property. The airport, however, was planned to be situated some distance away from the railroad.

The Phantom submitted that map to an intensive analysis, using even a violet ray to bring out every detail.

And then he found it!

It had been cleverly done, leaving little trace. But it was there!

Originally, this Government map had been different! The square plot of the airport had, instead of being so removed, actually bordered on the railway's property. The marks designating the original plot had been erased, doubtless by chemicals.

Nodding in sudden understanding, the Phantom rapidly sketched in that original plot. And then, partly across the square but mostly in the railroad property that immediately adjoined it, he wrote a single word-with a question mark after it. The word was:

Pitchblende?

In increasing excitement at his discoveries, he hurriedly viewed the other map showing the locales of the train sabotaging. Yes, most of it had taken place in the Southwest-in Kansas as a matter of fact, where the railway had its biggest Southwestern spurs, and where that streamlined train had been wrecked.

It had also taken place along other points of the many tracks, in other states. But Nevada had been neglected by the saboteurs! Not one spot was marked there.

Thrusting all his deductions temporarily into a recess in his brain to await further analysis, Van turned back to the immediate problem in hand. The exact location of the criminal's Long Island hide-out. He must follow that up. And there was something else, too.

On another table he now dumped out the stuff he had taken from the Piedmont Hotel room. Carefully he went through the collection.

Cigarettes. Currency-wads of crisp new bills. A little loose change; a watch. Keys, and an oblong card on which was printed:

GRAND CENTRAL TERMINAL CHECKROOM
NUMBER 138

It was the last item which most interested the Phantom. What had those thugs left in the depot checkroom? Here was something that warranted immediate investigation.

The Phantom called Police Headquarters, and in a moment was connected with Inspector Gregg.

"Inspector, I suggest you and some of your men meet me in the waiting room of Grand Central Terminal as soon as possible," Van said authoritatively. "I have to look into something there-and I also have some information to convey to you concerning the base from which the Tycoon has been operating in New York."

"What's that?" came the inspector's gruff ejaculation. "I'll be there all right, Phantom!"

Chapter XIX
Another Victim

Good as his word the detective chief was promptly on time. When the Phantom, his features once more disguised, entered the big concourse, stripped now of the waving banners that had given it a festive air, he saw the big, placid-faced inspector and a group of plainclothes men shifting impatiently.

The Phantom identified himself without having to show his badge, since he was expected here.

"Well, now, what's this about the criminal's base of operations?" the inspector demanded at once.

"I hope I haven't stirred up any false hopes, inspector." Van smiled tightly. "My information isn't too definite. And it can wait a little longer. I want you and your men to be on hand now, just in case there's any trouble. Let them spread out a bit, but watch me."

The command was carried out swiftly. Plainclothes men scattered about the concourse, amongst the coming and going travelers.

The Phantom walked straight to the checkroom counter. A uniformed attendant, youthful and sleepy-eyed, waited upon him. Van presented check number 138.

The clerk looked at it, then turned to the row of wire-wickered shelves. He took down a small black valise, shoved it over the counter. Van carried it away carelessly, feeling a sense as of anticlimax.

Inspector Gregg joined the Phantom to walk with him into the adjoining smoking room, which was almost vacant. Other detectives, at Van's command, made a screen around him.

Picking the lock of the valise as it stood on a bench, was a matter of seconds for the Phantom. The lid came open-and a low cry of amazement burst from the inspector, while the Phantom's eyes went to slits.

Stacks of engraved paper lay in the valise. Negotiable stock certificates of the Empire and Southwest Railway!

Hastily pulling on a glove, the inspector was already going through them, his heavy lips pursed as they always were in moments of climax. The Phantom pulled out another paper that laid beneath the stock. On it were cryptic figures-algebraic formulae, a few chemical quantities. And the name inscribed across its top was: "Donald Vaughan."

"Lord, what does this mean, Phantom?" said the puzzled inspector. "Stock placed in a check room? Who —"

"My guess," Van said slowly, "is that Donald Vaughan, the geologist, put it here and gave the check to one of the gang. That's how I got the check-from a dead gangster's room. I think we've uncovered the method of collecting extortion, though, inspector. The checkroom was used as the place of exchange."

"But that would be crazy; imagine using a public checkroom-Say, wait!"

Stirred to action now as the Phantom closed the suitcase, the inspector barked orders to his men.

They went to the checkroom. The sleepy-eyed youth was promptly put through a grilling. He disclaimed any knowledge of what had been going on. He couldn't remember faces, he said, and there were so many people. Van, looking at him, thought he was telling the truth.

Taking matters into his own hands, and dispensing with the formality of procuring a search warrant, the inspector barked orders for the whole checkroom to be searched for more such stuff.

"It beats me!" he told the Phantom. "I still can't understand how anybody would have the nerve to use such a place for his extortion collections."

"Why not?" Van asked, even as a new, vague, but disturbing apprehension began stirring within him. "Isn't it the last place we would have thought of looking? And accessible to anyone? Anybody could safely collect the loot, just as the men who had secretly to pay it could put it there unnoticed. If you ask me it was a most ingenious method. I suggest that you look up Donald Vaughan at once."

"They'll know up at the offices, probably, where to find him," said Gregg confidently, and dispatched a man there. "Well, one thing is sure. They won't be using that checkroom again!" He scowled heavily. "And now, Phantom, what about that information about the base of operations?"

"You can send word to the police in Long Island to search in two areas for a house of this description," Van said, and gave the description.

The inspector concealed his eagerness to be off-this news had evidently interested him more than the discovery of stock-as, on the heels of a plainclothes man, two of the men whom Van had seen in the upstairs office on the night of the tragedy in the concourse, came hurrying to the scene.

James Strickland, the florid-faced vice-president of the Empire and Southwest Railway; and Jenson, the mild, bespectacled secretary of the line.

"What is it now?" Strickland's voice was hoarse, agitated. "We've been here trying to check reports on that streamline train wreck-have our hands full. What's this about Vaughan?"

"Where can we get a hold of him?" It was the inspector who answered, for the Phantom hadn't identified himself to these newcomers.

Strickland was looking from the group of men outside the checkroom to the frightened checkroom clerk. He shook his head, jerkily.

"I don't know just where Vaughan would be at this hour —" he began.

"Why, he must be at his laboratory," Jenson promptly broke in. "He sleeps there when he's working, and he's been working all this week. It's on East Sixteenth Street." He gave the number.

"Okay." A moment later Inspector Gregg, having drawn Van aside, said in a low voice: "I'll send a couple of men there to see Vaughan. Let's take the trail of this Tycoon's base ourselves, and —"

"Let other men attend to that job," Van put in, his tone crisp, incisive. "And you-and plenty of police-come along to Vaughan's at once!"

Something in his tone stopped any protest the inspector might have intended making. He told one of his men to attend to communicating Van's message about the criminals' base to the Long Island authorities.

Minutes later, the inspector's car, in which he rode with the Phantom and several other men, was screaming through the scant night traffic, down and across town. Behind it came two prowl-cars with their bluecoat duos.

On a dark desolate street, in the shadow of tall factory chimneys and where the East River bridges could be seen etched against the sky, the cars with sirens screaming slid to a stop opposite a modern, trim building which looked almost incongruous in this neighborhood.

The Phantom and the police leaped swiftly to the curb, strode to the front door of the building. Van pushed a bell. They could hear it ring inside, but there was no answer.

It was the inspector who seized the handle, turned it. He gave an ejaculation of surprise as he found it unlocked, then yanked the door open and —

The concussion of the sudden, terrific explosion sent the inspector and several of his men flying backward, the Phantom with them! The house shook on its very foundations. Windows shattered! Smoke billowed out the open door.

Before the smoke had cleared, the Phantom, gun out, had leaped ahead of the other men into the house.

Flashlights went on in the hands of police who followed him, illuminating a large, devastated chamber.

It had been a laboratory. Now it was a mess of broken lights.

And then, one and all, the flashlights focused on the debris-strewn floor.

There, horribly mangled, and in a pool of blood, lay the body of Donald Vaughan, geologist.

He had been literally blown in two. The middle of his body was one sagging mass of broken bones and flesh. His squarish face, with its heavily pouched eyes, was distorted and twisted out of shape, blood frothed the purple lips.

The Phantom took in the gruesome sight in a flash and then his eyes roved fiercely about the flashlit room, taking cognizance of wrecked apparatus and particularly of one broken glass tube filled with a peculiar gilt foil.

His glance swept suddenly then to an open door, a corridor in the rear which the darkness there had at first obscured. The only exit.

His lithe body hurtled forward. Out into the corridor, to a rear door, his gun out. He yanked the door open, revealing a rear alley leading to the next block. He stopped abruptly. The dark alley was full of slouch-hatted figures, apparently just making a get-away. This he saw only fleetingly as he opened the door, for in the next instant he had ducked back.

Shots flamed from two directions. Gunmen had seen the door opening and were cutting loose, their guns giving the alarm to the rest.

From behind the door frame the Phantom grimly aimed, and his own gun blazed.

One of the thugs dropped in his tracks, pitched to the paving.

Then, just as the rest started to cut loose with blazing guns, police came pounding to the doorway.

"Get those thugs!" Van yelled. "They're the Tycoon's gang!"

He would never forget the faces of the men he had seen in that plateau experience in the Catskills.

The police leaped out. Shots from steady, flaming Police Positives shattered the night. The alley became a bedlam.

Gangsters fell, their life-blood spurting redly as they paid for trying to shoot it out and resist capture. Others tried to flee up the alley onto the next street, where they evidently had their cars. But police prowl coupes had already sped around to head them off, to blockade the alley.

The Tycoon's gang was caught between two fires. As if they realized that capture meant death, they fought like cornered rats. Two of the police were badly wounded —a bluecoat, writhing on the pavement with a side wound, and a detective hobbling bravely on one wounded leg while he still tried to fire his gun.

The Phantom himself was in the midst of the fray, and again the Nemesis of Crime was taking a grim toll. A face loomed before him in the gun-blazing alley-the twisted face of Maxie. Van took aim, only to see the thug go down before the gun of one of the bluecoats. But at the same instant Van saw another figure only too familiar —a flashy-dressed, dancer-like figure, the scar on his otherwise handsome face showing livid in the night. Slick!

The Phantom leaped forward, gun whipping up as he ducked a desperate shot from the gang lieutenant.

Again, he aimed.

And again he held his fire. For out of the swirling mass of figures, the acrid mist of powder-smoke, leaped a slender shape. Kitty, the gun moll! With a scream, she had leaped in front of the man who, though an underworld felon, was the man she loved.

And though Van knew she was a cold-blooded killer, he could not shoot at that slender shape.

Seeing that, Slick took cruel advantage of it. He grabbed the woman who had furnished him her own body as a shield. He started to retreat, dragging her backward with him; his callous answer to her love.

But evidently one of the zealous bluecoats hadn't seen that she was a woman.

She slumped so suddenly, with a stricken cry, that Slick could not hold her up to longer shield him. Like the cornered rat he was, he flung up his gun, aimed straight for the Phantom. But the Phantom beat him to it. Even as he was sidestepping Slick's bullet that whistled by his ear, the Phantom's own bullet found the cowardly Slick's heart.

As Slick's lifeless body sank to the paving, Van swiftly leaped forward. He caught up the limp, moaning girl, carried her out of the melee to the nearest place of safety. There he lowered her.

One look, even in the darkness, told him that she was beyond help. The bullet had entered too close to her heart.

In a moment she stirred, her eyes flickering; no longer cold, but frightened, like a child's.

"Slick!" she murmured. "Don't let them get you, Slick."

The Phantom leaned close, spoke softly. "Slick's all right," he lied. "They have taken him alive." But then he hardened himself, to take grim advantage of the lie. "Maybe it'll go easier with him if you speak up," he suggested.

"I'll talk," she gasped, even as the death rattle began in her throat. "It ain't his fault —I'm to blame." She too, was lying, and Van knew it. "He's just a baby, honest —"

"You posed as Nurse Keenan." Van forced his words to rap hard against that ebbing consciousness, even as the roar of guns was subsiding in the alley. "But you were also Nancy Clay. Right?"

"Yes."

"The Tycoon got you that job of airplane hostess, too? And you did the trick, didn't you?"

"Yes. I gave —" She broke off, a paroxysm shaking her slender body.

But the Phantom was unrelentingly persistent. He bent closer. "Do you know who the Tycoon is?"

Fear fanned the dying spark in the girl's eyes. "I —I thought I did-heard voice-saw-Guess I was wrong—"

Van leaned still closer. "Who did you think it was? Was it —" Into her ear he spoke a name.

She raised her head a little as if to answer-but before she did, a final paroxysm shook her body. Her eyes went dull, and she lay still.

It was just as well, Van reflected in that gruesome moment. For what he had on her would have doomed her to the chair—

Chapter XX
The Conference

When Van Loan turned from the girl's body, the sweating police were sheathing their smoking guns. They were standing about, looking foolishly idle as men always look immediately after a fray, when there is nothing more to do. Saluting the warriors, the Phantom walked back into the blasted house. "Well, we wiped 'em out!" Back in the shattered laboratory, where emergency lights had been rigged up by a hastily summoned riot squad, Inspector Gregg spoke tersely to the Phantom. "We got them all, thanks to your quickness."

Van's disguised face showed no triumph. Instead, his eyes were thoughtful, sober, and his lithe body, if anything, was more tense than ever.

Homicide men had come, were working about the mangled corpse of Donald Vaughan. The verdict of "death from bombing" pronounced by the stocky medical examiner, however, was superfluous.

"Now if we can only get the Tycoon himself!" the inspector gritted. And the thought sent him to a telephone which by some miracle had been found to be in working order. He called Headquarters.

"Any news from Long Island about that house?" he demanded. His grunt of disappointment was enough. "Okay. Well, keep in touch with them. I'll be at this number for a while."

He hung up. But hardly a minute had passed before the telephone rang insistently.

"Hello!" The inspector was back at the instrument. "What's that? You just got a news flash? Yes, I'll wait." He waited, his face hopeful. "Yes?" He listened, and the hopeful look turned to blank amazement.

With a short exclamation he hung up, turned to the Phantom.

"Listen to this." His gruff voice shook with excitement. "Just when the Long Island police were starting the search of the areas you suggested someone phones them an anonymous tip to go to a certain house in Elmore. They thought it was a crank, but went anyway. And it was the house you described. They raided it-but no one was there. They found that air-conditioned room, you described, though, with a lot of crazy-fangled machinery in it —"

For a moment Van's eyes were puzzled. "But they did learn something, didn't they, inspector?" he demanded.

"I'll say they did." The inspector sprang his climax. "Guess who owns that house. Winston B. Garrison-the railway president who's in the sanitarium. What do you say we interview him-and find out just how cooped up he is? Maybe he's been getting around more than we have thought!"

"Maybe," Van said noncommittally, remembering that murder in the sanitarium, and the faked trip to St. Louis.

And then his eyes gleamed with decision. He turned to the inspector hurriedly.

"Inspector, I'm leaving this case here in your hands for the time being. Do whatever you deem wisest."

"You talk as if you're leaving town." The inspector laughed.

The Phantom moved through the death-room for the door.

"I am," was his parting remark, spoken with grim purpose.

Half an hour later a surprised, haggard-eyed Frank Havens, who had hardly had time to express his relief at seeing Van safe and sound, stared up from his desk in the *Clarion* office.

"I've chartered the plane as you asked, Van," the publisher said. "But I can't understand your bolting off like this again! Leaving this case virtually dangling-just when it seems headed for a finish, with the gang caught —"

"I'm following the trail to that very finish, Frank," the Phantom told him determinedly.

He had been re-packing a bag with clothes he had thrown in hastily at his own apartment. He took out his Colt, snapped back the slide, cleaned and oiled the gun.

"I may be wrong, but something tells me I'm not. The Tycoon no longer has the jump on me. But I know he's not through yet, even with his New York mob wiped out, and unless I work fast —"

The ringing of the phone interrupted him. Havens answered it. He spoke briefly, listened. And his rugged face went suddenly taut with shock.

"That was Inspector Gregg, Van. He said to tell you, if you were still in town, that Garrison has disappeared. He's vanished from that sanitarium. Dr. Ferris is gone, too, And that's not all. The inspector has been unable to contact any of the other men involved. Sprague has left the Polyclinic and has vanished with the rest. It's as if everyone concerned has suddenly disappeared."

Even before Havens finished, Van's whole body felt rippling with impatience. He slammed his suitcase shut, speaking with gripping firmness:

"I expected this, Frank. It confirms everything. I was right when I said I had to work fast."

* * *

The railway depot of the Empire and Southwest's biggest line, a line hard hit by sabotage, was a concrete structure, by no means as imposing as the Grand Central Terminal in New York, but even more modern in its design and equipment.

The large, spacious office on the ground floor was an excellent place for a secret conference. Its windows could be closed as tightly as its door, for the room was air-conditioned, and the air that came through a wall vent was fresh and invigorating.

But the six men who sat around a table in the room seemed uncomfortable, despite this air. Not one who did not look tense, haunted and nerve-ridden.

Winston B. Garrison, his face gaunt, the skin like crumpled parchment, sat at the head of the table. The glass, which had held the morphomine he had just finished, was at his side. Next to him sat his physician, tall, dark-eyed Dr. Ferris.

James Strickland and Jenson came next, the latter busily polishing his glasses.

Then Paul Talbert, the wind-burned, mustached shoring engineer, and the shock-headed Leland Sprague, surveyor. Two scientists where there had originally been eight! And yet the secret bond which had held those eight so close now held these remaining two.

Talbert sat erect, but his eyes were bloodshot. Sprague was squirming uneasily, his lips twitching strangely from time to time.

"Well —" Strickland spoke, a little hoarsely. "Well, here we are, after two days in that train we had to run out so secretly!" He glanced at Garrison. "If you ask me this trip was foolish. What can we accomplish here?"

Garrison strained forward. "I've got to salvage my railway." His voice was a hoarse croak, but there was determination in it. "Though our lines have been virtually ruined, I was informed, from here, that the sabotaging has stopped since the wreck of the streamlined train. We've got to work out a plan! A plan!"

"Don't excite yourself, Mr. Garrison," Dr. Ferris said soothingly. "Just take it easy, and keep taking that medicine —"

"Maybe that medicine isn't doing him so much good," Talbert clipped, pointedly.

The doctor's dark eyes flashed. "Meaning —"

And of a sudden the room seemed to crackle with tension. Eyes clashed-eyes of suspicion and hostility.

Jenson laughed nervously, replacing his glasses.

"Now gentlemen, let's not start accusing each other. We've got to cooperate. The railway —"

"Damn the railway!" Sprague burst out shrilly, "I'm sorry I ever had anything to do with the railway." He laughed wildly. "If it weren't for the others —"

Talbert whirled on him. "Careful, Sprague. You don't know what you're saying. You know all of us, even when a murderer and extortioner was killing off our numbers, kept doing our jobs. We all tried to help Mr. Garrison put the railroad on its feet."

"Did you?" a new, crisp voice asked.

The group at the table whirled as if every head was jerked by strings, cries of alarm coming from several throats in unison. They had not heard the door open.

They gaped as a tall man in a black silk domino mask strode purposefully into the air-conditioned room-followed by four of the city's police.

The Phantom quietly closed the door.

"Keep your seats, gentlemen," he told the group. "I'm the Phantom, and I've come to get to the bottom of this whole ghastly intrigue."

Garrison looked as if he were going to have another of his spells. "But how-where —"

"You wonder at my opportune arrival?" The Phantom smiled grimly beneath his domino mask. "As a matter of fact, I preceded you down here by a full day. I've been waiting for you, and it was easy, with the help of the excellent police here, to check your arrival, and your meeting here."

"What do you want?" Garrison was still spokesman for the startled group. "Why have you brought in those policemen?"

"Largely to prevent any further crimes," the Phantom replied, with a grim smile. "To help me, if I need help, in stopping the Tycoon, once and for all."

Strickland gave a horrified gasp. "What? Then he is down here? He's followed us! God, he'll kill us all!"

"I'm here to stop him," said the Phantom. "And that's why I want to get at the truth. I asked a question when I came in this room —" His eyes swiveled to Talbert. "You were saying how you and the others wanted to help the railroad get on its feet. I challenged that statement."

Talbert's mustache bristled. "What do you mean by that, Phantom? We've all worked like slaves for the railroad. It was to our own monetary interest to make the stock we owned rise in value."

The Phantom made an impatient gesture. "I said it was time for the truth. Wherever there is a big crime like this, I've invariably found that a smaller crime is behind it. Or perhaps you scientists didn't consider it a crime to tamper with a Government map? Or to move the location of a Government field?"

Sprague gave a stricken cry. Talbert sat frozen, now, eyes cold with fear.

"You were men of science, but you were human-too human," the Phantom pursued, relentlessly. "Greed was behind that tampering. Greed made you move the field from the place you had first selected; made you do it so secretly that no one but yourselves knew that it was not the original site. Then it made you resign your Government posts and cleverly induce the Empire and Southwest Railway to take you on as technicians, in return for stock.

"You scientists had been selected by the Government to plan that airport and select its site because of your specialized knowledge. You, Talbert, because you know waterways; Sprague as an expert surveyor, Vaughan for his knowledge of geology, of rock formation; and so on. But when you got actually to work on the original plan of that airport, had selected the site, you unexpectedly came upon some rich deposits of pitchblende. Some of it was on Government property, but most of it was on the property of the Empire and Southwest Railway. Pitchblende! The ore from which the most valuable element in the world is extracted. *Radium!*"

Garrison half rose from his chair, eyes bulging. Strickland and Jenson gaped, and Dr. Ferris sat looking on like a confused observer. Which he was, in truth.

"Radium!" the Phantom repeated. "A word which signifies millions of dollars! A fortune for scientists who had hitherto made only a modest living. But their first fear was that it would be found before they could swing some deal which would give them a grasp on the pitchblende property. If the airport were built on that particular site, because some of the pitchblende was on Government ground, you would have to 'discover' it openly. So, to divert this possibility, you group of scientists, and there were eight of you then —" His gaze was bent on the two at the table. "—changed the Government map. As trusted Government men you had access to the Department of Commerce files, and could accomplish that.

"Then you went to Garrison, to swing the deal that would give you stock in the railway. And through that stock, partial ownership of the property —"

Garrison broke in then, his voice a hoarse croak.

"But they told me nothing of the radium! What I have said about their promise to modernize the line is true-that's why I gave them stock! No wonder they wanted it!" His nervous agitation was gripping him as he singled out one man. "Strickland! What did you know of all this?"

Strickland denied any knowledge. So did Jenson.

The Phantom's eyes were inexorable, seen through the holes of his mask. "The criminal who calls himself the Tycoon *did* know about that radium!" he said flatly. "It was the motivation for his crimes! It was the goal toward which his greed drove him, which led him to murder, to extortion, to sabotage! Radium! That was what the Tycoon was after."

Garrison rose totteringly from his place. "This-this is all-too much of a shock!" he croaked. He seemed like a drunken man. "I —I must beg to be excused. I —I have an errand —"

The police glanced at the Phantom, but he gave no sign, though his eyes had narrowed. And Garrison was permitted to leave the room.

Over his own doctor's protests he went out, closing the door.

The Phantom's glance swiveled to Talbert and Sprague, who had listened speechlessly to his accusations.

"Well, gentlemen. Have you anything to say?"

Sprague's wild eyes looked about. Talbert's tall, strong frame slumped a little. His voice came hoarsely, brokenly.

"What you have said is true, Phantom. I admit my complicity. All of us swung the deal with the railroad to get our fingers on that land. I helped change the map. But-but I swear I had nothing to do with the crimes that have now happened! I swear —"

A strange, groggy sound had come into his voice suddenly, as if he were talking in a daze. Looking about the table, Van saw that the faces of the others were going strangely weary.

Then his own superior physique felt it, and his heart went suddenly icy.

Something invisible was closing upon this room. And then his nostrils detected a faint odor in the air, like that of fresh peaches!

His eyes flashed to the vent through which the conditioned air was coming, the only inlet. He whirled to the paling police.

"Get everybody out of here! Hurry! And close the door behind them!"

As he spoke he was jerking the door open. Without waiting for the rest, he dashed out into the corridor of the station. The vent! He saw the piping-saw where it curved downward.

His lithe body hurled to a stairway leading to the basement, as he whipped out his Colt. In seconds he was down the stairs on soft-soled shoes, and the darkness of the cellar engulfed him. The lights were not on, but he could hear the whir of an air-conditioning plant.

Then, as his eyes accustomed themselves to the gloom, a shadowy figure leaped toward him with a wild animal-like cry.

Hands like talons clutched at the Phantom before he could aim his gun.

His antagonist was possessed of the strength of desperation.

But the Phantom, his own muscles flexing with the strength of rage, had his left arm free. His jabbing fist found the face in the dark-struck twice. Short, crunching blows.

Chapter XXI
The Dream of Power

Leaping to answer the Phantom's summons the police, followed by the whole group from the executive room who came rushing down to the cellar, found a strange, grim tableau.

The cellar lights were now on but the big air-conditioning plant had been turned off. Close by that plant stood a metal container-small, green-painted, a faint wisp of cloudy stuff emanating from it.

And several feet away, holding a half limp figure in a viselike grip stood the Phantom.

He spoke more with wearied relief than with triumph.

"Here," he said, "is the Tycoon."

The police guns promptly whipped up. Men gave one concerted hoarse cry of astonishment.

"Then it's Garrison!" Strickland yelled. "He left the room just before that gas came in! He came down here!"

"Right!" the Phantom clipped. "He did come down here! And there he is!"

He stepped aside, pulling his prisoner with him. On the floor, just coming to, was the railway president, cruel finger welts on his neck standing out bluely. Dazedly Strickland got to his feet.

"Then who is —" Jenson cried, staring at the man whom the Phantom held in that grip of iron.

Van stepped aside from his prisoner.

Police guns were covering the fellow now.

Every eye was staring at the man, bewildered, as they took in the gaunt body, the thin-haired head, the pallid face covered with thick, dark stubble, and the eyes that glared like live coals.

"Yes, gentlemen," Van's voice rang out, "this is the dreaded Tycoon. Otherwise known to you as-David Truesdale!"

Cries of amazed incredulity rose in protesting chorus.

"But it can't be Truesdale!" Talbert's hysterical cry rose above the tumult. "Truesdale's body was found in the airplane wreck!"

But Jenson, stepping closer to the prisoner, broke out with even greater vehemence: "It *is!* The Phantom is right! It's Truesdale! That beard can't conceal his face!"

"Truesdale!" Sprague screamed shrilly. "So it was you-you who were making me come at your beck-to your hideout-to —"

The glaring prisoner spoke then, his voice thick.

"This is all some mistake! I never heard of any Truesdale. I can identify myself. A mistake —"

"You made the mistake when you first gave yourself away to me, even though I had never seen you," the Phantom said flatly. "The game is up, Truesdale. Your ego-maniacal dream of power is ended. While you were stunned I found enough incriminating papers in your pockets to prove plenty." He handed one paper over to the police. "This list of names and hideout locations," he said, "will finish the mob you had working in this town and state. Just as your mob in New York was finished."

The prisoner's face drained of its last drop of blood. His dark eyes glared wildly.

"All right!" he shrilled. "You found me, Phantom! I knew you were on my trail throughout-knew that only you might ferret me out! I killed them-all of them! *And I'm not through yet!*"

Only a man fired by utter, animal desperation could have moved so swiftly, so unexpectedly.

Before anyone could stop him, David Truesdale, with a maniacal scream, made one mighty leap toward that green-painted metal cylinder.

He lifted it, his hand on the cap, his face like that of some satanic gargoyle.

Whether he intended to hurl it out at the whole group, with its content billowing out, or whether he intended to erase himself as well as the rest, could never have been told-for Van's gun barked then, aiming at the hand unscrewing that cap.

The hand let go as blood spurted from it. The other arm of the criminal still hugged the cylinder, as he cursed and screamed in pain. Then suddenly a horrible change came over him.

His body seemed literally to wither. His distorted face turned greenish. The life went out of his eyes as he slumped slowly to the floor.

Grimly the Phantom swung to the petrified group of men.

"Clear out of here-out into the air! That tube is still leaking! It can't harm you as long as you're not near it-but you can see what one whiff of it, full strength, has done to the devil who brought it here! The Tycoon is dead!"

* * *

"And so it was Truesdale, Van! But I still can't quite grasp the whole fiendish business!"

Frank Havens uttered those words of bewilderment as, two days later, he sat beside Richard Curtis Van Loan in one of the latter's purring touring cars which Van was driving uptown through Manhattan.

"Truesdale was after that radium, Frank," Van said. "Where the others had been content merely to get a share of the property, Truesdale was greedy enough to want all of it! A peculiar man, Truesdale. To his friends he seemed shy, meek. Actually he had a gigantic ego, a terrific greed for power and wealth. And so he planned his devilish crimes-planned them with all the thoroughness of a true scientist.

"His purpose was twofold. He meant to get possession of the stock from the other scientists who knew of the stuff, then to seal their lips. His second aim was to buy what stock he couldn't get by extortion, and this he could do if he lowered its value sufficiently, made it worthless to its holders. His sabotage was inaugurated in an effort to ruin the railway, in the belief that Garrison would finally be glad to sell out, provided he didn't know about that radium. And, since the other scientists had not yet told the president of the Empire and Southwest Railway, killing them would safeguard that secret. Once the murders began, the other scientists dared not talk anyway, for fear their whole intrigue with the Government map would come out.

"Truesdale planned to die-in the eyes of the world. He would be mourned as a victim of the criminal who already had been exploiting himself as the Tycoon. Later on Truesdale could assume a new identity. I believe now that he meant to use Leland Sprague as a sort of intermediary-to buy up the depreciating stock for him and do other such work.

"When I learned, from Sprague's shoes, that he had been to the Tycoon's hideout, at first I was suspicious of *him*. But later, I learned the truth. Sprague's blood showed that he had radium poisoning, had evidently contracted it during the experiments conducted at the site of the pitchblende deposits. And he was a cocaine addict. This, which your physician told me, was also confirmed by his blood. Truesdale gave Sprague that cocaine, playing on his illness, converting him to a drug addict so that he would have a man he could use as a slave.

"But to get back to the beginning of Truesdale's crimes. As I said he started them with sabotage of the railway, as soon as he and the others had acquired stock. His first mob —a mob led by Frenchy-operated in Kansas. The money they took from the wrecked trains paid them, and helped pay the second mob Truesdale organized in New York, with Slick as its lieutenant.

"Truesdale knew he must start his murders of the scientists-with himself apparently among the murdered-when he learned they were planning to tell Strickland and Jenson about the radium, after which it would be told to Garrison, who was then supposedly in St. Louis. They had all shrewdly figured that Garrison might react unpleasantly when they told him the real reason they had come into the railway. For Garrison was more interested in the railroad than in anything else. The idea was to tell Strickland and Jenson first, let them in on the fact that all would become rich by exploiting the radium land. With a solid majority they could win Garrison over.

"Truesdale, however, didn't want even Strickland and Jenson to be told the secret. The less who knew about it, the more chance he had of acquiring the stock.

"And Truesdale knew well enough that Garrison wasn't in St. Louis. For in organizing his New York mob, he had been fortunate to get the services of Slick's gun moll, Kitty, a female Jekyll-and-Hyde who had already built up a respectable role for herself as 'Shirley Keenan,' registered nurse. She was well-educated, clever-and I still wonder whether she would have gone wrong if she hadn't fallen for a rat like Slick.

"Garrison, ill from his worries over his failing railroad, was looking for a private nurse, and Truesdale knew it. The gun moll went for the job, got it. This enabled Truesdale to keep tabs on Garrison's movements.

"He learned that Garrison had ordered a big portion of his own stock from vaults in Chicago to be sent to New York. Garrison had already turned over most of the stock he had on hand to the group of scientists. The stock was to come by plane on the maiden flight of the new Harvey airliner.

"I don't know just how Kitty managed to get the job as stewardess, under the name of 'Nancy Clay,' on that airplane. But since Truesdale knew in advance about the flight and the stock order-from her spy work-she had plenty of time to apply for the job, and I believe she got it on her own abilities.

"Meanwhile, Truesdale saw his opportunity to accomplish even more during this airplane flight. He and Garth had gone out West to bring back some of the pitchblende to show the railway officials and convince them. They had the ore in a fireproof briefcase. Later I found a piece of it that Truesdale had failed to remove. That was what first gave me the hint that radium was mixed up in the whole ghastly business.

"With Garth and Truesdale taking the plane from Chicago for the final lap to New York, Truesdale was at last ready to launch his terrible crimes! He began to phone warnings to the other men, demanding both their stock and whatever papers on the pitchblende were in their possession. I found one such paper in Vaughan's satchel full of the stock.

"Truesdale pretended to receive the warnings himself. He acted terrified, his real purport being to spread a contagion of hysteria to the others, so they would meet his demands.

"And now he was ready. In their operations, the gang Truesdale had painstakingly built up used a plane of their own. They had a secret field in the Catskills, where that shack and radio were located.

"Having learned that Pat Bentley was to pilot the Chicago transport, Truesdale got hold of that *Hindenburg* record. Though how he knew of its existence only he could have told. We will never know more, but that's inconsequential.

"On the plane, the gun moll stewardess served drugged coffee to the passengers. Truesdale had not told her he was her boss, though as the Tycoon who knew what was coming, he knew he could insure his own safety. He could only pretend to drink the coffee. However, the girl overheard him talking to Garth. She thought she recognized his voice as that of the Tycoon, but even when she was dying and told me this, she said she wasn't sure.

"Some other member of the gang must have been a stowaway on that plane, for the girl needed help, and all the others aboard are accounted for. When the passengers were drugged, Truesdale also feigning to be drugged with them, the girl and the gangster who aided her cripple the radio, held up the pilot and co-pilot, and made them land on the plateau.

"The rest of that story you know. Three persons who should have been among the dead were missing, you remember. One was Bentley, one the stewardess, and the other, I assumed, was Garth. It was Garth I first suspected up on that plateau, especially since I had found a check of his for twenty-five thousand on the dead Joseph Ware. Now I realize that Ware was frightened and had sold out his stock to Garth, who made the check payable in advance. But to get back, I first accepted the corpse bearing the ring of Truesdale as Truesdale's.

"But by his own move, executed through his gang, Truesdale virtually gave himself away to me. I was to be burned and placed among the dead, to be identified as Bentley, the pilot, by the simple device of putting Bentley's identifications on my charred body. One thing I have learned about even the best criminal minds. That is that they tend to repeat themselves. It occurred to me then that if *my* body could be substituted for Bentley's, then another corpse-and the name of Garth came to me instantly-could be identified as Truesdale's by the same trick.

"But to follow Truesdale. With the plane down, he rushed to New York. Undercover he entered Grand Central Terminal and planted that bomb in the box which motivated the sign, also changing the strip so that it would flash his warning boasts. When the lights flashed, Vincent Brooks and John Eldridge went to investigate the box. The criminal probably counted on Brooks going there, since he was the inventor of the sign. The fact that two went was all the better for Truesdale's plans. When Brooks opened the box, the bomb went off, doing its work on two of the scientists the criminal planned to eliminate.

"Whether Truesdale was anywhere about when I had my set-to with his thugs in the terminal, I don't know. But it is certain he ordered them to follow Bentley and kill him. They were not expecting trouble in making their get-away without going through the gates. I appeared on the scene almost in time to stop that, but they did get away—then.

"Next came the murder of Joseph Ware, at the sanitarium. Ware, I believe, had found out that Garrison was there and not in St. Louis. No doubt he had gone to the sanitarium to tell Garrison the true story about the radium. But Truesdale followed him, killed him and escaped, while the gun moll, Kitty, now posing as Nurse Keenan, cleverly drew my suspicion to Garrison himself, by making it obvious he could have committed the crime. Garrison said later that he had dressed at her suggestion, that it would be good for him. But he had been too confused at the time to tell me that. Naturally she must have seen Truesdale then, too, but quite as naturally, not in his real character. Truesdale also was something of an adept at disguise.

"Fastening suspicion on Garrison was a part of Truesdale's scheme. The disgrace would help to further cripple the railway, lower the buying price of what stock he could not extort.

"Next, Truesdale learned that the airplane wreck had been found. He was not ready for it to be found. As I told you previously, he thought he had plenty of time to clear up that scene, to remove all possible clues, so his 'body' could be neatly found when he tipped off searching parties.

"He sent his gang there in a hurry, but I got there first. You know what happened there.

"When learning that the moll and the nurse were one and the same, I got into the shoes of Frenchy. I learned that the criminal had an active mob in the Southwest. It was they who wrecked the streamlined train in Kansas. Though Truesdale had planned to have it wrecked by being bombed from the plane I was on as 'Frenchy,' he was taking no chances of a slip-up, and his other men were on the job.

"Back at my laboratory I found how the scientists had altered the Government map you got for me. I had already analyzed the little piece of pitchblende, and the evidence of radium poisoning in Sprague's blood gave me final corroboration. From the other map, showing locations of the sabotage activity, I saw that one area in Nevada was untouched; also that the center of sabotage activity was Kansas. Where I had myself seen the vandalism at its worst.

"Now came the checkroom business, and the discovery of the extortion method, followed by Vaughan's murder. In the dead geologist's laboratory I saw shattered parts of an electroscope. I realized then that Vaughan had probably been making radium tests, and the bomb had been used as much to shatter his work as to kill him.

"But the gang who had committed this murder and who had destroyed the laboratory was trapped. They were cleaned up. The Tycoon must quickly have learned this, and realized that without his gang, operations in New York were temporarily at a standstill. So he tipped off the police about the house in Elmore, Long Island, for which I had already started them looking.

"The house proved to be Garrison's, making him the leading police suspect, which was what Truesdale wanted. Actually Garrison had not occupied it for years. Truesdale had rented it and had converted it into a hide-out, with the air-conditioned room. As you know, he was an expert at ventilating.

"From all this I deduced that Truesdale would now have to go out to the Southwest, where he had his other mob, if he wanted to continue operations. Nor was I surprised when it was reported that Garrison and the rest had 'vanished.' Truesdale had managed somehow to get word to Garrison that the sabotaging in Kansas had stopped, and that there now was a chance to repair the damage. So Garrison and the rest left for Topeka.

"When the meeting took place in Garrison's Topeka office, Truesdale was down at the air-conditioner, having knocked out the engineer. Through a vent he could overhear what was taking place in the room. When he heard me revealing the whole background of the crime he started mixing chlorine gas with the air.

"Garrison must have detected it, and thinking something wrong with the vent, gone down to investigate. Truesdale knocked him out, too. But by that time I had become aware of the gas and had hurried down to the cellar myself."

The phantom was slowing the car near Havens's apartment hotel. "And there's the whole thing, Frank," he said. "I still feel that it was Pat Bentley, bringing it to my doorstep, who helped most in its solution."

Havens sat back, a smile of heartfelt relief on his face.

"You've done a wonderful job, Van," he commented. "Bentley did not die in vain."

The car drew nearer to the curb when a girl's voice called a cheery greeting. Muriel Havens came across the pavement.

"Dad! And you, Van! Where have you been, stranger?"

"Hop in," Van invited, "and I'll tell you all about it."

Havens took the wheel then. Van and Muriel sat in the back. And somehow with Muriel beside him, Van forgot his fatigue, and how wearied was his brain that was still teeming with details of the ghastly affair his skill had brought to a solution.

"I've been sleeping most of the time," he drawled to Muriel. "You know, one gets bored."

But though his tone was the languid, idle tone which Muriel so despised, she felt his strong hand close over hers, taking it with brief but warm possession.

Yes, brief. For sooner or later, another baffling crime must break-and again Richard Van Loan would have to forget all human, all personal feelings, and hurl his energy and skill against a diabolical criminal.